"The empire is going t... shouted in desperation. "This is the end of the end! You said so yourself!"

"Not if Karsus succeeds!" She gazed at her cousin, who shouted threats at the ceiling as he floated higher. "He *will* ascend to godhood and save the city! Save the empire! He's the greatest mage . . ."

Candlemas only stared, unsure if his lover was trying to convince him, or herself. Then her words were lost as the building's ceiling blew off.

Tons of stone, slate, timber beams, granite, carved cornices, and other elements exploded upward like wheat chaff. High up, yet almost close enough to touch, frowned the cloud face of Lady Mystryl, Controller of the Weave, the stuff of all magics. And facing her, still shouting, was the presumptuous mage who would steal her power, usurp her place, walk into the firmament and take the throne of the gods themselves.

FANTASY ADVENTURE

The Netheril Trilogy
Clayton Emery

Sword Play

Dangerous Games

Mortal Consequences
(available April 1997)

FANTASY ADVENTURE

Dangerous Games

Clayton Emery

DANGEROUS GAMES

First Printing: November 1996
Printed in the United States of America.
Library of Congress Catalog Card Number: 95-62256

9 8 7 6 5 4 3 2 1

ISBN: 0-7869-0524-7

8570XXX1501

TSR, Inc.
201 Sheridan Springs Rd.
Lake Geneva, WI 53147
U.S.A.

TSR Ltd.
120 Church End, Cherry Hinton
Cambridge CB1 3LB
United Kingdom

**Dedicated to
Seamus, Powerhouse of the South**

Chapter 1

"There! It's nice to be—"

"Move!"

The pudgy wizard was knocked flying by a shove from the tall, scarred barbarian. Candlemas caromed off a table, slipped, and crashed to the workshop floor. The stumble saved his life, for a monstrous red insect had leaped to the table, scattering jars and crockery and priceless artifacts, clashing steely mandibles to snap the arcanist's head off.

Fighting instinct saved the barbarian's life. Mistrusting magic, Sunbright had unsheathed his sword before Candlemas could invoke the shift spell. One minute they'd been standing in a dusky rainy forest then, at a fast-rattled spell, they were whisked to a cluttered workshop with high, airy windows—a room besieged by a horde of rust-red insects as big as wild hogs.

Had Sunbright thought about danger, he would have been dead long ago. Reared on the tundra, where death was always just a whisker away, he reacted instinctively, attacking the menaces with might and sinew and the fighting agility bred deep into his bones. Training seized his hands and body. Before Candlemas even recognized the threat, Sunbright had attacked half a dozen marauders.

The great hooked sword Harvester of Blood flashed as Sunbright fell to slaughter. The insects were thick in the body and hunchbacked, like giant fleas. They *were* giant fleas, he realized. Myriad scuttling legs were pointed as daggers, claws bore pincers like a scorpion's, mouth-mandibles were jagged as broken razors. A dozen insects rushed the two men. Sunbright was hard-pressed to beat them back, both from himself and from the chunky Candlemas, whom the barbarian considered helpless.

The first insect to chomp onto Sunbright's iron-ringed moosehide boot lost its head to a downward slash. But even that was difficult, for their carapaces were thick as boiled-leather shields and they had few vital organs to shear. Sunbright barely wrenched Harvester free before another flea hopped up and clamped onto the barbarian's unprotected thigh. Yowling with sudden pain, Sunbright batted the thing from underhand, bowling it aside and slashing off four legs like brittle jackstraws. Yet the bug ripped a hunk of flesh free as it tumbled to land, upside down and twitching. The bug's blood was thick, reddish, pasty, and smelled acrid as burning garbage. Their alien smell filled the room, until Sunbright felt like some fly blundered into a spiderweb. He tried not to think about being sucked dry of blood, or being paralyzed and eaten alive . . . slowly.

Screaming a northern challenge, he slammed his great sword between the jaws of a charging insect, felt the hook hang up in the tough carapace of the skull. He stamped his boot into a face with multifaceted eyes— then a bounding bug crashed on his back, sent him sprawling, knocking his breath out.

Kneeling under the table, crushing a crystal goblet with his bare knee, Candlemas was not helpless, but neither was he happy. How had these giant vermin come to infest his workshop? And how to combat and survive them? Not that he had time to think, for a furious red insect with clacking jaws raced straight at him.

Candlemas was no fighter, but he could hurl magic as instinctively as Sunbright could sling a sword. The wizard's first reaction to these monsters was to push them away, and the spell he ripped off did just that. Locking his two middle fingers under his thumb so first and fourth projected like horns, he squalled the mystic gargle of a spell, invoked the name of Amaunator, and fired a wormhole at the bug not three feet away.

Before the wizard's hands a vortex like a gray tornado spun into being, writhed and twisted in the air, then sought the closest, densest object. With a tail like a bee's sting, the magic wormhole drilled through the insect like an arrow through a mouse. The thick, rusty, hair-studded carapace was bored open, and the mystic energy spiraled through the beast to erupt out its back end. In the process, the bug's primitive guts were churned to paste and sucked into the magic maw to disappear Candlemas himself knew not where. The stunned insect, half-deflated, collapsed onto the flagstones of the workshop.

But Candlemas yelled as another insect tore into his robe at the shoulder, seeking sweet meat and rich red blood.

Sunbright saw his blood mix with the rusty ichor of the giant flea's. He'd been nipped on the arm, gnawed behind his knee, and skinned along his scalp where it was shaved above his ears. A many-legged menace scrabbled at his back, claws and mandibles shredding his thick goat-hide vest, which so far had spared his spine. Another flea with a nest of sharp legs pinned his sword flat on the floor, while a third scrabbled at his elbow. More were no doubt gnawing his boots.

Stupid to be eaten alive by bugs, the young man thought with disgust. Hardly the stuff of legend.

Angry with the fleas' mindless attack, and at Candlemas, who'd teleported them into the mess, Sunbright let his anger grow, and harnessed it. With his free right hand, he hauled as well as he could onto his belly and punched the first flea in the eye. The multifaceted orb, like a mosaic of tiny mirrors, crunched under his fist. The bug was shoved backward and Sunbright could wrench up his sword. At the same time, a keen sting along his back told him his vest was destroyed. Pain fanned his battle rage.

Kicking both feet, grunting with the effort, the barbarian rolled right, dumping the monster on his back into the one at his elbow. Scrambling up, he found the two bugs idiotically gnashing at one another. Swearing in his guttural, icy tongue, he sucked wind and slammed his sword down, shearing through both bugs until his steel blade banged the floor and hashed the insects into a tangle of oozing parts. These bugs weren't so hard to kill, he reasoned. Just bulky, toothy, and persistent.

Behind him clattered jars and retorts, and Sunbright glimpsed a bug straddling a table, smashing crockery as it shuffled to leap on him. Sunbright slung his sword far back to slice the flea's head open from side to side, but the thing leaped too quickly. The table was upset so the edge crashed on Sunbright's toes, crushing them cruelly and making him yelp. Jerking his foot free, he made to kick the bug back to gain swinging room.

But the fearsome beast leapt into the air almost to

the barbarian's face, and spat.

A blob of brown ichor like tobacco juice splattered Sunbright's face. Caught unprepared, he hadn't time to close his eyes. Blinking furiously and clawing at his eyes, he found he couldn't see. Then the stinging glop began to burn, sear, until he shouted in pain and anger. And for the first time, fright.

He was blind.

Candlemas's wormhole spell worked on another flea, drilling it through and reducing it to a curved shell spinning on the stone floor. The pudgy mage grabbed the table legs to pull himself out from under, when a warning crash made him duck back. From above, a jar filled with brine crashed on the floor, drenching him. A silver scale followed. The destruction didn't bother him so much as the danger: this table was old and creaky, he recalled. But before he could slither clear, it crashed on his back, pinning him.

A flea nipped at his ear, so close he felt it tick like a cat's claw. With the monster's weight crushing him—how could bugs weigh so much?—he couldn't free his arm to conjure another spell. Normally he hated to employ the same spell repeatedly, for it was considered the mark of an amateur, and many of his spells were subtle, designed to turn opponents away, to instill fear, to enfeeble their minds. But these insects had no minds, only claws and teeth, and ravening hunger.

But now he'd be glad to hurl a wormhole, except he was trapped with one hand underneath him. The bug hooked a mandible into the back of his neck, making the arcanist shiver. It would tear open his skull and suck out his brains unless he got loose—

Then a crashing, smashing, crunching rattled all around him, and the flea was knocked clear, as was the table. Sunbright stamped on the arcanist's hand, making him gasp.

Still, Candlemas didn't waste time. Sliding on his knees under the far side of the table, Candlemas clambered up, shoving the empty hulls of dead insects away. How many of the murderous bastards were left?

He ducked as Sunbright's sword slashed sideways, scattered glass and pottery, and tore a chunk from the table's edge. Was the barbarian mad? Broken chips stung Candlemas's face, cutting his chin and eyebrow, making it hard to see for blood. Sunbright was under attack from four slashing, jumping bugs, but the barbarian slung his sword awkwardly, dinging a marble column, almost severing Candlemas's forearm, hitting nothing. The wizard shouted, "What are you—"

"I can't see! *I'm blind!*" A sob of panic drowned Sunbright's voice. Strong of arm and body, the barbarian was terrified of being rendered helpless. Now he howled involuntarily as a flea clamped its mandibles onto his knee.

"Get down!" Candlemas shouted. *"Drop!"*

Desperately the wizard racked his brain for some all-encompassing spell. Noanar's fireball would incinerate everything in sight, set off a chain of explosions that could level the tower. General Matick's shields were useless, for the bugs would just jump over or around. And they must be destroyed. Aksa's shatter? Ptack's brittleness? If Candlemas had a fault, he knew too much and became paralyzed trying to choose. Nor was Sunbright helping. Used to battling alone, the barbarian had no intention of ducking from a fight.

What to do? The insects were like hot coals tearing up his laboratory and the two men. Even now one skipped away from Sunbright to leap at Candlemas, and the wizard found himself stepping away from the threat. Heat wouldn't mean much to them with their tough, leathery hides. But the opposite . . .

Invoking Kozah, the Storm Lord, Candlemas shot his

sleeves, locked his fingers, and conjured. The spell took form instantly, for his fingers ached to the bone, then to the wrists, then the elbows. He couldn't hold this enchantment long—

A flea leapt. Instead of backing away, Candlemas stepped to meet it.

A slap to either side of its head did the trick. Veridon's chiller sank magic deep into the beast's core. Its rust-red carapace was suddenly brighter, reflected in morning sun from the high windows, as the insect was coated with a layer of ice an inch thick. Frozen solid, the thing tilted down and thundered at Candlemas's feet, icy legs and claws shattering against stone. Clumps of frozen bug landed on the wizard's sandaled feet, leaving a wet, chill, ugly feel on his hairy toes. Irritated, he kicked the thing away and dashed around the long table.

Sunbright had sunk his sword into another insect by sheer instinct, but he'd lodged it in the chitin behind the beast's round head and the keen hook had fetched up again. As the barbarian yanked and twisted desperately, another flea crashed into his chest, knocked him loose of his weapon. Sunbright was slammed on his back, winded. Grappling the beast, he only cut his fingers on its sharp claws.

Candlemas worked as fast as he could. He touched a flea before him on two spots on its back. The chill touch rippled through the beast where the hands touched, like an icicle hammered through its body. The creature's back end was frozen solid while the front legs scrabbled to whirl and attack. It would die shortly, Candlemas knew, but he skipped backward, for those living claws could still rip. Circling, cursing, he swung wide of the struggling insect and laid hands on the bug on Sunbright's chest. A touch at head and rump froze the monster instantly. The blinded Sunbright hissed as his fingers were frosted from the periphery of the spell. The bug fell with a clatter, small legs snapping like frozen twigs.

Candlemas scanned the room quickly. Hadn't there been a third—still alive?

He grunted as the bulky beast crashed into his back. Candlemas flopped atop Sunbright, who'd been uncoiling upright. The men banged heads, then the bug crushed Candlemas's face to the stone floor. His hands locked under him still retained magic, and Candlemas felt ice frost his rough smock and belly. Greedy mandibles gnawed at the back of his bald head. "Get it off! Get it off me!"

A gutty grunt answered, and Candlemas saw a big iron-ringed boot sail by. Leather thudded into the flea's belly and flipped it over. Sunbright followed, grappling madly like some drunk. He stepped square on Candlemas's rump before he stamped down hard on the insect's gut to pin it. The gasping wizard winced at the crunching, tearing noises, rolled far enough to see Sunbright, still blind, ripping wriggling legs and claws off the insect like dead branches.

When the last pair of legs had been yanked off, a red-bathed Sunbright reared back and rubbed at his eyes with his wrists. "Thank Selûne! I can see! But gods above, it stings!"

Candlemas pushed upright, cast about wildly for more insect enemies. But apart from the de-limbed one writhing impotently on the floor, all were dead, some drilled through, some frozen solid, some chopped to hash. Bug parts and smashed pots lay everywhere. Candlemas himself was wrapped in torn and spattered clothing, while Sunbright was painted head to toe in bug guts and blood, some of which was his own. His long shirt and goat-hide vest hung in tatters. Gasping, he pawed his red eyes clear and blinked painfully.

Sunbright asked, "What were you saying?"

Candlemas sank on his hams on the floor of his ruined

workshop and found himself in a puddle of ice water, the last vestiges of his chill touch spell. He sighed, "I said, it's nice to be home."

* * * * *

Stumping across the filthy, littered floor, Candlemas pulled tassels to ring faraway bells. Despite seeping wounds, fiery pain, and swollen eyes, Sunbright saw first to his weapon, scrubbing ichor from the blade and touching up the edge with a stone plucked from a belt pouch.

Harvester of Blood was Sunbright's weapon, his father's sword, forged in some unknown southern land. The shank of the sword was as wide as three fingers, but the tip swelled to a curved and brutal edge where the backside was cut away to a deep hook. A good blade for slaughter and mayhem: wide-pointed for stabbing and driving home damage, heavy-nosed for lopping and slashing, back-barbed for sinking into an enemy's vitals, then causing terrible damage twisting and ripping out. A weapon to destroy man or beast or pit fiend, and Sunbright had killed them all in his adventures since leaving the tundra. One reason he'd survived was because he always honed Harvester's edge before tending to his own wounds.

Before long, a clutch of lesser wizards and black-and-white-clad maids swirled in, wondering when their master had returned and exclaiming at the wreckage and wounds. Candlemas ordered the lot to shush, demanded hot water, rags, and brooms. Within a few moments, sculleries were stuffing bug carcasses out the window, mopping up blood and sweeping up crockery. Two wizards blathered apologies to Candlemas while two maids undressed him. When the women and girls made to disrobe Sunbright, the barbarian let them close enough to swab his eyes with deliciously warm and clean water, but when they picked at his leather laces and rags, he pushed them at bay with bloody hands.

The babble was horrendous, everyone gabbling at once.

The chief assistant arcanist, a green-robed woman named Kalle, apologized over and over, ". . . sorry, Lord Candlemas. We thought it best to move the breeding boxes here where it was quiet in your absence . . ."

A clerk called, ". . . Lady Polaris is asking for you, my lord. She says it's urgent and you must . . ."

Kalle's assistant, a older man in red robes named Gibor, blathered, ". . . just a tad too much magic in the wrong place. Instead of growing tougher they grew bigger . . ."

Sunbright brushed in vain at helpful maids' hands. "Candlemas, tell them to desist!"

"My lord, it's all this fool's fault. I had no idea—"

"Not true, Lord Candlemas, not true! She insisted we come up here—"

"How could you have been so stupid?" Candlemas roared at his mages as maids removed his sandals. "You know this workshop is saturated with magic—What is your problem, Sunbright?"

"They're trying to tear off my clothes!" Older maids tsked and younger ones giggled as they plucked ineffectually. They wore plain black-and-white gowns, aprons and caps, the house colors of Lady Polaris.

"What did you expect? You need a bath! Kalle, I'll have you scouring toilets if you don't come up with a better reason—"

"I can bathe on my own!" Refusing to strike the women's hands, the barbarian backed into a corner. Two maids giggled so hard they had to hold their stomachs.

"And you, Gibor! What kind of moron . . ." By now, Candlemas wore only a loin cloth. Maids scurried out with his torn, bloody clothing. None of the servants seemed to mind his paunchy, hairy near-nakedness. "What? No, you can't bathe on your own! A lord is never alone, or at least not often! A gentleman is tended by underlings!"

"I'm no gentleman!" Sunbright retorted. A maid sneaking up from behind caught his long shirt and ripped it up the back. Sunbright yelped. "Stop that!"

The clerk insisted, "Lady Polaris promised to bleach my skull for a birdhouse if I didn't tell you immediately . . ."

"My lord barbarian," pouted the head maid, Hamuda. "If you'll just allow us—"

"I'm no one's *lord!*" Sunbright barked. Sensing a draft, he looked back and saw his own white rump. "My shirt!"

"To blazes with Lady Polaris! I'll send to her when I get a moment! Salve this cut, will you, it stings like fury! Get used to it, Sunbright! You're one of the rulers of this castle now, even if you are my underling!"

Candlemas went on berating his mages. It was true he'd ordered experiments made on these fleas. He'd had a vague hope they carried germs in their guts that could counteract the "wheat rust" that was threatening famine, since they fed on the cows that prospered eating blighted wheat. The arcanist was getting desperate, for every other experiment had failed. But he'd never intended his workshop to be the site of the testing. There were laboratories, storerooms, and halls aplenty in this castle, more than in some whole towns. And certainly he hadn't ordered giant, man-eating fleas, though he had mentioned a magic grain-toughening spell he thought might help. Still, his underlings were supposed to think for themselves, not follow orders like drunken zombies. He wasn't Sysquemalyn, after all. "You two'll be flogged for your incompetence! I never—"

He halted, whirled in place by a mighty barbarian hand. Sunbright towered over the smaller man with a heart-stopping frown.

Up close, the wild man was frightening. Although his hair was bright blond—thus naming him—Sunbright wore only a topknot and horsetail, with his temples shaved close. He bore no facial hair, but made up for it with myriad scars: enough scars to stitch a tapestry, though he was not much over twenty years old. He was strapped with ropy muscle, tough as an oak tree and as hard to kill, for he'd been to hell and beyond and survived, killed more monsters than Candlemas could imagine. Blood-spattered and scraped, with his bulky clothes in rags making him look even wider and taller, Sunbright was a frightening sight. Candlemas knew he could handle this young wildling—most of the time—but there was a dangerous gleam in his eyes.

"Let's split that nut now!" growled the northerner. "I am *not* your underling! *You* came asking *my* help! I agreed to study with you to learn Greenwillow's fate, and to see if, together, we could solve our problems. But we're to be equals in all things. Is that clear?"

Breathing carefully, keeping his face neutral, Candlemas replied, "Of course. My mistake. Being steward of this castle I tend to give orders easily, and forget. All apologies. But I might point out, if you are to live in this castle, you'll need to conform to certain rules, certain . . . conventions."

"I see no need for any conventions, or rules!" Sunbright leaned close, and Candlemas reflected even his smell was wild: wood smoke, pine sap, and musk. "I seek to become a shaman, to free Greenwillow's soul from whatever slimy corner of hell she's been banished to, and to eventually return to my tribe to . . . well, never mind why. So I don't—"

"Yes, and I've plenty to do too," Candlemas dared to

interrupt. He needed to show some pride. "And that's why I asked you here! I need to direct these nincompoops in finding a solution to this blight—which is beginning to spread to barley crops and apple orchards—before nine-tenths of the empire's peasants starve to death! And I need to address the demands of Lady Polaris, may Tyche, our Lady Luck, see she prosper, because this is *her* Castle Delia you stand in! And I must also . . . well, enough about me. Just don't think—"

"I'll think as I please!" So intent was he on arguing, Sunbright failed to see the maids creep in. "Don't tell me how to think! Or what to do! We'll work together or not at all! I'm not some bull-whipped dung-shoveler you've cowed into subjugation! I'm Sunbright Steelshanks of the Raven Clan of the Rengarth Barbarians, and my tribesmen bow to no one, including each other. There are no freer people in all the lands of all the gods!"

"Fine, yes, wonderful," Candlemas sighed, "but this is not the tundra, and you'll do well to follow a few of our customs. Such as regular baths, especially when one is drenched in gore! Now, if you'll be so kind—is that better?—please follow Hamuda and her girls to the baths. Because you're now as free as a man can be." He looked downward significantly.

Sunbright glanced down. While he'd glowered at the steward, the maids had industriously peeled off the rest of his torn, bloody, trail-worn clothing. For a moment, the barbarian stood in only his ring-studded moosehide boots, then the giggling maids wrapped him in a soft robe of black-and-white.

Candlemas raised his eyebrows. With a snort of disgust, Sunbright snatched his sword from a table and, boots jingling, followed a bevy of fawning, laughing maids out the door.

Chapter 2

With no idea of their destination, Sunbright tramped after the frowning Hamuda with the giggling maids trailing. The twin girls were pretty, he noted, small, not one higher than his elbow, with short, dark hair, unlike the women of his tribe, who were mostly northern blonde like himself. The girls had pixie faces and white teeth, and looked alike, as if they were all cousins. They'd been recruited from one tribe, he reasoned, an idea reinforced when they occasionally whispered words in a language he didn't recognize.

The dark, shining hair peeking from under their caps reminded him of Greenwillow's hair, black as only an elf's can be. The memory sent a pang through his chest. Greenwillow had been lost, crushed or burned to death in a fiery chasm of a lesser hell. He'd seen it with his own eyes, yet somehow couldn't believe she was gone forever. Her spirit was out there still, he knew. But whether it was a forlorn lover or a shaman-to-be who hoped so, he didn't know.

Lost in thought, he realized they'd stopped. The girls stood behind, Hamuda to one side. They waited.

So did Sunbright. "What is it?"

For answer, Hamuda waved a bony hand at the wall. It was all white, broken by square lines. A sigil of some kind was painted on the wall. When Sunbright hesitated longer, the head maid swallowed a sigh and pushed the wall. The square part swung back to reveal a room.

"Oh!" Sunbright nodded. "It's a door! I've seen these in the cities."

To the accompaniment of fresh giggling, he was ushered into the small room. The air inside was hot and steamy and the walls were lined with white tile. Two more maids waited inside, wearing only short white smocks and wilted hair. At the center of the room was a raised circular rim. Sunbright approached, touched it. "Is this a well? No, a hot spring."

"It's a bathtub," rasped Hamuda. "If master would be so kind as to get in?"

"In?" Sunbright clamped his hands on the rim and leaned over carefully. "How deep is it? There's a hot spring near our summer camping grounds that's bottomless, and it gets hotter the lower you go. If you weight a trout with a stone on a line, you can cook it by sinking it nine arm-lengths."

A gasp sounded behind, one maid finally losing control and setting all four sniggering with hands over their mouths. Sunbright smiled too, until he realized they were laughing *at* him. He bit down on a frown.

Hamuda clapped her hands, stifled the girls somewhat, and shooed out the two in black. Sunbright was left with the two bathmaidens, who held fluffy towels as they gestured to the water invitingly. When he still hesitated, one slipped over the edge of the tub in her shift, demonstrating that the "spring" was only knee deep. Still frowning, Sunbright shucked the robe, kicked off his boots, and climbed in. Unused to the slick bottom, he almost slipped and brained himself on the opposite edge of the tub. The bathmaidens pretended not to notice.

The water was so hot Sunbright's toes tingled, and his many insect wounds itched and stung. Gingerly, he made to sit.

One of the bathmaidens asked, "Is it too hot, milord? We can add cold water." Stroking a finger along a silver pipe to one side, she breathed, "Wet!" Cold water spilled from the spout, then she shut it off. "Dry!"

Wondering, Sunbright touched the pipe. It was cold. Sunbright stoked the pipe. "Wet!" Nothing happened. He asked the girls, "What is the secret?"

"No secret, milord. Just a simple cantra to turn the spigot off and on. The water is behind. It just needs to be released."

Sunbright squinted in the steamy room. "*You* can work magic?"

Giggles. "Everyone in Netheril can work magic, milord. At least, everyone born and raised in the empire. It's . . . part of our being."

"Magic. Can-truhs. Spit-guts." Suddenly Sunbright felt as thick as an addled mule. And as out of place. "I have a lot to learn."

The girls nodded absently. One unbraided his horsetail to gently comb out sticks and specks. The other plied a washcloth soft as bird down to scrub wood smoke and blood from his face. Surrendering, Sunbright laid his head back on the tub rim and let the girls scrub him. Their quiet competence and dark hair again reminded him of Greenwillow and brought a fresh pang of loneliness. *She* would never have mocked his ignorance.

He sighed aloud. "So much to learn."

* * * * *

Candlemas's workshop had been swept, scrubbed, and aired, but the maids hadn't dared to throw anything away, so the fresh-wiped tables were heaped with the remains of his work and hobbies.

A dark, dumpy, bearded, balding, paunchy man, Candlemas knew he was no beauty, and took little regard of his looks. Despite his status and personal wealth, he wore only a gray wool smock, rope belt, and sandals when working and administering from his high tower. Vanity, love of clothing and jewelry, and lust for fine robes only distracted an arcanist from his studies, he believed. Candlemas was determined to study hard and soar up the ladder, to someday be as fabulous an archwizard as Lady Polaris herself. Perhaps then, when he owned his own floating castle and lands, and had his own under-mages slaving to resolve *his* problems, then he might succumb to vanity. For now, he could look like a shepherd and keep busy.

But a lot of work had been lost. Some of the broken jars and pots he recognized on the table had been vital experiments that he'd pursued for months. Growling at the callous idiocy of his underlings, he gathered a handful of trash, marched to the high windows, and pushed it through the mild shield spell that kept out the icy wind. He let it drop onto the fields or forest or whatever lay below. Though he was steward of all the lands visible from the castle, right now he didn't care what happened to them. They belonged to Lady Polaris after all, not him. Very little really belonged to him except his knowledge and studies; his hard work that had been destroyed, again.

He'd hurled out the last of it when Sunbright marched into the workshop. The young man's face was still pink from the hot bath, but clean, his hair neatly combed and retied, his temples neatly shaven. He wore his thick knee-high boots and an off-white shirt that reached to his knees with a wide belt of brown leather. The boy (as Candlemas thought of him) dressed as simply as he, like a son he might someday have. It gave the arcanist a glad feeling: if they agreed on simple clothing, they'd agree on much else, and accomplish more.

Candlemas glanced around his half-emptied workshop, then waved his hands. "Never mind the losses. Things can be replaced. Let's get on with your lessons. Now . . . the first step in conjuring magic is summoning it. So—"

"Where does it come from?" Sunbright interrupted.

"What?" Candlemas flexed his pudgy fingers. "Where does what come from?"

"Magic. Where does it come from?"

"The weave, of course. Now—"

"Where does the weave come from?"

"What do you mean, where? It just is. Like . . . the rain."

"Rain comes from the sky, from clouds. Clouds are full of water, as anyone who's climbed a mountain into a cloud can tell you." Sunbright stood spraddled-legged, arms folded across his chest. "If magic rains, where from?"

"It doesn't rain from anywhere," snapped Candlemas. "You summon it and it's there, to use as you wish."

"It must have a source. Everything has a source." Sunbright frowned in concentration. "Even the mightiest river is formed from the tiniest streams of the hills."

"Well, there." Candlemas absently picked up one of his

fine silver statues. It had been a medusa, but most of the snakes were broken off her head. He set it down again, unsure what to do with it. "Magic is collected from the thousands of tiny sources that make up the weave. If you can answer your own questions, why ask me?"

"I need the answers wizards have gathered over the ages. I have only the knowledge of my people, the barbarians of the tundra. They know many things, but not all, and I've much to learn. The girls showed me that."

"Girls? Oh, you mean the bathmaidens." Candlemas chuckled knowingly. "I imagine they can teach you a thing or two. Did you enjoy them?"

"Enjoy? No. I felt like an ox awaiting slaughter, too stupid to see the hammer in the butcher's hand."

"Butchery? Slaughter? The girls mentioned that?"

"No, of course not!"

"Then who brought it up? Hamuda?"

"No one said it. When I talk of dressing livestock, I speak of myself!"

"But—never mind." Candlemas rubbed the top of his bald head and moved to an empty table. From a pocket in his smock he drew a steel stylus, but he had nothing to write on and didn't know why he'd taken it out. Angrily, he put it away. "We're getting off the track. Now be silent and listen. How do you expect to learn anything if you keep asking questions?"

Sunbright blinked. "What?"

Disgusted with both of them, Candlemas growled, "See? That didn't make sense. You've got me babbling nonsense to your pesky questions. What I meant to say was, If you keep hurling questions at me, I won't have time to answer them. No, wait, that's wrong too, damn it!"

"Wait." Sunbright waved his hands. "Ignore the source of magic for now. What's the *price* of magic?"

"Price? Magic doesn't cost anything. It's free!"

"Free like what? Deer in the forest?"

"Forget the animals, would you? Is food all you think of? Jewels of Jannath, I wish I were twenty-odd again and had your appetite!"

"I wasn't talking of food, though now that you mention it, I am hungry. How old are you, anyway?" Sunbright was nothing if not curious.

"Old enough not to discuss butchery with a bath-maiden!" the mage retorted hotly. Plying magic, Candlemas had in fact lived three times the span of a normal life, but he didn't like to be reminded of it. "Can we get back to the lesson? When I say magic is free, I mean it's there for the taking by someone who can master it. Like the damned deer, if you will."

"I thought we'd forgotten the deer," Sunbright chided. "And I may just be a moss-brained barbarian, but even I know magic costs. Nothing is free. If you shoot a deer or an elk, you must lay it on its side gently, slit the belly to release its spirit, then stuff its mouth with lichens to feed the beast on its way to the other world. Otherwise it's offended, and won't be reborn to be killed again next year to feed your family. And then there'd be no more elk, and the people and timber wolves would starve, and so all. That's what I mean by the price of magic."

Staring, Candlemas sputtered, "What a barrel of blather! What superstitious claptrap! Elk aren't reborn to be shot again. Elk calves come from mother elk—bull elk know what to do with randy cows, at least! They make little elk. You can have as many elk as you like. They're free for the taking, and so is magic!"

Put out, the steward stamped to another table. Propped against a cracked urn was a painting of a boy teaching his dog to jump for a snack. But a giant flea's claw had punctured the boy's face. Furiously, Candlemas kited the ruined painting at a window. It rebounded off the shield spell and clattered on the floor.

He whirled. "Why can't you just believe me when I

tell you something? The knowledge I offer is the sum total of eons of study by the most learned mages of all time. Men and women so wise they transcend humanity to challenge the gods themselves! But if you question every little thing I tell you—"

"I don't believe anything I don't witness myself." Sunbright cut in. "I don't believe half of what I witness anyway. The eyes can be deceived just as easily as the mind, which you would know if you ever hunted elk in a spring fog near the ocean at sunrise. You'd loose a quiver full of arrows into wisps of fog and come home with nothing on your shoulders. And where would you be then? Hungry!"

"I don't need to go hunting!" Candlemas shouted back. He was unsure when the shouting had begun. "If I want venison, I ring a bell and tell the cook's boy. Hunting is for peasants! It requires no more knowledge than a cat pawing a mouse. It's instinctive. Any fool—"

"Fool? The hunters of my tribe are the smartest, fastest, toughest men and women on the tundra! The tribe counts on them—"

"Will you stop nattering about that misbegotten clot of lunatics who hunker on the prairie and gnaw knucklebones by moonlight? I'm sick of hearing about them! Forget them! That's in the past. You've been blessed by the gods, can't you see that? You're in Castle Delia, on the threshold of the entire Netherese Empire, with a chance to advance up the ranks of true nobility—"

"Nobles who hunt men for sport?" the barbarian sneered. "Nobles who starve entire cities without conscience? Nobles who dump garbage on sacred groves—"

"If you don't care to associate with nobles, why the blazes did you come here in the first place?"

"*You* invited me!" Sunbright jabbed a finger like a fireplace poker. "But I'll admit I need help. I scoured the empire for any sign of Greenwillow and failed to trace her! I was despairing of what to do when you came along—"

"I invited you here because I thought you showed promise! You've exhibited a natural flair for magic—or call it shamanism if you please—and I thought you could think! Instead you rant like a crack-brained child about birds and flowers, and clouds shaped like oysters!"

"Oysters?"

"Can't you get this straight? Can't you see your opportunity? The Neth are the greatest, most enchanted race ever to inhabit this sphere! We've learned all there is to know about magic, mostly. We've sweated and slaved to learn the rules of dweomer, to bend magic to one's will! Based on that—"

"But at what price! To lose your souls? To be heartless fiends, insensitive to suffering, like vampires come up from the ice holes?"

"Damn your ice hole! Vampires come from dark caves, not underwater! How will you ever learn clinging to these foolish beliefs? Can nothing I say penetrate that stony barbarian skull? Open your mind and *think!*"

"I'll not bargain a bear for his teeth! I know what magic costs! I've seen the old ones with their bent backs, their very hearts and livers shrunk beyond endurance from practicing the ways of the shaman, from healing the sick and tasting the wind, warning of storms and tracking the seals under the ice. No one twists magic to his will. Magic twists the twister until it ties you in knots. No one takes up magic unless he's willing to sacrifice their all for the good of the tribe. Yet you would have me believe that a wizard can reach out a finger and turn magic on and off like a spit-gut!"

"Like a what?" Then the arcanist sighed. "Never mind. We're getting nowhere. I had hoped this would be your first lesson, and we'd get through the elementary principles quickly. Instead I'm arguing the origins of magic!

"The question has been asked before, you know," Candlemas continued. "Wizards have sought the source of magic for centuries. Though the goddess Mystryl is certainly in control of a great deal of what comprises the weave, no one believes she controls it all. Certainly she didn't *create* the weave. . . ."

"Why not just say so, then?" retorted Sunbright. "I'd have accepted that answer!"

"What?" Candlemas was suddenly tired, as if he'd conjured an elephant from the far southern deserts. He wished he had. A mad mammoth might prove less truculent than this hammerheaded barbarian. "What would you accept?"

"That no one knows the source of magic!"

"Oh, very well. Here, let me say, 'No one knows what the source of magic is.' How's that?"

Sunbright folded his arms again. "Go on. I'm listening."

"Good, good." Candlemas dragged out a stool and sat down. But a leg was cracked, and he almost spilled onto the floor. "Uh, that's all for today. I'm exhausted. Come back tomorrow morning."

"Very well." The barbarian padded out of the workshop, sure and silent as a panther.

Candlemas watched him go. "Ye gods. What a bargain I've struck . . . what else can go wrong?"

A page, a young boy in a black-and-white tabard, scurried around a screen. "Master Candlemas? Lady Polaris wants you."

The pudgy mage stifled a groan. "That's what can go wrong."

Threading his tables and stacks, Candlemas came to a black palantir mounted on an eagle's claw stand. In the globe floated the shining head of Lady Polaris, his liege lord. Even Candlemas, who had lust for women but no love, felt a pang when he beheld her. Polaris had snow-white hair cascading around her face and shoulders. Her face was calm as a queen's, only far more lovely. She was the most beautiful woman in the empire, and grew more beautiful every year, a beauty that bespoke enchantment, though no one knew her secret. Her mysteries were manifold and unfathomable. Her stunning beauty made her master of any scene, and rendered men all but dumb, even filtered by the smoky glass of the palantir. Even the page boy was awestruck.

"Candlemas," she said without preamble. "How goes the solution to the blight?"

"Uh, well, milady." Polaris disliked negative news. "We're making progress—"

"Good." She dismissed the problem. "I need something."

Always, thought Candlemas. How many hands did she think he possessed?

"You must fashion a device to move bones without my moving or blinking or having to chant. In the shape of a brooch, perhaps, but nothing that will attract attention. I need it by the new moon. Have you got that?"

"Yes, milady. I'll get—" But the palantir had gone blank.

"Bones!" Candlemas swore. "What kind of fool does she take me for? The only bones she ever touches are dice! And while she's gambling and demanding my help, whole villages will wither and die! Where will she get money then, eh? Where?"

But Candlemas was ranting to himself while a wide-eyed page stared. "Get busy, boy." The boy scooted away. Candlemas chided himself, "And me too."

* * * * *

Sunbright didn't go far. There was something he had to do, and he'd been dreading it, putting it off. Now was the time to face it.

He stood in a stone-lined hallway cut by windows down one side. As with Candlemas's airy tower, nothing showed outside but the purple slopes of the Barren Mountains. Tightening his gut, Sunbright stepped to the window, braced both hands against the window frame, and leaned out to look.

The side of the castle dropped sheer for many stories, a dozen at least, all pierced by square or round windows. Far down showed the footings of solid granite. Below that . . .

The earth and dark forest far, far below.

Sunbright groaned involuntarily. His palms on the window frame were slick with sweat, trembling. He wanted to back away, but forced himself to stand firm. He'd known all along where he was, of course. He'd seen Castle Delia float over the southlands (for a tundra dweller, everything below the Barren Mountains was south), had known it was Candlemas's home. So when the arcanist offered to bring him "to his workshop," the truth had eventually dawned on him. Now he was here, and he'd have to adjust—

It was no good. His legs shook so violently his kneecaps drummed the stone wall. Stand here too long, and he'd pitch out the window like dice rattling out of a cup. Slowly, shuffling his broad boots, he crept away from the gaping space.

"Is something amiss, milord?"

Already spooked, Sunbright jumped at the girl's soft question. Backing against the inner wall, he willed his heart to stop pounding. Sweat trickled down his cheeks, dripped salt onto his lips. He must look a fool, he thought, the greenest of country bumpkins. Humility was not helping his pride this day. Earlier he'd had to have a water closet explained. He'd rather face a pack of starving wolves than live through that embarrassment again.

He didn't belong in this place. Room lights, water closets, running water, even drains that magically whisked away garbage were alien to him, as was the inhabitants' casual use of magic. Even the sweepers could nudge a dustpan along without touching it. Sunbright was here to learn magic from Candlemas, and he knew less than the slop boy who could spark a fire with a flick of his finger. Surrounded by magic-users, Sunbright felt like a trained raccoon at a market fair: it might wear clothes and do tricks, but it wasn't human.

The girl sensed the reason for his unease. Moving gracefully to the window, she peeked out, murmured softly, "It *is* high. Being in the clouds takes getting used to. I couldn't even walk past a window for the first month I lived here."

For something to say, Sunbright croaked, "How long . . . ?"

"Have I been here? A year and some months. I work for my dowry. My family had all girls and little money." She smiled, not to mock, but to comfort. Like many maids, she was small, pixieish, with short-cropped hair and natural curls now emphasized by dampness. She was one of the bathmaidens, and still wore a bulky black robe.

"Where . . . ?"

". . . is my village? It's very small, at the headwaters of the Ger, but in sight of Patrician Peak. Frosttop, we call it, not that it needs a name. Not many come our way."

Sunbright nodded. His breathing had slowed, and he mopped his brow with his sleeve. He hated being up in the clouds. His land was the tundra, table-flat, where a musk ox looked like a mouse standing on the horizon.

He'd been up high only once, and that accidently, on the back of a dragon, and he still screamed in his sleep when he recalled that trip.

Patiently, the girl waited while he gained his composure. "You know, my lord—"

"I'm no man's lord. Or woman's. Call me Sunbright. Please."

She bit her lip. "Very well, uh, Sunbright. You know, it's not often we have a visitor so tall and strong, so handsome and dashing. You make a girl wonder what the future might bring." As if scratching idly, she tugged open the fluffy black robe, revealing the soft upper curve of a modest breast.

Dully, the barbarian nodded. Without knowing why, he reached for her, and she leaned to meet him. But his hand didn't stray to her throat or breast. Rather, the knotty scarred brown hand stroked her hair along one side. She smiled shyly, confused by a gentle touch from such a fearsome man.

As if speaking in a foreign tongue, Sunbright said, "One day a fine and simple man with violet eyes will ask a drink of water, then marry you, get you with strong children, a round half-dozen. But you'd best get about it soon. It's unnatural to live here on high, suspended on naught but magic. T'will come a time when thunder tolls and these castles fall."

Surprise flickered in the girl's brown eyes, then fright. Sunbright felt her fear, and sensed it within himself. How had he made such a pronouncement? He'd spoken like a seer, a prophet.

A shaman.

Dazed by his own behavior, his hand dropped from the girl's hair. She bit her lip, excused herself, and bustled away, robe pulled tight around her neck.

Sunbright shook his head, laid a hand on the inner wall for support. The rough stone tingled under his fingers, as if he felt stone for the first time in his life. The floor too seemed full of imperfections: dips and whorls, and huge cracks where before it had been smooth.

Why was he seeing things so clearly, so brightly? Had someone cast a spell on him? Or had he cast one upon himself?

What power? What knowledge?

Why here?

Why now?

Chapter 3

Even Sunbright's nights were disturbed, for he
dreamt of Greenwillow.

Three nights now he'd dreamt of her, visions of love,
memories of battle, miles of travel they'd made together.

But tonight was different.

A dark forest was rife with roots and rocks, a foot-
tripping tangle impossible to see. Black boles surrounded him. But ahead, as if between prison bars,
flitted his elven lover. Greenwillow of the Cormanthyr
was tall and slim but with a woman's curves, her face
pale as milk, her eyes and ears slanted and exotic, her
hair flowing down her back in black billows. This night
she wore a sheer gown of white silk, embroidered all
over with elaborate runes and vines, and that was

strange, for Sunbright had never seen her in anything but emerald green and black leather armor. She tripped among the dark trunks like an errant bird, and he stumbled to catch her. Occasionally she cast a glance over her shoulder, but always tripped onward, eager to lead him. To show him something? What could it be?

Hard pressed to keep her in sight, Sunbright thrashed through the woods. In the pitchy night, he banged his shoulder against rough bark, stubbed his toes on roots, conked his forehead and scratched his face on branches. But Greenwillow sailed on, light as a breeze. They ran for dream-miles. Sunbright gasped for her to slow down, heard only his own panting. *"Greenwillow! Wait! Wait for me. . . ."*

The blackness began to change, to wane. A bright light like a single torch speared the night. It came from high overhead, gathering strength, banishing the blackness. Sunbright squinted, picked out Greenwillow only as a dark, slim silhouette against white light. Then it was too painful to look, so he plowed on blindly.

He grunted as he fetched up hard against an upthrust chunk of granite, skinning his knees. He slapped at the barrier to find a way around, found it rose only higher on each side. Cursing, shading his eyes against the fiery glare, he swung a knee on the stone to climb over. But the top surface felt strange: cold and very smooth. Too smooth to be natural. A quarried rock here in the forest? The wall of a ruin?

Backing, he felt the wall. Square everywhere. How . . . ?

"Sunbright, wake up!"

Greenwillow's voice, the first time in a long time he'd heard it, clear and sweet as a lark's warble.

He opened his eyes, and his blood ran chill.

The dreamer stood in the stone hallway of Castle Delia. The barrier he'd struck was the windowsill. Sleepwalking, he'd tried to mount it, climb over. With a gasp, he looked down. He'd have fallen a mile or more to the forest floor.

Gagging, Sunbright stumbled back from the open window. He clawed sweat from his face and eyes. But he still had to squint, for the fiery glare out the window was no dream.

High in the sky, slicing the night in an arc, was a shooting star. Even as he watched, it completed its journey from the heavens to the earth. The glare illuminated distant tall trees like twigs in a campfire—for just a second, then the light was snuffed out. Sunbright thought he felt the earth under his boots shake, but that was his imagination. He wasn't on the earth, but floating a mile above it.

On trembling legs, he staggered back to his plain chambers and tousled bed. He closed the bedchamber door and bolted it, then wedged a heavy chair under the latch.

He collapsed on the sodden bed, tried in vain to recall Greenwillow's face and sweet voice.

* * * * *

"What do you mean, you want to go down to the forest? There's nothing down there but—but trees!"

"I want to see a tree." Sunbright sounded petulant. His head ached and he was dizzy. He wasn't sleeping well, and never would until he stood on firm ground.

"Walk in the gardens! We have nine of them! What about our agreement, our working together? Do you know how many artifacts I have to interpret?"

"No." The barbarian's tone suggested he didn't care, either.

"I'll show you!" Candlemas ignored Sunbright's reticence as he marched across the big workshop.

Sunbright followed. Slowly he was learning his way

around Castle Delia, or Candlemas's small corner of it. The mage's realm was mostly this tower on one corner of the floating mountain that supported Delia. The tower was a dozen stories high, big enough inside for a chariot race on any floor. Candlemas's workshop occupied the topmost floor, a room bigger than Sunbright's village. Tables and screens and partition walls split the chamber into smaller areas, but always the high windows loomed in all four walls. The floors below, Sunbright had seen, contained more rooms and workshops where some thirty lesser mages worked at dirty, complicated, and arcane tasks per Candlemas's orders. The pudgy mage was an Inventive, he'd explained, one of the empire's leading experts at creating and destroying artifacts, and so a favored employee of Lady Polaris. Secondly Candlemas was a Variator, but the barbarian hadn't grasped that word's meaning. There were more flavors of magic in this society than colors to the forest, and everyone from the mightiest archwizard to the dumbest stable hand practiced magic. Everyone except Sunbright.

And this single tower was only a tiny fraction of the castle, for Candlemas's other realm of responsibility was steward, overseer of the holdings of Lady Polaris. Below and far out of sight were farms and orchards, plantations and ponds, mills and mines that belonged to this one woman who, it was carefully explained by the maid who'd fetched his breakfast, was one of the supreme archwizards of the empire, but not the uppermost: merely the tenth or twelfth. Archwizards spent most of the time scrambling to one-up their rivals, to step upon their enemies while climbing the ladder.

Like salmon hurrying to mount a cataract and spill into a fisher's trap, Sunbright thought.

Castle Delia was almost a square league in area, and the mansions, outbuildings, and battlements on it ran for acre upon acre, stacked six and seven stories high in places. Two hundred and sixty rooms made up the main house, a maid had breathed. Or so it was rumored: no one knew for sure. Over two thousand servants kept it tidy under the all-seeing eye of Umeko, Acting Chamberlain (the former chamberlain, Sysquemalyn, had vanished) for those few occasions when Lady Polaris actually visited. For it stunned Sunbright to learn that this vast castle was only one of seven such keeps owned and maintained by Lady Polaris, in addition to her mansions in many of the larger floating cities, including one in the capital city of Ioulaum. To the tundra-dwelling barbarian, who owned a sword and a blanket, the idea of so much wealth—and the power it brought—was incomprehensible.

And his difficulties with the city-mansion were immediate and irritating. For one thing, in the few days he'd been here, healing, resting, and arguing with Candlemas, he'd consistently gotten lost. Many rooms and hallways had no outside windows, being lit by magically illuminated globes. In such conditions Sunbright had no way to tell north from south, east from west. He felt like an addled child every time he fetched up in some dead-end hallway or dusty cellar, which was often enough. A maid had offered to assign him a boy as a guide, but the barbarian's pride had bristled at the idea. Eventually, he decided to stick to outside hallways to keep his sense of direction, even though the yawning windows with their precipitous drops made his stomach ache and his bowels pinch.

And now he'd told Candlemas he wanted to be on the ground a while, and had sounded whiny. If it weren't for needing to find Greenwillow, he'd climb the Barren Mountains and take up sheepherding.

"Here!" The wizard led him around a trio of ornate gold-leafed screens that depicted heroic battles and quests from the distant past. Behind the screen were odd statues and rolled rugs, glass chandeliers hanging from temporary wooden frames and a dozen or more mismatched chests, both plain and fancy. Planting his sandaled feet before one, Candlemas uttered a cantra to spring the lock and flung back the lid.

Sunbright peered. Inside were gadgets and gewgaws, velvet pouches, long wooden boxes, bundles wrapped in cloth and tied with ribbon. Candlemas plucked one up at random. To Sunbright it looked like something cut from a reindeer's guts, bulbous and tubular, but crafted of silver, now tarnished black in the crevices. "Do you know what this is?"

The barbarian shook his head.

"Neither do I," snapped the mage in disgust. "But it's magic. I have three apprentices who do nothing but detect for magic. Everything in these chests is enchanted, and I don't know what *any* of them do!"

Sunbright watched as Candlemas opened another chest, then another. Most were full. "Where did you get these things?"

"They're found in odd rooms in the castle, bought in markets, won by Lady Polaris in gambling dens, and from her neverending wagers. She wins a pot of gadgets and sends them to me, and *I'm* supposed to interpret them!"

Sunbright was mildly interested. "And do you?"

"Sometimes." The mage slammed the lid. "I work on whatever problem or question she hurls at me today, then drop it for tomorrow's emergency. Most I can fob off to underlings, but sometimes I must work nonstop to glean the workings of some piece of arcane junk. I once spent three weeks analyzing a jeweled poker-sort-of-thing. Polaris—excuse me—*Lady* Polaris insisted it would harden quicksilver to silver. Do you know what it did? It curled one's hair! It came off some fop's vanity table!"

"Why would someone want to curl their hair?" asked Sunbright.

Candlemas rolled his eyes. "Never mind. That's not the point." He swept his arms to encompass the jammed chests. "I had hoped you, with your promise of shamanism, could help me solve some problems. The wheat rust, for one. Blight, actually. One assistant thinks it's attacking rye now. Shamen are supposed to understand growing things. I had hoped that, among other experiments, you could assist me in sorting these gadgets, perhaps find one that cures plant disease. There are enchanted tools here that resemble farm implements. Maybe one deters crop rot. A magic sifter, or wand of rowan wood, or a stone that, buried in the field, sucks up evil influences. . . ."

Idly, Sunbright touched the top of an iron-strapped chest. The glyph protecting it shocked his hand. Sucking a scorched fingertip, Sunbright opined, "I couldn't even break one of these locks, let alone puzzle out your—gaj-dits. Blight is part of the natural order of things, you know. Plants grow strong, are attacked by disease, but fight it off and grow stronger. Or they die and are replaced. All things scribe the circle eventually, come from earth and return to it. Us too."

Candlemas rubbed his head, work-roughened, chemical-stained hands rasping on his bare scalp. "I don't need a lesson in barbarian philosophy. Yes, things pass away. And *I'll* pass away, and so will thousands of peasants, if we don't cure this blight! Don't you understand? If we can employ magic properly, we can undo all these ills and make the world a better place! The point is not to give in to despair, but to best it! Magic can solve *everything* given enough time and effort! There's no limit to its power!"

"Everything has limits," said Sunbright evenly. He fingered the nose of a statue, a bronze beauty holding a two-headed snake across her bare shoulders. "A touch to this statue wears it away, in a small way. This castle will be dust some day. Trying to stop the decline of things, or to hasten natural ways—hardening quicksilver to silver—never works for long, and usually backfires. If you would cure your blights, burn the crops. That's a natural cure and ends the problem. Let people move elsewhere and eat differently until new, clean crops appear. The land and people will be stronger for it. But to hope that a random tool from a heap of junk will solve your problem is silly. To cure an ill, you need only visit the source. Sit upon the earth, in the field, fast, clear your mind, learn how the grain eats of the earth, and why the disease works its evil."

"There isn't time." Candlemas stared out a distant window.

Sunbright continued, "And another thing. Where's your end of the bargain? You agreed to help me track Greenwillow's soul. How fare those efforts?"

The elder mage only waved his arms. "Again, there might be something in these boxes. Mirrors are the best thing I know for seeing to other worlds and planes. Telescopes sometimes, or kaleidoscopes. Glass eggs, too. There are probably six of each in these trunks, and more downstairs. And enchanted doors: there are five in the cellar, stacked against the wall. Feel free to fit them to frames and chant over them. By the time you're as old as me. . . ."

The barbarian peered at the trunks, frowning. "I'd give the same answer. A mirror might show some other world, but only that part desired by whoever enchanted it. So too a glass egg or door. To find Greenwillow, we'd need some part of her: a lock of hair, or a ring she wore for a long time. Shamans can learn the animal by reading a bone, or commune with the dead while sleeping on a skull. But we have no piece of Greenwillow. Only dreams."

That thought conjured the night's vision, a dark forest, Greenwillow's ghost leading him on to—what?

He interrupted himself. "I need to go to the forest."

"Fine, fine. Ask the birds if hollow wheat kernels are bitter, or if groundhogs can gnaw bare cobs." Candlemas waved a weary hand. "I'll fetch you at sundown."

He forked his fingers to invoke a shift spell, but Sunbright stopped him. "Let me retrieve my tackle."

"Why? I said I'd fetch you within hours."

The barbarian didn't answer, only turned for his chambers. Candlemas swore softly and slammed the lid of a trunk.

* * * * *

How proceeds the fire?

The fire amongst the humans? They seek heat, and we heap on coals.

Far below the earth, in chambers that had never seen sun, whirled a score of creatures like tops with diamond tails. Cruel gashes with rock-hard edges were their mouths, for they could eat anything found underground: roots, rocks, moles, hibernating bears, tombstones, and bones. But mostly they fed on magic, for enchantment ran through their very fiber. They were the Phaerimm, unknown to men, seldom seen, and even then invariably mistaken for dust devils. Usually they destroyed the observer, champed his bones and muscles to bits, leaving only scraps and stains in the wilderness.

I like it not. Piling magic on magic puts them at risk of burning out, but it endangers us as much.

We discussed that at length. There is no other way. We shall be safe. Their idiocy shall scour the earth, but not penetrate here.

If we are careful.

We are always careful. We must be, for we are so few.

We are the oldest living things on the planet.

All the more reason to safeguard.

The humans will be undone, have no fear. They are soft and cannot last.

Look how our drain spell sucks the nourishment from their food. Soon they will have naught to eat.

They'll eat each other.

All the better. Their bones will enrich the soil. And we will again hold the worlds above and below.

If we give them magic enough to choke.

The humans are foolish to use magic so freely. Don't they see it hastens their demise?

They see nothing, know nothing. They will burn out and cease to be.

This new magic we've pulled from the sky will add more dweomer than ever before. Mountains of magic!

For an orgy—a holocaust of magical energy!

But it will take time. Many revolutions of the sun.

Not so many. Not so . . .

* * * * *

It felt good to have soft earth and needles under his boots, to smell pine sap and wet moss, to hear warblers trill and red squirrels chitter, to feel the wind on his scalp. Sunbright felt at home.

But more exciting, he thought he recognized this stretch of forest.

It was hard to say, for he'd dreamt it, at night, when distracted by the vision of Greenwillow. But the folds of land looked right, the configuration of those two joined pines was familiar, and the spidery bulk of that bull pine called to him. His lover, his sweet elf, had floated that way, he thought. Always having lived more by emotion than by logic, Sunbright followed.

It felt good to touch nature again, and also to shoulder his traveling gear. He wore the heavy Harvester across his back in a new bull-hide scabbard and at his belt hung the warhammer of Dorlas, son of Drigor, a weapon he'd inherited and promised to someday return to the Sons of Baltar in the far Iron Mountains. A new goat-hide vest was laced across his chest and a bright green shirt hung to his knees. Around his waist was a thick, studded belt, and his tall moosehide boots with the rings and buckles were newly-blacked and the leather oiled. The workmanship of his clothing and tackle was exquisite, hand-stitched by Lady Polaris's seamstresses and saddlemakers. Not that he cared: he would have gone abroad in rags to tramp the forest.

And tramp he did, past trees like pillars, in a hushed, green-filtered, luminous light. He moved quickly, driving game before him, delighting in their quick fluttering. The flick of a deer's white tail as it bounded away. The snuffling of a badger dragging its striped head back into its sett. The twitter of chickadees tracking him from twig to twig. The slither of a green snake as it oozed around a bole and clung to the bark with its belly scales, tongue flickering. Sunbright breathed deep and laughed aloud, glad to be back, as if he'd been gone years and not a few days. The only dark cloud was the need to return to the floating castle high above like a squat stone cloud. But he pushed that thought aside and gloried in his freedom, like a child let out of school.

Walking for miles, he watched everywhere, naturally curious and trained to be cautious. At one point he halted, bemused. Drawing his sword, he hunkered alongside a pine, slowed his breathing, unfocused his eyes to better detect movement.

Something had alerted him, but he didn't know what. A sense of being watched or, oddly, spoken of. (Though he couldn't know it, he sensed the Phaerimm plotting far below the earth.) In time, doubting his own senses, Sunbright sheathed his sword and moved on, walking warily until he was half a mile away. Finally he dismissed the unease with an old adage. " 'Imagination is a two-edged sword: a blessing and a curse.' "

Pausing to rest, he lay flat and drank from a rippling stream, surprising a frog. He ate a meager lunch from a haversack, pressed on. Somehow he knew which paths to follow, for Greenwillow had shown him. In the same way, he knew she was still alive, waiting for him, helping him. Helping him find her.

Then, abruptly, he found his (their) destination. And it made sense, for the shooting star and Greenwillow's warning had broken his sleepwalking, kept him from pitching out a window.

Here the shooting star had plunged into a hillside, blowing open a crater like a tumbled mine shaft.

Easing his sword from its scabbard, though he sensed no danger, Sunbright paced forward. The forest here was scrubby, rife with pin oaks and mossy granite rocks taller than himself. Yet several rocks had been blown aside like dandelion fluff when the star crashed. The forest was hushed, for animals still avoided the area. Quietly, wary of hidden holes, Sunbright padded across old leaves, then onto fresh-turned dirt of yellow and brown. The hillside was not high, and the impact had split the top like a loaf of bread, leaving a large hole. Sunbright tiptoed to peek inside.

The bottom was ten feet down at a slant. Nothing showed but dirt. Considering the size of the hole, and being unfamiliar with shooting stars, Sunbright had no idea how deep the star might be buried.

He stood up straight and checked the forest all around, but saw nothing but a pair of cardinals chasing each other through a wild rose bush. The sun was one hand over the horizon, for he'd spent the afternoon walking. Now that he was here, he didn't know what to do. Once he called quietly, "Greenwillow?"

No answer.

Humming a love song to himself, he swept clean a rock and sat down to wait for sunset, Harvester across his knees.

* * * * *

"There you are! What's this hole?"

Sunbright rose to meet the arcanist. Candlemas, always curious, sank sandal-deep in fresh dirt as he climbed the low hill and peered into blackness.

"A shooting star landed last night. I saw it from a window." The memory of almost tumbling out made Sunbright's knees shake, but he clamped them straight. "I don't know how deep it is."

"Keeper of the Sun!" Candlemas reared back as if from a bonfire. "Feel that enchantment!"

Sunbright stood alongside, but felt nothing. "What? It's magic?"

"By Jannath's Tears, I'll say! My, it's—imagine how strong the magic must be if we can *feel* it at a distance!" The stocky mage jumped in place like a child offered a treat. "We must dig it up! I must have that star!"

Shrugging, Sunbright sheathed Harvester, cast about for some digging implement, for he wouldn't ply his sword as a shovel. Breaking a dead branch clipped by the fallen star, the barbarian slid down into the hole and dug. Candlemas helped, shoveling dirt with his hands like a dog. As the sun disappeared, he picked up a stone, muttered a small cantra, and set it glowing like cold fire.

"That's a handy spell," Sunbright told him.

"It's nothing."

The star was not deep, it turned out, not over two

feet buried. Sunbright missed it at first and started to dig around, until Candlemas stopped him. "What are you doing? Dig it free!"

"This?" The barbarian thumped the branch on the star. It looked like a plain, lumpy stone, burned black. "This can't be it."

"Why not?" Candlemas hunkered on his hams above the hole. "What did you expect?"

"Shouldn't it glow, like your rock there?"

A snort. "No. It was afire when it fell, like iron in a forge. It was snuffed by the dirt."

"Seems pretty ordinary for something so magical."

"And what's an emperor's crown but a hoop of pointed gold? Yet it can move mountains." The mage ran his hands over the burned, sandy surface lovingly. "My, my. I might get my own floating city after all. Imagine the value of this thing! I'll be *rich*."

"It'd make a fine anchor." Sunbright tried and failed to lever the thing up. "It's powerful heavy. Or else stuck."

"It's not stuck. Here, give me a hand."

But dig and grab hold as they might, the two men couldn't budge the star, though it was no bigger than a pumpkin. If anything, the star settled deeper into the hole they scratched, as if alive and wishing to hide.

Sweating, swearing, Sunbright opined, "You'll have to dig away the hillside, and hitch an ox team to drag it out. It weighs more than lead!"

"I think you're right." Candlemas's face and hands were sooty, his arms sandy to the elbows. "It must be made of . . . I can't think what. The densest metals are lead and gold, though the old books speak of adamantine being harder and denser. Still, this is the most solid stuff I've ever seen. I doubt your sword could scratch it."

"We'll never know," countered the barbarian.

The forest was dark. In a distant bog crickets chirped and peepers cheeped. Candlemas reached out, grabbed the small stone he'd illuminated, snuffed its magic and turned the hole black. "We'll return on the morrow. I'll have Damita from the stables bring a hitching rig and a stone boat. Then—"

"What's that?" Sunbright snapped his head up, out of the hole. "There's a rushing in the treetops."

"Night wind. It's—no, wait."

Candlemas squinted in the dark. The little star was glowing. Ripples of green light chased each other across its surface.

Sunbright glanced down, hissed, "You said it wouldn't glow!"

"It shouldn't!" Candlemas backed up, slid on sand, landed back on the cooling star. Eldritch fire illuminated his hairy toes. "It's magical, but—"

Near Candlemas's shoulder, Sunbright ducked as the rushing sounded again, louder, as if a giant bird beat the forest, hunting them, or a hurricane stirred the tree crowns. But the sound was loudest in the hole. The rushing came from the fallen star. "It's hissing! It's working! It's—"

"Get out!" Candlemas grabbed the barbarian's belt to haul himself along even while pushing. "Get out! It's going to explo—"

Green light flashed from the star, engulfed the two men, and winked out.

The smoking hole lay empty.

Chapter 4

Mouth open, hands clawed in an instinctive flinch, legs splayed to dive out of the hole, Sunbright stood frozen, unable to move anything, even his eyes. All that worked was his brain, and it wondered at what he saw.

The dirt and rock and black sky were drawn from solid objects to fine threads. A stone under his foot shrank and elongated, until it was a gray line like a pencil mark traveling from underneath him out of the hole, into infinity. So too went the dirt, and the nothingness of the hole itself. The night sky was shredded into splinters that sailed past him like black spears to mingle with strings of soil and tree roots that could encircle the world. All these objects stretched in two directions, all intermingled yet all separate, so Sunbright could follow the lines of each with his stiff and staring eyes.

Even Candlemas was drawn thin, like gold wire under a smith's tiny hammer, the outlines of the arcanist's body flattened and smoothed and stretched. Yet it was still the pudgy mage, Sunbright knew, whole and intact, but hair-thin. And so, he supposed, he must look to Candlemas. Sunbright shaved into a thousand splinters laid together like hair in a horse's tail.

They were moving and yet not moving. But if the lines of themselves were stretching from the hole to somewhere else, where were they going? Was this magic, or some other force? Certainly Sunbright had never heard of anything similar. Had the magic star somehow fashioned this weird not-spell? For it too was not an arm's length away, yanked fine, sailing through space, yet lying still as ever.

It was confusing, frightening, maddening. Sunbright wondered if it would last forever: certainly he felt like a granite statue. What if the fallen star sought to protect itself, and had suspended them in a spell forever? Could anything break it? Was this the ultimate curse, to stand and think unmoving for eternity? Could they be rescued, or even found? What if the hole collapsed about them, and buried them unmoving? How many seasons would pass before they saw sunlight again?

And if Sunbright stayed frozen this way forever, how would he ever find Greenwillow?

He stood for years, centuries, longer, waiting and fretting and wondering if this strange journey would ever end.

Then it was over.

* * * * *

Sunbright fell over and sprawled awkwardly on ornate tile painted with flowers in dozens of colors. He rolled on his shoulder and toes, shot to his feet, and whipped Harvester from its scabbard.

Before him was a skinny young man of average height, with tousled brown hair, grizzled beard, and sparkling golden eyes. With a bright smile, the stripling flicked his fingers in the air.

A striped cat as big as a horse reared on two broad cloven feet before Sunbright. Claws tipped appendages that were half-hands, half-paws. The cat's muttonchops and mane were white and stuck out at right angles. Its back was flaming orange with white and black stripes, and its broad chest blazed a snowy white.

The cat-man monster roared and slashed at Sunbright with finger-long talons.

Sucking in his belly, Sunbright skipped backwards, feet shuffling, butting aside a dazed Candlemas. He hoisted from knee-high to slash upward and across: he hoped to crease the animal if possible, or split its muzzle, but at least drive it back.

He missed as the cat leaped in the air. Hooves clattered as the beast landed, skipped to match Sunbright, and lashed out with a lower leg. A chitinous hoof tunked on Harvester. The blow rang like a sledgehammer's, knocking the heavy blade skyward. Before Sunbright could recover, the beast jig-trotted in place and kicked him soundly in the breadbasket.

Sunbright had barely hopped backward in time, and still grunted at the pain and fear of shattered ribs. The fighter sucked wind and hopped backward once more, forced to take the defensive. Behind that cat's muzzle lay a churning, thinking brain. Grasping his sword two-handed, he lowered the pommel near his short ribs so the long steel blade pointed straight. Unarmed, the monster would find it impossible to avoid a thrust. Or so he hoped. Meanwhile, he watched for an opening, marked a spot under the beast's arms and the pit of its lower belly.

All this in seconds, for the tiger-man slashed the air in dizzying circles, paw-hands a blur. Before Sunbright could lunge or duck, Harvester was again slapped aside, so hard the hooked tip caromed off a painted wall. The beast was too strong: it could crush him with a paw. But that was his mind recoiling. His sinews instinctively used the momentum of the impact against his assailant.

With a grunt of exertion, he dragged around the rebounding steel and added his own brute strength. Slashing backhanded, he slammed Harvester's barbed tip past the tip of clawed fingers to bite deep into the monster's neck. Hollering a nameless battle cry, he ripped downward to sink the hook in life-giving veins and tear them loose. And succeeded.

Frothy red blood gouted from the cat-man's neck. Red splashed the side of its face, soaking whiskers and pointed ears and white muttonchops in gore. More blood spattered Sunbright, rained on the wall and ceiling. The beast yowled in agony, but the sound trailed to a mew. Light sparking in its eyes winked and died. Sunbright barely skipped aside as the monster's back seemed to break and it plunged forward at him. A claw tore the barbarian's thigh as the dead thing's head struck the wall with a clonk muffled by thick orange-red fur.

Sunbright backed, panting, wary of any final kicks from those anvil-like hooves. He held his banged side, which throbbed with every sobbing breath. But he kept his sword ready for another attack.

There had been a young, tousled mage, he recalled suddenly, who'd flicked his fingers and—

"*You!*" The barbarian whirled. "You conjured that fiend!"

"Yes, more or less. But it wasn't really here, so it doesn't matter."

The young wizard wore an expensive but rumpled and frayed robe embroidered in green-blue and white lace. By contrast, his hair was a rat's nest, his fingernails cracked, gnawed, and filthy, his chin stubbly, his bare feet black with grime. And he needed a bath. Yet his eyes were golden, like melted gold swirling in a vat, and arresting. He smiled in a cockeyed way and waggled the fingers of one hand. The tiger-man disappeared, as did the blood on the walls, the blood on Sunbright's sword, and even the blood on his hands and arms. The barbarian felt a tug at his side, and realized the pain of that frightful kick had disappeared too.

"You—" Sunbright's breathing was still a sob, "that was an . . . illusion?"

"No. It was real, mostly. It hurt, didn't it?"

"Why . . . attack me?"

A bony shrug. "You had that curious sword. I just wanted to see how you'd fare in a fight."

"I'll show you how!" Sunbright slung Harvester far to the right to give it weight, swung it back hard, slapped his left hand on the pommel to add his own weight and cleave the interfering idiot in half. Harvester split the air, wind off its blade making a high keen—

But suddenly he was upside-down, his horsetail and scabbard flopping, blood rushing to his head, feet pedaling uselessly. He fought to focus on his target, saw the idiot fifty feet off across a tiled and painted floor, or ceiling. Sunbright growled in rage, but his voice was choked by a thickening in his throat. He felt helpless as a fox hoisted in a snare. Wordlessly, he cursed freely and long.

At the same time, the wary barbarian scanned his surroundings, automatically hunting danger, exits, things to use as shields and weapons.

But even upside down, nothing he saw made sense.

He rubbed his eyes with his free hand, twisted in the

air, searching for sanity. There was none to be found.

If he could trust his eyes, the room had no walls or ceilings, only floors on all its surfaces. Staring down—or, at least, in the direction that his horsetail pointed—he saw, looking up at him, a woman's face framed by a bowl of golden hair. Coolly, she said, "If you drop the sword, you'll probably descend."

Sunbright wasn't listening. He looked at his feet. Below his moosehide boots another woman with dark hair sat in an ornate chair at a table and scribed in a book. The barbarian could hear her goose quill scratching on uneven parchment. She never looked up at the man hovering an arm's span over her head.

Trying desperately to orient himself, Sunbright looked east, west, all around. The vast room, bigger than all of Candlemas's tower, was a wizard's workshop, he recognized, with much the same jars and books and odd artifacts, but people worked on every surface at right angles to one another. No, even that assumption was wrong, for none of the walls met at neat angles, but at random, cockeyed ones.

Sunbright struggled to understand. The vast chamber was like a beehive, in a way, with busy bees crawling everywhere upside down or right side up or sideways. He closed his eyes, which bulged, fit to burst like overripe grapes.

He cast about for the blonde woman and finally found her "overhead." He croaked, "What? What did you say?"

"Drop your sword."

"It's tempered. The tip will shatter."

Without a word, the woman extended a blunt hand stained and burned by magic-making. Sighing, Sunbright inverted Harvester and pushed the pommel three feet to her hand. She had to use both arms to catch it, it was that heavy. Gradually Sunbright sank until his hands touched the cool tile floor. Eventually he got his knees down, then clambered upright. He still felt airy, like a cloud, as if drunk, and his vision was clouded red from dangling.

The room didn't make any more sense standing upright. Overhead a dozen feet was the scribbler. Candlemas and the young wizard clung to a wall like flies fifty feet over and up.

Otherwise, the place was much like Candlemas's workshop in Castle Delia, only very much bigger. The same tables racked with bottles and jars, the same scales, even the same salty, punky smell of brimstone and saltpeter as Candlemas's tower. Yet where Candlemas's was largely plain, everything here was ornate. The walls and floor were an eye-blurring rainbow of colors and flowers, the ceiling fairly dripped with sculpted and painted plaster. All the tables were fashioned of brightly polished woods, many inlaid with lighter-colored wood or mother-of-pearl. Even the simplest objects were filigreed and tooled. Mouse cages were hand cut in tiny silver vines and leaf patterns. The wizard's purple robe was so heavily embroidered that no original material showed, only gold, silver, and purple threads interweaving in a dizzying array. All these lesser mages, forty or more within sight, were dressed that way.

Far off, the young wizard jabbered at Candlemas like a child. Candlemas nodded sagely. Sunbright picked up his sword, stood fuming, fighting to control his temper. He wanted to sound another war cry, race across the room, and split that interfering moron from crown to crotch. But he'd tried that and failed, been hung upside down like a ham. Another rush might find him anywhere: hanging upside down outside a window, for instance. And he wasn't even sure he could walk cockeyed, like a drunken mountain goat, to the spot where Candlemas stood.

To say something, he engaged the young apprentice. "Thank you. Who is that sawed-off snot?"

"Karsus." She turned back to her workbench, which contained a dozen cages where green mice ran inside wheels, then said over her shoulder, "This city is named after him."

"Moander's Mouth! After *him?* Why?"

"He owns it." A shrug. "He's the most powerful arch-wizard in the empire. The most powerful ever."

Sunbright stared, slack jawed. "That . . . *pimple?*"

"Aye." The apprentice, or whatever her rank, held a green mouse by the tail and gently lowered it into a cage lined with sandpaper. The mouse paddled its legs until it could run, which it did, frantically.

Nothing made sense, but Sunbright had to start somewhere. "Why are the mice green?"

"Karsus made them green. He reckoned it would make them run faster."

That made no sense, but he persisted. "And do they?"

"Oh, yes." The woman tapped a cage where panting mice whirled round and round. "In fact, they can't stop running. They run themselves to death. So I'm trying to find a way to slow them down."

Sunbright didn't know what to ask now. Absently he tried to map the room, but it only got madder. Off a ways, he realized, a floor had been inserted between two opposing floors. This intermediate floor was no thicker than solid boards, so people stood almost sole-to-sole, like reflections in a mirror pond. Sunbright shook his throbbing head.

The woman went on talking about her work. "Karsus wants the mice to be fitted with tiny baskets and strings on their tails. That way they can deliver dollops of heavy magic to the spaces between walls in old buildings. The globs could be illuminated so light shone through cracks at top and bottom to cast a softer glow.

But unless they stop sometime. . . ." She hoisted an exhausted mouse from a cage and dropped it in a box of rags, where it proceeded to burrow out of sight.

Sunbright felt like doing the same. "How do you get from here over to there?"

The blonde turned, her hair flicking on her cheeks. For the first time, Sunbright noticed that her eyes were different colors, one green, one brown, like some cats. She said impishly, "Well, you could jump, but that can be painful."

Reaching onto the table, she took a small jar and tossed it up. Sunbright watched it sail upward, hesitate, then shatter on the floor above. The scribbling brunette looked up indignantly. "Watch it, Seda!"

Sunbright was more confused than ever. The blonde pointed a languid finger. "Actually, you just walk to any intersecting wall and step across. You'll get used to it."

No, the barbarian thought, he never would. Shuffling his big, rough boots, he scooted toward Candlemas and—Karsus?

He paused a moment. If Karsus was the most powerful wizard ever, why hadn't Sunbright ever heard of him?

* * * * *

Sword in hand, the barbarian threaded tables, chairs, bookshelves, marble slabs, cages, iron sconces on tripod legs, telescopes, and more. Some wizards looked up curiously, but most did not. They'd seen odder things, obviously. Finally he reached another floor that tilted up at an angle. Gingerly he reached up, planted his foot, and stepped onto the next tiled floor. His stomach gibbered like a frightened animal, sent a burst of nausea into the back of his throat. Then he was across the magic barrier, for such it must be, and marching toward Candlemas and Karsus.

Regretfully, but at least proud of his self-control, he sheathed his sword before getting within striking distance.

Karsus was kneeling and babbling like a child. One dirty hand tugged at his hair, so much so it was ragged and short above his ear. His other hand stroked the star-stone repeatedly. "Exactly, exactly what we need! Exactly! All my experiments have been leading up to—"

The young wizard broke up, bounded and hopped on one foot before Sunbright. "Did you like my mutant? I bred him from a tiger and a dwarf! A big dwarf. I keep them in the cellars. Actually I just made him up from thin air. Actually a friend captured it in the southlands and gave it to me. People bring me lots of presents. They like me."

Sunbright couldn't see why. And three contradictory sentences in a row was a bad sign. On the tundra, this man would be the village idiot. Here in the empire, he owned a city. It said a lot about the empire.

"But you fought well. Why does your sword have that hook on the end? Would you like to fight in the arena? I could augment your strength, or give you eyes in the back of your head. You'd be famous! Women would love you. Men too . . ."

All Sunbright wanted was to squeeze this fool's neck until blood shot out his ears, but he clamped his hands on his belt and asked Candlemas, "What does this— person—want? Can we leave? Where are we, anyway? They say this is the city of Karsus, but I've never heard of it, and I've walked from one end of the empire to the other."

Candlemas nodded absently, but then rubbed his mustache. The young wizard blathered, "My city! Actually, it's named after my father, Radman. Mother wanted it that way. Of course, I've sold a lot of it, I think, so other people can live here. People never call it

Radman, though. Everyone wants to live here near Karsus the Great . . ."

The pudgy mage interjected gently, "Yes, this is Karsus, Arcanist Supreme, the greatest Inventive/Variator of all time."

"Which means he waves his hands and conjures things," replied Sunbright blandly. Karsus dropped back to the stone, sniffing it all over like a dog. "So what?"

"Um . . ." Candlemas was plainly embarrassed about something, and Sunbright wanted to throttle *him* now. He'd choke somebody soon if he didn't get answers. "As I said, this is the city of Karsus and, uh, Karsus has been experimenting with a new form of magic called 'heavy magic.' He's had some success, but needed a final ingredient to, ah, cement the process. And we've found it with this fallen star, because it's so monstrously heavy. So when we, uh, uncovered it, Karsus brought it here to him. He brought us, too, so we could explain where it came from." Candlemas sounded outwardly calm, but something in him trembled. With fear? Anticipation?

"So?" Sunbright's great scarred, knotty hands clenched and unclenched. He cast about the dizzying workshop again, with its busy-bee apprentices stuck to floors all around. The place made his brain churn. He wanted to go outside. But something was distinctly wrong. "He's got it! Collect your reward, and we'll go home!"

"That's just it," hemmed Candlemas, until Sunbright took a dangerous step forward. "Wait. Karsus fetched the shooting star hither with a spell. Through space but, uh, *time,* as well."

"Time? What in the name of—?"

Candlemas rubbed his beard. "Three hundred and fifty-eight years."

"*What?*" Sunbright looked down. Karsus was rolling the star like a child's ball. Apprentices came running like rabbits at his bawl. "Three hundred—"

"Fifty-eight years. It's the year thirty-five twenty here."

Sunbright shook his head. It had been the First Year of Owldark when he left his tribe, for they counted by the reign of clan chiefs. Or the Year of the Bright Snow, as some elders had named it.

"We've been drawn into the future, Sunbright, many generations past what we know." Candlemas's voice was urgent. "Everyone we knew in Castle Delia is dead dust. Back then, we would have disappeared, never been seen again. The castle itself was sold, Karsus assures me. Lady Polaris doesn't own it anymore, if she's even alive. He's not sure she is. There's nothing back there for us."

"Nothing for you." Sunbright's face was blank as he tried to sift the information. His people told legends of heroes who traveled from Now to the Elder Days, and met heroes of ages past. Was he doing that now? Better to hear of adventures than live them. . . .

"No. I had no friends in the castle, really, just servants. All I did was slave for Lady Polaris, and get precious little thanks for it." The pudgy mage sounded excited, almost like Karsus. "But this is better. Karsus has invited me to help him work, experiment! And the man knows more magic than anyone, ever!"

Sunbright looked where Karsus kissed the lumpy star. "The man has bugs in his brain! He can't even comb his hair."

"He doesn't need to. He's got five hundred mages working under him, in this part of the city alone! He's the most powerful arcanist the empire has ever seen."

"An empire run by a madman? How long can *that* last? Are we in another damned floating city? What if Bug-brain here sneezes at the wrong time and loses his concentration—what little he has? You'd need to sprout wings damned quick!"

"You don't understand genius." Candlemas rubbed his bald head. "Anyway, I'm staying here to work under him. Six months' study and I'll know more than Lady Polaris ever hoped to!"

"What about your wheat rust? Weren't you responsible for curing that?" Sunbright had so many objections and questions they just popped out of his mouth. It would take him weeks to sort out this madness.

"See? That's solved!" The mage waved a hand at the ceiling/floor. "That problem's three hundred years back in time! Someone else must have fixed it, or the empire wouldn't be here. And look how rich it's become! Look at the opulence of these work tables, look at the clothes on even the lowest ranked apprentice."

"What about my tribe? I've got to get back—" Then he realized. All the people he'd known would now be dead: his mother, Owldark his enemy, Thornwing, Blinddrum, so many others. He felt his throat constrict. Could a man be more cut off from what he knew and yet still be of this world? Feebly, he croaked, "What about Greenwillow?"

Candlemas huffed. "She's dead. We knew that already."

Within seconds Candlemas was hoisted by his smock, feet dangling as Sunbright rammed him repeatedly against a wall of curlicued plaster. "This is how you honor bargains? Make it someone else's problem? People starved or didn't, but it's none of your concern? Greenwillow's trapped in some hell and you slough it off? I'll tear your heart out, if you have one!"

"Wait, wait!" Candlemas fought to regain his feet, to loosen the stranglehold, to breathe. "I can't get you back! Neither of us can go—" His wind cut off.

"Is he distressing you?" came a voice from Sunbright's left. "Here. Let me. . . ."

Sunbright found himself standing in a street. Night

was falling. Gasglobes were just igniting, blotting out
the thousand stars.

* * * * *

"Mages! Hand-wavers! Sorcerers! Wizards! Bastards,
all of them! I'd like to pitch them off their own floating
cities, and hear their bones crunch when they strike the
villages and fields they so dearly love to dump on!"

Sunbright groused as he tramped the darksome city.
Needing to walk off his anger, he'd stomped for miles in
his moosehide boots. Harvester patted his back in a
companionable way, but nothing assuaged his black
mood. Once again he had no idea where he was, no idea
where Candlemas was, had no idea even if he were still
in the floating city of Karsus or even in the same cen-
tury, for that matter. But the **K** sigil for Karsus was
everywhere, so he supposed he hadn't been shifted far:
just out of harm's reach.

Walking should have spent his energy, but instead it
stoked his anger like a bellows. He cursed freely and
often, and stamped so hard his iron-ringed boots set off
a metallic *ching ching ching*. Unusual for a barbarian
on foreign soil, he didn't notice much around him, for
his mind churned with outrage.

Thus he stumbled on a crime.

Whirling around a corner, he almost bounced off the
back of a man vigorously kicking something. Three
men, in fact, holding mugs of ale to one side so as to not
spill. They grunted with the effort of kicking a tiny
something—a *child?*—with their heavy boots or wooden
clogs. They'd have done more damage if they weren't so
drunk, but as it was, Sunbright's bellow froze them in
mid-kick.

"Halt, you blackhearted swine! Else I split your
heads and suck your brains!"

They turned to see Harvester, the hooked tip glistening like a crescent moon. The "child" they'd been kicking sprang up and sped off. Seeing the tiny form run man-fashion, Sunbright wasn't sure it was a child.

"Hoy, help us!" A shrill whistle, and the door to a bar split open to spill light, pub noise, and more assailants.

"He's let our gnome escape!" called one of the kickers.

"Let's get 'im then!" came a roar.

Sunbright looked at a dozen angry attackers. He just had time to wonder what a gnome was before they swamped him.

Chapter 5

Three assailants or nine didn't matter to Sunbright, as long as he had Harvester in his hand. He'd killed more than that in one bad day in the underworld.

Briefly, he wondered if he *should* kill this lot. Cities were fussy about brawling and fighting with blades, and apt to throw everyone in a jail cell. And since the gnome (whatever that was) had fled, perhaps Sunbright should just flit around the corner and disappear too.

Then someone grabbed his sword arm from behind, another man stabbed a knife at his face, and a woman tried to kick his shins or groin. Smart or not, the fight was on.

His brawny sword arm was trapped above his shoulder so he tensed it to keep it from being twisted, then dealt with the kicker by lashing out with his own foot, blocking her kick and knocking the knife-wielder's arm away.

The narrow street was dark, the only light was the glow from a rose-colored lamp above the tavern door. Painted by the blood-red light, it was hard to distinguish his opponents, but the man looked rawhide tough, scarred, and knotty-jawed; while the woman looked young—still wrapped in baby fat. All three were drunk, which helped. Sunbright would have to test how strong they were.

Stamping his broad, heavy boot on the woman's toes, he pushed straight back to slam his rearmost opponent against the wall. The man, young and perfumed, grunted when he hit the wall, then again when Sunbright added to his grief by smashing his left elbow deep into the dandy's soft belly. When the lad doubled, Sunbright crashed an elbow upward into his teeth. Though the barbarian cut his own bicep, he managed to get his other hand free.

The closest attacker now was the woman, who was wailing about her injured foot. Sunbright distracted her by kicking her jaw out of shape. She whirled and slammed the cobblestones, moaning.

The tough man before him, coarse and smelling of onions, had stepped back when he lost his knife. Evidently he hadn't much stomach for fighting, or else waited for the reinforcements that were spilling from the tavern. They milled drunkenly, yelling, yet Sunbright saw a knife blade, a broken bottle, two or three clubs, even a trio of slim swords. Since he was free, the barbarian thought, now was a good time to disappear around a corner. Someone might get lucky with a quick jab, but Sunbright Steelshanks could run down a deer. He could certainly outrun this lot. He cast behind and left to see if the coast was clear.

A whisper from the dark alerted him. A metallic ching pinged by his ear. He had no clue what that portended, or how to defend against it. Suddenly, a weighted chain hissed around his sword arm. Before the cold steel had even wrapped fully, the man in the street hauled. Twisted links bit the barbarian's arm, and he was yanked forward.

He crashed on one hand and knees on the cobblestones.

"Kill 'im!"

"Kick his lights out!"

"He hurt Magda!"

"I'll pay for his hands! Cut 'em off!"

"And 'is eyes! Gouge 'em out!"

Boots, clogs, and soft shoes alike thudded into Sunbright's ribs, shoulders, and rump. Two clubs batted at his head, but the attackers were getting in each others' way. Sunbright didn't stay down long. Since they expected him to roll away, he went the opposite direction, charging them in a half-crouch, one hand guarding the back of his head.

Yet even in this desperate situation he was appraising his enemy and coming up blank. This mix of villains made no sense. There were perfumed fops with fine clothes and soft hands, men and women, and coarse working folk in near-rags. Sunbright knew enough about the classes to distinguish them by their voices and slang alone. Why were so-called gentlefolk associating with riffraff? Was everyone in this city as mad as the man it was named after?

Then he crashed among them, and left off questioning their motives.

One strong man still hauled on the weighted chain that ripped skin from Sunbright's arm. The man leaned back on his heels and hauled to keep the barbarian down and tamed, like a rebellious horse. The "horse"

fought back. Since the chain-wielder was the greatest
danger, Sunbright charged him. The man fell back, still
hauling, but the barbarian was faster. As soon as he got
slack in the chain, Sunbright dragged back Harvester
and stabbed the blade straight as an arrow. The man
dodged quickly to save his throat, but not quickly
enough. Harvester's barbed tip seared his neck. He
yowled once and dropped to one side, and Sunbright
smelled blood like sheared copper and knew he'd deliv-
ered a killing blow.

Shaking off the coils of chain, the barbarian whirled
on the rest—

And was smashed on his sword wrist by an iron-
wrapped club.

The blow was perfect, completely stunning Sunbright. Harvester clanged on cobblestones. Others had
fallen back. One young fop doubled over, vomiting stale
beer at the smell of blood. But someone yelled to rush
him and surged in. More than one would die in this
street, the barbarian knew. It mustn't be him, lamed
hand or not.

Scanning the red-splintered darkness, he inventoried
his opponents' weapons. His right hand was numbed,
perhaps broken, and pain flashed up and down his arm
like a forest fire. He couldn't make a fist, but he could
slap with it. His left hand snatched up the dwarven
warhammer, almost forgotten in its belt holster, in time
to block a jab at his gut. He batted a club aside with a
clack, stepped back, kicked, and forced his opponent
back temporarily. He stooped to retrieve his sword left-
handed, but someone hurled a bottle at his head and he
fell over in a squat. The hurler laughed and jumped to
kick, then yelped when she sliced her soft shoe on Harvester's keen edge. Sunbright kicked to his feet.

A shadow crowded him, thrusting awkwardly with a
long sword. He turned into the thrust, let the slim

blade pass under his right arm, and clamped down on it. The wielder, an incompetent who shouldn't even carry a sword, tugged to free the blade. Sunbright snapped the warhammer at his face, felt a satisfying chunk of iron on bone, and the swordsman staggered. Sunbright ducked behind him as the crowd half-rushed, half-hung back. The woman in the silken cape who'd cut her foot thrust angrily with her sword, and skewered her broken-nosed drinking buddy.

She yelped, "Sorry, Jules!" but Sunbright heard the sob of a sucking wound: a lung puncture. He propelled the stricken man against the swordswoman. They tangled with each other and fell.

He still had to retrieve his sword, but still had to watch his back, so he angled for the stone wall. Stooping his great height—he was half a head taller than all of them—confused them long enough for him to move. Along the way, he smashed the warhammer on a thug's hand and club, downward so the man beat his own knee. Sunbright shouldered him into the crowd too. It helped that the fops panicked and milled, and the thugs cursed. As he thumped against the wall, someone whisked a knife at him, but he sidestepped and the blade snapped on stone. He punched awkwardly, left-handed, skinned his knuckles on a brow ridge, then punched higher and bowled the man over.

Not bad for an unarmed, one-handed barbarian against nine street toughs (or toughs and fops), but he couldn't fight forever. If he could circle, kick, and punch clear to his sword, he'd reckon it a good night's work.

Then light spilled around the corner like daylight, a half-dozen gasglobes lined with mirrors.

A commanding voice hollered, "Right! Everyone stay where you are! Hands in sight! We're the city guard!"

In a city of madmen, Sunbright thought, this could be bad.

* * * * *

After the darkness, the glare was blinding, and Sunbright hunched one shoulder and turned away—though he still tracked the mob.

His guesses made in semidarkness proved true. The contrast between the street toughs and the fops was enormous. There were four street toughs: three men and a woman, and five young fops, two of them girls. The toughs wore cast-off clothing, ripped and ragged, work boots and clogs, though two were barefoot. They were tough as rawhide, sharp-boned and skinny as starved wolves after a long winter. They'd probably never had a decent meal in their lives. The fops had brocaded shirts, silk neckerchiefs, small, elegant hats with feathers or pearls, satin capes, tight breeches made of some material with a high sheen, and hand-crafted shoes of red or yellow leather. Perfumed, painted with eye makeup and face powder, with the softness of baby fat still upon them, they looked like mischievous children dressed up and let out to play.

Not everyone was upright. One thug lay on his back, his neck sheared by Harvester's tip, his life's blood a pool on the cobblestones. The drunken fop, the poor swordsman, lay groaning and clutching his chest where the girl had accidently punctured him. She squatted to comfort him, then nagged him for getting in her way. Others had walking wounds. Sunbright had scored half a dozen hits.

Yet the tundra dweller still couldn't understand. Why would privileged brats hang with footpads? Surely they didn't need the money: their clothing could have bought out a marketplace. Was this some perverted sort of bounty hunt?

The six city guards wore polished lobster-tail helmets, blue-green tabards, and metal breastplates adorned with the fancy **K** sigil. They carried short swords on their belts and silver-tipped clubs in their hands. Nor did he miss the braided red cords tucked into their belts: lashings for recalcitrant prisoners, no doubt.

"Weapons down, or you're dead!" the captain of the guards bellowed. Clubs and knives clanked. But as the gasglobes illuminated the street, the officer refined his manner, became almost gentle. "Now, then. What's all this?"

A fop in a yellow shirt and red cape spoke right up. "This beast attacked us! Look here, he's stabbed Jules!"

The bald lie stunned Sunbright. He should have run when he had the chance. The guards surveyed the damage, dismissed the dead thug with a sniff, helped stem the bleeding of the punctured boy, and sent a young guard running for a stretcher. The captain stamped a foot on Harvester, studied Sunbright curiously, so much so that the barbarian wondered how many of his kind they saw in Karsus.

"You were just out walking with your friends," the captain stated as if from memory, "and this rogue jumped you. Is that it?"

"Yes, exactly," lied the boy. He sniffed, drew his cape closer, which made him sway drunkenly. He added, as if by rote, "We'd be obliged if you'd handle the matter, captain." With no shame at all, he handed over a fat purse of blue velvet.

"What about these?" asked the captain, nodding at the three remaining thugs.

Another sniff. "Never saw them before. They were probably helping him, lying in wait for us, to rob us."

"You hired us!" objected a scar-faced footpad. "You needed muscle for your hellraising! You ordered us to kick that bloke to death, and knock down that gnome—"

His words cut off as a silver-tipped club smashed his

teeth in. He staggered back and another club crashed above his ear and felled him. Other guards waded in, taking turns smashing him down as if threshing wheat. The thug's face was pulped to bloody gobbets. A fop turned and puked up her ale.

"Keep your place! Don't argue with your betters!" chided the captain, though the thug was long dead by then. As he pocketed the purse, the officer addressed the fop. "My apologies, young master. . . ."

"Hurodon," snapped the lad, "son of Angeni of the House of Dreng in the Street of the Golden Willows."

"Oh, yes, sir. I know that neighborhood well. Fine people live there. But down here the streets aren't as safe as they should be, and it's our fault. We'll redouble our efforts from now on. Please don't let this unpleasantness spoil your evening."

"Certainly not!" laughed the fop. "The night is young, and we'll have plenty of fun yet! Come on, friends!"

Prepared, the guards yanked the tired thugs' hands behind their backs, lashed their wrists with the red cords, and shoved them to their knees. Two strong men arrived in light blue tabards that sported red **K** sigils, and they bundled the stricken Jules off on a stretcher.

"*Wait!*" Sunbright had been rendered speechless by this calumny, by so obvious a bribe, such a callous abuse of privilege by this fop, and such a barbarous beating, the most brutal he'd ever seen, on or off the battlefield. Now the objection was ripped from him. "You'd let these rich snots go free after they hired these thugs to kill people? What kind of blasphemous, decadent hole is this city—"

Words were useless. The fops pranced off, laughing with excitement and the joy of buying justice. The guards encircled Sunbright slowly, clubs bobbing in the air. Harvester lay in the street behind them. Sunbright had only a warhammer in his off hand, and a wounded right that throbbed as if a badger had gnawed it. The captain intoned, "Keep your place. Don't argue with your betters," platitudes to distract him. Clearly, they intended to beat him to death.

Just as clearly, he couldn't defeat these canny killers in uniform. His brain raced for a defense. Instinctively, he grasped what he'd seen succeed moments before, when the fop invoked privilege.

"Captain, know that I'm a guest of Karsus."

One guard snorted, but the captain paused. Obviously he didn't know who Sunbright was. He spat, "Prove it, then."

Gritting his teeth, Sunbright played the game. "I and another wizard named Candlemas were brought here from Castle Delia, by Karsus's command, because we unearthed a shooting star. Karsus needs it for his experiments. We're to give him information on finding the star. I've talked with one Seda, in his workshops. You can ask anyone there."

"I know Seda," muttered a guard. "From the House of Zee. She does work in Karsus's close circle."

Still unsure, the captain frowned. But the magical name had worked. He nodded toward the wider street beyond. "Very well, good sir. Go, and good luck to you. We apologize for any inconvenience."

Wary as a cornered lion, Sunbright slid along the wall until clear of their semicircle. Slipping the warhammer into its holster, he watched the guards as he picked up Harvester and backed into the main street.

His precautions were unnecessary. The guards had already forgotten him and had fallen to other work. As the captain divvied up the bribe, two guards slipped the braided cords over the heads of the two surviving thugs. Their bleats were cut off as the garrotes snuggled tight. Bug-eyed, the unlucky street toughs strangled.

Sunbright cursed as he sped off down the street, bloody sword in hand, after a certain foppish wretch.

He had debts to pay.

* * * * *

Hurodon and his well-dressed friends whooped with delight, carolled songs, and hurled jokes as they cut through a park lined with trees and gasglobes. They aimed for a brightly-lit ale shop at the opposite corner, but were interrupted.

A thick bush at Hurodon's elbow split open as if from a charging lion. A girl yelped, a boy cried out.

Sunbright Steelshanks burst from the foliage to grab Hurodon by the throat. The fop gargled as he was whipped off his feet and slammed against a rough-barked oak tree. His gang of friends dithered, drew their toy swords, yelled.

The barbarian's harsh cough cut them off. "Attack me, or call out, and I'll snap his neck!" He was panting from his quick run around vast blocks to get ahead of the party. His right hand, still numb, was tucked in his belt. He only needed one hand to tame this bunch.

Yet looking at them, he couldn't follow through on his plan, which was to kill them all. Certainly they deserved to die for their casual cruelty. They'd killed their hired thugs as surely as the guards had. But they were young and raised wrong, like puppies let loose to become wild dogs. Perhaps they could learn.

Hurodon hissed, "Let me go, you filthy muckraker, or I'll have you—" A squeeze cut off his wind.

In the lout's face, Sunbright rasped, "You sneaking milk-sucker! You nest-robber! You cache-thief!" Sunbright's tundra-born insults were lost on the boy, but not the berserker's intent. "You were born wrapped in sable! You think you can buy people's lives with your filthy coin?"

"I'll buy your death!" gasped the boy. "You'll be roasted over—"

Sunbright let go just long enough to backhand the boy, whose head snapped around so hard his ear was torn by rough bark. Then he was clamped and throttled again.

"You'll need to buy a new nose once I slice yours off and throw it to the dogs!" Sunbright assured him.

Never before manhandled, and always given what he wanted immediately, the boy blundered on, "You're a ghost, underling! My family will see you—"

This time Sunbright smashed him in the mouth hard enough to knock out a front tooth. Choking him again, so blood and makeup ran from the boy's mouth onto the barbarian's wrist, Sunbright shouted, "I'll knock out every tooth and then cut out your lying tongue!"

Finally, the boy was scared. Before, Hurodon couldn't imagine anyone hurting him, and now he realized that Sunbright was going to kill him then and there. But it was too late for Sunbright to kill him now, for the barbarian had decided to talk instead. Maybe he could teach this petty thug a lesson in honor. "Now, fish guts, for once in your miserable life you'll listen!"

Hurodon got the message. Mouth swollen and bleeding, he whimpered, "All right. But don't hit me again."

Sunbright was sickened both by his own actions and this poor excuse for a human. Yet he bore down. "You—and you lot too—you get yourselves back to the Street of the Golden Willows and you stay there! You're worse than those backstabbing blackguards you hired for your hellraising and left to die. They've been punished—at your behest—while you've gone on to more mischief. But you're lower than they, for you betrayed them, and that's the worse crime!"

Hurodon wiggled, and Sunbright shook him like a rat. Some of his friends couldn't meet Sunbright's glare.

The barbarian continued, "No longer. If I ever see any of you out after sunset again, I'll slit your throats and drop you off this mountain. Understand?"

"Yes," some of them murmured. Hurodon dripped warm blood on Sunbright's hand. He dropped the stripling onto the tree roots and, without another word, stalked off into the darkness.

His words were bluster, of course. He had no intention of tracking these dung beetles. But they'd sleep uneasily for a while, and might curb their ruthless hellraising in the future.

But not all. From far behind came Hurodon's mushy wail. "I'll get you! I'll see you dead! And all your family dead! I'll buy the finest assassins in the empire!"

Sunbright only shook his head. "Karsus's finest assassins and its finest youth," he said to himself. "This empire is naught but a rotten melon infested with insects. One good kick would crush it. And will."

He was more angry with himself than with the spoiled brats. This city life was infecting him, making him grow soft, for he'd committed the second-worst crime a barbarian knew.

He'd left an enemy alive.

* * * * *

Passing the narrow street where he'd fought, Sunbright paused a moment in curiosity.

The city guards had been efficient, at least. They'd laid the four bodies of the thugs at the head of the street, neatly in a line, heads out, even the pulped head of the man they'd beaten to death.

A bony mule hauling a long-sided wagon clomped to a stop near them. An old man and woman, both wearing gasglobe helmets, got out. Together they dragged the bodies and heaped them in the cart. The red lamp of the alehouse glowed as bloodily as before, and the noise from inside it was just as loud.

"What are you doing?" Sunbright asked.

"Eh?" The old man tilted his head. Sunbright asked again, louder. "Oh. Cleanup crew, milord. The local waste buckets are too small to swallow a body. We have 'ta take 'em to a locked room and drop 'em down there."

"Waste buckets? Locked room?"

The old man peered, as if to ask: where are you from? But he minded his betters. "Yes, milord. The city guard don't want no one stuffin' folks down the garbage chutes. So we take 'em to a locked stoneroom and slide 'em down there. The magic eats 'em up, makes more magic. Nothing left."

Sunbright still didn't understand how magic "ate one up," but it didn't surprise him the empire would feed on magic generated by its dead. A form of cannibalism, he reckoned it.

"Do you do this every night?"

"Eh? Oh, yes, milord. All night, every night. But we gotta be off the streets by sunrise or the straw bosses scream. But me and Mandisa, we're slow, but steady. Still, we gotta be off soon . . ."

"Why soon?"

"Oh," the man avoided his eyes, fussed with the dead men and woman in the cart. The old woman shuffled slowly, helmet lamp making a white blob bounce on the ground, and sorted through the trash on the street for anything valuable. "Some nights the city's more boisterous than others, is all. There's what, nineteen cleanup crews, all told. We're busy, but glad for the work."

Sunbright supposed they were. This man looked as starved as the bodies he'd loaded onto his cart. He didn't understand what "boisterous" might mean, but a casual comment had arrested his attention. "*Nineteen* teams work all night, every night, just to pick up corpses?"

"Aye, milord. 'Course, that's just the poor 'uns, you understand. Strangers or folks no one cares to give a funeral to. Good families take care of their own, of course. Some of 'em are even buried down on the ground, I hear tell. Now look at that, ain't that curious?" He took hold of a white object suspended around one tough's neck and broke the thong. Peering, waggling his head lamp, he still couldn't see, so he handed it to the barbarian. "What is that, good sir?"

Sunbright took the thing. It was yellowed by sweat and grime, but polished from lying between the dead man's skin and clothing. "It's a hunk of knucklebone. Too big for a deer's."

The old man waved a crooked hand. "Good luck charm. Worthless. Keep it. Ready, Mandisa?" He helped his wife climb onto the seat with creaking knees, checked that their next stop, according to the guards, was the Street of Lilacs.

As he clucked to the old mule, Sunbright asked, "Can you point me to Castle Karsus?"

The man squinted, nodded with the reins, indicating a yellow-lit structure high up in the distance. Sunbright nodded: he should have known. Of all the odd buildings in this city-state, it was the only one with tilted walls that met at odd angles.

The old man said another curious thing. "You better be off the street by sunrise yourself, young master. Rumors are milling again . . ."

"Rumors of what?"

"Oh, troubles in the marketplace. Same old same old. . . ." The deaf man slapped the reins and rolled away.

The barbarian found himself still clutching the knucklebone, the only artifact left of a man he'd killed for no clear reason, except that the man had tried to kill him. Somehow, it didn't seem a good enough reason right now. He pocketed the polished bone and trudged on.

His opinion of the empire sank lower with every new sight, if such were possible. Before the doorway of a large meeting hall, citizens had dragged a man with pointed ears by his hair, lashed him to a signpost, and doused him with strong liquor, probably brandy, for when they applied a torch, the man (or half man) ignited, to die screaming while the crowd cheered.

Sunbright saw it all in the length of a block. His legs wanted to run that way, but he stood rooted. There were fifty or more villains, yowling men, and shrill women. He couldn't save the victim, could only get himself killed. Wondering what had become of his pride, or common sense, he trudged until the flaming pyre was past. Farther on, he saw a man and woman sprawled in the gutter, their throats cut, their clothing looted. He saw starved horses hitched to glittering coaches, saw a row of gap-mouthed heads spiked on iron pilings around a park, some of them children's. He saw more children pick through garbage and fight with dogs for a bone, and city guards chase both with silver-tipped clubs.

There was no end to the corruption of the empire, he saw. It was built on the bones of the unjustly-treated dead, and the hunched backs of the dying living.

Back in opulent Castle Karsus, Candlemas was learning the opposite. And the same.

Chapter 6

One second Candlemas was pinned against a wall and throttled, then Karsus waved a hand and Sunbright flickered away like a snuffed candle flame. The pudgy mage dropped, lost his footing, and plopped on his bottom.

"There," said the younger mage. "He'll be a while returning. Servants are such a bother, aren't they? I turned one into an orc last week. The soup was cold."

Candlemas rubbed his throat and nodded absently. Sunbright was hardly a servant, nor was he a proper apprentice or even an equal partner. That was the problem with their relationship: neither was really certain how they meshed. The barbarian was too quick to hammer things for a solution: a man of pure action. Yet Candlemas, a man of science, was too quick to ply magic as a cure-all. Between them, he reflected, they should be able to solve any problem. Instead, they only seemed to end up stalemating, sinking deeper into a morass of trouble.

Karsus had wandered off, calling orders to attendants and lesser mages, sailing like a war galley scattering tiny ships. Massaging his throat, Candlemas trotted to catch up.

He soon forgot his troubles, for Karsus's workshop—which stretched over many *buildings*—proved a wonderland of spells and magic that Candlemas could only have dreamed of. Karsus had hundreds of experiments going on simultaneously, and kept track of each in his tousled head.

One room sported a stone fountain and pool. A dozen mages were at work, and when Karsus swept in, they scurried to show him their latest results. Holding hands in a ring around the pool, they chanted a short command. Instantly a rainbow fountained up from the center well. Streaks of color shot upward, fanned out, and spilled into the retaining pool. Karsus clapped his hands with delight, like a child, and Candlemas joined him. But there was more. The rainbow looked and behaved like water, but maintained its stripes. So as the colored fan hit the pool, the streams separated out, and made a swirling whirlpool of color: a circular rainbow.

A mage leaned over the pool, gesturing. "There's more, Great Karsus. Look!" Dipping his hand into the pool, he demonstrated that the color stuck to his hand. Fingertips stayed green, his palm blue, his wrist violet. Shaking his hand, the colors spattered on the floor to make a tiny rainbow—like from a prism glass—that slowly faded.

"I love it!" Karsus dipped his hand, painted the front of his dirty robe in stripes, painted Candlemas's nose blue. "My invention! Heavy magic! It works for *everything!*"

Karsus dipped in the pool, scooped a multicolored ball and hurled it against the wall, where it stuck. "They'll pay scads of money for this one. Everyone will want one for his garden. You'll all be rich, and the name of Great Karsus will be even greater!" Candlemas chuckled but shook his head. These lesser mages had accomplished something he never could have even attempted.

Quitting the room, Karsus sailed down another corridor. Candlemas was getting used to the archwizard's abrupt starts and stops, and scurried to catch up, but he tripped over a loose floor tile and crashed on his hands and knees.

Karsus scurried over to help him rise. "Clumsy, clumsy. Keep up, now. We've much to see, much to do." His sparkling golden eyes roamed around in their sockets. Candlemas found the effect unnerving. The man was either a genius or a lunatic, perhaps both.

The pudgy mage looked where he'd stumbled. Floor tiles had cracked and separated as the floor shifted. One edge was four inches too high. The crack even continued across the floor to one of the tilted walls, reaching with spidery fractures all the way to the ceiling. The steward of Castle Delia (or former steward) pointed. "Shouldn't you summon a mason to patch that? Someone could trip and spill—"

Karsus was thirty paces away. He never seemed to walk, only jog from one task to another. "No time, no time! We don't use masons anymore anyway. Wouldn't know where to find one. I'll have someone seal it magically. Brightfinger's stonebind should work! Come on, come on!"

With skinned hands and knees tingling, Candlemas trotted after. It occurred to him that hiring a mason would be cheaper than plying magic, but then, they had plenty of magic to spare. Yet no one seemed interested in maintaining the building, a fact he found strange. As steward of Castle Delia, he knew how quickly things deteriorated if neglected.

Then he was witnessing other miracles and soon forgot about repairs.

In a smaller room near the cellars stood a trio of female arcanists before a big, scarred, wooden table. In the corner, watched by a city guard, was a starved and shabby man shackled wrists to ankles. Clanking awkwardly, the man gulped down a bowl of porridge with his fingers.

A woman with blonde hair and a high forehead greeted him. "Great Karsus, we've perfected the spell you requested!"

"Wonderful, wonderful! Which one was it?"

"Imprisonment, milord," replied the apprentice patiently. "The more powerful version of Yong's imprisonment?"

"Oh yes, oh yes!" Turning, he said, "You'll like this, Candlemas. The city guards asked for it. Show us, show us!"

Candlemas nodded attentively, but he couldn't help but wonder about the prisoner in the corner. The man was nothing but skin and bones. The planes of his forehead and cheeks were sharp enough to cut, and his eyes were sunken and vacant as he licked the wooden bowl for the last specks of porridge. What was his crime? Had the city guards been starving him for months?

Smiling in the spotlight, the mage picked up a small globe of pale green glass. With one hand, she gestured to the city guard that he should stand aside. The nervous soldier retreated to the other corner. Lightly, the mage lobbed the globe at the prisoner. It broke on the floor with a quiet tinkle.

A whirling mist of green spun from the fragments, rose, expanded, and, like a hunting hawk, zoomed at

the prisoner. The man yelped as the magic touched him.
Instantly the green mist turned to a layer of slime that
spread on contact. The green raced up the man's thin
arms, spilled over his shoulders, chased down his
skinny body and closed over his head like a hood.
Within seconds, the man was encased in shimmering
green—and was suffocating.

Candlemas could see through the slime, see the
man's eyes bulge, see his mouth gape in surprise. But
as soon as it did, the green coating flowed into his
mouth. With slimy hands the man grabbed his green
slick throat, clawed at his mouth, pounded his chest for
air. He thrashed, beat his face against the floor, kicked
and jerked, all uselessly.

Karsus hopped in place, fists in the air. "Wonderful!
Even better than we hoped! Do you see, Candlemas?
Candlemas is my new special friend, everyone! Do you
see? The heavy magic takes the shape of whatever it
touches! So when he opened his mouth, it slipped right
inside to coat his throat—all the way to his lungs! Oh,
won't the city guard be pleased. This is just the thing
they need to halt the food riots."

Food riots? thought Candlemas.

Lungs emptied of air, the prisoner didn't suffer long.
Within a minute his twitching stopped. And as with the
colorspray magic, the green heavy magic gradually
flowed off him and evaporated.

Chuckling, Karsus went over the details. Why was
the magic green? The city had requested it be colored,
not clear, so they could identify it more quickly in a
mob. Karsus suggested it be changed to blue, his favorite color, and the blonde mage assured him it would
be done.

Again, Candlemas jogged as Karsus sped from the
room. But now his feet dragged, as if part of him were
reluctant to keep up. Indeed, his brain kept asking,

What had the prisoner done to deserve such a horrid fate? And how many more folk would it be used against?

The day wore on. Candlemas was exhausted, but Karsus never flagged. Indeed, as he displayed more wonders to his "new special friend," he grew more animated, until he jabbered nonstop and Candlemas's ears rang. Certainly he saw wonders, only some of which he even understood. In a separate, heavily guarded building, he watched teams of mages chant rhythmically to summon monsters. Lined in huge cages were things Candlemas had never known existed. A weird antelope with a brown-checkered head but a white-striped body. A twisted goblin-thing like a bag of broken bones covered with warts. A tank of fish, some thin as axe blades with luminous orbs of cold light. A three-foot salamander with a toothless mouth at either end. Birds with brilliant tails longer than their bodies. And much, much more. Karsus examined each, named people in the city who would pay for these freaks for their private zoos, and squealed with delight. Nor was his enthusiasm dampened when told that one conjured beast had howled so loud that three mages died from the sound before a guard speared the creature to death. Karsus waved their deaths away as necessary to research. Tugging one mage aside, Candlemas asked where the beasts were summoned *from,* but no one knew or cared. Candlemas shook his head in disbelief.

He witnessed demonstrations of spells and artifacts until he was dizzy. A tin triangle that shattered steel with its ping. A pair of mirrors that reflected one's image into infinity, but also showed one's age from infancy to old age, or in one mage's case, no image at all beyond age forty. A taunt spell that enraged another starved prisoner to beat herself senseless against iron bars. A worldweave spell that distorted all sizes and distances, until Candlemas looked like a mouse standing alongside Karsus's dirty foot. And much, much more, including a circular workroom where sixty mages analyzed a single object: the shooting star Candlemas and Sunbright had dug up.

Finally, when he could see the night sky through high windows, Karsus called a halt. Snapping his fingers, he summoned a page to lead Candlemas to his chambers. The stocky mage expected a room, and was grateful for the hospitality. He was astonished when escorted into a suite of rooms bigger than his workshop in Delia. There was, in fact, an entire household of fourteen servants, cooks, and maids awaiting his single word. Stunned, Candlemas called for a loaf of bread, cheese, and wine, and sat in a brocaded chair before a roaring fire. A maid drew off his sandals, a manservant washed his feet. He was so tired he could barely munch the bread—they'd brought five different loaves on a silver tray—and the wine made him groggy.

But he did ask the manservant, "Please, a moment. Karsus says I'm his 'special friend' because I've brought him a shooting star. But how many 'special friends' does he have?"

The butler tidied up the tray. Very carefully, he offered, "Karsus has many friends, for everyone loves him. But he always has just one 'special friend' at a time. Sometimes for a month, sometimes for only a day. One never knows."

Candlemas watched the man walk away, silent on a thick, embroidered rug. "Oh. . . ."

Drifting off in the soft chair, he wondered what had happened to Sunbright. And what would happen to him.

* * * * *

The next morning, after climbing out of voluminous

sheets and quilts, eating an opulent breakfast, and dressing in a fine short robe of brown and red brocade hand stitched for him that very night, Candlemas searched for Karsus but failed to find him. No one knew where he was, a common occurrence. Candlemas welcomed the fact, actually, for it gave him time to orient himself. Asking around in the vast echoing and ornate halls, he found a library run by a lesser mage with a squint and fuzzy red hair. She showed him racks of arcane books, mundane histories, and other such ephemera. Candlemas studied them all ravenously. He had three hundred and fifty-eight years' worth of catching up to do.

The more he read, the more disturbed he became.

It was late in the afternoon when a page cleared his throat and bowed to Candlemas. "Milord?"

"Eh?" Candlemas grumbled, shaking his head and rubbing his eyes. "What is it? You're not with . . ."

He stared. The young man wore a neat outfit of black-and-white like a jaybird's, not the shiny blues and greens of Karsus's household. Candlemas realized what the boy resembled when he was offered a card. On it was drawn a single black *P* with a white star in the loop.

"Is that . . . ?"

"Yes, milord. She bids you come right away. I'm to escort you."

Candlemas looked for irony in the lad's voice, found none, sighed and stood up.

"Very well, then," Candlemas sighed. "Lead on."

Near Castle Karsus's main gate—they walked half a mile through three linked mansions to reach them—waited a coach-and-four. The coach was white, piped with black, as were the coachmen and footmen. The horses were black with white blazes and exact white rings around their middles. Candlemas wondered if they were bred that way or painted. He muttered, "The more things change, the more they stay the same."

Once Candlemas had crawled inside, the coach rattled through the streets, whip cracking to clear the way. Outside for the first time, Candlemas got his first look at the city. Below this high hill, where Castle Karsus was sprinkled like a handful of cocked dice, lay the enclave, or city, of Karsus. Candlemas knew he was atop an inverted, floating mountain, and in the far distance saw other mountains, yet he was hard put to discern the drop-off. Karsus was more like a floating mountain *range*. And the buildings! Towers fine as pencils, elongated tubes that arched to meet high overhead, delicate traceries like crystal spiderwebs that spun in all directions, dozens of onion-shaped minarets in a row, each more fantastic than the last. The streets were uniformly paved with even cobblestones, gasglobes stood poised to light every corner, and parks and gardens interspersed the high walls around gorgeous mansions. Public fixtures were just as beautiful, from a shimmering fountain a hundred feet tall to bridges that looked like silver jewelry.

All told, the Karsus enclave made Castle Delia look like a lily pad. And Candlemas felt like a frog atop it, backward, ugly, and ignorant. What he'd seen in Karsus's workshops and read about in histories had humbled him. The lowest apprentice sweating in the workshops cleaning jars knew more than he ever would—probably as much as Lady Polaris had known when she was master of Castle Delia.

But he'd know more soon.

The carriage finally stopped by a black iron fence studded with white dots to resemble pearls. Beyond was a mansion of black stone and white mortar. But it took a while before Candlemas was admitted.

Oddly, the coach stopped on the wide avenue, and Candlemas was bidden out by a footman. Amidst a flurry of apologies, Candlemas was searched, groped by two white-gloved hands. Only then was he allowed inside the gate, where he was searched again by a pair of black-and-white guards, then escorted to the front doors.

Inside the mansion, the search was repeated, though more extensively. To an unbelievable degree. Braced by two guards, Candlemas was directed into a small room and ordered to strip. Wondering, he did so, even removing his loincloth. He was given a black-and-white robe, but the search continued. A maid went through his hair and beard with a comb, while a butler inspected each of his fingers, even pricking them with a needle to draw blood. Candlemas would have protested but for shock. After an inspection of his teeth, each one sounded with a tiny hammer, he was finally marched down a long corridor, handed to two more guards, marched farther, and so on.

Eventually he reached the top floor. A maid said, "Lady Polaris awaits you," and opened the door. Wondering, Candlemas went in. He was already half shielding his eyes. Remembering how stunningly beautiful Polaris had been three centuries ago, he imagined she must resemble a goddess these days.

So his mouth fell open in shock as he entered the chamber.

The light was dim, filtered through thick white curtains. The room was vast but cluttered, mostly with couches and low tables. At the far end of the room, reposing on a wide couch heaped with pillows, was someone who reminded Candlemas, vaguely, of Lady Polaris.

Except she was huge. Massively, obscenely fat.

The formerly beautiful face was lost in rolls of suet. Jowls suited to a hog framed deep-rooted, pouchy eyes and protruding lips. Her frost-blue eyes were lost under triple lids. Her hair looked dry enough to break, like frosted grass. Her body sprawled on the cushions, propped in a dozen places by flat pillows. From under her black gown stuck an ankle like a ham.

"Candlemas!" Even her voice dripped with fat, curdled and choked, unlike her cool tones of centuries gone by. Her skin, Candlemas saw as his eyes adjusted, was blotchy and veined from years of debauchery and gout, too much wine and fatty food. "Candlemas! You wretch! Where have you been? Have you been searched?"

Reeling with shock, the pudgy mage found it hard to respond. Slowly, he grasped her point. He and Sunbright had disappeared three hundred and fifty-eight years ago and had never been seen or heard from again (he supposed). Until today.

"Yes, I was. Um . . ." he groped for a chair as he groped for words, but found only piles of pillows. Begging pardon, he sank onto them. He couldn't stop staring at his transformed liege.

"I've been busy," he finally said, "in a library, lately."

The obese lady nodded as if that made sense. Grabbing with sausagelike fingers, she crammed a handful of sugared dates into her mouth. Drool chased down her chin, but she didn't seem to notice. "When I heard you were in town, I sent my card immediately. Have you solved my problem of the scrying glass? I'll need it for tonight."

"Scrying glass?" Candlemas didn't know what she meant. The last problem she'd tossed in his lap was the flipping-bone-dice conundrum. But this . . .

"No, wait. That wasn't you I assigned, was it? It was, let's see—that dark girl. Behira."

Oddly, this memory lapse shocked Candlemas the worst. One thing Lady Polaris had possessed above all was a keen mind that never forgot the smallest detail. Now she couldn't even recall her hired help's names. He watched uneasily as she picked up a mirror and finger combed her frizzled hair.

Absently she murmured, "I need the glass because there's a new form of assassination going around. They hire desperate people to sacrifice an arm, then fashion a simulacrum concealing poison until they can close with the victim . . ."

Candlemas remembered each of his fingers being pricked to draw blood. Assassinations?

" . . . I'm a prime target, of course, the choicest of the nobility. They're all jealous of my beauty." She preened in the mirror as she spoke, her forearm jiggling with fat. "Everyone hates me for my beauty, but they love me too. Or pretend to. They all want my secret, but they shan't have it. But poor Baron Onan. He was disemboweled and strangled with his own guts. Hung from the bedpost. That won't happen to me! Have you been strip-searched?"

"Yes," Candlemas told her again. Ye gods, was every noble in this city insane?

"Good. You'll need to be searched each time you enter. I'll abide no assassins near me, and you can't trust anyone. They all hate me, and love me. But you'll need to fashion that scrying glass. There's a ball tonight at the House of Danett. There'll be candle matching, and cards, and only the spyglass can help me win. I've got my eye on Mika's stable of race horses."

Candlemas nodded absently. Among the histories he'd read, he'd seen the name Polaris once or twice, marking how she'd made fabulous wagers, and often lost. Fifty years ago, she'd lost Castle Delia wagering on a yacht race. It was Castle Bello now, a hunting lodge for some other noble.

He'd read more facts, none of them pretty. Like Lady Polaris, the empire had declined immeasurably in the past three hundred years. Growing problems had been ignored, had reached the crisis point, then gone beyond.

While there had always been a huge gap between noble and peasant, lately it had grown insurmountable. A tiny cadre of wealthy and decadent archwizards brutalized the starving poor. Food riots were crushed with clubs. Down on the ground, unchecked blight, excessive taxation, and mismanaged and stolen funds had forced even prosperous folk to abandon farms and wander. In the wake of the blight came famine. Mills and mines crumbled, fields reverted to briars and weeds, and as the human populace suffered, they blamed outsiders. Dwarves, gnomes, and half-elves were persecuted atrociously, or killed outright.

Yet despite losing the source of their wealth, the Neth had grown even more callous and barbaric. They'd increased the Hunt, slaughtering whole villages and roads full of destitute pilgrims. Any sane voice of reason within the nobility had been silenced by assassination or banishment. The once proud Netherese had only three preoccupations: gambling, garnering status and wealth, and avoiding assassination, which was commonplace and ghastly.

In short, Lady Polaris was a perfect representation of the Empire of Netheril: self-consumed, bloated, ingrown, oblivious to rampant decay, and fuzzy minded.

For a while, reading, Candlemas had considered returning to Castle Delia, and his own time—if that were possible. Troubles hadn't seemed so insurmountable back then. But the castle, his home, though he'd never thought of it that way before, was gone, sold off.

Another thing disturbed him, too. Nowhere in any book did he find any mention of his name. Which meant he'd never been famous, never amounted to anything. Which meant working for Lady Polaris had netted him exactly nothing.

Dropping her mirror for more sugared dates, she interrupted his musing. "Well, why are you sitting here?

Get busy on that glass!"

Grunting free of the pillows, Candlemas gained his feet. Bowing, he stated, "My pardon, milady, but that's not possible. I'm in the employ of Karsus the Great now. I'm his"—not *special friend*—"confidant, in a matter of great importance. One that will allow him to finish his experiments."

"You work for Karsus?" The fat lady's voice went small as a frightened child's. She cast about in the dim room. "Karsus? Did he send you? Are you here to as-sass—Get out! Get out, now, before I have you killed! Get out, get out!"

She screamed in her raw, raspy voice. Frightened by her insanity, Candlemas fled for the door. As a maid yanked it open, he sailed past and ran down the corridor. Heart pounding, he ran all the way until he stood in the evening street, bent over and wheezing. And weeping, though he didn't know why.

Chapter 7

Sunbright dreamt.

Before dawn, exhausted by the long, confusing day, he'd found a park and crawled under some bushes to catnap. Jumbled dreams immediately seized his mind— images of women in many forms.

Greenwillow was there, walking in an ethereal forest, first in her green shirt and black armor, then in a misty gown, then naked, as he'd seen her only once. But this was no erotic dream, for she kept moving, shifting like the mist itself, cool and serene as a mountain waterfall. Where was she?

Later, as night rolled over the vision, she grew taller, her eyes sparkling like stars, until she loomed across the sky, filling it from horizon to horizon, not smiling now but frowning. What had he done?

But suddenly she was small, scarcely coming to his breastbone, close enough to touch, yet slipping behind him again and again so he couldn't catch her. As he stupidly craned his head, he could glimpse only one green, sparkling eye, for the other was shaded, or dull, or milky white, and she'd turned shy and hiding. What did that coyness signify?

And where was she going, this ever changing Greenwillow? Whenever Sunbright got close to her, she skipped away, light as a fawn, leading him on. On to something. But what? There wasn't anything he wanted except Greenwillow, yet she evaded him. Was there something or someone else here? How could there be, when he knew no one in this world?

Chasing the elf's shifting, lithe form, he begged her to wait, grabbed at her, but she slipped behind a laurel bush with a giggle. He batted it aside, brush thrashing, crashing, whipping in his face, stinging his hands—

—and woke himself up.

He lay in the park, with the sun leaking over the horizon, in a city high in the air, far from home. Alone.

* * * * *

As the wind died just before dawn, Sunbright halted to sniff. Something was up. Trouble brewing.

Treading the early morning streets toward the jumble of Karsus's compound, he passed unmolested, as he had all night. The few night dwellers had steered well clear of the tall barbarian loaded with weapons and spattered with others' blood. City guards had studied him, but his noble bearing and firm stride gave them pause, and he was leaving their blocks, which suited them fine. As the east tinged red, the roisterers of the night stumbled home under city guard escort, like vampires fearing the sun. Now the only folks abroad were

merchants with pony carts or porters with barrows:
fruit sellers, bakers' apprentices, butchers' boys, deal-
ers in frozen fish. (How fish could be frozen solid in
warm weather Sunbright didn't understand.) They converged on the central market with its tables and corrals
and stalls and kiosks, settling into traditional spots and
setting out their wares. Yet filtering in came city
guards in polished lobster-tail helmets and blue-green
tabards emblazoned with the **K** for Karsus. All of them
carried silver-tipped maces, and they grunted from the
sides of their mouths. The merchants also whispered,
uneasy at the large number of guards.

In all the nervous preparations, Sunbright was
mostly ignored, and had tramped halfway across the
marketplace when he felt the first hint of danger. It was
a whiff, a scent, a prickling along his neck that warned
him he was being watched. Something was lurking like
wolves in the bush, or a panther braced to spring from
a tree. The feeling was all around. Yet turning a circle,
he saw only stalls and pennants and slit-eyed guards
with ready maces.

Then the sun topped a mountain peak, the bright yellow splintered by a thousand distant trees. A dome
upon Karsus's mansions burned golden as if ignited by
the rays.

And a roar went up from the shadows around the
marketplace.

Instinctively Sunbright drew his sword, which he'd
paused to hone by the light of a street globe, and surveyed his surroundings for shelter and escape routes.
Behind him lay a long line of wide-eyed frozen fish. Opposite were bushels of wheat and corn, and fresh loaves
of bread like fat swords. The marketplace floor was
square tan cobblestones. The stalls were flimsy, mere
poles and canvas, with the occasional small wagon, a
maze of sticks and canvas. It was hard to pinpoint the

roar—whatever it was—as it came from all around.

Then he saw the threat, ragged and dirty and howling, surging in from all sides like a storm tide. It was the starving poor of Karsus, and there were hundreds of them.

Women, men, children flooded the marketplace and snatched at anything resembling food. Clad in cast-off nobles' clothes or the scantiest, most colorless rags, they outraced one another and the city guards and the market sellers, who swept their goods into sacks or wagons while grabbing for short swords, meat cleavers, or long, weighted clubs. Sunbright saw that the poor had planned this raid well, for each wore one or two sacks strapped to his chest or back, so their hands might be free to grab and stuff and grab again. Grimy hands scrabbled like flailing octopuses, like demented weasels in a henhouse, in a frenzy of bloodlust.

Yet for all their mad rush, they were marvelously organized. One woman with an eye patch and queerly gold-glittering hands even stood in one spot to shout orders and encouragement. She caught Sunbright's attention, though he wasn't sure why. Something about her eyes—had he dreamt of a woman with one starry eye? Her hair was dark, like Greenwillow's. She took nothing, only watched over the others. And something familiar and white winked at her throat—but in one glance he couldn't identify what.

A man stiff-armed a fishmonger and scooped three whiskered catfish into the sack hanging about his neck. A barefoot boy leaped upon a table, avoided the clumsy slashing of a short whip from a baker's girl, and popped round loaves of bread into twin sacks hanging at either hip. A crone threw sand into a merchant woman's face and slapped red cheeses into her own sacks, then jammed three more into the backpack of a rawboned girl alongside. A huge man, a giant, but blindfolded, was led by a elfin girl to a stall of hams and sausages. As the giant flailed blindly with a staff that made butchers jump out of the way, the girl filled pouches on his legs and back with stolen meats. A yellow-haired scoundrel whirled a weighted chain overhead, making corn merchants duck, so he could snare, one-handed, fat sacks of yellow meal that he stuffed down his shirt. Another man hurled jars full of something that, when the jars broke, stank so abominably that food sellers retreated retching. A pair of girls, twins with stiff topknots like Sunbright's, upended a table onto an old woman so they could snatch up flitches of bacon in a scrap of canvas.

There were more attacks and distractions, some of them magical, and Sunbright remembered that anyone born in the empire could enchant. A crone, obviously a hedge wizard, fanned her fingers to hurl what looked like water into the path of two carters, except they slipped as if on oil and couldn't rise. A girl with red pigtails held on to a fallen banner so the other end rose like a snake and enwrapped a burly butcher from behind. Elsewhere Sunbright saw clouds of purple and blue smoke, a spinning lightning bolt, a brace of phantom horses charging.

All this happened within seconds, hundreds of poor battling scores of merchants and robbing till their sacks were filled, while Sunbright stood stupefied at the spectacle.

Then the city guards rushed in, and the killing began. While the poor had just upset and driven back the merchants, the guards had no such qualms. The burly men and a few women charged into the ragged folk with silver clubs swinging. A club smacked the side of one man's head and caved it in, dropping him like a shot goose. Another club broke the wrist of a woman clutching a ham. As she dropped it, and bent to grab it with her good hand, a blow landed on her neck, driving her facedown onto the cobblestones, dead. A boy running down tables had his legs swept out from under him, was brutally kicked as he toppled to the ground in a tangle of skinny arms and legs. The guards could ply magic too. A crackling hand shocked a raider senseless, an indrawn breath sucked another off her feet, a glob of spittle darted unerringly to smack a thief in the eyes. Guards worked in pairs, two or four or six, watching each other's sides and backs, driving hard with heavy boots, shouldering the poor aside and down, smashing and breaking bones at will.

A gaggle of raiders stormed by Sunbright, who hadn't budged an inch in all this hurly-burly. They swept past like a wave around his waist, for he towered above most Neth. The twin girls flitting past flicked his elbows with their topknots. The lone barbarian was left to face six stampeding guards with bloody clubs, who would bull over anyone in their way.

That suited Sunbright.

It was gut reaction, not reason. If the poor needed food so desperately they must steal it, they deserved it. And the guards had no right to kill them for so necessary a crime. And these brutes enjoyed their work.

So Sunbright welcomed combat, a chance to strike back at the callous rulers of this city.

A barbarian shriek split the morning air to rise above the roar and stampede. Planting his big iron-ringed boots, Sunbright swept Harvester behind him with two hands, shouted again, *"Raaa-vens of Rennn-garth!"*

Too late the guards realized this big man wouldn't flee. Two of them braked, almost falling. Two sheared to the side. Two, angrier than their comrades, drew their short swords to match their clubs.

They died first.

Harvester of Blood sliced the air, hissing as its

glistening blade sheared through an ironwood club, slammed into the first guard's neck, and carried on to bat the club of the next man, who reeled in shock from the gout of blood that erupted into the sky, and from the thud of his partner's head at his feet. The sword edge cut the club deep enough that Sunbright's tug ripped it from the guard's hand. The soldier ducked and stabbed with his short sword, aiming for the barbarian's gut. But Sunbright had whipped his sword straight back, pommel high against his shoulder, and stabbed back. Longer arms and a longer blade scored. The guard was skewered above the breastbone by the terrible, hooked tip of razor steel. His own fetched-up club battered his chin, though by then he was already dead.

Chanting an ancient battle air, Sunbright hauled back his sword and whirled in a fast circle, though he shuffled without picking up his feet lest he trip or slip in blood. It was a good thing he instinctively guarded his back. A female guard was chopping at his kidneys.

Tilting Harvester down, he caught her sword on his steel with a frightful clang and screech. Dishing her thrust to one side, he flicked a quick chop at her chin. She hollered and flipped her head back, but not fast enough. Harvester cleft her chin from underneath, laid open her lips so bloody teeth gleamed, and knocked her onto her back.

Her partner, a square-jawed brute, tried an attack that almost worked. Reaching over his shoulder, he jerked loose his lobster-tail helmet and flung it at Sunbright's face, followed with a quick killing thrust to the groin. But the barbarian had fought too many battles to flinch. Still gripping Harvester in two hands, he snapped his wrists up to deflect the polished bowl with a clonk. At the same time, he leveled Harvester only slightly. The lunging guard ran his own belly onto Harvester's keen tip. As Sunbright spun to his right, the sword's barb ripped a furrow across the man's guts and liver.

Sunbright was still turning, still guarding his back, but four guards were dead and the other two gone. He was alone, temporarily, in a pile of bloody dead. Cowering merchants hunkered behind spilt tables while distant guards clubbed the wounded to death, for most of the poor had fled to the shadows whence they'd come. The food riot was over, and soon Sunbright would be the only one standing with a bloody sword amidst a hundred angry guards.

But not everyone had fled. The one-eyed woman— again Sunbright glimpsed that tantalizing white bauble at her throat—struggled to drag a yellow-haired man who'd fallen and broken his leg. The blind giant, hampered by his bulky loads of food, jabbered at the tiny girl, and groped for the fallen man. Guards spotting the quartet saw them and shouted to close in.

Instantly Sunbright was among them, sheathing Harvester, butting the giant aside, grabbing up the broken-legged man, and pitching him over his shoulder. By the time he'd balanced the man, the one-eyed woman was waving a glittering gold hand at them from yards away. "Run, slue-foot!"

Heavy boots sounded behind him. Hunkering forward under his burden and grabbing the giant's elbow, Sunbright dashed through a maze of upset stalls, rolling vegetables, and slippery fish. The one-eyed leader paused at a narrow alley between two brick walls and slapped her comrades inside while watching the onrushing guards. She spanked Sunbright through into semidarkness, then shoved his hams from behind to keep him moving.

But as he'd zipped past her, grappling to keep the injured man on his shoulder, Sunbright had glimpsed the white shininess at her throat and finally recognized it.

It was a knucklebone.

* * * * *

When Candlemas trudged back to his suite of rooms, thoroughly distraught by he knew not what, he found yet another calling card lying on a silver tray next to his canopied bed. This bore an **A**, a letter for once not so ornate as to be misread. The simple, neat monogram made him already like the bearer. But who "A" was he didn't know.

A maid finally told him that the monogram belonged to one Lady Aquesita, and that her footmen had requested Candlemas visit, when he had the time. Now he had only exhaustion from a day of reading, and his nerve-racking interview with Lady Polaris. Kicking off his sandals, he climbed into bed and tried to forget everything.

But the morning was bright, a hot bath and splendid breakfast brought him alive, and wearing yet another new robe, this one red with brown trim, he summoned a page girl to lead him to Lady Aquesita, whoever she might be.

It turned out she lived in one of Karsus's mansions. He had many, for he was the most important man in the empire, no matter what the other nobles might want to believe. It was a good mile walk down stairs and up ramps, out one door and across expanses of flagstones and gardens and lofty balconies until he arrived at Lady Aquesita's "chambers", which were, in fact, a whole separate mansion. Along the way Candlemas wondered what she wanted. Everyone in this city, he'd concluded, wanted something. Already he'd been approached by many folk currying favor with "Karsus's special friend." Aquesita, he supposed, would prove no different.

Yet when the page led him down a gravel path to the lady's mansion, Candlemas was impressed by its neat severity. Painted a lovely rose color, it lacked the usual overdone bric-a-brac and garish paint. Coming from the overly ornate realms of Karsus, this refreshingly plain house was like a breath of fresh air.

His admiration grew when they passed through the main doors—with no guards barring assassins—to a large, open room painted a plain white and decorated mostly with green plants and flowers. At the far end, sitting at a small glass topped table, sat his hostess, who rose to meet him.

"Good day, Master Candlemas. I am Lady Aquesita. So kind of you to come."

Never good at court manners, Candlemas bowed awkwardly, briefly kissed her hand, and accepted a seat in a delicate ironwork chair. Shrewdly, he studied his hostess, wondering what she wanted of him, while she fussed with tea and raspberry tarts.

She was no beauty. Plain, round face, dimpled mouth, with brown hair piled on her head, she had a figure blocky as a barrel, and pudgy hands. But her smile seemed genuine, and she was not slathered in makeup as were most women and men in this place, nor were her eyes two different colors; the latest fashion, he'd been told. And her clothes were rich but severe. She plied her sunny smile so much Candlemas began to worry. She must want a powerful lot. Candlemas accepted herbal tea and a tart, and tried to guess what.

A person's chambers told much about the occupant, he knew, so he put his keen scientist's eye to observing. What he found was a pleasant surprise. This and adjoining rooms were light and airy, and faced out on a long stone balcony overlooking gardens that ran out of sight to hedges and rose bushes, outbuildings and gazebos. The high doors were wide open, admitting sunlight and breeze and the breath of flowers. There were almost as many plants inside the room as outside, and the effect was to surround one with natural beauty. Scattered about the room too were many gorgeous artifacts such as Candlemas himself collected (*had* collected) back in Castle Delia. A graceful muse arched grapes over her head. An illuminated book lay open on a rosewood stand. Carved lions flanked the doorways. Glowing tapestries covered the walls. A crystalline dragon spun in the breeze, a goat between its front claws was a tiny clapper giving off bell-like tones.

Stunned by this quiet beauty, Candlemas kept turning, making new discoveries. A faint giggle. "You admire my trinkets?"

Flushing like a country bumpkin, Candlemas jerked upright in his seat, slopped rose hip tea on his robe. "Oh, yes, yes. Very much. I, uh, collected things like this, uh, long ago."

She was pleased by his admiration. "The cream of the empire, I hope. Most folks follow the latest fad, discarding what was new last year for newer trash this year. I pick and choose, seek out the Neth's finest works, and keep them here, safe. Years from now, I like to think, people will know what was beautiful and appreciate my efforts."

"Yes, I'm sure," he agreed. She made Candlemas nervous, though he couldn't think why. "That's, uh, noble of you."

"Or selfish?" she countered. "Trying to buy my way to fame? But someone needs to tout the empire's better side. Don't you agree?"

"Yes, of course." Candlemas agreed again, nodding like a dog begging a treat. "Uh . . ."

"Why have I requested you visit?"

Embarrassed by her directness, he fumbled with his cup. Even it was exquisite in a simple way, paper thin, painted with a single songbird so real it looked alive. She laughed, and he liked the sound. Looking up, he studied her more closely. It was then that he really noticed her eyes: a soft golden brown.

"You've found me out," she teased. "I'm cousin to Karsus. His only living relation."

Ah, thought Candlemas, but then, what could she want? Surely she could have anything in the city with a snap of her fingers.

"I know you're Karry's special friend, at least for now. Gossip travels faster than hummingbirds through this castle. But I won't ask much. It's just that, as his only family, I like to keep abreast of what he's doing."

"You want me to, uh . . ." Candlemas fumbled for a polite word.

"Spy? No. No secret knowledge between us, no sneaking around. No, all I ask is that, while you're his friend, I might ask his progress. What he's thinking, what he's up to. I'm responsible for him, in a way, because he's not really responsible for himself."

That Candlemas knew. Karsus was a lunatic, albeit a genius.

"If it's a bother," she went on, "please forget I asked. It's just that, with no other family, and servants being deferential, and seekers currying favor, it's hard for me to get the truth about my own cousin sometimes. An honest opinion would be so helpful. And you seem forthright—"

"I'll do it," Candlemas blurted, though he wasn't sure why. For some reason he wanted to help while she, unmarried and childless, looked after the mad genius like an older sister. "I'd be glad to come see you—no, I mean—"

"Thank you," she interrupted. A soft hand touched his wrist. Cool, it sent tingles down his spine like an enchantment. "I would be very grateful."

"It's no trouble. You're welcome. I'll come, uh, soon. As often as you wish."

Something sparkled in her eyes. Amusement? Mirth? Was she laughing at him? He couldn't tell. He finished his tarts, wishing there were more so he might linger, but finally excused himself.

The page girl had to take his hand to lead the way back. Candlemas couldn't understand why he was befuddled. Had she potioned his tea? Cast a spell on him? Clouded his mind with some illusion?

"What a remarkable woman!" he told the page girl as they walked, really speaking more to himself than to the servant. "Keenly intelligent, conscientious, noble, sacrificing, handsome in an unadorned way, with not a speck of decadence! It's like finding a flower growing in a rubbish heap! Imagine . . ."

The page girl was only ten, and said nothing, but she hid a woman's smile as they passed up the gravel path.

* * * * *

Grunting, shifting his groaning burden while his shoulders were rubbed raw, Sunbright followed the ragtag thieves deeper and deeper. To where, he had no idea.

Trotting down an alley, they'd taken an abrupt right through a broken wall into blackness, dropped into a cellar beneath what smelled like a disused tannery, scurried behind a mound of dirt and dropped to their knees—the blind giant barely fit, and Sunbright had to push the injured man before him—to clamber through another broken wall, then turn tightly and drop beneath even the cellar. Stooping, Sunbright tripped down a sloping tunnel until they reached a natural cavern.

A blue-white light came from their leader, the woman with the eye patch, who'd set aglow her leather vest with strokes of her hands. A thief's cantra, Sunbright assumed, in a city where even dung shovelers used spells.

As the cavern narrowed, they passed through a cleft, then walked a rounded pipe that would accommodate a coach-and-four inside. And so on, twisting and turning until the barbarian was thoroughly lost. There were pipes, drains, tubes, caves, cracks, shelves, platforms, iron staircases, troughs, tunnels, pits, stone steps, and more.

Eventually they passed from a tunnel onto a sheer drop-off like a square cliff. Fifty feet down winked oily wetness reeking of sewage. All of the party panted except Sunbright, so the leader called a halt, silenced them while she listened (cupping her ears in a queer way that suggested another cantra) then demanded to see Lothar, the yellow-haired man with the broken leg. He had gone limp from pain and Sunbright laid him down, straightened his limbs, and untangled the weighted chain wrapped around his arm. The blind giant, the tiny girl, an old crone, the twin girls, and a boy all ate, digging out stolen corn cakes, breaking, and sharing them.

The one-eyed woman striped her hands around, causing leather and stone and even flesh to glow eerily, then ordered the giant to hold Lothar down while she worked on his leg. Even unconscious, the man groaned in pain. As she sweated over the leg, probing the break and hissing under her breath, Sunbright studied her.

She wore only leather: a tightly laced calfskin vest and breeches, and she went barefoot. Her only jewelry was the knucklebone cradled between her small breasts. The jewel-like glitter of metal came from the solid brass knuckles with cruel serrated edges that she wore on her right hand. Scars told the story of her life. Dozens of them crisscrossed her arms, striping her dusty feet, and spotting her face like chalk marks. One deep scar split her right temple, no doubt the slice that had ruined her eye and necessitated the leather eye patch. Her chin

and nose were small, her dark hair unkempt and cut
short, and when she tilted her head, Sunbright noted
the slight points at the top of her ears. That, and a hint
of slant to her eyebrows, told of elven blood. In only the
short time he'd been in this city, he knew how people of
mixed blood were treated. Short and slim, she barely
came to his breastbone, not that he could stand upright
in these tunnels.

Her examination of her comrade's leg complete, the
leader instructed Sunbright to pull Lothar's leg while
the giant held on. Tugging the leg muscles straight,
then the bone ends into line, they got the limb splinted
with rags and fragments of wood they'd picked up along
the way. Only then did the leader sit back and accept
some stolen food.

Sunbright could contain himself no longer. "Who are
you people? Did you lead that raid on the marketplace,
or was it just an unplanned uprising? Where are we?
Where are we going? What are all these passages down
here?"

The leader sat back on her heels and glared with her
one good eye. It was green, Sunbright thought, though
the confusing glowing light made it hard to say for sure.
Blank faced, she studied him. Sunbright doubted she'd
ever seen anyone like him before: tall and tanned and
topknotted, dressed in far northern clothes, laden with
a sword almost as big as she was. But he could read
nothing in her face; it had been schooled to reveal
naught. Instead she shot back, "Why did you help us?"

Her voice was surprisingly low for so small a thing.
The others munched.

Sunbright waved a hand and said, "You needed help.
I haven't been here long, but I don't like the city
guards."

"Where are you from?" She shot the questions like
darts, her good eye boring into his face.

"The tundra, though lately the high sierra."

"What are those?"

"Eh?"

"What are those places?"

"Oh, uh . . ." He'd been asked about his distant homeland before. "The tundra lies in the far north, where the
land is flat to the horizon, with no trees, and cold most
of the year. The high sierra is the slopes of the Barren
Mountains. Pine forest, red pines, and chert."

The woman glanced at her comrades. Reaching in the
crone's pouch, she withdrew a thawing fish and skinned
it with a long knife plucked from a back sheath. The
crone croaked, "Down on the ground."

"Yes," he said, then suddenly it struck Sunbright.
"Haven't any of you ever been on the ground?"

The leader asked, "So you only followed us to escape
the guards?"

"Wait a moment!" Sunbright growled, spreading a
broad hand, outlined darkly against the blue-white eldritch light. "Why do my questions go unanswered?
Who are you people? What're your names? And where
do they get frozen fish in the height of summer?"

The leader sliced fish into raw strips, handed them
around. Sunbright took one absently, munched the cold,
rubbery flesh. It sang of sea salt, another mystery, for
they were easily a hundred leagues from the ocean.

The woman said, "We'll lead you to a pipe that leads
outside. You can return to your friends above."

"I don't have any friends in this city!" he snapped.
"Well, one, perhaps, but he's caught up with Karsus."

Silence crashed down. They even stopped chewing.

"You're a friend to Karsus?" asked the leader, her
voice low.

Sunbright swore under his breath, then said, "Would
someone answer my questions? Who are you? Why do
you wear these knucklebones around your necks? I see

you all bear them. I've got one too!"

Digging in a belt pouch, he produced the polished knucklebone drilled as a pendant. "I found it on the body of a fellow who swung a weighted chain like this man's. I wondered . . ."

Sunbright let his words trail off. The silence that had fallen over the strange band seemed to thicken, though the barbarian never would have thought that possible. One of the children—the little girl—took a step back, glancing meaningfully at the leader. The little girl was afraid. A cold chill went down Sunbright's back. Now what had he done?

"You're the one!" shrilled the leader. She exploded to her feet like a startled cat, blade outthrust. "Rise and draw, you bastard! Defend yourself!"

Chapter 8

Hunkered on his heels, Sunbright snapped up nearly as quickly as this hellcat. He held out both hands, fingers spread, saying, "I don't have a knife. And I'm the one who did what?"

The one-eyed woman lunged. Her knife—the black blade was a foot long and tapered to nothing—stabbed for Sunbright's middle. Instinctively he slapped to knock her arm wide. But she'd anticipated that and, dipping her hand under his, whipped in close. Surprised by the catlike riposte, Sunbright jumped back, but his back rapped a projection of the tunnel corner and his head banged a pipe in the ceiling. He felt a bee sting. Her blade had pinked his red shirt and belly.

Her hand jerked back to thrust again, but the barbarian batted hard and low, cuffed her head, and staggered her. Still, she'd seen even that move coming, and had almost ducked out of the way. Squatting low as a toad, she flicked in and sliced his inner thigh just above the knee. Sunbright knew that strategy: a few deft cuts would weaken his legs and topple him. He was still pinned against the wall and the low ceiling, and still unarmed. Harvester's pommel ground on stone.

The thief sashayed back and forth, hypnotic as a snake, ready to strike. Her face and ragged hair were illuminated by her glowing vest. She muttered curses under her breath, and Sunbright knew they were not mere bravado. She was truly angry with him, wanted to gut him. Why? Because he'd killed some mugger up in a city street?

Before he could even frame a question, she lashed out again.

Straightening her back, she struck high to stab at his face. He flinched back and smacked his head on stone again, though he tried to slap her hand aside. Instead he felt searing, grating pain as the blade slid through his left palm. For a second he saw almost a foot of needlelike steel jutting from the back of his hand, then he whipped his hand off the blade. A good thing, too, for she twisted the blade deftly to sever his tendons. If he weren't so quick, she'd have destroyed the hand.

He was like a bear swatting at a hummingbird. One good clip would kill her, but it needed pure luck to land. He forced himself to ignore the bleeding cuts and watch instead the blade, which he now realized was of elven craftsmanship. Where had she gotten it?

The woman stooped and jabbed for his left knee. He crooked the knee aside, smashed down with a fist for her head, and hit only air.

He could draw his own knife, but no, she'd still carve him like mutton. She was hot to fight, and he wasn't. Some kind of shield would be better, a chair or net, or even a pair of sticks. Despite her mad ferocity, he didn't want to kill her. Rather, he wanted to question her. More likely she'd cut his throat.

Wary, fumbling with his right hand, he drew Dorlas's warhammer and held it close by the steel head. By flipping the leather-wrapped handle he might deflect the blade sideways and get in a shot with a fist or boot. He'd hoped that, with only one eye, her depth perception would be poor, but she seemed to know exactly how far to thrust and how to keep clear.

But he was thinking too much, and needed to react. Battle-lust cooling, she hesitated to get within his grasp. After two rapid feints, she scored with a long cut down his left forearm. Blood welled, ran down his arm, dripped from his elbow. Red wetness from his punctured hand had already flowed there.

Sunbright didn't mind the blood, he had plenty. But a few more cuts would weaken him. Her anger was mystifying, puzzling. He fought to keep himself from getting angry at this blind attack.

Shuffling awkwardly in the semidarkness, eyes tracking everything, the fighters—one reluctant, one determined—assessed their chances. The one-eyed woman continued to curse, breath whistling. Sunbright wondered if he should waste breath on reason.

A flicker, and he was pinked on the back of his right hand. A snap of the hammer handle, and her blade clicked aside, then again. A thrust at his knee and he sidestepped, returned with a quick kick of a boot too thick to pierce. Aiming true, she slit his knee just above the leather. A punch from the hammer made her hook her head aside. A feint at his throbbing, bleeding left wrist again, then a lunge for his guts. A move to block with the hammer handle—

—and his bloody left fist came down like a boulder from a mountaintop to smash on the back of her head.

The woman was driven flat as a tent peg, so fast and hard her face slammed dirt.

Frustrated, worried, Sunbright had lashed out, and immediately regretted it. But he stamped down hard on her hand and the knife blade before doing anything else. The woman lay still.

"First time I ever saw that happen," rasped the crone.

"What happened?" asked the blind giant, worried.

The tiny girl whispered, "She's down."

The twins with the topknots faded into the dark even as the giant shot to his feet. Though blind, he could gauge the ceiling, and didn't rap his head as Sunbright had. He clenched monstrous hands and growled, "Let's see if you can knock *me* down!"

"Hold on. I don't want to harm anyone . . ." Sunbright called. He held up his hands, his left welling red, his right almost as bad. ". . . or *be* harmed. I just want answers."

Holstering his hammer, Sunbright squatted and plucked the knife from the woman's limp grasp. It was elven work all right, the handle of black polished wood chased by silver wire, the pommel and hilt filigreed. He slipped it into the back of his boot.

The crone hobbled forward to lift the knife fighter's head. The thief stirred, moaned, blubbered. Her nose was mashed and swollen, dripping blood down her face. She was covered with dirt. Sunbright had almost snapped her neck, had smacked her face into the dirt hard enough to leave an impression. He chided himself. This was no way to make friends. Didn't anyone in this city want to talk instead of fight?

The crone fussed and mopped the woman's bloody, dazed face. The leader croaked, "Where is he?" Sunbright admired how she still strove to place her enemy and determine his danger. He just backed away and hunkered low. Using his own knife, he sliced ribbons from his long shirt and awkwardly bandaged his left hand. It hurt now, sizzling as if on fire.

The crone ordered the giant to pick up the injured Lothar, then told the twins to carry their groggy leader. Sunbright was being left behind. He stood up and they all tensed, wary as stray dogs.

"I'm coming with you."

"What makes you think that?" wheezed the crone.

The barbarian sucked wind through his teeth, fought down a simmering anger at everyone and everything in this city. "I won the fight, I get what I want."

"What do you want?"

"Answers."

The old woman shrugged, turned, and pointed the way down a narrow slope. "Come on, then."

* * * * *

The strange and wounded party crept on like sewer rats, threading deeper into the guts of the city. Finally they reached an iron door that the giant heaved aside. Beyond lay a chamber in which the slightest noise echoed in Sunbright's ears. Someone snapped a finger to set a glowlight burning.

The rocky cavern reminded the tundra dweller of a rookery. Floor, ceiling, and walls were a jumble of pockmarks deep enough to hide in. The twisted cavern ran for some distance, out of the range of the glowlight cantra, then seemed to dip. The air was surprisingly fresh, even breezy, until the iron door clanked back in place. Rocks and planks made tables and seats where more rocks had filled holes and made the floor tolerably level. The "furniture" encircled a fire pit. Dotted around the cavern, like rooks' nests, Sunbright saw blankets and bedding. Odd bits of junk such as split paintings and soiled tapestries were decorations. A colony for these thieves, then, them

CLAYTON EMERY

and three other misfits already here: a burly man, a balding woman, and a girl with red pigtails.

They'd already laden the table with their stolen food, and now the incoming party added more. Lothar was put to bed with a bottle of brandy for his pain. The leader—Sunbright still didn't know her name—was propped against bales of old cloth. Water dripped at the back of the cave, and the crone wet a rag and mopped the leader's bloody nose. Sunbright hunkered on his heels, arms across his knees, and watched.

"I'd like to ask some questions, and get answers for a change." he asked the crone, "Then I'll leave you alone."

"Ask away."

The old woman's face was a mass of wrinkles, but her white hair was drawn neatly back and pinned. Her clothing consisted of a single voluminous dark robe, an all-encompassing garment that would keep out rain or sun and keep in heat. Most of the thieves wore the same. Only the part-elven leader wore thin leather, as if she were impervious to the subterranean chill.

Sunbright got busy asking his questions. "What's your name?"

The woman cradled the leader's head, dabbed off blood. "Call me Mother," she told him. "Everyone does."

"Are you really any of these folks' mother?"

"I was a mother once. It suffices."

Sunbright grunted, settled more comfortably on his heels, and asked, "What's her name?"

"Knucklebones."

"Huh? What kind of name is that?"

Mother mopped dirt from the woman's hair as she said, "What's the toughest bone in any animal's body?"

"Oh." Sunbright replied. Dogs and wolves could eat any part of any animal, crack any bone for the marrow, except knucklebones. "Is that why she wears a knucklebone pendant?"

"And because she's good at the game of Knuckle-bones. And because she wears these," she said, indicating the brass knuckles on the young woman's right hand, filed and shaped to fit her fingers like multiple rings. Mother picked at her own throat, tugged up a thong, showing a glimpse of white. "But we all wear these. The badge of her family."

"You mean gang."

Mother shot him a look from under thin eyebrows and said, "Don't be impertinent."

"My apologies."

Sunbright squatted with his back to the iron door, one ear tuned lest it move. The other thieves were dividing or storing the food in stone jars with wooden lids.

"Family it is. And the man from whom I took the knucklebone. He was a member of your family?"

"And her lover," replied Mother. Gently, she stroked her finger along Knucklebones's nose. Sunbright saw the fingers glow a pale red, saw the swollen flesh slowly sink to normal size. Mother was a hedge wizard, he supposed. Or else minor healing was just another spell everyone knew. "His name was Martel. He went into the garbage chutes, I take it."

"Yes." Sunbright may have damned himself, but said, "I stumbled on a street brawl. He was out to kill me, tangled me with his weighted chain so he could stab me. I think. I was confused. I didn't want to kill him."

"Explain that to her when she's up," replied Mother evenly. "But I'm not surprised. We should stick to thievin', not hire out to the noble brats for their hell-raisin'. Knuckle' didn't want him to go. They argued, and he didn't come back. We heard why."

Sighing, Sunbright changed the subject. "You live by thieving. Why not work?"

"There's no work," she laughed. "Only for friends of

the nobles. This city is about played out, ready to collapse under the weight of the nobility. They've eaten away their foundations, you see, let termites bore through their homes."

"And you're the termites?"

Now Mother sighed. She dragged loose cloth around and covered Knucklebones, who was in and out of sleep. Sunbright hoped he hadn't caused her brain damage, or injured her spine. "No," she told him, "we're nothin', rats livin' off garbage, just a nuisance. It's the nobles who're their own worst enemy. They'll drown in their own sewage."

"I don't understand."

"You really are from far away, then. It's this way all over the empire," Mother said, creaking upright and fetching two bowls of porridge a girl had warmed by the fire. She and Sunbright ate with their fingers. "The nobles're greedy. They've always been so, but as time goes by, their appetites increase and they want more. They take it from the commoners. Eventually they take too much, the commoners starve, and then the nobles do too. But they never see it comin' and never try to stop it.

"How much of the city have you seen? How many shops closed? How many people out of work? The workin' class has been taxed—robbed—out of existence. Leather workers and milliners and blacksmiths couldn't pay their taxes, so their shops're taken and they're thrown out of work. They starve a while, then choose: die or steal. The ones caught are executed or thrown into labor camps and worked to death. Anyone who complains about the oppression, bards singing or printers selling broadsides, or minor officials who know the poor're also silenced, banished, or killed outright. The city guard are nothin' but murderous thugs, out to collect graft and kill anyone who raises his eyes to a noble. Their watchword is 'Mind your betters.' And down on the ground, they tell me—I've never been there—it's better, and worse.

"Worse," she continued, "because farmers're thrown off their land and made to wander. But here, we're like fish in a pool, all fightin' for crumbs. Folks can't work, so families split up to find food. Children are abandoned . . . look at these lost souls Knucklebones has taken in. And the high-and-mighty archwizards don't care, they only demand the guards grind down harder, punish more terribly."

Sunbright interjected, "But all that food in the marketplace. And the goods?"

"For nobles only," Mother sighed, shaking her head. "Their cooks and chamberlains're the only ones permitted in the market once it's open. Any commoners comin' near would be beaten to death by silver. Oh, there are some folks still makin' things. The archwizards have private workshops and hired artisans. They have cooks to prepare fabulous food for their endless parties, I'm told, and craftsmen to manufacture toys. Certainly they make flyin' disks for the Hunt, so the nobles can kill peasants on the ground. They lark and game like blind children. But the nobles skate on thin ice that's bein' licked away from underneath by a changing tide. They can prop the empire with brutality, with magic, with money—but it can't hold up forever."

"So what's to happen?"

Mother shrugged, said, "One day, sooner or later, the ice breaks. And the empire crumbles. And us at the bottom'll be crushed first.

"But the nobles'll have a mighty rough landin' too."

* * * * *

Sunbright asked all the questions he wanted, for Mother liked to talk about big ideas, and her brood was not mentally inquisitive. They were too concerned with staying alive. The big man was Ox, once a wrestler, until his eyes were gouged out by city guards. His tiny daughter was Corah. Their wife and mother was rumored to be dead, spirited off the streets one night in one of the guards' many random sweeps. Aba and Zykta, foundlings, were the topknotted twins. A skinny boy was Rolon. Others came and went, Mother explained, and Knucklebones commanded them all. Their rules were simple: defend and share. They stole when they could, avoided the guards daily, fought when necessary, and occasionally brawled with other gangs under the city, but not often. Life was tenuous, yet the poor showed one another mercy. No one else did, not the noble archwizards, and not the gods.

Sunbright nodded, deep in thought. For all their cooperation and organization, these folks were incredibly vulnerable. Even knowing little about the city, he could think of a dozen ways the nobles and their guards could crush these thieves. They could pump heavy gas such as infested coal mines down the tunnels and suffocate them. Or pour in oil and set it afire. Or loose trained dogs, or assassins guided by wizard eyes. Even a spell to divert a lake and flood the caves would do the job. Right now, the thieves only lived at the sufferance of the nobles, who were too preoccupied to wipe them out. He wondered if Knucklebones had considered these macabre threats, and planned for them. Or if she simply crossed her fingers and prayed.

Sunbright learned more. Which archwizard families ruled the city. How they all deferred to crazy Karsus, and curried his favor for magical trinkets and new spells. Where the guards bunked and how they patrolled. How the thieves managed to avoid capture and death. How they could trip traps and time the guards' rounds. How to penetrate a building sealed against the weather. Even how the fish was frozen. Out in the ocean were weirs, floating fish traps that funnelled fish inside. When an edible fish entered, it was instantly shifted hundreds of miles to a huge room spelled with a Veridon's chiller, then separated out and sold.

As they talked, Mother tended Sunbright's hurts, sealing the deep cuts, smoothing the lesser. The barbarian gnawed strips of raw fish to fuel the healing.

Sunbright marvelled at the clever uses of magic, but Mother warned, "Yes, but, see, magic is the empire's downfall. They use it for everything, and no one thing can solve all problems. But I'm tired and would rest." She creaked upright, dragged her hood around her head, and patted Knucklebones's blanket into place.

"One more question, please," Sunbright begged. "Whence comes the fresh air?"

"Oh, that. Rolon!" The skinny boy pricked up his ears. "Show our guest where the air comes from. He should find that interesting."

The lad waved a hand toward the end of the tunnel, and Sunbright picked his way over the uneven floor to follow. The boy skipped like a goat from rock to rock, sometimes in pitch blackness. Sunbright plodded after him, slipping and banging his knees often, and his head occasionally.

"What spells do you know?" Sunbright asked the boy.

"Eh? Oh, not many. Healing, mostly. And I'm learning to talk to animals."

"That's not much. I know catfeet, and color, smokepuff, mouse, tangle. Lots of spells. Knucklebones knows 'em all, though."

"I'm glad. You must need them." He swore as he skidded on a slippery rock and barked his shin.

"Are you a good fighter?" the boy asked.

Sunbright smiled at that, said, "I haven't been killed yet."

"Good. We need a good fighter. There's things down here like to kill us."

"Oh? What things?"

Sunbright found that curious. Mother hadn't hinted of any dangers.

"Uh . . ." the boy hesitated at a taboo topic. "Never mind. You come from down on the ground?"

"Yes."

Sunbright didn't press about the danger, but marked a mental slate to ask more later.

By now, there were no more pipes or tubes or man-made structures, only broken rocks. Oddly, the tunnel grew larger the farther they went.

"How long you been in the city?"

"Just a few days."

"So you don't know anything about how to live here?"

"No. That's why I need a guide. Someone like you."

"Don't worry, then. I can show you everything there is in Karsus."

"Wonderful."

Suddenly the barbarian realized he could see Rolon's silhouette, then his features. The breeze was fresher in his face. Ahead was daylight.

"Here we go," said the boy.

Turning a corner, they saw white light reflected off gray rock. It came from a huge hole in the floor of the tunnel. That confused Sunbright, for he'd been expecting a hole above.

"Better crawl," warned Rolon. "This is scary."

The boy dropped to his knees, then his belly, and wriggled to the lip of the hole. Wondering, Sunbright crept alongside, his guts in a knot. He'd finally figured it out.

Sneaking his nose past the rocky lip, he looked *down* into open air, to the ground a mile below. From this dizzying height, he could see green and gold rolling hills and distant slate-blue mountains. Edging the hills were crooked stone fences marking fields, and a trout pond. Then, between him and the ground, he saw a gray hawk's back. The high-flying bird was between them and the earth. High winds whirling into the cave gusted in his face and made his eyes water.

Sunbright groaned involuntarily. He'd known in a vague way he was on an inverted floating mountain, but to actually see it was the stuff of nightmares.

Suddenly he had a driving need to get back to the ground. The urge was so strong, for a second he pictured himself leaping up, diving through the hole, falling, falling, falling . . .

Stomach twisting, Sunbright rolled over to eclipse the sight. He clung to rock with both hands. Something on the ceiling caught his attention.

"Oh!"

"What?" the boy asked, looking up.

Sunbright pointed to long, shallow scratches in the smooth stone above. "This was a bear cave when the mountain was upright. Those are claw marks."

The boy peered, then looked back over the edge. "You live down there?"

Sunbright rolled, looked again. The idea of a bear cave, a familiar, homey image, helped anchor him, cheered him. "I did," he said. "Though not here exactly, and not in this time. But yes."

"You get eaten by bears down there, I heard."

"No," Sunbright chuckled. "At least, not many do. It's a fine place. I'll take you there someday."

"You will?" The boy's voice was a pipe of excitement.

Sunbright was surprised himself, but he meant it. "Yes," he said. "Living in the air, under a poisoned city, is no life for a boy, or anyone. It's too far from the natural order of things, the way the gods laid out our lives. I have no idea what, Rolon, but we must do something.

Your lives here are too fragile. A good start would be to get down there.

"But to do that," he muttered, "I'd need Candlemas. . . ."

* * * * *

When the two returned, Knucklebones was waiting. With a nod of her head, she steered Sunbright back down the tunnel and Rolon away.

Out of Rolon's earshot, she told the barbarian, "We need to talk."

"Very well."

Sunbright waited patiently, and for some reason, this irritated her. Her single dark eye flashed as she demanded, "Can you fight that well all the time?"

In answer, he extended both arms, showed her scars beyond counting. "I've gained these and lived to tell it."

"Can you steal? Thieve? Find things without getting caught?"

Honest, he shook his head and told her, "I know naught about thieving. In my homeland, we gather the supplies we need. Sometimes it's easy, sometimes a struggle, but no, we've no need to steal anything. But I can learn."

She puffed. "What *are* you trained in, besides brawling?"

Sunbright scratched a scar idly. Knucklebones had illuminated stripes along her wrists for light, but their ghostly glow did little to light their faces. "To tell the truth, I was training to be a shaman."

"A what?"

"Oh," Sunbright fumbled for words. "Um. A healer among my people, but more than that. A warrior, but more a prophet, a seer, a reader of portents. Dreams are very important, for they teach us—"

She cut him off with a wave of her hand and said, "Why was your training interrupted? Did you rebel against your teacher?"

"What? Oh, no," he said. Now he fiddled with his hands, jamming his thumbs in his belt. "You learn on your own by embarking on a spirit quest. But I lost the ability to learn along the way."

"How?"

"I was sucked dry by a—" He stopped and looked around uneasily. This tunnel could match the Underdark, and be just as haunted. "—by a thing that sucks spirits. I lived, but there's, uh, a hole in my soul. It's a wound that won't close."

Like the ache in his heart for the lost Greenwillow.

"Just what we need," snipped the woman. "A big booby with holes in his guts and probably his head. Well, we'll let you stay until Ox feels better. After that, just remember I give the orders, and you better hop to."

"Agreed," said Sunbright solemnly. "May I ask you a question?"

Immediately suspicious, she snapped, "What?"

"How long have you lived in these tunnels?"

"Since before I can remember. I'm a foundling. Do you know what that is?"

The shaman-to-be ignored the sarcasm. "Where did you get that knife? It looks elven."

"It is, I'm told. It came with me, inherited since forever."

And without another word, she stalked off down the tunnel to the homestead.

Sunbright was left talking to himself in the dark. "Another thing I forgot to add. Shamans are teachers. But you need to have the student listen in order to explain something. . . ."

Chapter 9

Karsus was away. No one knew where. With all the inbred intrigue of the empire, Candlemas first suspected that everyone knew but wouldn't tell, but even pestering folks couldn't make them spill secrets, and he concluded that really, no one knew where Karsus had gone. This was both mysterious and frightening, considering how heavily the empire depended on the man.

Assigned no particular tasks—no one could even guess what Karsus wanted Candlemas to do—the friendless mage wandered the halls, laboratories, workshops, animal collections, and libraries. Everywhere were fascinating magical works, most of which he couldn't understand, but idleness made him itchy. At least, slaving for Lady Polaris, he'd had too much work to be bored. Uselessness was a new sensation.

Finally, he sought out Lady Aquesita. He told himself he was merely being useful, seeking out Karsus's only living relative for practical advice. But in fact, he had a nagging doubt something else pushed him. Another weird sensation he couldn't finger.

By now he'd oriented himself somewhat. Karsus controlled the top of a low hill called Mystryl's Mound by some. There had originally been two mansions atop it and a half dozen smaller ones encircling it. As his importance grew, Karsus had bought or been given all of them, and the city had erected an encircling wall and called the entire complex Castle Karsus. The eccentric magician had then, as if to put his own stamp on it, had the buildings linked and modified and added to, with some torn down or turned at a crazy angle, until the whole sprawl was brain wrenching to look at. The most disturbing aspects for Candlemas were the doors that opened from third floors into midair, or the winding staircases that just stopped.

But Lady Aquesita had been given a smaller mansion—Candlemas suspected she'd coveted the gardens—stripped all rococo from her sight, painted it a lovely rose, and concentrated on improving the grounds. So his sandals crunched on plain white gravel as he wended his way to her "simple cottage" of only sixty-odd rooms and its acres of gardens both symmetrical and wild.

A manservant conducted Candlemas to a stretch of garden behind a tall screen of blue-green spruces. There Lady Aquesita directed a dozen gardeners in the planting of a wagonful of cuttings and small bushes. She wore a gown of spring green that featured gold lace tucked and folded to hide her ample curves. She was issuing clear and polite orders for the plants' placement when Candlemas rounded the corner. Oddly, she stopped in mid sentence to brush back her hair and smile brightly.

"Good day, milady." Candlemas found his stomach fluttering as he spoke, as if he'd eaten rye bread and beer for breakfast. "I, uh, just came to see you. Or, how you were doing. Or, rather, uh, whether you knew where your c-cousin was. Karsus, I m-mean." Damn it, why was he stuttering?

Aquesita licked her lips and fussed with her hair some more. "Good day, Master Candlemas," she said brightly. "I trust you're well."

She glanced at the servants and gardeners, told them to carry on, then took his arm to lead him along another path. Candlemas supposed she had some secret to convey. He found the touch of her cool hand tingly, as if she were enchanted. Or enchanting him.

"I'm so glad you've come, Candlemas. I wanted to show you some of my work. I like to show off my gardens, and I get so few visitors."

The mage nodded vaguely. He'd come to ask about Karsus, though. Or had he already? He couldn't recall. What was *wrong* with him?

She seemed to read his mind, saying, "Oh, Karry is away. That's Karsus, my little cousin. No one knows where, least of all unimportant me. But he'll return shortly and throw the whole castle into a tizzy. But I suspect you want something to do in the meantime. You seem the responsible, productive sort I so admire. I suggest you find an unused bench and work at whatever you like. Any of the apprentices will fetch whatever you need. Karry has nine hundred of them, I think he said once. I'm sure someone as clever as you can think of lots to do."

Candlemas found himself grinning like an idiot. He hadn't felt clever lately, actually the opposite, since he knew less magic than most of the apprentices. But her words made him feel clever, against all logic.

"That's kind of you, Lady Aquesita. I was wondering—"

"Please, call me Sita," she interrupted. Her smile seemed brighter than the sun. Her cheeks rounded nicely, he thought, and were dimpled at the corners enticingly. Funny he'd never noticed that on a woman before.

As they strolled along a blue slate path, Candlemas suddenly wasn't concerned about Karsus at all, only walking and talking with Sita. Perhaps the outside air had infected his brain, sucking out the nourishment. His feet felt lighter too, and the grass and flowers smelled heavenly.

"Oh, I can keep busy," he assured her. "But what did you want to show me? I'd love to see anything you find interesting. What were you directing so competently back there?"

Strangely, she blushed, and tightened her grip on his arm, tugging his elbow to brush her round bosom. When Candlemas jerked away, she deftly drew him back and said, "Speaking of work, that's more of mine. As I mentioned before, my lifelong project has become the gathering of the cream of the empire. Inside, I've tried to collect the most beautiful artifacts our people can fabricate. Out here, I collect their natural works."

She stopped at a long raised bed of small flowers, all the colors of the rainbow jumbled in soft petals.

"These, for instance," she continued, "are every variety of pansy I've been able to locate. I correspond with a great many people, you see, and humbly ask that they send me cuttings. They do, of course, from all over the empire. When I started this bed, there were only the white and the purple. But see how many others the Netherese have bred? I try to cultivate every useful and beautiful plant for the betterment of our empire. Really, in my own small way, I emulate my famous cousin."

"Admirable. Wonderful." Candlemas fingered the pansy petals as he spoke. They had a fine fuzz that softened their brightness. "And this is no small effort. Anyone would admire your taste and good sense. You must be the talk of the empire."

"Oh, no." Aquesita rubbed her nose to hide a flush. "No, I spend more time alone that anything else. There are sometimes whole series of balls held and I'm not even invited, just forgotten . . ." Her voice trailed off, sounding infinitely sad to Candlemas. He wanted to do something to assuage her loneliness, but for the life of him, he couldn't think what to do.

Aquesita sniffed and wiped her eyes while Candlemas looked elsewhere. Here, raised beds surrounded a croquet green with a babbling fountain in the center. Bushes with huge white flowers screened more gardens. The mage started when a pair of white-spotted deer no more than knee-high padded from under the bush to crop foliage.

The lady went on, "It's good to have a cause and busywork. Between corresponding, managing the rest of Karry's estates, and encouraging artists at the guild, I'm never very lonely. And of course, I see Karry when I can. He can be difficult—not ornery, you understand, just preoccupied—but I try to steer him toward creative, helpful magic projects, not frivolous and destructive ones. But he loves to pursue everything, and . . . well, you must know how it is."

Candlemas nodded, not smiling now. He thought of the ragged prisoner suffocated in the testing of an imprisonment spell, the random conjuring of strange beasts from who-knew-where, and how one had killed three apprentices with its unearthly screech.

But Aquesita was talking. ". . . Karry will be hailed as the empire's savior in time. With his abilities and the guidance of wise rulers, the Netherese Empire will stretch beyond the horizons, expanding ever outward to the far seas. We'll bring peace and justice, and—but silly me, I'm rambling. Perhaps, when things settle down, there'll be a need for all these plants, and new beds faraway where they can prosper."

"Well, please then," he said, "show me more." Her bright smile rewarded him. Candlemas covered her cool hand with his own as they walked the gardens, she pointing out this and that plant, he murmuring appreciatively. But he felt a shiver as from a cloud. From hints and glimpses he'd seen of the empire, it was neither prospering nor bettering the world. Food riots, obsessions with gambling and assassination, the casual destruction of the poor, insensitivity to growing problems . . . if the empire were to grow to new heights, its "wise rulers" had better see to shoring up the foundation first.

And may the gods have pity if mad Karsus really did rule the empire.

* * * * *

"Push this up. But quietly."

Shifting Harvester's scabbard and bracing his feet, the barbarian put his back against the stone grate and heaved upward. Instantly one of the twins, Zykta by the scar on her cheek, stuck her head past him like a topknotted gopher. "Clear!"

"Slide it over," said Knucklebones in her low, dulcet voice.

Sunbright obliged, grunting, and stood up in the hole. Zykta had already climbed through. She hunkered on her skinny hams in the dark cellar, peering at oblong shells on the floor. Sunbright sniffed and asked her, "What are those? Dead cockroaches?"

Knucklebones elbowed him aside, deftly slapped her hands on the rim and vaulted through the hole like a wildcat. The barbarian felt the caress of her warm leathers. Her lean muscled neatness reminded him of Greenwillow. She squatted in bare feet and inspected the round carapaces. "We catch them and kill them," she explained, "then spread their shells on the floor near our exits. If they're crushed, we know someone's been sniffing around."

"Hmm. Smart."

Sunbright levered himself through the hole. Although lean for a big man, he had trouble wriggling through. That was why the giant Ox hadn't come this time. Normally, Knucklebones had explained, he lifted the heavy grates that were the gang's best protection against assault.

Sunbright shuffled aside while the rest of the gang hopped up. Aba, the other twin; Mother; Rolon toting Lothar's thin, weighted chain; a sunken-chested man named Hute who coughed whenever he talked. And Sunbright, clubfooted and clumsy compared to these silent thieves. When he accidentally trod on a cockroach, making the tiniest crunch, they all froze, then turned to stare. Their eyes were ghostly in the phosphorescent light cast by Knucklebones's hands.

"Make noise in the wrong place and our heads will be spiked around the archwizard's park!" Knucklebones whispered harshly.

"Sorry."

The party crept up broken stairs to a floor littered with trash. The old building reeked of cold fires and urine. Sunbright peeked past Knucklebone's slim shoulder and asked her, "What was this place?"

"Bookbinders," the thief answered, "A woman named Roni and her family. Friends. Guards confiscated her goods and tools for taxes. She couldn't work, so she took her children to the edge and jumped."

"Edge of what?"

"The edge of the city," she snapped. "What did you think, the archwizard's wading pool?"

Sunbright shook his head absently. In two days amidst these thieves, Knucklebones hadn't once mentioned his having killed her lover, Martel, nor their fight, nor offered thanks for his rescuing them from the city guards.

Lacking anywhere else to go, Sunbright stayed in the homestead. Talking to Mother, he learned more all the time. He was tolerated, but doubted he was considered a member of the gang. He didn't know what he was, except a barbarian out of time, too far from the tundra, stranded under a city suspended too damn high in the air. The thought of someone jumping into that mile high void turned his bowels to water.

Squinting in the dim light, Mother waggled her fingers as she crept to the door and broken crockery and splinters were brushed aside as if by an invisible broom. Another thief's cantra, Sunbright realized. They had over a dozen between them. What did he know? Minor healing.

Knucklebones crouched by the door, lithe as a seal. She put her slanted eyes to a crack through the door, eased it open and shooed out a twin. Others waited, then there came the squeak of a rat trapped under a cat's paw. Sunbright found that amusing: a city wildlife call. Silently, one by one, with Knucklebones watching everywhere at once, the party slipped outside. Sunbright was last, and scuffed as he stepped. Knucklebone's hissed order to, "Pick up your feet!" cut the night.

Outside, the street was black. Sunbright had been told the mission, a raid on a butcher in a district where nobles' servants shopped. This shop preserved meats like ham, bacon, and sausages. Good for the larder, Knucklebones explained, good to trade with other scavengers. Sunbright thought it simple enough, but Knucklebones seemed tense as a bowstring—though the barbarian had barely said a dozen words to her, so he couldn't claim to know her. Neither could Mother, she said, who'd known her for four years.

Sunbright picked up his feet and crossed the black

street after the part-elf. The twins occupied opposite doorways with thin pipes in hand. Mother had somehow climbed atop a stone lintel, and hunkered on arthritic knees like a weather-beaten gargoyle. The barbarian couldn't see Rolon, but heard the clink of his new weighted chain. The sound drew a sharp hiss from their leader. The man Hute was out of sight. Sunbright felt a small hand on his belt buckle, was guided into a niche between buildings. Strong fingers signaled he was to draw Harvester and hold it ready, then Knucklebones was gone.

Sunbright tuned his ears until he heard ringing and probed with his eyes until he felt blind. He was used to night hunting in a forest, where he could feel hooves fall against soil and boot soles, smell oncoming game by fur and musk, and sense the wind on his cheek lessen as game closed. But this *city* was alien, bound by stone flags and hard walls that cut and trapped the wind. He could only guess what his teammates were doing.

He heard a fizz and saw a white light outline Knucklebones's tousled head for a second. Some magic lock defused? Then he heard the clattering of a key.

A savage growl, deep and low-throated, from a wolf or big dog, echoed around them. The growl stopped as the dog's mouth clamped down, then changed to a frenzied snarling as the beast worried flesh and bone. Knucklebones gasped.

Keeping quiet as he could, Sunbright streaked across the narrow street. By sound he located the thief, on her back, straddled by a mastiff.

There was more movement. Mother was suddenly across from him; one of the twins scooted past, bent low. They didn't seem to be doing anything so, still silently, Sunbright hoisted Harvester, aimed as best he could, sent up a prayer, and struck.

The heavy, keen blade cleft the dog's spine with a

meaty smack. The animal flopped limp atop Knuckle-bones, who grunted at the weight. But before Sunbright could jerk the brindled hound loose, slicking his hand and forearm with blood, the thief had wriggled loose. She whapped at his elbow and whispered urgently, "Go back! There were two of them!"

"Two of what?" he whispered.

But she was pattering for the disused bookbinders', rallying her troops with chitters and low whistles.

A voice behind Sunbright stage-whispered, "Stand or die!"

The barbarian whirled. He hadn't even heard the enemy approach. It was a pair of city guards, starlight and the glow of distant gasglobes flaring on polished helmets. Ahead galloped a tongue-lolling mastiff, twin to the dead one at Sunbright's feet.

Oh, he thought. Two dogs, one to attack and one to fetch help. But why need the city officials be silent too?

Then he had his hands full, and his feet.

The dog bounded, mouth open, and snapped for Sun-bright's knees even as the guards split to bracket him. No clubs now, but short swords. Instinctively the bar-barian dropped to a fighting stance, feet braced and pointed out to allow him to swivel to both flanks. His boot thumped the dog's big foot and almost tumbled him. The guards, partners in practice, swung at the same time.

To shrink from one blow was to drive into the other, so Sunbright gritted his teeth and took it. Flicking Har-vester at the right-hand guard, he deflected the blow with a tiny *ting* of blades. He'd ducked his shoulder and curled to avoid the other swipe, but felt the cold, bloodcurdling kiss of steel as it sliced open the muscle of his upper arm.

Sucking wind, he swung his left heel up hard to kick the dog in the stomach or crotch, to get it from under-foot. The mastiff yipped at the thud and skipped its bony back up, jarring Sunbright's own rump. But as it hopped clear, he decided to use the beast in defense. Hooking his foot, he caught the dog above the hock to stop it and stepped back alongside its head. The maneuver put the dog between Sunbright and the left-hand guard for just a second. In that second, the barbarian lashed at the guard on his right.

Eager to strike, the man came too close and over-reached to thrust straight with his short sword. The whole weapon wasn't as long as Harvester's blade. Sunbright aimed below the guard's blade and arm, and drove the wicked hooked point into the man's armpit. The guard gasped, whimpered, but Sunbright used the sword's great weight to free it, adding his own muscle to wrench down. The barbed hook tore tendons and arteries. Hot blood gushed along the blade as the man's heart emptied.

At the same time, the other guard struck. Sunbright felt the blade split his goatskin vest, pierce his shirt, and slice his skin above the shoulder blade. It was a glancing blow, but one that burned like cold fire. Sunbright even used that advantage, whipping around so the short blade fetched for a second in his leather. Seeing his mistake, the guard let go of his weapon. Too late. Harvester slammed into his belly, bowling the man back and spilling his guts. Another blow sheared half through the falling man's neck. Sunbright wrenched his blade free, and the guard fell like a tree. His polished helmet slammed the flagstones with a crunch.

Panting, throat wheezing, wounds aching, blood singing, and ears ringing with a battle high, Sunbright tracked back and forth with his sword, wary, seeking another enemy. But there were none, as part of him had known. The guard dog was gone. So was Knucklebones. In fact . . .

He stepped away from pools of blood and cooling bodies,

put his back against a shop front. Where was everybody? The whole battle had been waged in an eerie silence that he still didn't understand. He was used to hollering war cries and epithets, and just plain noise. Now the whole block seemed deserted. It was as if Sunbright and the guards were ghosts who waged war in a dead city.

Scanning, listening, peering, he found no one. Thoughts of ghosts and barbarian superstition caught up with him. It had been in just such a dead block that he'd once crashed into the Underdark, a misty non-world where a wraith had almost sucked the life and soul out of him. He still wasn't recovered from its effects, and sometimes wondered if that wraith still hunted and haunted him across leagues and years—

"Sunbright!"

The barbarian jumped so high his sword point tinked on the stone lintel over his head. The voice had come from alongside his elbow, sudden as a panther attack.

It was Rolon, the skinny boy. "That way."

"Right! Yes." Leaving ghosts and dead men behind, Sunbright shuffled in the direction that the boy had pointed. Behind him he heard stealthy chinking as the boy looted the guards' bodies. Sunbright was content to get his breath back.

Another tiny shadow hustled people into the ruined bindery. Sunbright was last in, but Knucklebones paused to fix the door and erase all sign of their passing. Their last act was for Sunbright to hold Mother up through the hole. With her finger-sweeping cantra, she scattered the trash and dust evenly across the floor again, and replaced the dead cockroaches.

It was only after they'd passed deep into more twisting tunnels, some so low the barbarian had to go through them doubled over, that he realized they hadn't accomplished their goal of stealing meat. They'd gotten nothing except a handful of coins and wounds.

And more. For when they reached a pocket with stone walls where Sunbright could stand erect, he caught hell.

The party was lit by the strange blue-white stripes that Knucklebones employed. Now, in this small space, some disused cellar or stone foundation, the small thief whirled on him.

"How could you be so *stupid?*" Her face was hard, her one eye glaring, her lips pulled back from her teeth. She rapped with her brass knuckles on his chest, yet still kept her voice pitched at a whisper. "How could you endanger us so? You've doomed every person in this party!"

"What?" Sunbright had cleaned and sheathed Harvester, and stood with his left hand across the slice on his shoulder. "I saved your life!"

"Temporarily! We never kill city guards. It's insanity! You'll bring sniffers down on our heads! They'll hunt us down like terriers after rats."

"Sniffers?"

More damned city magic, he supposed. His ignorance angered him, but her attitude angered him even more.

"That dog was poised to tear your throat out, or bite through your face! And those guards wouldn't have spared you! They'd have hacked you to crow fodder—"

"Bah!" She scoffed, waving a gold glittering hand. "The dog was no threat. I could have slipped out from under it, and the guards . . . why couldn't you just knock them down? You'll have the whole cadre after us now! They always avenge—"

"No one told me!" Sunbright bellowed. This was the first real noise he'd made in hours. Instinctively the other thieves shushed him. "No one told me not to kill guards. I thought you hated them. And why was everyone so *quiet?* Even the dogs didn't bark!"

"Fool! Don't you know anything? That district is

famous for quiet. The nobles like it that way. Even the guards are trained to never make noise, and the dogs have their voice cords slit. How have you survived this long? Killing those guards will prove fatal. But that's all you can do, flail away with that sword! It's how you killed Martel, wasn't it?"

"What?" he whispered, the change in topic confusing him. It was the first time she'd mentioned her former lover. Was this city madness, thief strangeness, or woman contrariness? "That was an accident! He was out to kill me . . . I think. I'm not sure what happened!"

"*Damn you!* You've ruined everything!" Hauling her elbows close by her ribs, the thief leader slammed him in the chest and breadbasket with tiny fists weighted with brass. Sunbright grunted, huffed, sucked wind, but took it. The blows hurt, as if someone were pounding him with a rock. On the other hand, his stomach and chest were hard as an oak tree, and she wasn't really pounding him, he knew, she was just beating out her frustration. So he waited patiently, suffered, and wondered about women. He hadn't understood Greenwillow's whims most of the time. Was that because men were thick or because women were enigmatic? Or something else? For a shaman, he thought, he didn't know much about people, especially female ones.

Shooed by Mother, the other thieves melted away. Sunbright was bashed more than forty times before Knucklebones wound down. She was crying, her soiled and dusty cheeks wet with tears of rage and frustration, and whatever other turmoil she suffered. Sunbright reckoned her tenuous life had finally caught up with her. The stress and strain of watching and worrying over her brood, the constant threat of sudden and gory death, the need for a brave, tough face for her followers and other gangs must have been difficult to bear. Though the barbarian had his own problems—

loneliness being utmost—but he didn't envy her. At least, he had no one else to fret about.

Finally she stopped pounding him, let her knotty arms hang limp by her side. Her small bosom heaved for breath and control. The magical light of her leather vest made shadows rise and fall on the stone walls around them. Tears dripped from her cheeks, and she snuffled and wiped her nose on her wrist. A sob escaped.

Finally, Sunbright knew what to do.

Reaching slowly, so as not to startle her, he gathered Knucklebones in his arms, pulled her against his sore chest. The top of her head barely came to his breastbone, and he bent his head to kiss it, as one might a child. Her hair was dusty and cobwebby from threading these dim tunnels, but still she smelled sweet, like a whiff of wildflowers, though she'd probably never seen a wildflower in her life. Greenwillow had smelled the same, Sunbright thought with a pang. Maybe all women did.

"Don't cry, seal pup," he comforted the sobbing thief with his mother's words. Knucklebones felt like a leather sack of bones in his brawny arms, her back hard, her ribs prominent. When he stroked her shoulder, he felt old, raddled scars like an alley cat's. But her skin between the scars was soft. "Don't fret, wildflower. I'll protect you."

For the briefest moment, she clung to him like someone buffeted by a hurricane. Her sobs quieted.

Then abruptly she crooked her elbows, slammed him twice in the gut, hard enough to rock him.

"Don't touch me! And don't protect me! I don't need anyone!"

Snarling, she turned on her heel and stalked off. Sunbright wiped his forehead and sighed. Then hurried after her. If he lost sight of this crazy woman, he might never find his way out. Out of this mad city of mad people.

Chapter 10

Sunbright dreamt.

Everywhere was a blue-white glare like the heart of a star, as if he'd been sucked into the white void where the evil arcanist Sysquemalyn had once hurled him. The glare made his eyes smart like ice glint, but the flare was everywhere. When he closed his eyes, whiteness throbbed through his eyelids.

Then, there was one dark spot. Silhouetted against the glare walked a figure, pacing like a panther stalking across a glacier. The figure was female, rounded top and bottom, nipped at the waist. At first the shape looked tall, and he thought it was Greenwillow finally returning. But as it closed, the figure shortened to no taller than Knucklebones. Then the ghostly being was close enough to touch, and she was of middling size, like neither woman. So who was she?

Her skin was white, shaded blue by the star-glow, but her hair was dark, as was Greenwillow's and Knucklebones's. Did this woman too boast elven blood? She wore a white robe with long blue points stitched on it, as if wrapped in the light of an arctic star. And her eyes . . .

They burned with a cold fire like northern lights, all blue-white, so bright Sunbright saw every eyelash in stark relief. Who was this star-eyed woman? And why did she seek him?

She didn't speak, but gestured with a white hand outlined with a blue-white glow, as if a cold halo enfolded her, as he had enfolded Knucklebones in his arms. The hand pointed, and Sunbright's eyes followed, no longer smarting from the eldritch glare.

High in the sky floated a city. The island enclave that was Karsus. He knew it by the jumbled dice aspect of the mage's mansions on the highest hill. In this toy city, a star-shaped building glowed too, but Sunbright didn't know it.

The sky picture reeled, and he stared down from above while his stomach lurched. People like ants ran through the streets in mindless frenzy while a huge round fountain boiled red. Another flicker, and he saw a portion of Karsus's hill explode. Dirt cascaded in an avalanche, and rocks big as houses careened down to crush human and building alike. And from the gap, like maggots from rotten meat, tumbled skulls in the hundreds like a child's marbles. Another flicker, and he was blinded by long, narrow, flapping wings. White storks, he realized, fluttering from their nests and niches high above the city, driven out by some magical blast, so the homeless birds squawked and keened and wheeled like seagulls while the people pointed and stared.

Then the people were gone, the streets empty, deserted as they'd been on the butcher shop raid. And again, Sunbright felt a pang of loneliness, an ache that sank to his bones and marrow, as if he struggled, trapped under an icecap, hunting a hole in the ice, until seawater filled his lungs, chilled him through, and sank him into the depths.

Brain awhirl, Sunbright tossed and fought, groaned in his sleep. Who was she? What did she want?

The star woman showed him more, and he understood less and less as the pictures flashed by. He squinted at her white face, under her halo of dark hair, past her brilliant eyes. First her face was elongated and pointed, like Greenwillow's. Then softer, rounded, but crisscrossed with scars like Knucklebones. Then she resembled both, then neither.

Reaching, Sunbright touched her cheek. And the skin split away, seared by a blue-white flare that made him flinch. But not before he saw the skin dissolve to leave only the stark white bone of a staring skull.

"Wake up! Wake up, you great oaf. You're dreaming."

Sunbright sat up so fast he smacked his forehead on an outthrust rock. Gasping with pain, cursing, he flapped his elbows to ward off the probing hands. "I'm awake! Leave me be."

"Vale of Faerûn, but you make a lot of noise! How's an old woman to get her beauty rest?"

Holding his aching head in his hands, Sunbright peered about. The rookery homestead was quiet. The fire was out and only a thin trickle of smoke stained the air. A single stripe of light illuminated the craggy room. Sunbright was huddled in a niche, bundled in a rat's nest of fabric, rugs, and rags. He was wringing with sweat, still dizzy and confused by the mysterious woman and the apocalyptic dream. What did it mean? Death and destruction? For whom? Why were three women melded in his mind? Were these prophecies or simple mind mush?

A shaman, he knew, lived and died by dreams. Visions of the future and the past, the nearby, far off, and unknown. Or sometimes simply nothing. But as a shaman-to-be, Sunbright couldn't interpret them, especially when they occurred in a future city he knew nothing about. But then, that was the curse of dreams, wasn't it? A mind could see them, but never understand until too late.

Shuddering, he climbed from his nest and stumbled to the fire, prodded the coals, blew, and fed splinters of wood scavenged from above. Mother sat beside him, huddled in a blanket over her thick dark robe with its many folds.

The two stared at the fire awhile, then she said, "Knucklebones has had a hard life. We all have, but hers was worse than most. Children of mixed blood are shunned in the empire. Elves hated. No one knows how she came here. Born of woman, to be sure, but abandoned right off, must have been. She just grew out of the dust somehow, refusing to die, like a weed between flagstones, pushing and battering a place clear to gain sun."

Sunbright nodded but said nothing. Knucklebones at least had a home. He knew where he was from, but couldn't go back. Not yet. Not until he was a full shaman, and there was little chance of becoming such in a cursed city of flying stone, or of finding Greenwillow, if she lived. Three of them then, lost souls, each alone, yet somehow linked. The dreamy, star-eyed woman would know, but she hadn't talked. And the dream city had crumbled. Knucklebones was the exact opposite of Greenwillow, short and scruffy, not tall and glamorous, but they interchanged in his dreams.

Sighing, the lonely man stared at the flames and tried to quiet his mind.

* * * * *

It was days later that Karsus sailed into his maze of workshops, shouting orders, asking questions, and demanding news, never explaining where he'd been. Nor did anyone ask.

Candlemas heard Karsus was back and sought him out. He'd followed Lady Aquesita's advice, simply taken over an unused workshop, cleared a space on a bench, and settled to work. It wasn't long before he found himself in the same situation he'd had in Castle Delia, only worse.

For one thing, endless numbers of artifacts littered Karsus's workshops. Candlemas had had a strange collection of stuff, but his was a child's toy box compared to these items. There were so many, most completely unidentified, and more arrived each day from the far corners of the empire. Where to start?

And how? Candlemas knew magic, like everything else, advanced from simple forms to complex ones over time. But he'd been pulled out of time, and his knowledge was ancient. Here arcanists specialized in Inventives, Mentalisms, or Variations. Candlemas had been an Inventive, and still was, if basic knowledge counted. He understood the classes of spells, or arcs, how deep into the weave one must go to access them, whether they drew dweomer from the winds or the spheres or artifacts or each other.

Necromancy drew magic from dead souls. Planar magic tapped weird beings men could barely comprehend, and never control. The gods made their own magic and sometimes shared it. Mystryl maintained the weave, the balance and interconnection of all things. There was sea magic and mountain magic and forest magic, and so on. Magic everywhere, in fact, if one knew how to see it. But Candlemas knew about as much about modern magic as a woodcutter knew about finished carpentry. He'd walked into a play during the last act, struggling to know everything and learning nothing.

The worst was heavy magic, Karsus's own invention. No one could explain it with satisfaction, and Candlemas suspected that no one but Karsus understood it, and perhaps even he didn't really. (Scary thought.) To Candlemas magic was a force, a soul, an idea. To shape magic was a blessing and a gift from the gods, a sacred responsibility. Karsus had made magic a commodity. That the mad mage could manufacture globs of wiggly, clear magic seemed absurd, like a child catching a jar of wind, or a man donning a cloud as a robe. Yet it worked. Karsus could bottle magic and sell it in the marketplace like olive oil if he so chose.

Karsus had lived for three hundred and fifty-seven years, having been born only a year after Candlemas and his barbarian companion had been stretched through time. Since then, many types of magic had come in and out of fashion. Now all of Karsus's recent work hinged on heavy magic. In fact, he talked constantly of how heavy magic would destroy his "enemies." Who these enemies were and what they intended no one knew, and many suspected they dwelt in Karsus's brain alone.

And finally, Candlemas found himself distracted by thoughts of Aquesita. He woke up from dreaming about her, wondered what she ate for breakfast while he ate his, saw the color of her golden-brown eyes in illuminations of books and tapestries, thought of her when he saw flowers nodding in the sun outside a window, considered what she did in the evenings, and, as he dozed off at night, wondered if she thought of him. Surely this preoccupation with one woman was unhealthy.

Since reaching adulthood, Candlemas had been too busy for one woman, and had no desire to be ordered about by one. When a man wanted a woman's charm, he could hire a barmaid or a chambermaid for the evening. Night was the time for love sport anyway, yet here he was, in the middle of the morning, absently pawing a necklace of shark's teeth (or whatever they were), staring into space, unaware he'd even picked it up. Such muddleheadedness was troubling.

So he was glad that Karsus was back, and went searching for him. He found the archwizard in the high circular room where three score mages puzzled over the fallen star Candlemas and Sunbright (and where was *he?*) had unearthed.

Karsus stood six deep in lesser mages. His hair was more disheveled than ever, sticking out all over; his golden eyes were glittering, but sunk in black pits, as if he hadn't slept in days. His gestures were more erratic, and he'd almost pulled all the hair out of the left side of his head with nervous tugging. But he seemed pleased as the chief mage demonstrated their progress.

"Great Karsus," the woman rattled, "as you wished, we plied a cold chisel to free some star-metal, used simple heat to puddle it and forge a crucible. Into that crucible we poured heavy magic, and let it steep for two days, while chanting round the clock over it."

Mages gave way to a scarred table. The chief dragged over a silver scale, all ornate fig leaves and vines, made sure it balanced properly, then set down her crucible of lumpy gray star-metal. As Karsus watched, she took up a redware beaker and plied a wooden scoop, brushing the top level with a finger as if the stuff were flour. Yet the magical mass held together like calf's foot jelly, clear, jiggly, utterly weird, like a block of hard water. It even refracted light like water, so objects on the other side were distorted and shrunken. Heavy magic, Candlemas knew. The woman placed a dollop on the left scale. Then, with the appropriate air of drama, scooped an equal dollop of magic from the star-metal crucible onto the right scale.

Instantly the right-hand scale plunged and crashed to the tabletop.

"Heavier magic!" crowed Karsus. He danced in place with clasped hands. "Super heavy magic! More magical magic! Wonderful!"

Like a boy playing in water, he repeated the experiment time and again, shoving the dollops of heavy magic onto the floor where they landed with squishy plops. "Oh, won't my enemies be discommoded by this. They'll be expunged, vanquished, crushed, hammered, smashed, broken. This will drive them clean through the earth's crust to . . . well, to whatever's beneath. Oh, I can't wait!"

People stirred uneasily at the mention of Karsus's imaginary enemies. Sensing unease, he lectured while playing. "They're down there! I know. Draining the life from the soil. Out to kill us all! Especially me, because I'm the savior of the empire. I'm the greatest arcanist ever born, and they know it. But it's easy to understand. They're jealous, you see. Well, when they're dead, they won't be jealous any longer. And I'll have their magic. At least, I hope so."

Karsus chortled and babbled and toyed. Mages ran helter-skelter around the room and congratulated the chief mage. Candlemas noted that the super heavy magic Karsus had dropped was mashed into the spaces between the flagstones. What would the magic do there, he wondered? Evaporate to make the air tingly with magic? Would mice that burrow through it become imbued with super heavy magic, so they might be undigestible to cats?

Suddenly he wondered how Aquesita might use the stuff. If a transplanted plant were to have its roots first dipped in heavy magic, say, could you render the roots magnetic so they would attract iron and other nutrients to make them grow? Wouldn't Aquesita be pleased if he thought up—

"Candlemas!"

Karsus had tossed away the wooden scoop.

"Candlemas," the archwizard trumpeted again, "I said, tell me more about this fallen star. What's it made of?"

The pudgy mage blinked. Daydreaming when the most important mage in the empire wanted him. Not good.

"Uh, made of? Oh, uh, metal. No, you said that. Uh, iron, I know, for it showed rust. And some very hard metal, probably nickel."

He was glad now he'd spent some time in this room, listening and taking mental notes. He walked toward the star.

"It would have to be hard metals, for soft ones would have burned up. As it was, it was sizzling hot when it landed, for it fused some sand—"

"I know that! I was there when it landed."

Candlemas whirled around so fast he almost fell. Karsus was imagining things again. "Uh, master," he mumbled, "you were here, and pulled us across the years—"

"No, I think not." Karsus spoke with one hand on his chin while his other hand tugged and twirled his hair. "No, I was there, in some other form perhaps, since this body wasn't born for a year or so—maybe a squirrel—and I knew to pull this star down from the sky."

"Oh, yes, I see . . ."

Candlemas found himself backing away, checking the exits.

"I'd agree, Great Karsus!" chimed an apprentice, toadying. "Only *you* would dare harness such power!"

"True. Only I."

Karsus walked around the star, inspecting it. Candlemas wondered what would come next.

"I know!" the archwizard cried. "Only a genius such as I could conceive of this. We'll make the entire star into one giant crucible. T'will save time and get on with discombobulating my enemies! A Stoca's feign or Smolyn's seer coupled with a Zahn's location to find the softest parts, and a Proctiv's dig such as the dwarves use to find water. In one fell swoop—"

"No!" bellowed Candlemas.

But Karsus raised both hands and gabbled fractions of spells, until suddenly a green-white bolt was crackling between his fingertips. With a laugh, he flung the bolt at the magic drenched star.

Candlemas dived under the heaviest table. Not that it would do much good. The whole top of the inverted mountain would probably explode, reducing him and Karsus and Aquesita alike to floating dust.

Several things happened at once.

At the last moment, the chief mage had hurled some sort of shield spell at the star. Karsus's green-white bolt spanked off the star in an eye smarting electric crackle. Karsus had his hair and eyebrows crisped as the bolt sizzled overhead.

But like lightning, the contrary and muddled bolt went to ground, between the flagstones, where lay pounds and pounds of discarded heavy magic. That magic combined with the bolt to turn it bigger, but more confused. Candlemas saw green fingers of energy like giant grass blades spike up from between the stones. One spike seared a hole big enough for a man's fist through a three-inch oak table. Another sheared a woman's arm off. A third shattered a chandelier overhead so the heavy iron latticework crashed down on another unfortunate apprentice. Yet another bolt squirreled up a table leg and danced from artifact to artifact along the table, so an iron gauntlet clenched shut, a glass globe gave a glimpse of the future, a magic sword rang like a bell, a ring's sapphire turned from blue to red, and there were many more whimsical magical oddities.

Not so funny was that several flagstones erupted from the floor to batter half a dozen people. Candlemas had the sole of his sandal slapped by a chunk of stone.

Yet nothing compared to the final effect, as one super energized bolt ricocheted and struck the star from behind.

The ring's stone turned to powder. The gauntlet went dead. The palantir burned out. The magic sword lost its luster. One mage clutched his chest, cried in agony, and collapsed. Another shrieked and covered her face. A third went howling mad and ran out the door. And Karsus's robes suddenly sported great ragged holes that showed dirty white flesh.

Yet the mage was exultant. He danced, shouted, waved his hands, sang, and laughed like a lunatic. Ignoring the groans of the wounded, the clattering of dropped things, the crackling and smoking of several small fires, he jumped in place and clapped his hands.

"We've got it! We've got it! Imagine the possibilities! My rivals will be powerless! Completely powerless! They'll be babes for the slaughter! We'll be *invincible!*"

"What?" Candlemas coughed as he crawled from under the table. He was surprised to find he couldn't stand. That slap on the foot had sprained his ankle, come close to shearing it off. He helped up the chief mage, who'd also dived under the table. "I don't understand. What does he mean? What happened?"

"The magic went dead." The woman rubbed her nose, found it was bleeding. She pitched her voice low. "It's happened before. Karsus, Great Karsus, once before, cast a Volhm's drain on a barrel of heavy magic. He sucked all the power from the mythallars and almost dropped the city out of the sky."

"Sunrest," muttered a man. "The city of Sunrest had a mage competing with Karsus. We guess he tried the same thing, because the whole city of Sunrest dropped and shattered."

"The whole mountain?"

The chief nodded, put her head back, held out a bloodstained hand, and waggled her fingers. "Look at my ring. It was a gift from my mother. Rub it and it sings like a nightingale. But it's dead. Permanently."

"All the artifacts in here are dead," the other mage concurred. "Oh, Kas and Zahn! My experiments! How far did it reach?" He ran from the room and had to leap over a dead man to get out the door.

Candlemas could only stare. Finally, he said, "That man who clutched his chest—"

"—had an erratic heart. A chirurgeon implanted a heavy magic massage spell that squeezed his heart gently, endlessly. It stopped. Nibaw there, I suspect, was using magic to keep her face looking young. And Karsus seems to have stitched his clothes with magic thread."

The chief yelled at someone to fetch water, either for her nose or the fires.

Candlemas watched the mad mage Karsus chortle with glee, tapping his head and listing dire fates for his imaginary foes while his skinny bum stuck out through a rent in his garment.

Candlemas was alone, but muttered aloud, "I've had enough for one day."

Limping, he made for the door.

* * * * *

Later, washed and splinted, fortified with a small brandy and leaning on a borrowed cane, Candlemas limped through the long journey to Lady Aquesita's abode. He told himself he went only to consult about this latest madness of Karsus's, since she was his cousin and, sometimes, keeper.

He hoped she didn't giggle in her knowing woman's way at his bald excuse. Actually, he liked her giggle too.

When he was shown into her study, he found her instructing an artist on how capture the afternoon light while simultaneously dictating a letter to a secretary. Yet when Candlemas was announced, she dropped both tasks and sprang up like a newborn fawn. Her smile faltered at his distressing limp. Nothing would do but he must sit immediately while a servant fetched a cool drink and a pillow for propping his foot. Candlemas objected to all the fuss, but secretly liked it. It was such a pleasure to see Aquesita he felt no pain.

He explained how his injuries involved Karsus's latest mad blunder. As his story drew to a close, Aquesita gnawed her plump lower lip. Her comment was odd. "More bad news . . ."

Candlemas was instantly alert, and jerked forward so suddenly his foot rang. He asked gently, "What troubles you, Sita?" (How naturally that name came to his lips in a crisis.)

"Portents, dear Candlemas," she said. Her pudgy hand stroked his pate. "I do so admire a man with a smooth scalp. Have I told you that? It's a sign of great intelligence, I think. And very sexy to boot. But alas, there are portents no one likes."

"Who? What?"

"I'm not altogether sure who's divined them."

She sat on a low stone railing, patted his shoulder, and left her hand there.

"It was either the sages of Mystryl or the Keeper of the Eternal Sun—you know, what's his name," she continued. "There have always been prophecies, of course, especially when donations are slack. The story about the fountains of blood that will precede the fall of the empire is one. Skulls will rain like hail is another. But this one . . . several sages have dreamt of a woman with starry eyes who blots out the sun just before the city falls."

"Which city?" asked Candlemas, already knowing the answer. "Not this one. Not with you in it!"

"No, silly, not us," she tried to sound soothing. "Some other city, I guess. Sunrest fell, you know, everyone in it killed through a magical mishap. And there's more. I correspond with a great number of people, you know, and many have mentioned the storks being disturbed, that they're not laying as many eggs as usual this spring.

"The white storks are the blessing of the empire, you know. 'The Eyes of She Who Shapes All.' That might be nothing, too. But spells have gone amiss, I know. Midwives are worried that babies are stillborn or freakish, but of course no one can show one. But someone mentioned the loss of the 'first of the brightest,' which is supposed to mean stars, we think. It's hard to say. The gods work their will, and we mortals bear up."

"You've nothing to fear," Candlemas said suddenly. He took Aquesita's pudgy hand and patted it. "I'll see that no harm comes to you."

"You will?" Her smile lit up the world as she said, "That's very kind of you, dear Candlemas. That's the sweetest thing anyone's ever said to me."

The mage didn't know how to reply, but didn't need to. The two just sat and stared. And each would have sworn the other's eyes were lit with stars.

Chapter 11

Down in the bowels of the earth, tornadoes like stone cones plotted.

The super heavy magic works its will.

The one named Karsus will blow himself and all the others to destruction soon.

Good. He alone among the humans can sense us.

And the humans think him mad because he rails against us.

All the better.

The Phaerimm had hatched their plot over many generations of humans, leading Karsus to the star-metal and a new application of heavy magic. In all that time, some of these ancient beings hadn't even stirred from the black cavern.

But who is this star-eyed woman with her warnings?

A deity, one of theirs. Not one of ours.

Can she warn them in time?

We'll see she doesn't.

I wonder, can this new super heavy magic penetrate even to our domain?

Best we not find out.

They will destroy themselves long before that.

Perhaps. But we'd best be ready to strike if need be.

We're ready.

* * * * *

Sunbright woke with a start when a small hand with metal on it touched his leg. "Get up, outlander! Something's hunting us!"

Tumbling from his nest of rags, the barbarian grabbed his sword and scabbard before putting on his boots. Knucklebones had shaken him, the brass knuckles across her palm like a branding iron on his bare skin. She was already padding from the cavern, having shouldered aside the iron door.

Sunbright followed, his body alert, but his mind still groggy from another night of dread premonitions. It was one drawback to being a shaman, he knew; they lived in dreamworlds as much as in the real one. Knucklebones had drawn only the smallest stripes of illumination along her wrists and ankles. Sunbright thought that cold light trick the handiest cantra he'd ever seen. He'd have to ask to learn it. If she would deign to teach it to him.

Moving up, he touched her ever so slightly, then whipped his hand back. Sure enough, honed reflexes spun her around with the black elven knife outthrust.

"What?"

"What are we after? How do you know we're being hunted?"

"There're pigeons' eggs in the tunnels. Pigeons always lay in pairs, so the eggs are linked. We steal them from nests in the eaves. Half the pairs lie in my bedchamber. Should someone step on a distant egg, the one over my head breaks and wakes me."

Very neat, Sunbright thought.

"Any idea what hunts us?" he asked her. "Have you been hunted before?"

"At times, when the guards are angry," she said. "Like when two of their members are hacked to death in the street."

Obviously this was Sunbright's fault, she felt.

"Sometimes it's dogs," she continued, "sometimes ferrets. They're not hard to mislead. We lay false trails, walk across mats at crossings and then roll them up. They've never found us yet."

Then why not just do that now? the barbarian wanted to ask. But she'd already moved off, her lean back and buttocks in worn leather reminding him of a mountain goat. He wondered how hard her interior was, for he'd glimpsed a woman's heart earlier. Now he was intrigued.

At cross tunnels, which might run up, down, at angles or even down as pits, she paused, sniffed, listened, and laid her pointed ears against the dirt. But the broken egg had told her that one certain tunnel had been breached, and she steered for it. Once they had to climb a cracked slope with hands and toes. Sunbright's moosehide boots slipped treacherously.

When the tunnel flattened, Knucklebones laid an ear to the floor again, then froze. Slithering on her belly, she inched to a bend and peered around. Sunbright had to lie atop her, half mashing her, to get a glimpse.

He had no idea what he saw.

A pack of city guards with batons lit by cold light waited behind a strange, crouching something. It was hard to see, being stone gray, but resembled a giant spider, or part spider, part man. It had carved features, a frowning elven face with a stone mustache, but the head was hollow. Inside, behind the eyes, rustled a scruffy gray-white shape. The animal's ratty tail slipped out one eye socket, then whisked back in. To Sunbright it looked as if a possum were caged inside an effigy of a black elf. Yet this statue bore six double-jointed limbs with claws like a crawfish. The statue crouched, nose to the ground, sniffing as a possum would.

Knucklebones bumped Sunbright off with her rump. The barbarian slithered backward. Kneeling, the thief drew his head down, planted her mouth on his ear. Her warm breath sent a thrill of ecstacy through him, despite her daunting words.

"That possum's a sniffer. Their noses aren't that much, but magic makes them smarter, so they talk in squeaks. The statue is some kind of golem that follows the possum's movements."

Sunbright nodded as he sniffed her natural perfume: wood smoke, sweat, and that curious breath of wildflowers. He patted his sword pommel to ask, do we fight?

A pause while she thought, then, "We'll lay a false trail in Blackwater Bog. It's confusing enough. But if they pass that, our hideout is endangered."

Sunbright tapped his chest, made a walking motion with his fingers. Can we lead them astray?

She shook her head, told him, "We've used it too many times lately. They don't fall for the 'cripple fleeing' anymore." But he thought he detected warmth in her tone, as if she appreciated his offer of sacrifice. With a dirty hand, she urged him back down the tunnel.

Since he'd skidded coming up, Sunbright pulled off his boots, tied the laces together, and slung them around his neck to descend the cracked slope. Noise of a slip would bring the guards running. Farther on, before a five way intersection called Blackwater Bog, Knucklebones bade him urinate on the passage floor. She then stepped in it barefoot and padded up a tunnel leading away from the stronghold. Sunbright waited, and moments later she returned, having washed her feet in a puddle. Now she crab walked half up the sloping tunnel wall, grabbing at cracks for support. Signaling he should crouch, Knucklebones squatted and vaulted across the intersection, into his arms. Catching her by torso and thighs, he found parts very soft indeed. But she immediately pushed away and tripped down the tunnel for home.

Farther on, she paused to listen and think, muttering, "This is very bad. Sniffers are one thing; they breed fast and cost nothing, but some top-notch mage worked hard to bring that golem to life. I've seen them used as pickets by doors, to slam axes on thieves, but I've never seen one act on its own, even with a possum thinking for it. The guards want us badly. We may have to abandon the homestead."

Her whispered tones laid the blame squarely on Sunbright, but he refused to take the bait and protest. He only waited until she shrugged and said, "Can't be helped. Let's lay an ambush."

She skittered off down the tunnel—and blundered into another crab-clawed golem.

The thing immediately whirled on Knucklebones, stone legs churning, claws clicking. The thief piped in surprise, but recovered instantly. Doing the last thing it would expect, she leapt in the air above the claws and landed nimbly on its broad back, strong toes latching on.

Sunbright saw two claws snap for him. Reminded they were stone, he flipped Harvester and slashed with the back of the blade, for a cubit-long edge below the hook was unsharpened and double thick for strength. He couldn't swing outright, for he was stooped in the tunnel, but the tempered steel clipped off one clawed arm at the joint like a lobster's leg. The other claw was batted down, and when the golem snapped again, he swiped sideways and broke that off too.

"Brace yourself!" he rasped, and squatted so he could swing overhead. The next leg in line was anchored to the ground, so his blow wasn't diminished, and it broke off clean. The golem lurched wildly on one corner leg.

Knucklebones, in the meantime, had struck at the beast's brain. Reaching along the monster's stone head, she slid her long, thin knife into the eye of the elven mask. The trapped possum shrilled and died, then the shell of stone flopped on its side. The stone legs stopped twitching. Blood oozing from the black eyehole made Sunbright turn away.

"Not so tough," panted Knucklebones. She hopped over the thing's back, staying clear of the severed claws lest they snap shut.

"Why shaped like an elf?" he asked. Sunbright's curiosity extended to all things. "Why not a spider or a—"

"Who knows? Tradition? Some old story? Probably the necromancer's recipe showed an elf on the page. Now, what to do?"

The carcass needed disposal, since it was a clear sign they'd been here. Knucklebones rubbed her nose.

"See if you can heft it," she said, "If so, we'll pitch it down the mile hole."

"Mile hole?"

Sheathing Harvester, Sunbright bent, and hoisted the thing on his back. It was heavy, a couple hundred pounds, but he could walk hunched over if he was careful.

Knucklebones swabbed up a trickle of the possum's blood from the cave floor, even bent to lick up the last traces, then scuffed the spot with her foot. Sunbright marveled at her diligence, the incredible lengths she took to protect the trail to her homestead.

"The drop through the sky," she whispered.

Sunbright recalled the ancient, inverted bear cave, and his first real glimpse of the earth, where he truly belonged.

Knucklebones mused in a whisper. "Worse news yet. *Two* golems to hunt us? We've never been this great a nuisance before . . ." She turned to glance at Sunbright.

Staggering under his burden and irritated by the thinly veiled accusation, he snapped, "What?"

She padded on, more alert since being surprised.

"Our lives were quiet and orderly until you came along."

"And shaky," Sunbright growled. "But you've guessed my secret. Shar Nightsinger, goddess of perverse winds and ill luck and petty revenge, bid me make your life a seething hell."

Did she chuckle, or did he just imagine it? "In that case, I'll burn a beggar in her honor. What—"

With a gasp, she put down her head and ran. Sunbright heard nothing, for his ears were less sharp than a part-elf's, but her urgency made him drop the golem carcass and pelt after her.

The iron door to the homestead lay flat on the tunnel floor. From within came shrieks and shouts and curses. Knucklebones sailed over the door, and Sunbright stomped on it to follow.

Inside the rookery, half a dozen spider golems harried Knucklebones' thieves while city guards killed with glowing clubs.

* * * * *

Candlemas included, every mage and apprentice had to drop their experiments and turn to a new task: the exploration of super heavy magic. Yet, as many expected, exactly what was required was unclear. Projects were thrown into motion while Karsus ran from one to another, hollering orders, then dashing off in mid sentence only to return moments later with countermands. The only consistency was his ranting about "war machines."

Soldiers arrived with sledges stacked high with bizarre tools of mass destruction. These contraptions had lain dormant in warehouses, or under barracks, and a few were dragged from caves under Karsus's own mansions. Why Karsus wanted to resurrect war machines when there was no immediate threat to the empire was not explained.

Candlemas was present at the first official test of a modified war machine, and it frightened him.

A ballista, a giant crossbow shooting spears twice as tall as a man, had been hauled by soldiers and oxen onto an outside balcony. Normally its great arrows were just sharpened logs. But Karsus had coppersmiths and armorers fashion an arrowhead of copper sheets that measured three feet across. And was hollow. The mad mage himself oversaw the fitting of the great arrowhead to the log and, from a dozen blueware crocks, poured into the hollow point a startling quantity of super heavy magic tinged a fiery red. He explained that, previously, heavy magic would dissipate if catapulted through the air, but this heavier stuff should cling together. Hammering down the lid, Karsus daubed a brush and, chanting and giggling, painted an elaborate rune on the red-gold metal. Karsus then ordered the ancient sergeant manning the ballista to aim for Emperor's Park, which from this balcony was just visible past tiered houses and trees. Stone-faced, the grizzled veteran tolled off orders and a warning to stand clear. An axe fell, and the restraining rope parted.

With a *BRONG* and *WHOOSH!* the giant arrow split the sky, rocketing across the heights. Its tail chased its head until it began to spin end over end. It disappeared behind the trees and—

Everyone grunted as a massive explosion rent the air and made the balcony tremble. A geyser of dirt, grass, and rocks cascaded upward in a fan, then rattled back down. Candlemas thought he saw a body, arms and legs flailing, among the debris, but wasn't sure.

Laughing, Karsus took center stage. "See? It works! I can increase the power of exploding runes a thousand-fold, blow a huge crater where my enemies are hiding, then another and another until they're flinders! Oh, and think! There's more! Invisible arrows that couldn't be shielded. We could create tornadoes—that would fix 'em! Once they're spinning, shift heavy magic into them and increase their power, until they can split a mountain! Or better, power sinks to draw off my foes' magic and turn it against them. Yes, we must work on that—"

Karsus and his usual hangers-on—toadies all— sailed back into the workshops. Soldiers wrapped the slack ropes of the ballista and departed. Candlemas went in the opposite direction from Karsus.

Yet war madness was catching. Mages talked openly about punishing "Karsus's enemies," though no one had a clue who these enemies were. Everyone plotted new methods of destruction, egging each other on to greater hopes for devastation. Bubbleheads argued that improved war machines would dishearten the enemy, causing rivals to capitulate without a fight, so the empire might stretch her borders and grow even greater. Yet at the same time, they acknowledged that pockets in the north were exhausted of magic, thinned so badly that floating cities couldn't drift near for fear of plummeting. To the former steward of the former Castle Delia, it seemed folly to plan more magic mischief when their own city's existence was precarious already. But like children, Karsus's cronies were addicted to their dangerous games and couldn't quit. Until someone, or all of them, were hurt or killed.

Later that day, even working alone, Candlemas was almost killed by someone else's stupidity.

He was working down the hall from the star chamber. No one wanted to work in that cursed space lest corrupted magic queer their experiments. Candlemas puttered. He hoped to fashion a magictight compartment of star-metal to contain super heavy magic. At least that way, they could safely store the stuff and keep fools from tampering with it.

A scream rang out and Candlemas ran. A brilliant flare lit the hallway, pouring from the door of one workshop, and Candlemas squinted at a fierce blaze consuming the floor.

One mage had been burned to death, shriveled to charred meat. Another crawled aimlessly, shrieking as his robe flared out of control. Candlemas ran back to his workshop and grabbed a thick rug. Others had gathered in the hall to gape, and he bulled them aside to wrap the rug around the burning man and snuff the flames.

The rug immediately caught fire. Shocked, Candlemas ripped it loose and hurled it away, but his sleeve ignited. While others stared stupidly, Candlemas tore his sleeve free by main strength. Singed skin made him gasp.

The burning mage had died. The stink of charring wood and scorched flesh, and his own brush with disaster made Candlemas queasy. He blundered out the door. At least, he soothed himself, the fire had dropped through the table to the stone floor, and would now extinguish.

But someone shouted, pointing, "There goes the stone!"

Candlemas gaped. The fire was burning through the flagstones. And still going. Creeping mages jostled to peer into the hole and the fools burned their feet on nolten stone. Craning, Candlemas saw the fire burning on the next floor down. Later he learned it had just kept going, until it burned through the cellars to create a pit where it cooked for three days before sputtering out. Reconstructing the experiment, Candlemas and others learned that the two dead mages had infused a flaming sphere with super heavy magic, creating an unquenchable fire. They'd bragged beforehand that Karsus would be pleased, and reward them for their discovery. Karsus was indeed delighted with the news, but never asked the names of the dead.

Candlemas wondered if he weren't the only sane mage in the castle. Or if, by remaining, his own sanity was in question. . . .

* * * * *

Sunbright had the fight of his life, and mostly in the dark. He only prayed he was shearing enemies and not friends.

It was a question of which was more dangerous, the sniffer-driven golems or the raging guards. The possums had the instincts of animals, which was to flee a battle if possible. But they were trapped in the rookery and panicked. Their scrabbling, tearing claws were like threshing knives amidst wheat. Sunbright saw a nest of bedding shredded to rags and kicked against a wall. He hoped no one was in it. It was almost impossible to see with only one light, "Knucklebones's night-light," a mere stripe on the rock wall. The guards brought their own light, enchanted batons that glowed in the dark. Sunbright judged that a foolish tactic, for he had only to chop six inches below the glowing wand to lop off a hand—when he guessed correctly which end to strike at. Still, the guards' other hands clutched short swords, and soon they tossed the wands away.

Rampaging guards attacked sleepers in niches while Sunbright dodged blows from all around. Twice he tripped and tumbled over a black golem. He'd shorn one man's hand, leaving, he guessed, five guards still fighting.

And somewhere were Knucklebones's gang. He heard a chain clink and ching, knew Rolon swung the weighted end, and for once a guard shouted. Oddly, the most competent person was Ox, who, blind, knew the rookery better than anyone. He'd batted a guard with his staff, hoicked the man off his feet, and probably burst his guts, but Ox blundered into a golem that clamped his ankles and tangled his feet. Another guard's baton thudded onto the blind giant's skull. Whether or not he was stabbed to death after that Sunbright didn't know.

Occasionally he glimpsed Knucklebones, bounding like an alley cat, stabbing and twisting with her black, elven blade. But he heard too a shriek and burble, and guessed some woman's lungs had been pierced.

They had to finish this dustup quickly, for more guards might spill through the door at any time. Currently he stood between two guards who took turns jabbing at him from the dark. He flung his sword to his right, but had to whip it back quickly to guard his left. And he was stuck. He'd blundered into a hole and tangled his feet in wicker food baskets. Trying to jump free only banged his knees. He wasn't even sure if the guards were stuck in the same hole, or crouched alongside it. He considered drawing Dorlas's hammer and flinging it, then crawling over a guard if he toppled. But how would he know?

He felt a kiss alongside his ear, the cold breath of steel and a near miss, and let go Harvester's pommel to grab. His hand closed on a sleeve and he jerked the man off his feet and hurled him into his partner. Sunbright was rewarded by double grunts, but when he stabbed in that direction, he struck nothing. Cursing, he slapped his palms flat and kicked to jump free of the hole. His boot touched another foot. Groping, he clunked a wagging helmet, realized what it meant, then slammed the heel of his hand under the helmet to keep the guard flat. Guessing, he used his free hand to ram Harvester into a solid body. Whether he killed another guard underneath, or that man was gone, he couldn't tell.

Stone claws nipped at his boot, and he caught his balance and kicked viciously. He hurt his toes but toppled the squirming beast into the hole he'd just left, or at least he thought he did.

Crouching, sword in two hands, ready to strike anywhere, he listened. The noises had died down. Scuffles, skittering, a gurgle, were all he could hear.

Risking the chance, he called, "Knucklebones! Light!"

In answer, glowing stripes the width of a woman's hand flared along one wall. Immediately the small thief slid away, circled, striped elsewhere. Sunbright found even that tiny illumination smarting after so much darkness.

Then he could see, and wished he couldn't.

Two dead guards lay interlocked near him. A spider golem kicked six legs helplessly in a hole. Another guard was face down over the fire pit, another moaning from Ox's punishing belly smash. Knucklebones had stabbed the last two, and stood over one with a bloody blade.

But Ox was dead, his neck hacked half through. Lothar, with his broken leg, had been plucked from his bed and stabbed. And Mother had been run through the lungs.

Face grim, Knucklebones called and the children, trained to run at the first sign of trouble, came creeping from the shadows: Corah, crying over her dead father, the topknotted twins Aba and Zykta, Rolon dragging his weighted chain as if it were too heavy for him.

"We must bury the dead," Sunbright muttered. But tradition was thwarted, for there was little dirt. "We'll do something—"

"No, we get out," Knucklebones interrupted. She reached into a wall niche and withdrew stout sacks with straps, proceeded to fill them with food and small purses of coins. "More patrols might come any minute. Children, fetch what you can. We'll not return."

Sunbright stared, disbelieving, as even tiny Corah left her dead father and dug in the bed they'd shared. Circling the corpses, he grabbed Knucklebones's arm. She whirled with a hiss like a cat's as he demanded, "No funeral? Not even a minute to mourn? That's damned hardhearted—"

The woman's one eye blazed as she wrenched free and spat, "Better hardhearted than dead, country mouse! Hard hearts kept us alive, until you got here!"

The words stung, and Sunbright drew back. Miraculously, he was the only one not ready to go, for the mute children had gathered meager possessions and withdrawn through the door. Knucklebones stumped under the weight of a single sack, turned and pronounced, "*Wisht!*" The room went black, leaving Sunbright in darkness.

Tramping over the dead, he jogged to follow the tiny entourage. Corah, very small, called, "Where do we go?"

"To another stronghold," replied Knucklebones over her shoulder. "I've scouted it—"

This time Sunbright interrupted, "No."

The one-eyed woman glared, but he continued, "We're not going to hide in these tunnels any longer. We're going where people belong. Down to the ground. To freedom."

Chapter 12

A hand clamped over Candlemas's mouth, jolting him
from a sound sleep, terrifying him. The huge hand
pinned his head, rendering him powerless as a child. As
he blearily fought for breath and vision, he saw that
there were several people hovering around the big
canopied bed. Were these assassins?

"Can you remain quiet?"

The voice and barbarous northern accent were familiar, and Candlemas nodded. His heart continued to
race, though, as if it would never slow down.

Dragging himself upright, he saw it was indeed Sunbright. With him were a scruffy, short, one-eyed woman
with an elven cast to her, and four filthy children
dressed in rags and carrying satchels. Questions over-
rode indignation, though Candlemas pulled the blanket

CLAYTON EMERY

around his ample middle. He slept naked, while these intruders were villainously clothed and armed.

"Where have you been?" the pudgy mage whispered.

"Adventuring." Sunbright talked in a whisper as well. He sat on the edge of the bed and it creaked under his weight. The elvish thief stroked the bedposts and made glowing stripes that cast a wan light.

"I see you've been treated well," the barbarian said, "Can you have food fetched? The children are hungry."

"What?"

Candlemas rubbed his eyes. He noticed that Sunbright had a few new, livid scars and wounds wrapped in dirty bandages, but was otherwise the same.

"Who are these people?" he asked, "How did you get in here? What have you been up to? How have you managed to survive in this city without any money or contacts?"

Sunbright answered with a snort, then, "Get some food and we'll tell you. It's an interesting story. And I'm hungry too."

Grumbling, Candlemas tugged on a robe and rang a bell. While the visitors hid, he ordered a night maid to fetch a platter, enough to last him all day if necessary. She left without a word, returned shortly with a silver platter heaped with loaves of bread, cheese, wine, fruits, cold sausage, raw vegetables and sauces, even delicate jam tarts.

Sunbright and the rest came out of hiding, the children gazing wide-eyed at the food. When told to dig in, they ate like wolves. Sunbright stuffed cold roast into a hollowed loaf and tore off chunks with strong white teeth.

Candlemas took mulled wine, sat in a wing chair, and said, "Now will you tell me what you've been up to?"

Sunbright told him, leaving out nothing. The list of dead guards made the mage shake his head. When the barbarian had finished, Candlemas related some of his work, marveling at the contrast between them. Sunbright battled spidery trackers and killer guards in the sewers while Candlemas perched in luxury and explored esoteric magic. It was hard to believe they spoke of the same city. Candlemas didn't mention Aquesita.

The northerner nodded at Candlemas's observations, as if they confirmed his own suspicions. He picked up a bottle and smashed the neck against the table edge, for he didn't recognize the enchanted corkscrew next to it.

"So this Karsus is the wild-eyed nit who pitched me out into the street? And he just builds magical things and destroys friend and foe alike, and no one stops him?"

"It's even more insane than that," Candlemas sighed. "Karsus has no friends, only slithering toadies who slobber after him like idiot dogs. I suppose he has foes—other mages or archwizards—but they're nothing compared to him. Karsus has whole teams of mages dusting off war machines and enervating them with this new magic. He's like a boy in a sandbox, building tiny cities and stamping on them. And there is no one to stop him. All the archwizards in the city bow to Karsus. He owns whole tracts of the city anyway. He built it. And no one dares speak out for fear of assassination. You remember Lady Polaris?"

"The white-haired woman who got us out of hell?"

Sunbright didn't see Knucklebones's one eye go wide.

"Aye." Candlemas sipped wine. "There's enough of her now for three women. She hides all day in a dark room preening and stuffing herself like a pig. She has no concept of the danger the empire's in, and doesn't care. She's probably representative of all the archwizards."

Sunbright nodded. The children had stuffed themselves until their stomachs were round and their heads drooping. The barbarian ferried them to Candlemas's huge bed. The mage didn't comment on how they dirtied the sheets.

Returning, Sunbright said, "The empire's rotten to the core, and I know, for I've seen the core. I've felt this abuse of nature and magic, and had visions of destruction—whole cities collapsing—so it can't be far off. It emphasizes your words."

Candlemas waved away dreams. Hard facts interested him more, and he had plenty. He found himself echoing Aquesita, defending her position. "It's not all bad, and need not lead to devastation. Magic can be a force for good, too, don't forget. Tamed, it's the most powerful force in the universe. It's Karsus who's abusing it. Were he to disappear, the empire could regain its senses and climb to new heights—"

"No." Sunbright cut him off, shaking his head. "All things come to an end. A tree grows tall and strong, crowding out its neighbors, but it always grows too large eventually, and rot sets in, and the core collapses, and a strong wind knocks it down to destruction. Its children may take root, may survive and grow in their own way and in a new direction, but the tree is dead and gone, its body serves as food for the young ones."

"A simplistic view. Something for a shaman to lecture children with," Candlemas snorted. "The empire has much greatness about it, and it's not dead yet."

What would Aquesita think of those words?

"I may be an ignorant barbarian, but I have eyes." Sunbright nodded toward the bed, where petite snores whistled. "Those children were abandoned by their parents, or orphaned by your empire's guards. A race that feeds on its young won't last more than one generation, let alone forever. And you said yourself no one's opposing Karsus and his cronies."

Candlemas was disturbed by the simple logic. He

wondered if Aquesita knew anything of abandoned children. Wondered, too, if she'd ever wanted children of her own? And did he? But he was daydreaming.

"How did you get into the castle?" he asked Sunbright, trying to clear his mind by filling it with a few facts. "It's covered in glyphs at night, and patrolled regularly."

Sunbright nodded to his traveling companion. "This is Knucklebones, another child of your empire, but one it can't kill. She sneaked us in here. Actually, the children had no trouble either. I'm the clumsy one."

"How do you do?" said the mage formally. Knucklebones only nodded. Rising, she left the table and slipped out into the hall. "Where's she going?"

The barbarian raised his palms. "I've no idea. I ask her questions, and sometimes she answers. She's had a hard life."

Haven't we all, thought Candlemas unkindly, saying nothing but, "So what are you about?"

"We're hiding." Sunbright sorted through the food as he spoke, looking for whatever would keep and storing it in a haversack. "I've killed so many of the city guards I suppose I'm an outlaw, though I don't think any have escaped me to report back. Your city's guards are the scum of the earth. They'd crush a child's skull under their boots and turn it in for a bonus."

"It's not *my* city," Candlemas corrected. But he thought of Aquesita. It *was* her city, the good parts anyway.

For answer, Sunbright only looked around the opulent suite lit by stripes of white light. The mage found himself stammering, "Karsus is—is grateful we, uh, retrieved the, uh, fallen star, is all."

Sunbright grinned like a wolf. "I've got scars and dead companions to attest to his gratitude."

Miffed, Candlemas banged down the goblet. "To get

back. What are you about?"

Sunbright popped grapes in his mouth, then used a goblet of spring water and a satin napkin to swab grime off his wounds. "I'd like to get down to the ground with these little ones. It's not safe in the city for us. For some reason Knucklebones can't guess, the guards actually expended time and coin to fashion those spider golems to kill us. I'd like to ask you—please—to work your shifting spell and get us down to earth. We can't use a transgate, whatever that is, according to Knucklebones. But we must leave, so we came to you for help, though we'll be parting company now."

There was a touch of regret in his voice.

Candlemas was surprised by a pang too. Sunbright was not exactly a friend, but was more than an acquaintance, and a familiar link to the past. Certainly Candlemas had no friends here. Except Aquesita.

Thought of one woman made him think of another. "What about Greenwillow?"

"Greenwillow . . ." Sunbright breathed the name as if it contained his soul, ". . . I don't know. We're so far out of our time—"

"Have you thought of returning?"

The barbarian jerked, dropped his filthy napkin.

"Is that possible?"

Candlemas had surprised himself again.

"Well," the pudgy mage answered, "it just popped into my head. I don't know . . . Karsus brought us here with a chronoma—a time travel spell. I'd heard stories about the concept, everyone had, but never seen or read of it done. Yet he seemed to do it on a whim, so it must be doable. What I don't know is: can *I* do it?"

"Or get Karsus to do it?" Sunbright offered. "Or show you how?"

The mage rubbed his bald head, rose, and paced. "I don't even know if *Karsus* even knows anymore how he did it. Half his magic is instinctual. He simply imagines a spell and it happens. They say he could firefinger—a cantra—at age two. At twenty-two, he was the youngest archwizard ever, and now he's three hundred and something!"

Sunbright squinted. He'd known that mages lengthened their lives magically, but hadn't realized how much. To him, and his people, sixty years old was ancient.

Candlemas continued to pace in bare feet. "If I could convince Karsus," he thought aloud, "—if I could get near him—I might be able to learn the spell. Might . . . their magic is so advanced here, I should be lucky to scrub tables."

Sunbright nodded, for the first time realizing how tough Candlemas actually had it. In a way, he was a barbarian among mages.

"But you could learn it? And send us back—"

"Us?" Candlemas stopped him. "I don't want to go back!"

"You don't? Why? If you're an ignorant peasant here and an important man back there? And this empire's going to crash around your ears. What's keeping you here?"

Candlemas wouldn't answer, though her name was on his tongue. Aquesita. Even her name was heavenly.

"Never mind. I'll try to learn the spell, and we'll work out a way to stay in touch. In the meantime, I can get you down to the ground. I think."

"We don't want to go to the ground," retorted a low voice.

The men turned, startled. Knucklebones had opened and shut the door and walked up behind Candlemas without either of the two men noticing. A bulging sack hung over one slim shoulder. She set it down with a chink.

Sunbright nodded. "What's in there?"

"Nothing that'll be missed, much. We're not going down to the ground. You can go by yourself."

"We've decided this already," Sunbright sighed. "On the way here. You said the city is making a special effort to kill you, or me, or both of us, though we don't know why. It won't be safe anywhere. We must get down—"

"I can buy us safety for months with this." She cut him off, then nudged the bag with her bare toe. "Go without us. We wouldn't like it in the wilds. We're used to the city."

"Used to the city?" Sunbright's voice rose. "Living in tunnels like rats? I can find us a friendly village, maybe even the descendants of the Rengarth. Or we could build a cabin, let the children run free in the woods, teach them to swim in mountain pools, see they eat good, healthy red meat and grain still warm from the fields."

Knucklebones didn't answer. At the bed, she pulled back the covers and roused the children. Still more asleep than awake they nevertheless rolled out of bed and picked up their meager belongings. The thief opened a carved chest against one wall, pulled out expensive and ornate clothing that had been hand stitched to Candlemas's measurements. Summoning the sleepy children, she stripped each of their dirty old rags and fitted them with warm, serviceable clothing, the many folds of cloth tucked and belted. Seeing they'd picked up their dolls and satchels again, she retrieved her sack of hard currency and, without a word, slipped out the door, leading the four children by the hand.

Sunbright shrugged his heavy shoulder scabbard and belt into place and grabbed up a last loaf. "I go with them. We'll come back once she thinks it's safe—and we've worked out our differences."

But Candlemas, who didn't believe in omens, had a sudden premonition of disaster. Maybe it was the black night, maybe the wine, but he worried. "Wait!" he called, "Take something so I can find you."

Sunbright stood in the doorway. "Make it fast. Knucklebones could outrun a reindeer on the flats."

Frantic, Candlemas cast about, finally reached behind his ear and ripped loose a tuft of his meager hair. He closed it in the barbarian's palm. "Burn that if you need me. Then get up high somewhere."

Sunbright nodded, and with his belt knife, cut a lock of hair so blond it was almost white. Handing it to Candlemas, a strange wistful look crossed his face. He shot out a massive, scarred, and calloused hand, and gave the mage a squeeze that bruised the skin, whispering, "Thank you, friend."

Then he was gone, and Candlemas was left alone to wonder about many things, but about himself most of all.

* * * * *

Knucklebones made three turns in the dark, then ordered Sunbright to break an inside shutter. They slipped through the window into a garden. The barbarian was amazed at her ability to track inside, in the dark. He couldn't have found his way outside in an hour, and she'd chosen a different route from the one through which they'd entered.

Along a path under dark trees they tripped, Sunbright the noisiest one in his moosehide soles, which were wearing thin with all this pavement walking. The tundra dweller knew only that they tended downhill until he looked up at the stars. Bad enough to be floating in the air, but the entire island revolved ever so slowly, constantly confusing his sense of direction. But the stars at least were fixed, though this was a southern sky. The Sled and Cappi's Cat were stretched lengthwise along the northern horizon.

Knucklebones and the children had disappeared around a corner. The stargazer had to trot to catch up. He found Knucklebones perched like an alley cat between the spears of a wrought iron fence. She reached down and caught the children by the scruff to haul them over. Sunbright admired her quiet strength, her calm poise. He grabbed the spears to vault up and over, but she stiffened, sniffing the air.

Abruptly she pushed Sunbright back down, then hissed to the children as she handed them the loot sack, "Get to Sleeping Gunn! He'll take you in." Then she hopped down beside Sunbright, snagged his vest front, and led him along the fence to a globe-lit corner.

He asked, "Why are we going where it's light?"

"Lead them away from the children!"

Without pause, she dashed across the street into an alley. "Pull that hammer," she whispered. "We'll need it."

"Who's coming?" he asked. Her tension was catching.

She vaulted a puddle that Sunbright splashed through.

"Trackers!" she breathed. "Rushworth and Pericles's crowd!"

Sunbright hadn't seen or heard anyone. He could see even less in this black alley. He started to whisper, "How did you—"

"They've a special soap they wash in to remove human scent. But nonhumans can smell the soap."

She ducked down an alley just as dark as the first and up three long steps. Sunbright could barely keep from falling. She was fleet and nimble as a deer, and with only one eye, he marveled.

He ran into her thin, bony arm, blocking his path.

"In here."

She jerked open a door and they passed within. Sunbright smelled polished wood and dust, books, a trace of food grease. It was no combination he knew. "Where are we?"

"Academy of Mentalist Study. A college. It's always open, but they'll know that too. Suck in your gut!"

"Who? Why?"

As they edged around a wooden corner, Sunbright felt bile burp at the back of his throat. His head felt empty, as if he'd suddenly been hung upside down again. He could tell from barely audible echoes that the room was large, and they were not alone. Knucklebones was counting shelves as they passed.

A light flared in the center of the room.

Sunbright gulped. He thought "center," because the room used all six surfaces as floors. The room was huge, taking up the whole building like a cave, and intermediate floors had been built here and there, jutting from other floors at angles. Bookshelves stood head high on every floor, and open spots with tables and chairs broke up the center. Above their heads on an in-between floor, like a fly stuck to the ceiling, was a man with a fierce red beard and horsetail, and dark, unadorned clothes. He flicked his fingers and sent more balls of glowing energy spinning through the room. So Knucklebones wasn't the only one who could illuminate with her fingertips. With his free hand he tapped a silver coin on his belt.

"You're getting slow, Knuckle'," the man offered. "I got ahead of you."

Knucklebones didn't argue, only fled between bookshelves, leapt like a mountain goat, and gained another "floor." Chasing her, Sunbright was staring at the top of her head for an instant, then he stumbled and righted himself on what had been a wall. His eyes and stomach liked none of it, but he kept running.

To no avail. Every floor had a door looking out on a corridor, and each doorway was blocked by a man or woman. Green capes were thrown back to reveal a skull and crossbones painted on their black shirts. In the eerie light of the drifting glowlights, the crossed bones showed jagged breaks. Knucklebones backed into Sunbright.

The redheaded man quit the left-hand floor, strolled to a doorway, and slipped past an assassin. Sunbright assumed the tracker had found them, and now came the killing. The assassins toted either crossbows with silver-tipped quarrels or long bullwhips forked at the ends like a snake's tongue.

One of the assassins, a woman with blonde hair pulled back tightly, called, "You can leave, Knucklebones. The Bonebreakers have no quarrel with you, and you're not in the contract."

Sunbright drew Harvester and looked for a screen against crossbow bolts. It wasn't easy to find one, for the glowlights cast wide, square shadows that chased one another. This was a bad place for a flatlander to be fighting, he thought.

But even as his brain began to sing with a battle high, he marveled that Knucklebones knew every building in the city inside and out, and that everyone knew her.

The thief called, "Who bought you?"

The blonde shook her head while snapping the safety off her crossbow. But behind her came a crow of laughter. A young fop in a brocaded shirt, satin cape, small hat, and face powder stepped out. He panted, obviously having run to see the show.

"I hired them! Same as I bought the cooperation of the city guards. You killed a fistful of them, didn't you? But they wiped out your nest, I hear!"

For once, Knucklebones didn't know somebody. She asked Sunbright, "Who?"

"Hurodon, son of Angeni of the House of Dreng in the Street of the Golden Willows," growled the barbarian. "My biggest mistake so far. I should have torn his head off in the park."

Hurodon laughed. "If she's your friend, I'll pay for her too!"

The blonde woman nodded, called, "Sorry, Knuckle'. Nothing personal. *Loose!*"

As the four crossbows shot, Sunbright shoved Knucklebones headlong into a rack of books. The freestanding shelves had no backs, and the barbarian shoved hard. The thief catapulted into the books, knocked them out the other side, and tumbled after them. At the same time, Sunbright used the impetus of his shove to backpedal out of harm's way.

The four bolts arrived almost simultaneously, and acted like nothing Sunbright expected. They were mad as the rest of the room.

One bolt thumped a book sliding across Knucklebone's back. The red book was thick as a knapsack, yet the bolt penetrated so the head projected out the other side. A second bolt Sunbright spanked away with the flat of his blade. It shattered and clattered off the bookshelves. The third he never saw, for he was distracted by the fourth.

Unbelievably, he saw it strike the wooden floor but not break. Instead it ricocheted, bending in a curve for an instant to speed at him. A slap and sting banged his ham, and he knew he was shot. It was painful as a bear's bite. But it was a small bolt, and if he broke off the head—

"Don't break it!" Knucklebones screamed, diving through the bookshelf at him. "It digs itself deeper! Hold still!" And she yanked the barb free, the head bloody and clinging to shreds of Sunbright's meat. *That* hurt, like fire jabbed into a wound.

From somewhere he heard, "Close! Nock!"

"Split up!" Knucklebones yelled. Headlong she dived over the heap of books to take refuge in partial shadows.

"No!" shouted the barbarian. But she'd whisked out of sight.

Cursing, he knew why she'd done it. Thieves didn't fight, they fled. And if one of the gang were caught, splitting up would see the others free. So be it. He didn't have time to argue.

He ducked, then skidded on his boots and aching butt around the end of a bookcase. At the command, "Loose!" he jerked the bookcase down onto himself.

An enchanted bolt slammed the floor by his head, bent and spanked into the air. But it only tagged a cascading book, nicking the corner and spinning away. Another bolt splintered a wooden shelf.

A third ripped through his thigh.

Gasping at the searing pain, he reached behind his thigh, grabbed the shank of the arrow—it was made of some queer, pliable material unlike anything he'd ever felt—and ripped downward.

As if watching someone else suffer, he saw the black fletching protruding through his thigh disappear into the tanned flesh. A flare of agony blazed through him, then the arrow was clear. He hurled it away, red with his blood, sucked wind, and struggled up to find two assassins with whips closing at either hand. And Knucklebones nowhere in sight.

Sunbright tracked both of the assassins, flicking his head from side to side. He pushed the pain in his thigh out of his mind. Of course, it wasn't the first time he'd been shot with an arrow. As a boy, practicing, learning with the other boys, he'd often limp home, his aching body resembling nothing less than a pin cushion of little toy arrows. But then, these weren't toy arrows. . . .

Keeping Harvester poised before him to strike either way, he tried to anticipate the assassins' next move. But these two, a man and woman, had worked together before.

At a "Hup!" they both curled their arms and lashed out perfectly in time. The black coils snapped at Sunbright, too close to his eyes. He jumped, but was caught by both wrists. Immediately, like wranglers taming a wild horse, they set their feet and pulled with the full weight of their bodies. Sunbright fought to keep from being spread-eagled, but he knew this was just a delaying tactic. They were merely holding him for—

—here they came. Two crossbowmen jogging through the stacks of books to aim and pierce him through.

He was pinned, surrounded, helpless and about to be shot. There was no way out.

Then he remembered. There was one more way. . . .

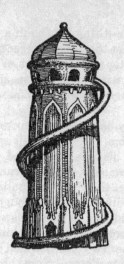

Chapter 13

Black lengths of leather dug into Sunbright's wrists as the two Bonebreakers yanked so hard and viciously that the barbarian couldn't get a grip to shake them off. He was hard put to hang on to Harvester, and couldn't angle it to slice the thongs. The weird glowing lights bobbing throughout the room like will o'wisps cast long and short shadows that revolved like manic dancers, yet he saw two assassins take aim with their crossbows. He was blocked or threatened in every direction except from above, so that's the way he went.

With a mighty grunt, Sunbright clambered up the bookshelves. He wasn't sure what to expect, but if people could run across the "ceiling," and one "ceiling" was an intermediate floor not twenty feet away, then he could get there if he were desperate enough.

And he was certainly desperate enough.

Planting a big boot on a stout middle shelf, he vaulted up the bookcase, took a wild stab for a higher one, grabbed it, and gained the top. Books cascaded off the shelves and into the path of the increasingly reluctant Bonebreakers. He was dragging them along by their whips with brute strength.

One of them let go, the handle of his whip jerked from his hands. The other managed to hang on as Sunbright gained the top of the shelves with both feet. A crossbow bolt flew by and the barbarian jumped into open space.

The one clinging whip jerked him off course so he ended up flying sideways, but he clearly saw and felt the weird transition. One second he was leaping upward, as ungainly as a yak trying to take flight, the next he was free of the pull of the library floor and grabbed by the magical gravity of the one above. His stomach flipped, he tasted bile, then his feet and body were hauled upward, which instantly became downward.

Sunbright flung out a hand, kicked, bounced off the edge of a bookshelf, and crashed hard onto the floor. At the last second he'd cradled his head; a good thing, for his elbow clipped wood so hard that pain flashed up and down his arm like lightning. His boots slammed down, and Harvester jarred across his lap, slicing his shirt and nearly killing him.

He'd been banged and slammed in a dozen places, but he was still alive and fighting, growing angrier every moment. As he scrambled to his feet, he thought about how he and Knucklebones were hunted, and how Ox, Mother, and Lothar had died, because a spoiled brat had connived to repay an injury, and the city guards had colluded with him. All the corruption of the empire was conspiring to kill Sunbright, and the few decent people he knew, so the corrupt might be sated with revenge. If he got the chance, he'd kill a dozen for every one of his companions who'd died. And Hurodon would suffer the most, in gruesome ways only a barbarian could invent—and have the guts to apply.

But for now he held his anger, using it to fuel his fight rather than being blinded by it. First, he should untangle himself.

Two whips were coiled around his wrists. The loose one he left in place, concentrating on the woman who had managed to hold on all this time. The whip went straight up into the sky like an inverted fishing line. She stood directly above him, still hanging on to the whip, yanking to keep him off-balance, and shouting to her comrades to shoot. Two of the assassins, a man and a woman, were nocking their crossbows while the one who'd lost hold of his whip ran for an intervening wall.

Good enough, thought Sunbright with glee. He could strike back.

Bracing a knee against a bookshelf, he grabbed the thin, black whip and hauled with all his might.

The woman shrieked with surprise as she was jerked off her feet. She'd stupidly passed the handle's loop over her wrist and now she was following it upward. Her free hand grabbed for purchase as she sailed past a nearby bookshelf, but the gravity of Sunbright's floor caught her.

She plummeted straight down and landed on her head and shoulder with a sickening crack. As she crumpled, the barbarian added a vicious, finishing stomp to her bent neck.

Above, someone called out that he was ready—a crossbowman.

Stooping, tearing the whips from his arms, Sunbright grabbed the woman's body and lifted her to his shoulder. A crossbow quarrel thumped into her chest. The other shooter, now poised overhead, took aim while

Sunbright grunted and pitched the dead woman.

It was the reverse of before. Now the woman traveled upward, flopping like a doll, until the opposite gravity snagged her. Like a sack of grain she landed atop the crossbowman, who bleated and tried to jump aside. But he'd been standing between two tall sets of shelves, as Sunbright had noted. The dead woman tangled the living man, and the barbarian was already running, wondering where Knucklebones had got to.

He charged across the floor, which was much like the other ones except for a threadbare carpet, and reached a spiral staircase that was enclosed on all sides, probably so climbers wouldn't get dizzy and topple off. The inside of the staircase was dark, for the glowlights had drifted away as they began to fade. He briefly considered hiding here, but rejected the idea. He had to keep moving so his enemies couldn't regroup and surround him. Knucklebones had that part right.

He stumbled over something filling the stairway. His knees thumped onto flesh. His hand landed on a cloth soaked with warm blood. He knew it wasn't Knucklebones, who wore all leather, so it had to be an assassin spiked by her elven blade. That made two dead. But where was she?

He exited the top of the winding stairs and found himself near a corner, the juncture of three "floors." Off to his right was a door out to the main corridor, but whether it would be upside down or right side up he couldn't guess. Inside this building, nothing made sense, as if a mad builder had impressed his will onto wood and stone. It further frustrated his desire to get away, but he knew not where.

Motion flickered at the corner of his eye. An assassin with his crossbow pointed upward, cocked and ready, skulked along the left-hand wall. It was the man who'd lost his whip. He'd obviously recovered the crossbow from the assassin whom Sunbright had thrown the woman onto. From the upper right came another attacker, one who'd drawn a wavy bladed knife. They obviously hoped to box him in, distract him long enough for one or the other to strike.

Sunbright struck first.

He snatched Dorlas's warhammer from his belt and flung it at the crossbowman. He waited only long enough to hear it thump flesh, then whirled right and charged the knife wielder.

The assassin was evidently not accustomed to his prey running at him and froze for just a second. Stabbing people in the back hadn't prepared him to defend against a screaming barbarian with a menacing, hooked sword. The assassin swiveled his hips, made to jump aside, but moved too slowly.

Harvester of Blood split the assassin's guts and rocketed out his back. Sunbright jerked his head aside so as not to run onto the wavy blade, but the man, mouth open, vomiting blood, had dropped his knife. It was his last act.

Still charging, Sunbright spun the dead man around and used the body as a shield. Harvester still protruded from the dead assassin's back when the second crossbowman—a woman, actually—leveled her crossbow at him and shot. The magic bolt ricocheted off the floor, actually bending like a fishing pole before seeking flesh. But it only lodged in the rear of the dead assassin.

Sunbright charged back. He hoisted Harvester's pommel to his chest and the keen blade sliced free of the dead man's bowels. The barbarian kept running, letting the sword trail behind him, then employing its weight to sling up and over his shoulder.

The woman had fumbled her reloading, unnerved by the target's mad, fast defense. Now she turned and ran, so Sunbright saw only a fluttering cape in the dying light of a glowlight sinking up ahead. It was enough. Howling, he slammed Harvester overhand and smashed it down on her shoulder, splitting her back to expose white ribs, and knocking her sprawling. Sunbright charged so fast he over ran her and had to hop her writhing body. It didn't writhe long, for he grabbed Harvester's pommel in two hands and slammed it point down into her kidneys to cleave guts and liver. If she didn't die immediately, she would before the hour was out.

Panting, the warrior backed into the shadows, scanning, counting, and thinking. Five dead, no, six with the one Knucklebones had spiked. Where was the last? One was laying in the staircase: the blonde leader? Would she have deserted her flunkies as their mission went to pot? Would Hurodon be nearby? And where was Knucklebones?

Straining to hear over his sobbing breath and pounding heart, he scuttled backward on flat feet to keep moving. As he crabwalked, he trailed a hand and found the warhammer he'd flung. That was no mere weapon, but came with a debt to pay.

His rump thumped a wall. Holding his breath, he listened. After a space of silence he heard a scuffling, then a sharp cry from the other side of a doorway.

Trying to run fast but remain quiet, Sunbright raced for the door. A glimpse outside made him blink, for the corridor was upside down to the floor. He had no idea how to make the transition from one floor to another. Must he jump up again? Or crawl around the edge? How did the students who worked here manage? The doorway and threshold themselves were wide, and as he sprinted through, he felt the familiar and sickening jar to his guts as the room flipped. But he was through and standing on the sandy, worn boards of the hallway. Evidently the door was charged with an inversion spell that snapped one upright. He gulped bile and carried on toward the sounds of distress.

Knucklebones and the blonde assassin chief grappled in a corner of the hallway. There wasn't much light, only a rectangle of moonglow or the fading luminescence of a gasglobe at one end of the hall. They couldn't have been at it long, for Knucklebones's knife was unbloodied. The Bonebreaker held a sai in one hand, the elongated horns of its hilt holding the elven blade at bay. With her free hand the blonde stabbed stiff fingers for Knucklebones's eye. The thief dodged her head, fast as a snake, while she clung to the assassin's cape and tried to tangle her arm. From behind both came a screaming and pleading to stop, but Sunbright couldn't see from whom.

"Knucklebones!" shouted the barbarian as he ran, sword held in two hands. *"Duck!"*

The thief heard and obeyed, letting go of the cape and jerking her blade from the prongs of the sai. The blonde saw the danger and tried to drop and scrunch behind Knucklebones herself, but the thief flicked her dagger upright, and the assassin flinched back.

Sunbright's sword slammed her across the midriff, cutting her to the spine.

The warrior heaved the heavy trunk off his blade and the assassin crumpled in two halves. Blood had exploded out, fanning over Sunbright's arms and Knucklebones's back as she skittered away. But Sunbright noticed none of it, for he'd seen, in what he now knew to be moonlight, who cowered in the window niche.

Hurodon. The spoiled brat who'd instigated all this.

Hands outthrust, the fop had only time to wail, *"Don't!* I can pay!"

"Aye, that you can!"

Sunbright caught him by the shirt front and yanked him upright. Slamming the young man against the wall, he dropped Harvester to tear the dandy's coin-heavy purse off his belt.

"You'll pay!" the barbarian roared. "Live by the purse, die by the purse!"

With one hand he grabbed the fop's chin, digging iron fingers into his cheeks. Hurodon opened his mouth to scream, and Sunbright rammed the velvet purse into his mouth. He choked and gagged, but the barbarian drove the purse farther in with a heavy fist that also broke teeth. Without a single glance, Sunbright hurled the brat out the window, arms and legs flailing like a doll. A thud and a tearing noise came from below, then nothing.

Knucklebones peered out the window while wiping blood off her face. Hurodon hung, impaled like a bale of hay, across the upright spears of a wrought iron fence.

"That was stupid," she mumbled, spitting blood off her lips. "That purse could've—"

"Some things," Sunbright cut her off, "you can't buy."

* * * * *

Grabbing their weapons, Knucklebones led them out of the building and onto the street. They conversed in whispers as they slid down more alleys, always tending downhill.

"How'd you kill that assassin in the stairwell?"

"Traction to mount the inside wall. Smokepuff to distract him."

"Those are cantras?"

"Yes," she snorted in disgust. "Children learn them in the cradle."

He kept close behind her in the black alleys. "Don't run away from me again. We have to stick together, to protect one another."

"Don't tell me what to do, groundhog, or how to fight!" she hissed. "Your noble barbarian tactics don't work in the city, country mouse!"

That remark panged Sunbright, for Greenwillow had

often called him that. "If we separate we'll be run down and killed."

"If we stick together we all die, you idiot! Only a fool stays to fight. You wouldn't last two days without help."

"I know," he said contritely. "That's why I don't want to separate from you."

"Why?" she asked, flicking him a sidelong glance. "What's it to you?"

"I—you remind me of someone."

"Pandem's Pardon!" she sniped, then spat, "Now I remind him of someone! Who, your mother? Forget what you learned down on the dirt. There are no hero's legends here, no last stands for honor and glory. It's run and hide and steal and don't die!"

Angrily she trotted ahead, and Sunbright was hard put to keep up. He gasped to himself, "Perhaps this is no legend, but there's something noble in you, little Knucklebones. . . ."

* * * * *

Soon Knucklebones led Sunbright onto a low bridge where she scanned in both directions, then vaulted over the edge. They landed in shallow water with a gravelly bottom. Sunbright had seen such streams before and had assumed that someone somewhere set up a magical pump to collect water and let it trickle downhill through the city. There was no end to the enchantments here, but he wondered that the archwizards believed they could exploit magic endlessly.

Under the bridge was a culvert. A grate jammed with trash was welded across it, or so it looked until Knucklebones pronounced "*Wash-ti!*" and sprung the fake welds loose with a cantra. Passing within the culvert, she signaled that Sunbright should muscle the heavy grate back in place, but suddenly froze him with a firm hand. Advancing, she knelt and sniffed along the walls above the water trickle, then ordered them back out.

"There's a wet dog smell. Dogs don't run wild down below . . . we poison them." She paused, sniffing again, then continued, "It must be guard dogs. That's why we haven't seen any city guards in the streets. They're all down below."

"What?" Sunbright asked. He was amazed she could know so much from the slightest clues. "Will the children be safe?"

"Aye. Sleeping Gunn uses a warren of false lofts between warehouses at the docks. . . ."

She chewed her lip, thinking.

"Hurodon's bribery can't affect the whole constabulary, can it?" Sunbright asked. "He couldn't have bought them all!"

"I don't know . . . they've done this in the past, used everything they have in one or two days to sweep the sewers and tunnels. The city council orders it, though they're beholden to Karsus. . . ."

She backed from the culvert, ankle deep in cold water, with bare feet. For the first time, Sunbright saw her tremble with fatigue and hunger as her nose tracked back and forth. Clearly, she was stumped.

He started to say, "Perhaps it's time we—"

Dogs barked, not far off. Two of them in tandem. Men and women shouted. Knucklebones stiffened, her single eye bright, and began to pick along the stream to hide their scent. Sunbright went too, but he saw that the stream soon ducked under a street, an underpass too low to crawl through. At least for him. Knucklebones could probably squirm through a mouse hole.

At the barrier, Knucklebones hopped nimbly up to street level. But the dogs' baying was louder, and now they saw activity, for a yellow glow from the east heralded dawn. As Sunbright gaped, the street globes began to fade.

"We could return to Castle Karsus," he suggested, "hide in Candlemas's room."

"Not by day. Perhaps the docks."

She started downhill again, but Sunbright snagged her thin arm. Tired, she didn't shrug him off.

"What?"

"The ground. We can rest there, repair. Think what to do next."

"Think about what?" she flared. "You think too much. There's survival and nothing else, you great oaf! What do you expect of me, that I aspire to own a house, servants, a coach-and-four? I'd trade your thinking and plans for a warm beer!"

Sunbright let the baying of dogs answer for him.

Knucklebones sighed; a shudder traveled through her whole body. "Very well," she conceded. "Try it."

The barbarian moved off between buildings and knelt. From inside his fire tin he extracted a lock of wiry hair, struck flint and steel, and dropped the hair into the flame to flare and turn to ash.

* * * * *

"Ouch!"

Candlemas slapped the back of his head. A horsefly or bee had stung him—then he realized. Sunbright's signal: the burning of his hair. A call for help.

"Good thing I follow up on my promises," muttered the mage. "I might be stodgy and boring, but I can deliver when asked. . . ."

He'd spent the last few hours asking questions and searching, searching, searching. Karsus's mansions were so huge no one knew them entirely, and there were constant rumors of secret rooms harboring a harem of elven women, a treasure trove including the emperor's crown, a dragon skeleton complete even to its teeth, and blue platforms that could transport one to other worlds.

Perhaps those things existed, but all Candlemas found were rooms of dusty, old-fashioned furniture, chests of faded clothing, and mouse nests. Nothing to covet, so far, but the rumors said that a large room had an outside door—

He found it. In a room like a boathouse, wide and airy, there hung from the rafters gliders like giant butterflies. They were fashioned from welded tubes of some mystery metal he couldn't identify. For once, there was little ornate about them, only the mildest curves and filigree imparted to the pipes and joints. Each glider had three sets of wings: one forward of where a person could sit, another high over the seat, and the third in the rear. The seats were baskets of woven cane. Two seats, usually, though one model sported nine seats with the pilot in front. Flitters, people called them, or gliders, or windriders. There had been a craze for soaring years ago, he'd been told, and every household had boasted one or two down at the docks. But careless, drunken flying sent too many crashing a mile to the ground, shields and levitation spells notwithstanding. And the thrill crazy Netherese grew bored quickly. The only flying they did now was on gold plated dragons, enchanted discs, and giant birds, to hunt humans to death.

Candlemas scratched the itchy spot on the back of his head. Now what in the name of Selûne would power them? A simple flight spell? Could he remember one. . . . ?

* * * * *

Sunbright whirled, poised at the edge of the roof, and kicked viciously. The guard dog yelped and tumbled backward onto the lower roof, bowling its handler back too.

The barbarian ducked a crossbow bolt and dashed across the low roof to where Knucklebones perched behind a chimney. Sunbright peeked and saw guards' helmets shining in the morning sun, just below the rampart.

"We've got the advantage," he puffed. "They're just doing a job for money. We're fleeing for our lives."

"Not much farther, we aren't," gasped Knucklebones. She studied the next wall, gazed at the roof. "Those are slates up there. Slippery. I've got a traction cantra, but you—why did your friend insist we get up high?"

"Don't know."

Crouched behind the chimney, Sunbright honed nicks from his sword blade while he waited for the guards to rush. "What are they waiting for?"

"Reinforcements. A dozen slingers and archers will fix their problem, which is us."

Sunbright nodded gloomily. Fatigue was catching up with him, too. He couldn't remember when he'd slept properly, what with nonstop threats and apocalyptic dreams. He heard dogs growling and snapping, hot to kill something, then shouts of joy as reinforcements arrived.

He tightened his sweaty grip on Harvester. For only the second time in his life, his sword dragged in his hands. The other time had been in hell, where he might return any moment.

"What's that?" Knucklebones whispered as she peered at the roof behind him.

"What's what?"

Sunbright only heard barking.

"That whirring noise. . . ."

Even the guards heard it now. Dogs whined. Sunbright glanced up and saw a giant dragonfly flutter over the roof. Trapped inside it, as if half digested, was a bald, pudgy man.

"Candlemas?"

"Come on!" the thief called.

Energized, Knucklebones scrambled for a handhold, vaulted up to the slate roof, and over. Cursing, but curious, Sunbright bounded after her, slipping and sliding in his worn moosehide boots. He rolled over a section of coping and found himself on a flat, black roof warmed by the morning sun.

The giant insect had released Candlemas, Sunbright saw. Vomited him out as too fat, perhaps. The mage was waving them on, calling out, "Hurry up!"

To Sunbright's wonder, Knucklebones hopped into a wicker seat in the beast's belly. Candlemas began shoving the barbarian, who asked, "What are you doing?"

"Get in!" Candlemas ordered, "I'll see you off!"

"Off what? In what?"

"Shades of Shar, it's a flying machine! Like those golden winged things the Huntsmen use. Get in!"

"What?" the barbarian asked incredulously. "Where are we going?" Sunbright had planted his feet like a mule, and Candlemas couldn't budge him.

"You're going to fly to the surface. It's what you—"

"*Fly?*"

Candlemas grunted as he shoved. In her seat, Knucklebones fiddled with two sticks that tilted the wings in two directions.

"It's what you wanted!"

"But . . . I thought . . ." Sunbright was speechless. "I thought you'd just . . . wiggle your fingers and shift us! Like you did back at Castle Delia."

"Have you got bugs in your brain? The whole enclave is warded against casual magic. You think they'd let people just shift in and shift out when everyone's terrified of assassination? You'd have to go through a transgate, and that's not possible! So, get—*in!*"

With the mage pushing and the thief pulling, somehow they got tall Sunbright folded into the seat. Candlemas began to shove the machine off the roof. Slowly it picked up speed, sliding on thin metal runners.

"I changed my *mind!*" Sunbright wailed.

"Too late! Good luck! Just steer the . . . whatever-they're-called and you'll spiral down like a maple seed!"

The barbarian tried to climb out, but Knucklebones clung to his vest.

"I'll take my chances with the dogs!" Sunbright screamed.

"What dogs?" Candlemas asked, then, "*Aiieee!*"

A pack of slavering guard dogs had bounded another way and been loosed onto the flat roof. Howling, bark-ing, growling, they dived for the two refugees in the glider. Candlemas had fallen on his face, and it was just as well, for a dozen dogs trampled over his back in a frenzy.

Sunbright reared back, crashed on his bottom in the wicker seat, knocking the flying machine so it tilted, then fell off the roof.

Everyone screamed at once, including a dog that had leaped into Sunbright's face. Knucklebones hauled back frantically on both sticks while Sunbright grappled the savage biting, kicking dog. With a tangled kick, he booted the animal straight up into the air.

A rattling glassy tingle sounded as the upper middle set of wings crumpled. The dog tumbled free to crash in the bushes of a garden below. The glider kept falling, soaring outward, skimming treetops, scraping a rocky slope.

Then it sailed off the edge of the floating mountain that was the Karsus enclave and soared into the free, naked, untrammeled air.

Sunbright screamed all the way down.

Chapter 14

The barbarian couldn't see, but he could feel them dropping like a shot duck. He'd tumbled backward onto his rump into the woven seat, so his huge boots stuck out of the side of the tiny vehicle, almost as high as the crumpled wings. He was screaming that he didn't want to fly.

Knucklebones was shouting too. "Turn around, you idiot! Lean out there and *grab that wing!*"

"Lean *out?*"

Sunbright could barely hear her for the rush of air. The flitter hummed like a bowstring in the punishing wind. But it wobbled, too, and waffled and sideslipped and spun and shuddered. They were falling, as Candlemas had said, in a spiral, like a maple seed, but the tubes and struts and flimsy wings vibrated so badly

Sunbright's teeth clattered. Or perhaps that was fear.

"The damned wings got crumpled!" the thief shrilled. "Grab them before they break off and we fall!"

"We *are* falling!"

Sunbright scrambled to drag his boots in and get his rump in the seat rather than his shoulders. But the wild bucking made the task as difficult as mounting a running horse.

"I mean fall like a *rock,* you fool! We're almost gliding now!"

"What do you know about flying?"

She didn't look at him, but peered all around with her one good eye. Her hands were never still on the twin sticks that banked and tilted the wings.

"I know enough to waggle these sticks, and see where those wings are bent and not straight! Grab 'em or we're dead!"

She punched his shoulder for emphasis, the brass knuckles stinging.

What the hell, the fighter thought. They were going to die anyway. And it wouldn't hurt much when they struck—no more than a cow felt the axe in its brain. Grabbing metal tubes not thicker than his fingers, he hauled himself upright—

—and almost started screaming again.

The ground, the entire world, was much closer than it had looked from the inverted bear cave behind Knucklebones's stronghold. Yellow-green fields below gave way to dark forests on the slopes of the purpled mountains that loomed here and there. He wasn't sure of any direction because the whole scene swung in wide, wobbly circles. Below his outthrust boot was nothing but air. It was insanity to fly, he thought again. This was worse than clinging to a dragon's ear.

Another thump rapped his shoulder blades.

"*Graaaaab!*" Knucklebones shrieked.

Clumsily holding on with white knuckles, Sunbright craned overhead. The wings were fashioned of some clear material like glass, only pliable. Laced throughout them were thin wires like the veins in a dragonfly's wing. When the guard dog had crashed into the wings, they'd bent and fractured. Spidery cracks ran through them, and two ends were curled up. Swearing and praying—which was the sky god?—Sunbright unglued one of his hands, reached, and tugged at the wings overhead. They thrummed in his hand, like the flanks of a horse, and the barbarian reflected that the designers really had mimicked a dragonfly when they'd built these. He had to pull hard to drag the wings into position. More of the glassy film crazed, and wires broke. The craft shuddered worse than before, and the barbarian felt terror that they might crumble in his hands.

But as he held on, amazingly, the craft stabilized. The worst of the jostling died away. Only a faint moan and hum was left. Knucklebones hissed as she tugged on the control sticks, but even Sunbright could tell the craft had leveled out, no longer diving, but properly gliding. The ground was so close he saw crows flap out of the tops of elm trees at their approach. Maybe they'd live. The barbarian sighed with relief.

"Thank the gods!" he said, and let go of the wings.

"Don't let go!" screamed Knucklebones.

Twin snaps sounded like whipcracks and immediately they plummeted again.

"Whoooooaaa!" Sunbright screamed as he grabbed wildly for the wings, but the fractured parts snapped off and blew away. As they disappeared, long strips were torn off, then the topmost pair split down their length. He snatched for the edges to hold them in place, but they crumbled into splinters.

Knucklebones was screaming hysterically, something about, *"—going to hit—"*

Trees reared up and clawed at them like monsters with giant, leafy hands. Branches snapped and ripped and slashed. The flitter disintegrated around them. Sunbright made a wild snatch for Knucklebones, to see if he could pull her against his chest, but she was gone. Tubes and wires studded with leaves crashed into his face, smothering him, striking his skull.

* * * * *

Daylight dappled by leaves fluttered before Sunbright's heavy eyelids. His head throbbed abominably, so badly it jarred him awake. He reached to rub his temples and found his arm pinned. It burned too, as if scorched by fire, and ached in a few spots. In fact, all of him ached. But he didn't worry about that—pain never killed anyone, his teachers had loved to note—but being pinned did.

No matter their situation, they had to get clear of this wreck quickly.

Struggling, kicking, grasping, all silently, he fought to open his eyes and clamber free of whatever mess he was tangled in.

Rotating his head, he slowly pieced together the scene, learning among other things that he hung upside down. The flitter had crashed in the branches of an elm tree and still hung there, perhaps thirty feet above the ground. It was in shreds, much of the framework wrapped around his body, with steel fittings and iron leaf edges cutting cruelly. Blood welled in several places, so he'd been unconscious for only a few minutes. Nothing seemed broken, but he ached so much it was hard to be sure.

He cast about for Knucklebones, found her under his right hand, also wrapped in split wicker and tubing. He wondered vaguely if some protection spell didn't linger in the framework, some ward that wrapped the flyers and shielded them in a crash. It wouldn't surprise him. Nothing did when it came to the Netherese and magic.

The warrior gave an experimental rock to see if the flitter dropped any farther, but it hung firm. It had fallen as far as possible and fetched up tight. Carefully prying with strong blood-smeared fingers, he twisted the framework away until he could sit up. Breathing fully again, with his head no longer throbbing, he ripped and tore to free Knucklebones, after first leaning by her cheek to make sure she was still alive, breathing. Her eye patch had ridden up on her forehead. The bad eye was exposed, milky white, with no pupil, and vaguely familiar, though Sunbright couldn't place the vision. Grimacing, he slid the dark leather tenderly in place before tugging her free of the wreckage.

He made a quick check for weapons and found Harvester still home in its back scabbard, Dorlas's warhammer still holstered—he was glad he'd taken the time to stitch them so well—and Knucklebones still had her elven knife. Two blades would keep them alive.

Sunbright hoisted her in one brawny arm. As an afterthought, he wrenched loose a hunk of tubing laced with delicate wires. He could already think of many uses for it. Little else comprised the flyer, and that was smashed to flinders, so he climbed down the tree. Knucklebones was hardly a burden. Sunbright judged she weighed about as much as a lynx. She was certainly as feisty.

Clutching her rag doll limpness, holding overhead with a scratched arm, he crabwalked along a branch, reached the trunk, and picked his way down one-handed. Finally he jumped the last five feet, and felt an unexpected jolt of joy at feeling the earth—the real Earthmother—under his feet. The rush was so exhilarating he wanted to shout with pleasure.

Instead, he scanned his surroundings, looking and listening, then trotted away with Knucklebones across his shoulder.

He'd gone about two miles, mostly uphill and away from watercourses, toward a knot of pines that topped the next hill, when she began to stir, then fuss and struggle to be put down. Sunbright only cooed, "Rest. I'll carry you to safety. We must keep moving."

But she objected, pushing and shoving feebly, squirming so much he finally set her down. She promptly collapsed, but caught herself before tasting turf. Sunbright waited patiently for her to orient, meanwhile he honed Harvester, though it was already razor sharp.

"Where . . . are we?" she groaned, shook her head, and scraped at blood from scratches around her eye.

"A forest." he answered casually. "I'm taking us to cover while scouting for materials."

"Cover? Why? Enemies? Materials?"

Even though her body was weak, her brain fought to defend itself by asking questions, gathering information.

Sunbright didn't argue, just sheathed Harvester, plucked her up across both shoulders like a gutted deer, and trotted quicker uphill. The trees here were maples, their rustling leaves heavier on the south facing side. By jogging from trunk to trunk and slipping behind to the side with fewer branches, he could zigzag quickly.

"I don't know what kind of enemies to expect," he whispered as he puffed along. "But once the forest settles back from that disruption, everything from shrews to vultures will come scavenging. I'd rather learn what's about from a distance."

"What . . . materials?"

"Flint, a likely spear, moss, alder or willow or ash—"

"Flint?" her groggy voice came to his left ear. Despite the rough trip, her head was comfortably pillowed on her hand. "Start fires? What's . . . moss?"

"No, to make spearheads. Gray flint will do to start. It's easier to flake. White or yellow is better, but I doubt we'll find any this high. We need a streambed for that. Moss is for wounds, to keep down infection, and to disguise the smell. But I dislike these woods. The signs are odd."

"Odd . . . ?" But she lapsed out again.

Panting, but glad to run freely for miles without limit, Sunbright reached the knot of pines atop the hill. Crouching, he wove his head back and forth until he found what he wanted: a blowdown. One of the taller trees had toppled in a strong storm. Circling the crater left when the roots ripped out, Sunbright tracked along the high trunk until he found a slot they could slide under. Laying Knucklebones gently on fallen brown needles—how he loved their smell!—he plied the warhammer to break off brittle branches, then laid them butt up against the trunk. In minutes he'd cleared a space big enough to prop Knucklebones against the tree. Turning outside, he broke and laid more branches, and heaped pine needles across the top, but carefully, so as not to dig up deeper needles with their darker color.

He slipped inside, found that the lean-to let him sit up. He piled more needles around Knucklebones for warmth, for she was still groggy. A strut-shaped lump had formed across her forehead, turning a livid purple.

"Stay here and keep quiet," he instructed. "I'll fetch us food." The handful of rations he'd picked from Candlemas's tray had been lost when his haversack was torn in the tree.

Knucklebones started to protest, but slipped into unconsciousness again. When she awoke, Sunbright was hunkered close. Sun slanted through the brown roof at a low angle. She'd slept most of the afternoon away. In the meantime, Sunbright had been busy. He had a brace of dead rabbits and a porcupine, an ingeniously folded box of birch bark that held water, two long, slim staves, and various rocks of different colors. He was industriously slicing a rabbit with his belt knife against a slab of bark, eating every other slice.

The barbarian extended a red hand with a thin strip. Wordlessly the thief took it, though she made a face.

"Can you eat it raw?" he asked.

"I've eaten sewer rats," she replied. "But we always cooked them."

"I won't risk a fire yet. I don't like the looks of these woods."

"What about them?"

Knucklebones was uneasy. She'd never been on the ground in her life, never even known anyone who'd been there—except Sunbright. The earth felt curiously alive under her rump, and the wind hissed incessantly in the trees overhead, talking in its own secret language, speeches alien to her city bred ways. And though she'd been unconscious, she knew they'd come miles. Back in Karsus, she'd known every inch of open space, both above and below the streets, had visited the insides of hundreds of buildings, illicitly or not. But this world was so wide. How much farther could they go? How could any one person ever know it all?

"I'm glad—" she stopped as he looked up, "glad I'm with someone who knows the forest."

The barbarian worked off the rabbit's skin, began to gently scrape the inside.

"I don't know the forest well," he told her. "The taiga and the high sierra, those are the places my tribe visits on our yearly round. This forest is similar to one I knew up north. Though many things are different, I think we can win through."

"How did you catch those animals?"

"Snares. I used wire from the wreckage across a rabbit

trail, then set them again. The porcupine I knocked down with a stick and clubbed. They're so easy to catch my tribe considers it unsporting. But they're good eating when you need it, and we can use the quills later. I've got materials for a simple bow, but I'll need a few hours to assemble one. The arrows will only be good for short range. There are fish in a stream farther down we can gig, or else drop snakeroot in the water to bring them to the surface. But I can't decide if we should stay on the ground or move into a tree for the night. There's bear scat around, but I think it's black bear, not brown. Black bears are harmless, while browns will attack if provoked. No sign of panthers, but this forest is . . . troubled."

"Troubled?"

She remembered his muttering about signs, reflected that for someone who claimed to not know the forest, he knew quite a bit.

"Look," he said and inverted the rabbit skin to show her the eyeless head. The ears looked long and silky and normal, until she noticed a second smaller pair. He showed her a beetle an inch long. When he parted the carapace, the wings were crumpled. "I've never seen or heard of a four-eared rabbit. And beetles are the harbingers of the earth. They're so common, any corruption suggests dangers or sickness hereabouts."

Knucklebones muttered, "It's not the Dire Woods, is it?"

"What?" Sunbright froze. "What's that?"

The thief shook her head as if in dismissal, said, "An old story. Karsus, when he was first fooling with his heavy magic, conjured up such a huge amount that it began, I don't know . . . sucking all the magic from the city, so much the whole enclave tilted in the sky and was in danger of falling. This was years ago.

"Karsus levitated the heavy magic and sent a Tolodine's gust of wind to blow it off the city. It fell, and the city came upright, saved, but after that Huntsmen warned that a reach of High Forest had been struck by the magic. It rolled downhill, scattered all over, and poisoned the place. They called it the Dire Woods after that. Wulgreth, a renegade wizard living there, was turned undead because the magic . . . did something. I don't know what."

"It severed his link to life," Sunbright judged. "These mages extend their lives unnaturally with magic. A dash of corrupt magic like that could remove the life, yet leave the body living—undead."

He shuddered with a barbarian's fear of zombies and liches. But logic prevailed. "True," he mumbled, nodding. "It could be true. It explains the signs. We're not in the Dire Woods, but they're not far. These corrupted animals have strayed from it, or else the bad magic leaked out. How's your head?"

"What? Oh."

Knucklebones touched her forehead, swollen far out by a bruise. She flinched at the pain, tried to rise, but fell back, dizzy. "I wouldn't have this," she accused, "if you hadn't let go of those damaged wings. But we should move."

"I know," he said, smiling, "and I'm sorry, but we won't move yet. Rest."

Darkness had fallen. Sunbright worked by feel to wrap the game in their skins and lay everything where he could find it in the darkness. "Sleep," he whispered, "I'll guard."

She didn't argue, only laid down gratefully as he slid the curtaining branch up and scooted out. Lapsing into glorious sleep, she reflected that, even if she were trapped on the ground, it was nice to have someone watch over *her* for a change.

* * * * *

They camped in that spot for several days, Sunbright catching game and fish, repairing their meager possessions, explaining the way of the forest to Knucklebones. Everything was new to her, and frightening, but they were content to relax and not be hunted.

Too good to last.

Knucklebones came wide awake in their lean-to when, late at night, something smashed its head into her sanctuary.

Knife in hand, the thief rolled out of danger even before she knew what was attacking. Something with a long neck and clashing jaws crashed through the lean-to, scattering pine needles and breaking branches. A pointed snout full of dagger teeth nipped at her heels as she dived like a rabbit for the end of the shelter. Where Sunbright had stopped breaking branches, some were snapped off against the ground while others stuck out whole. Into this tangle of jackstraws the young thief vaulted, until she'd left the raspy-voiced monster behind.

What *was* it? And where was Sunbright?

She heard him shout, the mad, barbaric hollering he made in battle. Was he fighting the toothy beast, or something else? His voice came from the wrong direction, so there were more fiends. Or worse. Flickers of torchlight came and went, so people attacked too.

Wriggling on elbows and knees, Knucklebones followed the tree trunk until she came to a hollow and slithered under. A canopy of brown branches hid her. Readying her knife for a quick thrust, keeping a branch as a screen, she peeked up and out.

The scene was like nothing she'd ever seen in Karsus.

Hunched and brutal men in ragged skins encircled Sunbright. With them were—Knucklebones didn't know what. The beasts were lizards, clearly, with black eyes and shining white teeth like a shark's, and hairless, dappled hides. They were taller than a man, like giant birds without feathers. Saddles with high cantles were strapped about them and they had reins around their snouts. She noted the men wore the hairless skins of the same beasts, seeing clearly by the light of torches held in tall brackets on the rear of the saddles, raised high to tower over the riders' heads. The light wobbled and danced across the forest floor and tree trunks as the lizard mounts tried to kill Sunbright.

The raiders had been four men on four mounts, but Harvester's flashing blade had already killed one lizard and two riders. It was the riderless lizard that had hunted Knucklebones. Perched atop the fallen trunk, Sunbright was surrounded by survivors. The lizards snapped their teeth, threatened to snatch him with long claws and rend him. Just as dangerous, the two ugly men plied short two part spears. A long handle like a throwing stick had a ring around one end, and the stabbing half of the spear slid in and out of this ring. By craning backward, the men could fling the throwing stick at incredible speed, yet yank it back in a second to fling again. Sunbright was already nicked in half a dozen spots, bleeding freely. It wouldn't take much more to weaken and topple him—unless Knucklebones helped.

She couldn't see how, though. In the city, she would circle under cover, get in close to stab from behind, then retreat to safety before being caught. As it was . . .

Sunbright held Harvester in his right hand and kept his left hand outthrust for balance and defense. He had the tree trunk to himself, a tall and solid platform, but he was clearly surrounded with nowhere to retreat. Hurled by a mounted rider, a spear shaft flew, and he sidestepped. The mounted men had the range now, were accustomed to the torchlight, and worked together. As Sunbright sidestepped one thrust, the other rider stabbed from behind. Sunbright caught the flicker at the corner of his eye and slung Harvester backward to bat the thrust away, but the move netted him little, for the rider simply tried again.

The barbarian changed tactics. As the first man thrust, Sunbright swiped and grabbed the shank. Surprised, the man held on, and Sunbright pulled for all he was worth. He flew forward into the face of the lizard thing, which flinched instinctively. In that second, he whipped Harvester up and over. The heavy tip chopped the rider on the shoulder, cutting to the bone so the man dropped his two part spear with a grunt.

Sunbright crowded the lizard beast so it couldn't pull its head down to bite. He snaked Harvester alongside and sawed into its neck, but as he struggled, he realized a fatal error.

Unlike the others, this beast had two heads.

A searing jolt jarred his left arm as he was bitten hard. Teeth like fishhooks ripped his flesh, tore muscle, jerked, and twisted savagely to open a vein. Sunbright grit his teeth to keep from screaming and backed toward the other head to drag the cut. Harvester came with him, and he hauled the pommel back into his gut to twist and slam the beast's neck. But the first head undid him, snapping shut on his wrist. At this rate, he thought, he'd be torn in half.

Then the bleeding rider on the thing's back smashed his spear down on Sunbright's head so hard the shaft broke in three places. The barbarian dropped.

All this happened before Knucklebones could plan an attack. Forest fighting was unknown to her, and her first inclination was to run anyway, leaving the unlucky to die while the rest fled and lived.

But she'd delayed too long, for the riderless beast, questing for fresh meat, circled the tree and found her.

The thief bleated as the lightning fast head stabbed, fishhook teeth clicking shut an inch from her face. She dropped down and made to scuttle back under the tree trunk, but the lizard was faster. At a crash of parting brush she felt the teeth latch on to her bare foot. She shrieked at the pain, jerked, but couldn't free herself. Whipping around to stab with her knife, she only fetched up in branches with sharp points. For a second, panic froze her, for she harbored a special horror of losing her one good eye, and she could easily pop it amidst these splintered branches.

The long necked beast planted bird-like claws and hauled with rapid jerks. Its power was unstoppable. Dragged by her gashed and bleeding foot, the thief was yanked from the shelter as branches snapped and rained.

Barely was she exposed to cool night air before a heavy shape crashed both knees on her spine. She smelled wood smoke, stale sweat, and rancid grease. Still wriggling to get free despite the agony in her shredded foot, a meaty fist bounced off her skull, stunned her, sent waves of white-hot pain through her bruised forehead. Rawhide cords bit her wrists, wrapped so tight her fingers went numb.

She was lost on unknown ground, a prisoner of savages, bleeding, wounded, heartsore. And Sunbright might be dead.

Knucklebones wished she were back in the sewers, taking her chances with spider golems and brutal guards.

Chapter 15

"Sir?"

Candlemas whirled, startled. The woman had entered his workshop silently, even opening the door without his knowing it.

He'd been daydreaming, thinking of Aquesita and when he might visit her. Too, he wondered about Sunbright and that young, one-eyed thief. Were they safe on the ground? And how might he locate them if the need arose? Or would he never see the barbarian again? And why did the loss pang his heart?

And now this girl jarred him from his daydreaming, then stunned him with familiarity. She resembled a young Lady Polaris: white-haired, slim, beautiful in a perfect, porcelain way. But this woman, girl really, had none of Polaris's cold aloofness. Rather, she seemed to cast a warm glow despite her cool looks.

"Sir," she said, in a voice no less beautiful, "do you work with Karsus?"

"Wh-What?" Candlemas stammered, trying not to stare. "Wh-Why, uh, yes. I was his, well, he, uh, called me his 'special friend' for a while. I imagine he's forgotten me by now. Why do you ask?"

Funny, he felt flustered by her star-eyed beauty. Women didn't usually affect him, though Aquesita had possessed his thoughts almost to the exclusion of anything else.

"I was just curious," she answered simply. The girl was slim, almost skinny. A plain gown, unadorned against fashion, hung almost straight from her bony shoulders. "I'd like to know about this new heavy magic of his. Powered by the metal from a fallen star. Has it really given his research a huge jump?"

"Why, yes, it has. Distilling magic by containing it in a crucible of star-metal increases its power. Mages are working now to learn the limits of this super heavy magic, but there doesn't seem to be any. The larger the container and the longer the magic steeps, the heavier it becomes. Like tea growing darker . . ."

He talked on and on, babbling as he did in the presence of Aquesita. The girl listened intently, starry eyes boring into his as if she were reading his mind.

Once she asked, "You must be aware that when Karsus first conjured heavy magic, decades ago, he temporarily disrupted the flow to the mythallars, and the city came close to plummeting. They say he's embarked on a new course, something never before attempted. Any idea what that might be?"

Candlemas shook his head. Her question puzzled him. What, in the annals of magic, had never been attempted before? There was nothing new under the sun.

"Why do you ask? Has Karsus told you anything?"

"Oh, no!" she giggled suddenly, like a child. "I could never get close to Karsus. He'd know me in an instant!"

"But . . ." Candlemas started to say as he backed against the table. It was as if she'd turned cold, but hot inside, like one of Sunbright's polar bears off the icecap. "How? Who are you?"

The frost topped girl stepped closer and said, "My name is Mystra. I was named after the goddess. But better you forget me." Quickly, she leaned forward and pecked him on the cheek. He stood dazed, unmoving.

He was still standing that way minutes later when a sound came from the doorway: a genteel clearing of a throat. He shook his head, dizzy and frightened, though he didn't know why.

Aquesita stood in the doorway. He was surprised, for she'd never visited him in the workshops before. She toted a cloth-covered basket over one arm, and Candlemas saw the top of a wine bottle projecting from it. She'd planned a surprise picnic! Despite his blurry thoughts, he smiled weakly, delighted to see her.

But her short round frame was very erect, her plump mouth creased by a frown. She snapped, "Well?"

"What?" Strangely weak, Candlemas held the table to keep from tottering. "Well, what, dear?"

"Don't you 'dear' me!" Her voice held the whip crack of generations of noble birth. "I saw you kiss that girl! Is that what goes on here when you claim to be working, you consort with hussies? Fondle the apprentices?"

"What?" Candlemas scanned the room. "What girl?"

"In this room, not thirty seconds ago!" Her plump finger stabbed downward, her golden-brown eyes flashed. "She kissed you, and you kissed her back, and she flounced from the room right past me without a word!"

The man wondered which was the worse crime for a woman, being cheated or being ignored. But he hadn't a clue what she meant. There hadn't been any girl. And he always wove personal wards to keep enemies at bay. No one could approach without his knowledge, certainly not close enough to kiss him. But then, his magic was outdated. . . .

"Do you intend to explain," demanded Aquesita, "or just stand there with your mouth open?"

"A spell," Candlemas whined. He felt tipsy, no, drunk. "She . . . I never saw her—must have enchanted me—"

"Pish! You think I wouldn't sense her enchantments? I am cousin to Karsus, you know! I haven't anywhere near his abilities, his genius, but I can detect magic with both eyes shut. She was nothing but a paltry wench with no more magic than my parrot, and skinny besides!"

This was bad, Candlemas knew. He was in trouble with a woman over something only a woman understood. And plump women hated skinny ones worse than poison. But *what* girl?

"The least you could do is apologize!"

Aquesita's voice contained a sob, and Candlemas found hope in that. At least she cared enough to cry over him.

"Sita, please. I'm sorry," he said, though sorry for what he didn't know. "I'm sorry if you're upset."

"Likely!" she blurted. "Likely not! You're . . . you're . . ."

Then she was gone, whirling down the hall in a flurry of skirts and tears. When he made to follow, the door slammed in his face, almost whacking his nose.

"What?" he asked himself. "What did I do? What did she do? Was there a she at all? And if so, why did she kiss *me?*"

* * * * *

Jouncing belly down across a saddle woke Sunbright, and there was pain. Agony tore at every nerve and churned his guts so he vomited down the scaly flank of the raptor. He was horribly thirsty, his throat felt like sandpaper, his tongue was foul. Bound with rawhide, his wrists and feet throbbed as if they'd explode. Only an iron will and stubborn pride made him study his surroundings.

The big lizard picked delicately along a trail on two thin, mincing legs. Sunbright was tied across the empty saddle. He had killed the rider back at the pine tree. Ahead tripped two more raptors, with riders. Knuckle-bones was trussed across the cantle of one of them. Setting sun slanted long through the woods, so Sunbright knew he'd been out most of the day, and they'd traveled far through a forest like nothing he'd ever seen.

Like some nightmare, trees grew every which way. He barely recognized some. As the lizard (bird?) plodded along, he watched a red pine pass. The tree had laid down, its scaly trunk like a serpent, until the end suddenly forked and sprawled in all directions. Some pine needles were excessively long, others stunted. After that came a sassafras tree with leaves like broken hands. Patches of a green ground cover, which Sunbright's people called rabbit-creeper, were tipped with spines like crabgrass.

The prancing lizards flushed a badger hiding in the underbrush. The poor animal was both balding and tufted with coarse gray feathers. Sunbright saw more corruption: mushrooms big as dinner plates and blood red, a frog with four eyes, a purple flower that drooled saliva, and an oak tree whose branches had broken from fifty-pound acorns. He recalled his painful discovery that one of the raptors had two heads.

So these must be the Dire Woods, where Karsus's twisted magic had landed and wrought havoc with trees and flowers and animals. Even the presence of raptors argued skewed magic too, for the old lizard beasts had been dying out for generations, almost prisoners of deep swamps and bogs. Yet here they thrived.

And people? Sunbright hadn't noticed much in the battle by torchlight, but in the dying daylight he noticed the savage rider ahead also sported deformities. The back of his square head had a bald spot like a scar. His elbows bore painful-looking bone spurs that stretched the skin. And his bare feet had only three toes. He must have been born in these cursed woods.

So a whole tribe of savages must inhabit this diseased forest. And Knucklebones and Sunbright were their prisoners, probably not for ransom, perhaps for slavery. But there were plenty worse fates.

Sighing, the barbarian hung his head and rested, harbored his strength for the ordeals that were sure to come.

It was long past dark when firelight announced a camp. One of the savages cupped his hands and bellowed a cry of recognition and boasting. Someone called back, and Sunbright barely understood the words. Then a flock of savages surged around, and it pained Sunbright to look at them.

One man was blind, with no eyes at all, just flesh over empty sockets. A woman had no lower jaw, just a hole in her face ringed by teeth. One child had no arms, while another had three. About half the tribe—forty all told—sported deformities. Most wore skins while some went naked, and still others wore cast-off clothing probably taken from prisoners. Many carried knives of iron or steel.

Jabbering mutants capered around the prisoners until the raptors danced nervously. One rider explained, in garbled words, that Sunbright had killed two fighters. Immediately their families began to wail, and the whole tribe beset the barbarian, slapping, pinching, tearing his hair, gouging at his eyes with filthy thumbnails. Hanging head down, Sunbright dodged as best he could, bit, kicked. But the wailing frenzy increased. Soon he'd be pulled down and torn to shreds. He heard Knucklebones yelp as someone ripped her dark hair. Laughing at his misery, a rider slashed Sunbright's bonds and heaved him off the saddle. Still bound hand and foot, he flopped in cinders and dust, was kicked and stomped with horny, bare feet, prodded with knives, rammed with spear butts. Someone wrenched his hair and jerked his head back while another put a flint knife to his throat. He kicked, flailed with his arms, bit an ankle, got kicked in the teeth. He couldn't see for dust and feet, and soon he'd be blinded. He hoped Knucklebones had the sense to cut her own throat before she was skinned alive.

The kicking, beating, and prodding stopped. The crowd fell away. Sunbright pried his eyes open to see why.

A great hand came down, caught the front of his tattered goatskin vest, hoicked, and slammed him to his feet.

A giant faced Sunbright. The man was a full head taller than the captive barbarian, as broad across the shoulders as a wagon, with hands as big as snowshoes. A massive, shaggy head was covered in coarse, red-brown hair. He was brimming with energy, but curiously lifeless, for his skin was a ghastly white, his muscles knotted but grainy. He wore almost a full raptor skin. The white scaled breast hid his own and the warty hide covered his back, hanging to his knees as if he'd hollowed the animal out and climbed inside. A necklace of raptor teeth like white fishhooks clattered around his neck.

But his eyes Sunbright noticed most. They were dead white with gray flecks, like chips of granite. Sunbright couldn't understand how the giant could see, yet the eyes bored into the barbarian as if taking his measure.

Superstitions welled in the barbarian's mind, made his flesh crawl. He'd seen many frightening things tonight, but this fiend was the worst. It must be Wulgreth, once a mighty wizard who'd lived too long by infusing himself with magic, until the day Karsus's corrupted heavy magic blanketed these woods and erased his life, leaving him animated, but not alive. Undead.

Abruptly, the giant shoved Sunbright to crash on his rump in dust and ashes. He saw by smoky firelight that the camp was only a jumble of huts and lean-tos and brush piles scattered through a grove of stunted oaks. On the outskirts were tipsy corrals holding raptors who hooted and squabbled and battled amongst themselves. The central fire pit sprawled like a black smear, and garbage and bones littered the ground. At every step, flies rose in clouds.

The giant addressed his tribe, hollering in their guttural accent, thumping his chest for emphasis. Wulgreth was king. Claimed right to first fight. Owned one-eyed girl. She'd be wife, or (to laughter) dinner. Did anyone contest that and, so, want to die?

There were no objections. Wulgreth bawled orders, and Sunbright was manhandled by half a dozen men and women. His remaining bonds were slashed so his hands and feet prickled with returning circulation. Before he could fight back, he was stripped of everything: Harvester and scabbard, belt and warhammer, haversack and canteen, vest and shirt. Even his knucklebone pendant was ripped away and his worn moosehide boots were shucked off. The iron rings would be priceless goods to these destitute savages.

Painfully, his clumsy hands and feet almost useless, Sunbright rolled to his knees to rise.

A huge foot almost kicked his head off.

The barbarian heard the scuff of a bare sole, saw the flicker of motion by firelight, and ducked just in time. Still, the kick creased his shaved temple and stunned him. Flopping on his rump, he heard the tribe howl with glee. His crippled hands and feet cramped, but he had to rise or be stomped to death. Gasping, he rolled to one side, felt the earth shake as Wulgreth crash-landed with both feet where Sunbright had just lain. Mutants cheered.

Hobbling, Sunbright crouched on numb feet barely in time to meet Wulgreth's charge.

Screaming, the giant ran at the barbarian with both fists locked. Sunbright limped aside, flung up both hands to deflect the blow. Uselessly. Fists like rocks hammered his shoulder, almost broke his collarbone. He was knocked aside like a doll to bite dust again.

This wasn't a fair fight, he reflected bitterly, it was a massacre, a savage beating such as Karsus's city guards might inflict. And it was Karsus's magical mistake that had turned Wulgreth into this hideous form. The arms of the Netherese Empire were long, grasping, callous, and cruel.

Sunbright spit dust, rolled to all fours. Some feeling had returned to his hands and feet. If Wulgreth could fight dirty. . . .

The giant had been crowing, arms in the air, calling his own name as a battle cry, exulting in wild applause and shrieks. Now he marched across the dirty arena and reached for the barbarian's horsetail to yank him upright.

Stooping, Sunbright clutched a double handful of dirt and ash, threw them into Wulgreth's dead stone eyes.

To no avail. The giant barely blinked, snagged Sunbright's hair and dragged him close. His scalp burning, Sunbright crowded the giant, bunched his fingers and rammed them into the brute's throat. The jab would have killed a normal man, crushed his windpipe, made him strangle.

Ignoring the blow, Wulgreth waded in, smashed a

forearm across Sunbright's throat, and snatched the back of his neck. Choking, the barbarian struggled, beat Wulgreth's head, kicked his knees and groin and instep. Nothing worked. The undead man couldn't feel pain. Meanwhile, Sunbright would either be strangled or have his neck snapped.

Yet Wulgreth didn't want to kill his plaything. Instead, he shifted his grip, locked Sunbright's wrist, sucked wind, and shoved.

Sunbright's arm snapped at the elbow. A double bone in his forearm jutted through the skin. Blood spurted. But the magically infused Wulgreth jammed a horny thumb against the wound and sealed it, though the bone still bent crookedly. Sunbright was oblivious to the details. Electric pain coursed through his body and blotted out everything else.

Enjoying the torment of his victim and the cheering of the tribe, Wulgreth stamped on Sunbright's foot to pin it, then wrenched the broken arm high overhead. Grinding bones broke anew, then Sunbright's ankle popped.

Released, the barbarian collapsed to jeers from the crowd. Wulgreth's stony hand crashed down on Sunbright's chest and broke ribs. More blows pulped other bones.

Shock and pain flooded Sunbright's mind like a tide, and he blacked out.

He awoke to a buzzing, like bees. A whole hive, it seemed, crawled over him with red-hot stingers.

Then a stick pried at his eyelids. He fought it, but couldn't move his head, which was tied in place. When his eyelid was finally dragged up, he saw a child holding a smoldering stick. Other children swarmed around him. He was staked on the ground, spread-eagled, near the fire. Urged on by adults, the children picked up coals and burning brands to tentatively scorch Sunbright's flesh. It was a lesson in torture. Sunbright smelled his own flesh burning, gargled a cry at this unending nightmare. At least the pain couldn't get much worse, he thought vaguely.

Then a boy dropped a red coal on his eyelid, and he learned about pain.

* * * * *

Hours later, Sunbright, or what was left of him, was dumped in a hut alongside Knucklebones.

The thief started from a near trance. So far she'd been ignored, left as a plaything—or supper—for Wulgreth. With her shredded foot, bitten deep by the raptor, she could hardly stand, let alone flee, even if she weren't surrounded by enemies. She'd merely hunkered with her arms around her knees, head down, trying to ignore Sunbright's torture, wishing she were elsewhere. Once, when a scream had ripped out, she'd uncurled and bolted from the hut. But a man and woman guarded her, and she'd been clubbed flat, kicked savagely, and booted back into the hut. Since then she'd blanked out the world.

Now it was back, in the form of a bleeding and burned Sunbright. The savages had given up, unable to keep him conscious. Now they sat around the fire and crowed of their triumphs. They laughed in their cruel recitations, and promises of more to come.

Toughened by a hard and harsh life, Knucklebones could stand almost anything, but this wreck of her companion was beyond endurance. His bones were broken, hair singed off, body seared in half a hundred places.

Yet he was alive, croaking, "Knuck . . . ?"

"Yes, yes!," she sobbed, "I'm here!" She cried real tears for the first time in her life. "But there's nothing I can do!"

"Water . . . please . . ."

Weeping, Knucklebones crawled to the hut door. On

her knees, she begged her guards for water, using hand gestures. They both laughed, and when she came closer, kicked her in the face. Tearfully she told Sunbright of her failure.

"S'aright . . . Not to blame . . . Harmed you?" His words were mushy, for even his tongue had been burned, and he stared at the roof of the hut as if blind. Probably he was.

"No, no, they haven't, but . . ."

She couldn't believe he, tortured and abused, thought of her safety. Oh, she thought, how cruel the gods were to send her such a man and then snatch him away! Or how cruel were *people*.

These last few hours had wrought wonderful and awful changes in Knucklebones's breast. Of course she'd had friends in the sewers of the city: Ox and Lothar and Mother, other unlucky souls like herself. And she'd had lovers too. Too many to count when your life was measured in days. Men who'd enjoyed her body but never touched her heart, and then Sunbright had literally dropped upon her like something from a dream. A tall, bronzed man, hard and tough as an oak tree, tough as she was, yet with a gentle and kind spirit even the city couldn't crush. He'd followed her everywhere, looked after her, cared about her, and she hadn't shown him a jot of gratitude or sympathy, for the iron that protected her heart was the hardest part, and she was afraid to open up lest it crack and leave her helpless, snuffed out by the cruelty of the city.

But in the hours she'd hunkered here, she'd prayed to every god she knew, but mostly Mystryl, Lady of Mysteries, Mother of All Magic. Mystryl was the goddess of lovers, and the poor, and those in dire strife. Never had Knucklebones been in worse trouble, nor cared so much to see someone else helped, and been herself so helpless.

And worse than useless, for she had no comfort for him.

She touched his singed scalp, recoiled at the clammy feel of his skin, hot and cold and wet and dry at the same time. He raged with fever while shivering with chills. For lack of anything better, she peeled off her leather vest and laid it gently on his scorched breast. "I don't . . . What can—"

"Try to . . ." his voice rasped, ". . . find knife or stick. Kill . . . yourself . . . before start on you . . ."

"Yes, I will," she whimpered. "I promise. I will, Sunbright."

"*Oh!*"

She flinched in sympathy with his new pain, but he was shaking his head in wonder.

"Wha—What is it?"

"Never . . . said my name . . . before . . ."

Then he sighed and blacked out again.

It was true. She'd only called him by nicknames. All this time, even "Country Mouse," which she'd never even thought of before meeting him. In her own way, she'd been cruel, for he was as lonely as she was, homesick and far from his home.

He lay still, barely breathing, just a trace of husky whistling.

"I promise you, Sunbright."

She would kill herself, and take Wulgreth with her, though she doubted it was possible. He was a zombie king, a wizard lich, undead, and how to kill one of them? But she'd try. She'd keep herself alive to try. And remain alive while Sunbright lived.

Which wouldn't be long, she sobbed. It was clear Sunbright was dying.

Chapter 16

"Now, watch!" yelled Karsus. "This is one of the cleverest uses of all!"

The mages, Candlemas among them, stood on the balcony of a mansion overlooking a bridge that spanned a canal. A lesser mage waited with a bucket. Karsus waved a hand, and the mage walked onto the bridge, then chanted as she upended the pail. Candlemas didn't see anything happen. The bridge was slate flagstones on a stone foundation, and the bucket's "water" actually super heavy magic, but it left no wetness. The magic just seemed to disappear. Still, the mage crept gingerly along the bridge's railing until she reached solid ground. Candlemas scratched his bald head. He didn't see any effect.

Yet Karsus almost danced with glee, rubbing his

hands, giggling. Other mages waited patiently. Karsus gave a call, and down the path from the opposite side a stable boy led a white horse. Karsus waved him on and the boy stopped at the edge, pointed the horse to the bridge, cooing and patting it, then slapped its rump.

The horse tripped across the bridge, got about halfway, and plunged down through the center. It vanished for only a second, then reappeared underneath whinnying in fright, then crashed, half in and half out of the canal. It thrashed and kicked its back legs, shrilling. One of its front legs was bent at an acute angle.

Karsus howled with delight, "See? It's one thing to create a phantom bridge. It's another to pour heavy magic on a *real* bridge that dissolves the stone and instantly takes its place! You could use it anywhere: a staircase, a street. You could fashion half an acre of a phantom plaza, say, and stampede people into it and drop them right off the enclave! And once you'd made up the magic, you could hurl it in catapults so it dropped out of the sky and mimicked whatever it hit. You'd have invisible potholes and death traps all over the enemy city! Or put it in the privy. Wouldn't that make a rare joke, a phantom toilet seat! Oh, think what you could do!"

Candlemas thought of a few applications, and wanted to apply some to Karsus. That horse had a broken leg. And although he knew horse leeches could do much with magic, repairing a horse's complicated, delicate leg was out of the question. That animal would be destroyed, its throat cut for no reason other than for Karsus's egomaniacal demonstration.

Yet one of Karsus's crawlers offered a more insidious way of killing with heavy magic. Insinuate heavy magic into someone's ear, then call a charm to flip the "magic dagger" at a right angle, tearing a great channel through the brain. Candlemas couldn't help wonder if someone hadn't tested that one already.

There were more deadly tricks in days to follow. One apprentice drew praise when he constructed a block of heavy magic a foot high and six feet long. For the demonstration, the block was colored a very pale yellow, like a box full of sunshine. The block was infused with Aksa's disintegrate spell. The eager youngster picked up a wooden stick and swiped it at the block. At the end of the swipe, he'd lost a foot of wood. This trap, he explained, could be laid across any narrow street or sidewalk. With the yellow dye removed, it would be almost invisible, impossible to see at night by gasglobe. And just lying there would do its work.

"I know," Karsus crowed. "I know how it would work! Only a genius of my stature could discern this. If someone walks into it, his *foot* would be instantly disintegrated! He'd lose a limb, fall down, and bleed to death. Even someone with working wards might miss it because it's so low to the ground. Oh, and think! You could make two layers, with a dimensional door behind them. If his foot is snipped off and he falls, he'd tumble in and vanish entirely! Oh, very clever, Krikor, very clever! You may sit at my right hand at dinner tonight!"

The youngster beamed. Candlemas rubbed his bald head.

More mayhem was created: incendiary clouds like slow billowing fireballs, masses of bright lights that pulsated fast and slow, able to hypnotize, or blind, or induce seizures. There was a transportable Proctiv's rock-mud transmution spell that could dissolve a whole hillside. "Mice mines": Karsus's green mice, released with tiny packets of heavy magic to infiltrate houses and cause random explosions. Even pointed slivers of heavy magic that could be inserted into fruits and vegetables. Overnight they would convert sugars into natural poisons like arsenic, nightshade, or belladonna.

It was too much for Candlemas. Once, when Karsus was striding down a corridor babbling about the success of the latest experiment, he blurted out, "By Jergal's Quill, Karsus, what *is* all this destruction for?"

The wild-haired mage stopped capering and stared with golden eyes.

"Who are you?" he asked blankly. "Oh, Candlemas! Yes, you were my special friend. Well, since it's you, I'll tell. But you must promise to keep it a secret."

The pudgy mage wanted to swear, but refrained. Fifteen mages trailed Karsus with an equal number within earshot. Beaming, the archwizard forgot about the oath of secrecy and stage-whispered, "This is something the city council has been toying with. You know them, always busy." Catering to Karsus's whims, Candlemas knew, but he leaned forward as if enthralled. "Anyway, and don't tell a soul, they're thinking of starting a war."

"*War?*"

"Shhh!" Karsus waggled a finger. "Don't be a blabbermouth! Yes. I asked them if we might use these war machines on the borders, but we're at peace with everyone, drat it, and our neighbors would take offense if we attacked. Soooo, we're going to stage a war between *cities!*

"Ioulaum has agreed to partake, and one other, as yet to be named. It shall be a battle between the first and greatest. The first city, that's Ioulaum, since he was the first to float one, and Karsus, which is the greatest city because it's named after me!"

Despite Karsus's shushing, the mages in the corridor were buzzing, and others leaned out of doors and windows for the news. Candlemas rubbed his scalp and found it sweaty.

"I don't think—"

"Oh, you don't need to!" Karsus cut him off. "All the city councilors agree with me. It will be great sport!

And allow us to playtest our new weapons for when we *do* seek to invade a neighbor. Also, the councilors reckon it will distract the populace from the famine—keep them from starting food riots and other trouble!"

"Great sport." Candlemas kept his voice cool. "Except that people will die. Children will die."

"No, no, no. Not *important* people, no archwizards, just commoners! Though some of the noble sons want to test their prowess in battle, it's said. Instead of dueling in the streets, they can do it on the battlefield, once we have one. Anyway, everyone's very excited, and buying new clothes and weapons and medals, and getting ready to host war balls and celebrations! It'll be simply grand!"

"Grand," echoed Candlemas weakly. Karsus's entourage swept away, jabbering and laughing and making bets and plotting mischief.

How, the pudgy mage wondered, in the name of the gods could anyone think a war was fun? Hadn't they read any history, visited any ruins, heard stories of death and devastation? War was not a village football game, where you chose sides and donned costumes and fooled around until you were tired, then drank the night away. It was death and insanity.

But then, no one in the city was sane except him.

And Aquesita. With a pang, he wondered what she thought of this war nonsense. He couldn't know, for she refused to see him. He'd been turned away from her door by bodyguards, had his letters sent back unopened, even had flowers returned. All because he'd kissed a phantom girl. Or perhaps some other reason he didn't know. Old as he was, he was new to this love business.

Love and war, he thought grimly. Neither made sense.

* * * * *

Sunbright was dying.

He knew he was dying because he didn't care. Only people with a spark of life worried. Once past that barrier, the journey turned interesting, he found, for he was sinking into the earth. On the floor of the hut lay the burned, broken hulk of his body, and far below sank his spirit, moving on to a new life, or the next plane, or wherever.

Dimly, he wondered where. His people had many legends about death, all contradictory. That a spirit entered a nearby being just born, a musk ox, or a bluebell flower, or a baby; so the living, especially children, must be polite to any living thing, for it might be an ancestor. Or that one's spirit traveled to a distant mountaintop and joined the wind, blown around the world eternally to observe and occasionally visit, which explained ghosts. Or that one's spirit simply went to a spirit world to stalk spirit elk and spear spirit salmon. Sunbright had always fancied that last idea.

Instead, he sank. Idly, he watched roots pass by, then a mole, a rock, then yellow sand. Odd, but perhaps the spirit world was below, not above. Spirits could go anywhere, after all.

Too bad he had to leave Knucklebones alone, but then she was alive and so no concern to him. Certainly the living cared little for the dead. He wondered who he'd meet in the spirit world. Old friends? Enemies? His father, Sevenhaunt? That star-eyed woman of his dreams, whoever she was? Was she Mystryl?

Greenwillow? Perhaps so, if she were truly dead. Sunbright had never really believed she was, but now he might find out. Unless, of course, she weren't dead and he were, in which case he'd never find her.

That slowed his sinking. Perhaps he didn't want to leave life behind . . .

But something was happening around his feet.

The underworld or afterlife had begun to shine. A faint glow illuminated his toes (like Knucklebones's glowlight cantra), then his legs, then his whole body. What caused the glow?

It was greenish and deep, like the ocean when his tribe hunted seals in winter. An underground ocean? Was there such a thing? Why green? That was the color of nature magic, wasn't it? But why here? This part of the world had been saturated in heavy magic, a corrupt force rained down by Karsus in his mad experiments. Why the green—

Then he got it.

Every place had its own magic: forest magic, sea magic, sky magic, mountain magic. Candlemas had argued that all magic was the same, a simple force like fire that could be used for good or evil, or just its pure self, as fire could torture a man, or cook his food, or forge his tools.

This healthy forest had possessed its own magic, long ago, before corrupt heavy magic rained from the sky like black snow. But the forest magic hadn't vanished, or been consumed. It had simply been crushed deep into the soil by the heavier magic.

Hence this faint green ocean, like an underground reservoir. It had collected here and drawn more nature magic to itself, as streams ran to the ocean and became one.

So Candlemas was wrong, he thought. Too bad Sunbright would never be able to tell him.

But why had Sunbright been drawn to this spot? He was dead, or dying, beyond the need for magic. Besides, as a shaman he was a failure. He'd lost a good part of his soul to a wraith in the Underdark, and had never recovered it. So even when alive—

—Unless he were still alive, and only sending his spirit winging, flying out of his body to search for knowledge and portents, help and hope.

Astral projection, some called it. Dreamwalking. Spirit sending. Ghosting.

What was the knowledge his spirit sought? That the flood of corrupt magic was only temporary? That it would eventually peter out, and the natural magic return, though it might take decades? Scant comfort to the cruel mutants caught in its web, or their undead leader who clung to a mockery of life.

Or was the knowledge for *him?*

In a way, Sunbright reflected, the hole in his soul left by the wraith was like the corruption in the forest. The gap in his spirit kept him from realizing his true potential, as the corrupted magic blocked the nature magic.

So, could this forest magic help him? Was that why his spirit sank here? Or had it been steered here by a benevolent god or goddess? Wasn't this the sort of miracle visited by Mystryl, Mother of All Magic, who controlled the Weave that formed the base of all magics?

If that were the case, and he belonged here, then he should use the magic as intended. As shamans used it, for healing, for reading the future, for protecting the tribe and the balance of life between people and plants and animals, wind and water and weather, between sky and soil.

Could he use it?

What had he to lose? Wasn't he dead now? Or dying?

Contemplating, Sunbright laid back in the vast ocean of green-tinged magic, like a bather giving in to the sea's embrace, so he floated on top of it, let it run over him and around him and through him.

And while surrendering his body and spirit, he let his mind drift. Far out went his senses, smell and sight and sound. He heard the chuckle of the magic, like currents on a riverbank or waves on a sand shore, in the voice of birds and the cries of children at play, in the hiss of the wind through mountain passes, in a whisper—the voices of Greenwillow and Knucklebones. He smelled the magic, the green of it, like growing grass in springtime, and the breath of flowers—the scent of Greenwillow and Knucklebones—the tang of pine in the high sierra, the fruity yeast of grain in the fields. He saw the green of magic in the curl of flowers, the turn of a bat's ear, the busyness of a squirrel scaling an oak, the break of a cloud readying to rain, the exquisite diamond cut pattern of snowflakes, and the swell of a woman's breast and hips—the curves of Greenwillow and Knucklebones.

Lying, listening, smelling, feeling, Sunbright came to know the magic of nature as few men or women ever had. For he'd surrendered everything, eschewed everything, even his body and life. And going where others feared, he learned how green magic, and man, and the world, fit together.

And how to link one with the other with the other . . .

* * * * *

Knucklebones sat with her arms wrapped tight around her knees, head down. Sunbright was a scorched lump alongside her. Hours before he'd given up his ghost, sighed one last time in a grotesque death rattle, and expired. Knucklebones was alone now, lame with a festering foot, unable to flee, surrounded by enemies with fiendish plans.

And now the greatest of them filled the doorway of the tiny hut.

Wulgreth stared at her with stone dead eyes. He still wore his lizard skin robe with the scaly white breast, but he'd belted Harvester of Blood awkwardly around his middle. Knucklebones's own dark elven blade was thrust through the other side, and her fingers itched to snatch it.

The lich lord bent for a second, prodded Sunbright in

his eye with a sharp fingernail, drew no response. Dead as cordwood. Wulgreth said something she didn't understand, a guttural growl. He waggled a craggy hand, signaling that she should follow.

Knucklebones felt partly dead already, for she'd blanked Wulgreth out of her mind, refused to acknowledge he was real, or that Sunbright was really dead. So the rough hand snagging her hair and dragging her forth surprised her, as did the agony of her hair being ripped out by its roots. She'd thought she was beyond feeling, but the dragging of her skin over dirt, the twisting wrench to her hair, and the thumping of her festered, swollen foot shook off her self-induced trance.

Was she to be wife or supper? Which was worse, not that she had a choice? If he were to gut her and eat her, he'd need to ply a knife, and that gave her hope, for perhaps she could wrest it away and—what? Pierce his throat? Hamstring him? Carve out his heart? He was undead, and probably impossible to hurt. But she'd try.

If she were to be wife, she'd kick and scream and punch until she was clubbed unconscious. He'd never defile her body without killing her first.

Once she cried out: "Sunbright!"

She wished he could fight alongside her, give her courage, make her feel again. But a heavy hand slapped her face, almost dislocated her jaw, set nose and tongue bleeding. She couldn't even bite him, for it wouldn't hurt—

What was happening?

Lying on one hip, her head hoisted by her hair, Knucklebones felt the earth tremble, as if a mythallar engine stuttered.

Whatever it was, the sensation was new to the tribespeople, for they howled and gibbered in fear. Some fell and clutched the earth, crying like babies, babbling in fright. Others clutched trees. Wulgreth let go of Knucklebones's hair so her head thumped the dirt. The undead wizard cast about, but couldn't find the source of the disturbance.

The campfire winked out, leaving them in early morning blackness. There were more howls and screams like demented monkeys, then the fire returned, a bright cone shining up from the blackened pit. But no, not fire, for this light was greenish. Knucklebones stared. What was it? No force or light she'd ever seen, though it resembled her own glowlight cantra, but a thousand times brighter.

The fire pit split open as if from an earthquake. The light was very bright, but by squinting Knucklebones just made him out. Straddling the hole, a hole big enough to swallow a man, or spit one out, was Sunbright, hale and hearty.

His bright blond hair was combed neatly into a horsetail with the temples shaved. His red shirt was restored, thick and soft, laced over with his calfskin vest brushed smooth. His boots were solid, the iron rings that the savages had fought over restored and stitched tight to jingle musically. His belt buckle shone, and Dorlas's hammer lay tucked in its holster. Even Harvester was returned to its master's back. Half prone, Knucklebones could see Wulgreth had lost it. As he'd lost his confident swagger and prideful stance. He was clearly flummoxed by this miraculous return of a vanquished enemy.

Knucklebones didn't understand either. A quick glance showed, by the light he shed, that Sunbright's body no longer lay in the hut. So this was no angel, no spirit, but the real man truly restored. Then she recognized his voice.

"Wulgreth!" called Sunbright. "Prepare!"

Chapter 17

"There! How do we look?"

Enthusiastic applause.

Karsus had arrived this morning in his latest finery. Instead of his usual ratty robe, he wore a blue-green tunic with a bold **K** emblazoned on the breast. The military cut sported a high, embroidered collar and stiff jutting wings at the shoulders. A jewelled baldric hung from one shoulder and banded his waist, and a silver sword with a tiger head pommel rattled at his side. On his head was a helmet of boiled leather, so laden with silver and gold wire it kept tipping over the mage's wild golden eyes. Add to that his frazzled hair sticking out from under it, and that his neck and bare feet were still filthy, and the effect was ludicrous, as if the village idiot had stumbled into a chest of old uniforms.

Candlemas applauded with the other toadies, and hated himself for it. By approving and helping in this war nonsense, he was furthering the empire's insane plans.

Though "plans" was too adult a word to give to these proceedings. The new craze for warfare was more like the antics of boys dashing though gardens with sticks for swords.

Yet everyone partook, for the empire had been hideously bored and seized on this new game with both hands. Tailors and seamstresses and milliners throughout the city hired extra help and slaved night and day to fashion military style clothes for the empire's elite, and male and female archwizards down to the lowest apprentices competed to wear the wildest designs possible, until the streets and glittering balls resembled peacock farms.

For all their hasty preparations, no one was sure if war had officially been declared, for no shots had yet been fired. But the "enemy," Ioulaum, Karsus's sister city, had drifted up from the west until its buildings could be plainly seen. Candlemas was surprised at how small it was. He'd seen it once, over three hundred years ago, and it had seemed huge. It was, in fact, scarcely a tenth the size of the city of Karsus. It was the first floating enclave, created and ruled by Ioulaum, one of the oldest known wizards. At this range, his high-turreted castle resembled a king's crown. It looked strange sitting atop an inverted mountain, nothing more than a cone of rock hanging in the sky, oddly contrasting with the real, upright mountains in the far distance.

But Ioulaum was girded for war, people said, and everyone must prepare. Even dowdy Candlemas had been coerced into donning a yellow robe with bright red stripes, and a wide, studded belt hung with a long dagger he'd found hanging on a wall in his chambers. A little round hat wobbled on his bald head, and stiff boots cramped his toes. It made him miserable, for he hated finery and fluff.

Miserable too because he couldn't show his new garb to Aquesita. She still refused to see him, and he pined until he could think of nothing else. His best hope was his latest letter, a long, slobbering missive of apology, though he was still unclear of his lover's crime. It hadn't been returned, so presumably she'd read it. He hoped so.

"Candlemas! Are you daydreaming?"

"What?"

He shook his head. People stared at him, some glaring because he dared to nod off before Karsus. The archwizard didn't seem to notice. He was familiar with bubbleheads. "Yes?" Candlemas said, "A hundred pardons, O Great Karsus."

"Uh, uh!" Karsus tilted his head back to see under the brow of his bulky helmet as he spoke. "*General* Karsus! The city council agreed unanimously to declare me commander in chief for the duration of this great struggle for survival in which we are engaged."

More applause.

Candlemas stifled a groan. Of course the stupid turds on the council would vote for that. They'd grant anything Karsus wished. As for a "great struggle," Candlemas was appalled at how seriously people took it all. They'd even dredged up old grievances with the people of Ioulaum, feuds dead for centuries, as an excuse for aggression. The city of Ioulaum favored eagles as their mascots, it was said, and eagles preyed on white storks, the beloved symbol of their "homeland," Karsus. An old border dispute had been dusted off. Foolishness about an abandoned valley that belonged to Karsus's grandparents but that Ioulaum had "usurped" to mine for silver. Another cause for war between cities floating in the sky!

Even the ground below was disputed. The peasants

there farmed for Karsus, mostly, but Ioulaum had sent raiders into their territory. Every ill the city suffered, from poor tasting water to peeling paint was blamed on Ioulaum. All foolishness, of course. What did Aquesita make of it?

But Candlemas had drifted off again while Karsus jabbered. " . . . Major Candlemas. No, that lacks something. Ah, *Colonel* Candlemas! Better sounding, is it not? Yes, I've asked that you oversee the first repulse of the villains who dare defile our beloved land."

Candlemas (Colonel?) blinked and sputtered, "M-me? I-*I'm* to lead a m-military expedition? I don't know anything about tactics! I've never . . ."

Karsus stared at an iron sconce above the mage's head. "You were a steward, weren't you?" the archwizard asked. "That means you know how to ride a horse and oversee peasants, or whatever stewards do. It won't be a bother. Just go with the lads and stand behind them in case of archers. There's a military tactic! See them off, then return in the boat."

There was a brief space of silence, finally broken by a cheerful Karsus, who said, "Off you go! When you return, I'll give you a medal!"

Staggered, Candlemas stared. But the ring of frowning faces told him to keep mum and do as he was bid. If he balked, plenty of other toadies would take his place, and Candlemas might find himself out on the street. What would he do then?

Not that he knew what to do now . . .

"Very well, Great, uh, General Karsus. I hear and obey."

Feeling a total fool, he threw a sloppy salute. Karsus clasped his hands and giggled with delight as Candlemas marched off down the corridor in his tight boots, trying not to sigh. Leading a raid? Well, how bad could it be?

It took a while for the carriage driver to find the right

dock in the right part of the city, for the war had everything discombobulated. Wagons jammed intersections and soldiers tramped hither and yon, drilling. Furthermore, to add to the immediacy, city guards with red armbands stopped and searched wagons and carriages for "contraband" or "needed war matériel." This was, of course, an excuse to do a bit of pilfering in the emperor's name. If indeed the war were intended to distract the populace from rioting, it was working, for he saw no signs of dissent. Of course, anyone protesting the war was hurled into prison as a spy and traitor.

Eventually Candlemas spotted troop boats arrayed at a dock. Each was a long, narrow wooden hull like an oceangoing dromond, or open peapod. Instead of sails or oars it wore a long metal foil stretched overhead from horizontal masts, designed to catch the sun's rays. Candlemas didn't know how it worked, except it was powered mainly by magic. Ostensibly in charge of this raid, or counterraid, against Ioulaum's troops, Candlemas tiptoed toward a clutch of young, gaily clad officers. They hadn't a clue who was in charge, but stood around boasting of their triumphs to come.

Finally Candlemas picked out the most elderly, grizzled, and scarred sergeant in the ranks. He introduced himself, stumbling over "Colonel" Candlemas, and told the sergeant to take complete command. The old man sighed in gratitude. He had had enough of idiot officers changing their minds by the minute.

Candlemas watched the preparations and got his first good look at the empire's finest troops. He was shocked. He'd imagined what he'd seen three centuries before: tall, square-jawed men and women scarred by training and battle, cool and steely-eyed, capable of slaying men or monsters. The Netherese Empire hadn't been built on dreams, after all, but by plying effective tools such as hard trained, capably led, and well rewarded soldiers.

But here were either gangly, underfed youths who'd fled farms and alleys, or else fat, slovenly "veterans" who'd found a soft life in the barracks.

The officers were mostly bored nobles' sons seeking adventure and an eye-catching uniform. The only hope for the empire were the sergeants, but while most had combat experience, the empire's last thrusts had occurred decades ago. Worse, soldiers and officers were cocky, confident of success, eager to fight, happy to be doing something instead of gambling and arguing in their barracks. Candlemas watched the sergeants shake their heads and mutter portents of doom.

But eventually the troops were marched aboard, the landing ramps drawn up. The small navy crew called orders, and the ships drifted, ghostlike, from the docks without a bump or tremor.

In less than half a minute, disaster struck.

Candlemas never knew what hit them—some kind of heat ray, probably—but the sheet metal sail overhead suddenly blistered and curled. A horizontal spar burned through, and the sail snapped and ripped the other spar off its mount. The ship plunged.

Candlemas gagged, prayed, screamed, and cursed Karsus in tones that would have shocked a mule skinner. No one heard him, for they all screamed too.

Safeguards, he thought. There had to be built-in safeguards to rescue them. He'd been sitting at the stern, now the highest point, for the ship fell nose first so steeply that soldiers were wrenched from their seats. Swords and spears pinwheeled among the ranks, cutting flesh and chipping wood. Helmets clattered, shields bonged, and a battle pennant unfurled to flap desolately over the chaotic mess. Candlemas tried to guess whether or not to shift out, now that he was free of the enclave's wards, or stay put. To shift was dangerous because he was traveling so fast. He'd be moving just as fast at the other end and likely collide with a tree or the ground. He felt so seasick he couldn't think straight.

Then magic shields kicked in like a giant pillow to cradle the craft, so it hit the ground gently, relatively speaking. One second they were falling, bodies free as birds, the next they were wrenched to a halt so hard Candlemas's molars bit through his tongue. A grinding smash came next, and a tree branch punched through the hull like a treant's fist. Men and women suffered broken limbs, shattered jaws, and multiple cuts when they fell into the nest of unsheathed weapons. Men were groaning, cursing, swearing, crying, when the shouts of the sergeants cut through the noise. A grizzled veteran kicked out the door chocks and the landing ramp fell away. Soldiers crawled or ran to get out of the wooden death trap.

Almost crying from the pain of his punctured tongue, Candlemas hobbled down the ramp. Outside were trees with broken branches and shed leaves, for they'd crashed in the forest. The pudgy mage saw sergeants kicking, hoisting, and slapping the stumbling soldiers into line, ordering the hale ones to stop whimpering and bandage their comrades. The puking, crying officers they simply ignored. Spitting blood, Candlemas looked to see whom he could help.

Screams. A charred smell of scorched flesh filled the air, an autumnal whiff of burning leaves. There was nothing to see, but soldiers died where they clustered. Barely visible heat ripples tickled the air as men and women felt their clothes, then their skin and hair, ignite. Painted **K**'s on their breastplates curled and smoked, then each person became a ball of writhing flame, then a melting pool of blackened fat.

The heat ray, the mage knew. Firing from Ioulaum on high. Someone up there didn't know this war was only supposed to be a game.

The broken wooden hull beside him smoked and

burst into flame. Men and officers died like flies under a burning glass. Candlemas stuck out a hand, latched onto a screaming soldier's shoulder, flicked his hand in the air along with a chant, and shifted.

Now he and the boy stood at the edge of the forest with grain fields running away from their feet toward a central road. High in the sky, at opposite ends of the valley, floated the sister cities. A quarter of a mile up in the woods, flames marked the destruction of the troop landing. In a rye field another ship landed successfully, and soldiers ran helter-skelter for cover behind rock walls, ignoring the shouts of their sergeants. The crew manning the troop ship waved frantically to lift before the heat ray found them.

Leaving the soldier to join his comrades, Candlemas aimed, shifted himself alongside the ship just before the landing ramp was hauled up. "Wait! Wait for me!" A brawny arm caught him by the tunic, hoisted him aboard to drop on his face in the bottom of the empty ship.

All the way back, he kept his fingers crossed lest the heat ray strike them, all the while praying to Amaunator, Keeper of the Sun. If he got back safe, he promised, he'd drop a year's wages into the temple coffers, and never fly again.

* * * * *

Wulgreth gave a shout and hurled at Sunbright the first thing that came to hand. In this case, Knucklebones.

One hand entwined in her short dark hair, he caught her by the neck, grunted, and flung her. She gave a shriek of fright, terrified her neck would snap, then flew through the air like a rag doll.

But she slowed in midair, hung suspended, then gradually drifted to earth near the sundered campfire.

Sunbright helped her rise. His brawny hand caught her small, calloused one, and she felt a queer thrill run through her breast that had nothing to do with magic.

"How did you—what was—"

"Feather fall," Sunbright answered. "I thought of goose down and applied its magic to you, and the spell took. I don't know how I did it."

Standing, leaning on his arm, Knucklebones noticed something odd. This was the real man, returned alive and well, but his face, eyes, skin, and fingernails all glowed with a bright green tinge. It reminded her of the first blush of leaves in the emperor's park. He looked like a paper lantern lit from the inside, bright as any campfire.

"What's this glow?"

"Nature magic," he said simply. "I'm infused with it. I don't think the effect will last, but it should keep us alive. Watch out!"

Wulgreth's tribe, exhausted by their debauchery and night of torture, had crawled from their huts and grabbed up crude stone and iron weapons. They ran to the edge of the fire circle, then stopped and stared. One man pointed a seven-fingered hand at Sunbright and grunted. Children hid behind their parent's legs.

The man they'd tortured to death had returned as an avenging angel.

Only the magic-user was not awed. Wulgreth let out a bellow, snatched Knucklebones's black knife from his belt, and charged.

Several things happened at once, too fast for the thief to follow.

The black knife disappeared from Wulgreth's hand and appeared in Knucklebones's. Blinked there, obviously, by the will of Sunbright. At the same time, the barbarian drew his sword, and Harvester of Blood had never shone more brilliantly. Light flashed from the blade like a sunrise. Suddenly empty-handed, Wulgreth snatched up a log as thick as a man's leg from the fire pit, but that limb too was spelled. As Wulgreth swung it overhand to crush Sunbright's skull, the barbarian stroked his hand in the air, aiming for the log. Wulgreth lost his grip as the log aged a hundred years in seconds, snapped, crumbled to punk, and rained down as splinters and dust.

Waving empty hands, Wulgreth charged with brute strength and blind fury. Brushing Knucklebones gently aside, Sunbright reached over his head, then skipped back.

Immediately there came a snap and creak, then a groan as dirt and roots ripped and popped as if caught in a hurricane. A long shape loomed over Knucklebones's head, then a crash jarred her to her knees. Dust and cinders whirled around, stinging her eyes, tickling her nose and making her snort. Sunbright carefully lifted and propped her up, and made an idle swipe with Harvester. A giant branch hung over their heads to trap them in a leafy prison, but the keen sword lopped it off so they could pass.

Knucklebones rubbed her eyes and stared. "Wh-What—" she stammered. "What happened?"

"I pulled down a tree," Sunbright said simply. "It was diseased, and can return to the soil faster this way."

She stared. Smack across the center of the camp lay a tree that been leaning to one side. Sunbright had merely gestured, and brought the thing toppling like a dying forest god.

Now he waggled Harvester so the gleaming blade bobbed in the air. He was calm as an oak tree himself, despite the fact that they were surrounded by enemies. Knucklebones wondered at his calm air of certainty and lack of fear.

She breathed, "You've changed!"

"Yes." he agreed. "I'm a shaman." He smiled, and

even his teeth radiated light, so she was reminded again of a paper lantern. "Finally."

Thrown off-balance, stunned by the magical attack, and trapped by the intervening tree, Wulgreth howled in rage and indignation, leaped into the air to crash down on packed dirt, beat his chest like an ape, and hollered his fury. His great hooked hands flexed as he ripped his lizard skin costume from his breast. Sunbright waited, unmoved and unafraid. Knucklebones clutched her familiar knife and crouched behind the newly-risen shaman.

Sense overcoming fury, Wulgreth saw that his antics didn't frighten his opponent, and quit. Instead, he stooped and latched onto a great rock with his craggy hands, grunted, and hoisted it high over his head.

Knucklebones shrieked, but Sunbright only snapped his fingertips together. The boulder burst into dust, like the tree limb, aged eons in less than a second. It spattered into dust around Wulgreth's head.

The lich lord stood stunned, blinking grit from his stone dead eyes. His followers oohed and aahed at the display, marveling that Sunbright could so oppose their invincible leader.

Knucklebones trembled. "We should flee," she told him. "If you can use magic, you could shift us far away, can't you?"

"No." Sunbright didn't look at her as he spoke, but watched his opponent. "I owe the land here for my salvation. I must repay her, make repairs as I can." He cast about at the dark woods, as if they were more important than a mere battle.

Talk of repaying the land sounded like mystic mumbo jumbo to the thief, the vague mutterings of a priest cadging offerings. But she said nothing, only waited to see what he—and Wulgreth—would do.

The lich lord spread his feet wide, arched his back,

tilted his head, and screamed. A long, keening undead screech that went on and on, setting Knucklebone's teeth on edge and making her spine crawl.

Her fear increased as, sprouting from the ground like horrific mushrooms or dropping from the branches or shambling from the dark, crept a handful of monsters awful to look at, painful to behold, for all were dead like him. Dead and deadly.

From the ground oozed a long skeleton, nothing but spine and ribs and a tiny human head with glittering black eye sockets. Cutting its way free of the earth was a small, dumpy man, but with four arms thin as sticks, blind white eyes, and mandibles clicking in his mouth. From the dark floated a pair of bulbous bags like ruby balloons, though with stinging tails that lashed as if eager to poison the living. Humping from the shadows came a short, stinking zombie lacking legs so it hobbled on hands and stumps. Dropping from the trees came a ball of arms and legs and tentacles and branches that grasped and writhed but had no body to speak of. And from the sundered campfire rose a wisp of smoke no wider than a shadow, a tall gangly thing that changed shape constantly as if unsure what it mimicked, though its hands were always long, scythe-like knives.

Knucklebones's teeth chattered as the undead things clustered around, weaving and bobbing, awaiting their chance. She'd seen horrors, but never anything to compare with these. More than ever she wished she were back in Karsus's sewers.

But Sunbright was undaunted, even laconic. In an even voice, he told Wulgreth, "These threats will avail you naught. This forest has suffered enough. Banish your fiends and yourself, get hence and begone. This is an abode for the living, not the dead."

Beside himself with anger, Wulgreth leveled his arm and screamed, "*Attack!*"

Chapter 18

"Candy! Candy!"

Candlemas stumbled down a landing ramp, bruised, bloody, singed, and thoroughly rattled. Who was calling him that silly name? He didn't know anyone—then a warm bundle bounced into his chest. Soft arms were flung around his neck, his sweaty, sooty face was smothered in plump and delicious kisses. Struggling to stay on his feet, he wrapped his arms around the woman's broad back and hung on. When she paused for breath, he saw who it was.

"Sita! Aquesita?"

"Oh, Candy, I was so worried, I had to come see you!" she sobbed. Tears of joy and relief spilled down her cheeks. "When Karry told me he'd sent you into battle, I couldn't believe it. But it was true! Oh, I'm so proud of you, my darling. So glad you've come back to me unhurt."

"I'm not quite unhurt," his words were mushy, his mouth sore. "I bit my tongue when the ship crashed."

"Crashed?" The word brought on a new flurry of tears, kisses, and hugs. "Oh, my poor, brave soul!"

Stunned, and not just from knocks in the head, Candlemas hung onto his ladylove and basked in her praise and attention. Her broad back was comforting, her modest bosom, pressed to his dirty uniform, exciting. Awkwardly he kissed her hair, stroking it with smudged hands, murmuring what sweet nothings he could conjure.

This made no sense; his brain whirled. For days, Aquesita refused him an audience, returned his letters and flowers. Now she ran to his arms because he'd been in danger. Was this love madness, woman contrariness, or male thickness? He couldn't begin to guess, so he just gave into it and let himself be pampered.

The coddling included a ride in Aquesita's long carriage, plain white but painted with vibrant, intertwined roses and vines. Lolling on red cushions, Candlemas sipped wine that stung his swollen tongue and watched the hustle and bustle of the city pass his window. He'd done his share. War wasn't so bad, he reflected, if these were its rewards.

He shifted idly, seeking a muscle that didn't ache. Moving sent a faint whiff to his nostrils: the stink of burned flesh. Rocking forward, he gagged on his wine, spraying it on the floor and the hem of Aquesita's blue gown. With the smell came the memory of screams as men and women burned to death, hair and flesh igniting. Suddenly his hands trembled so badly the wineglass stem snapped and cut his fingers. That could have been him, crippled and unable to flee the heat ray. He could be ashes fertilizing a forest right now.

Slowly, head down, he breathed deeply while Aquesita cooed and stroked his back. Best to not think about the raid, the disaster. Hollowly, he said, "I'll be all right. I just need a minute. And a . . . bath. What's—" He stopped himself. No, better not ask about her just yet. Their separation might be a sore point. "What's the latest gossip?"

"Gossip?" Aquesita laughed uneasily. "You know I don't follow gossip, dear Candy. I've no interest in who sleeps with whom, or who's gambled away his or her fortune, or who's lashed whom to ribbons. There are finer things in life to consider, and nobler pursuits. No, there's—wait! There was one unpleasantness that's newsworthy. Certainly it's a scandal. Did you ever meet a silver-haired woman named Polaris?"

"*Lady* Polaris?" Candlemas snapped upright so fast it made him dizzy. Cradling his aching skull, he said, "I know her—knew her. Worked for her once, long ago. She's a cold thing, a heart of ice, single-mindedly dedicated to her personal pursuits, with no concern for anyone else. She could be empress some day." If she lays off the food, he added mentally.

He kept thinking of the slim, calculating Polaris of old, not the bloated, preening, self-deluded pig he'd met in this time.

"She'll never be empress," Aquesita said. "She was assassinated last night."

"A-Assassin-Assassinated?" Candlemas sputtered as a fresh stab of pain shot through his head. "Dead? *Polaris?*"

The plump hand caressed his shoulder. "I'm afraid so," she cooed. "I never knew you worked for her. Yes, she died in a new and peculiar way. Someone devised a spell that injects a sliver of heavy magic into fruit without a trace. The magic turns the sugars into arsenic, or cyanide, I forget which. It was candied dates did her in. How unfortunate. It'll throw the empire into a tizzy, everyone fretting over new methods of assassination . . ."

Her pleasant voice droned on, but Candlemas didn't hear. He couldn't fathom the concept. Lady Polaris, once the most beautiful woman in the empire, and perhaps the most powerful—she'd bailed him and Sunbright out of hell with two fingers—dead, snuffed out, fit only for worms. It didn't seem possible.

And Candlemas was partly responsible. The "splinter of heavy magic poison" idea came from Karsus's new experimentation with super heavy magic, which in a way, Candlemas enabled by uncovering the fallen star. Of course he wasn't totally responsible, perhaps not at all. He was a victim of the new magic as much as she.

But he felt sorry and unhappy, though he'd never have believed it . . . and worried, and fretful. The empire, this war, Karsus's mad manipulations that brought certain disaster, it had to stop. Or else Candlemas had to leave it behind.

Sunbright was right, he realized suddenly. He, they, should return to their own time. It was the only sensible choice. There was no place for him here, no future, not with the empire hurling itself to destruction. He owned nothing, owed nothing, had nothing to hold him.

Except Aquesita.

Sensing his unease, the woman leaned close, her soft bosom pressing his arm, sending a tingle through him. "Dear?" she almost whispered. "Is something wrong? Shall I stop the carriage, or take you to a healer?"

"No, no, I'm fine. Better, anyway."

He sat up straight, though the weight of the world seemed to press his shoulders.

"Aquesita, do you . . . would you . . . is there . . ."

Patiently she waited, eyebrows arched, red mouth parted invitingly. Her eyes sparkled, and for a moment Candlemas imagined she thought he was asking to marry her. That couldn't be, could it?

"Yes, dear?" she waited.

But Candlemas didn't know what to say, so only enfolded her tightly, and hung on to her softness, inhaled the perfume of her hair, and wept like a lost child.

She patted his back, murmuring, "There, there, love. It's all right . . ."

* * * * *

Knucklebones was snatched off her feet by a bronzed hand and plunked in a crotch of the fallen oak. Sunbright's speed made her dizzy, and he moved faster all the time.

A flash lit the night as moonlight, starlight, and firelight all reflected off the blade of Harvester of Blood. The wide, nose heavy, hooked blade had never burned brighter, the steel polished to a fine luster, the whole glowing with the eerie green-tinged nature magic Sunbright had embraced. Like a winter moon descended from the sky, like white fire, the blade swept after the encroaching snake skeleton. One smash sent brittle bone fragments sailing in all directions so they rained like pointed hail. The blade flashed again, and the floating balloon things were punctured, sheared through. Red smears on the blade were quickly wicked off, leaving only a whiff of marsh gas and stingers that flopped to the ground and writhed like lizard tails.

Wulgreth was hollering, screaming, ranting. Knucklebones didn't know if he shouted encouragement, orders, or just noise. He thrashed against the fallen oak, furiously splintering branches in his craggy hands, climbing, pointing, and shrieking at the same time. The small thief clutched her elven blade close and waited for an opportunity to strike, but these undead menaces were beyond her capabilities. In Karsus, she'd have run ten blocks by now. And Sunbright held the center of the battle, and nothing could get near him for his whirling blade.

The dumpy manling with mandibles plied short knives in all four hands. He slashed the air and keened like a seagull, distracting Sunbright until others could strike. The shadeling slithered under the tree to circle behind, and the amputee zombie dragged itself up close to strike with a rusty cleaver it wore on a thong down its back. Sunbright watched them all, still calm, but singing the battle anthem of his people.

As she watched and waited, stunned, Knucklebones felt a thrill in her breast, an admiration for this man who possessed not only strength and intelligence, but gentleness and the will to win, to learn, to delve into magic and make it his own. Too, she felt a sudden and surprising yearning to hold him close, a rush that made her belly tingle. Mighty queer feelings for a disastrous battle in a darksome, haunted forest.

The attack coalesced when the knitting yarn tangle of arms and tentacles dropped from a tree onto Sunbright's head. Immediately limbs began to wrap around his eyes and mouth, to blind and smother him while the other fiends rushed in for the kill.

But Sunbright took it all in stride. Still watching his enemies, he squirmed his left hand up along his neck and cheek, halting the tangled thing's cruel embrace. Biting through a ropy arm, then wrenching, he ripped the thing off his head. His skin was torn and rasped, for the tentacles were as abrasive as a squid's. Sunbright wore a mask of his own blood, but as the thing coiled around his bicep, he smashed down hard to grind it against his ribs, crushing it in his armpit.

The four-armed manling scissored pipe stem arms wide, slid them between Sunbright's legs, and sliced to hamstring and cripple him. But the barbarian snapped his free hand on the juncture of two of the manling's arms, flicked his wrist, and broke both arms so they dangled and flapped uselessly.

The cleaver-wielding zombie scuttled like a crippled crab to hack at Sunbright's backside and spine, and here Knucklebones got her chance. Hopping up and skipping along a branch, she might get behind the thing and yet be out of reach of Sunbright's long, flashing sword, or so she hoped. Crouching, she latched onto the zombie's tattered robe to jerk it backward and pierce its throat.

The rotten cloth only tore in her grip. Grunting, the zombie spun faster than she would have imagined and the pitted, nicked cleaver came at her. The undead thing grunted, and Knucklebones saw with horror that its tongue was missing, cut out long ago. Up close the fiend was unspeakably repulsive. It stank of the grave and had only patches of skin to cover its yellowed skull, yet a deadly unlife glittered like moths in its eye sockets. Knucklebones wanted to shriek, but that would only get her killed, so she put her energy into striking instead. A short stab with her dagger, and the blade sank to the hilt in the zombie's neck. With a lurch and wrench, she jerked the blade toward herself and down to sever windpipe and vein. The blade tore free, the dead skin tearing like old, gray leather.

The hideous wound did exactly nothing to the zombie, despite the fact that its head was half severed. The glittering moth eyes only bored deeper into Knucklebones as the cleaver whipped at her head. Still crouched, she stumbled backward, hooked her swollen foot on a branch, and fell. That left her legs exposed to the zombie's chop. She'd be as legless as it was in a second.

Sunbright still had the tangle ball pinned in his armpit, for he hadn't the necessary second to rip it loose. The thing's arms and tentacles slapped, rasped, and sucked frantically at his arm and side and neck and thighs. The bitten off limb flailed, spraying black blood like octopus ink, and the limbs seemed to be growing, thinning and elongating. Two sucker-covered limbs wrapped around the barbarian's knee and yanked upward to trip him. Sunbright ground his arm tighter against his ribs, making the thing squirm, and tried to ignore it. The dumpy manling with two broken arms was hot for revenge.

All this took place by the eerie light of the barbarian himself, for the green-white glow still surrounded him. Too, in the east and high up, dawn sent rose-yellow tendrils of light onto a low overcast slit as if with a knife.

Knucklebones glimpsed all this as she flopped. The zombie made to chop at her leg, but she whipped it free before the cleaver struck. It cleft instead the branch she'd tripped on, the dull steel chipping through bark to white wood. Its stinking evil had first terrified Knucklebones, but now infuriated her. This zombie had been a bastard in life, too, she would bet. Scrambling on her butt and hands like a crab, she kicked hard at its brow, avoiding the mouth of broken teeth. The sturdy blow rocked the thing, but it didn't tumble. It was heavier than she'd guessed, as if the flesh had taken on the denseness of its tomb. Another quick kick glanced off its skull, shearing away rotten flesh and exposing fresh bone. For a moment, Knucklebones thought she'd vomit. Instead, she crabbed away from it.

Sunbright grappled with the yarn ball that flapped and flailed like a mad octopus. Snatching another limb with his free hand, he put it to his mouth and bit through that also. He spat, lips black with blood. The dumpy manling chittered at him with a high, rabbitlike keen. Sunbright had no desire to kill it, for it was obviously under the thrall of Wulgreth. But the yarn ball was becoming a problem, raking his skin raw where it touched. Sunbright feinted at the manling, a quick jab to make it fall back.

The manling did scuttle back, cradling its broken

arms across its chest. With two good arms it slashed the air viciously, but long as those pipe stem limbs were, they couldn't reach past Harvester without taking damage. Another swipe of the glowing blade made it hop back on short, stumpy legs and bare feet.

That step landed it on the stingers severed from the gas bags.

The manling yelped as if it had stepped on hot coals, then yelped again as the barbed stingers jammed into its dirty yellow feet. Screeching, it caught the sawtoothed barbs and ripped so blood flowed. But now its tiny, skinny hand was poisoned.

Sunbright grabbed another handful of arms and tentacles and branches to bite again, but the yarn ball creature was learning, and its pseudopods coiled around his hand like a bullwhip. When the tentacles retracted the barbarian's arm was jerked back tight to his own shoulder, and more coils trussed him. So it was stalemate, Sunbright thought. He had the thing pinned, and it had him half trussed. Cursing, he whirled to see how Knucklebones fared, and where Wulgreth had gotten to.

The upshot was not good. As Knucklebones scrambled to her feet, knife in hand, and backed from the truncated zombie, Wulgreth clambered over the trunk to snatch her from the rear. She'd be a hostage, Sunbright saw. He made to shout a warning, but a coil slapped around his mouth from chin to cheek, tightening too fast for him to bite. He cast a quick glance to his left, saw the four-armed manling had toppled, screeching and rubbing its feet with dirt. No enemies behind. But hadn't there been—

The shadeling struck.

All this time the smoky being had skulked close and low, biding its time. Now it leaped, like a shadow cast by a candle on a wall, and landed on Sunbright's back.

The barbarian caught the flicker of it, but at first felt nothing. It had no weight, no substance.

He felt the attack in his mind.

Suddenly his head seemed empty and echoing. His thoughts were a jumble, spinning as if a tornado had infiltrated his skull. The shadeling sifted his thoughts so it could know him, intimately, down to the last squib of his life. Because—he saw the threat now—it intended to suck his mind dry, take his place, and kill him.

To Knucklebones it looked as if Sunbright had grown another head, one rasped and bloody, one clean and fresh. Behind him clung something like a shadow, initially black and dim, but now taking on color and thickness and a life of its own. The thin mass adhered to the barbarian's back, and yet was separating from him, so that behind his bright blond horsetail, another head and neck and set of shoulders took form. The eyes of this shadow mimic were not Sunbright's, but hard and glaring and cruel, single-minded of purpose, dedicated to death. The barbarian struggled with the yarn ball even as the shadow being gained strength. The thief could have wailed. How to defeat an insidious foe like that, especially when she had her own stump zombie to fight?

Knucklebones watched as the zombie scuttled after her. Her knife couldn't hurt it, so she needed something else. Sunbright would say to use whatever was handy. She jumped and pounced on the branch chopped by the cleaver. Wrenching it loose, she circled back to the tree trunk. The branch was long and leafy as a giant broom, and thrusting it into the brute's face flustered it. If she reversed it quickly, perhaps she could slam the point through its chest. A stake through the heart killed vampires, legends said. . . .

A strong, cold pair of hands clamped around her

throat and lifted her, throttling, into the air. Knuckle-bones kicked, clawed at the hands, and raked her elven blade across the cables in the back of both hands. The razor sharp knife creased the skin but would not cut, as if she sawed on hardwood. Wulgreth gurgled by her ear, a noise of fury. He didn't shake her, nor snap her neck, but kept her alive and still. A hostage to subdue Sun-bright. Still kicking, the one-eyed thief wanted to cry with frustration. Wulgreth too used what was handy to defeat Sunbright, and successfully, for the barbarian's gentle heart would not allow her to be harmed. Oh, to fight something living that could be hurt and bleed!

Sunbright fought for sanity as the shadeling picked his mind apart. Already he was forgetting things, unable to recall his homeland, or his mother's face, or how he'd come to be a fugitive in the lowlands, or an outlaw in the floating city. This evil nothing monster would seize control of him, strip his mind, leave him a hulk, like the zombie that now stumped toward him to chop at his legs. Knucklebones strangled in air as Wulgreth watched the battle with stone dead eyes, and Sun-bright's spirit faded away, his mind sucked dry as an empty cocoon.

Desperately he tried to think of an escape, butting his head and slashing over his shoulder with only one hand, for the damned octopus arms wrapped tighter than ever. Nothing worked, he couldn't touch the shadeling. But it could touch him.

Or someone else.

"Knuckle', hang on!" he bellowed.

Through a veil of his own blood and skin raked by the yarn ball, he saw her kick in answer. But her single eye was haunted and helpless. She saw no way out. And he was weakening, losing his mind and strength as the life and soul drain grew stronger.

But Sunbright had an answer.

He dropped Harvester so the blade fell flat on the dusty, leafy ground. Giving the yarn ball another fast squeeze, he squatted, and grabbed the stumpy zombie.

The thing's fluttery moth eyes wrinkled as Sunbright caught it by a sturdy arm and hoisted it one-handed. It was vastly heavy, and made him grunt, almost fall to his knees. The rotted stench made him gag, but he ignored the stink and furious twitching, pitched the undead tomb guardian over his shoulder to crash over his back—right into the not-Sunbright face of the shadeling.

The shadow being's spell was interrupted as the zombie got in the way. The barbarian hadn't been sure it would work, but the phantom claws sifting his brain were suddenly gone. As if breaking free of a spiderweb, he jumped to get clear.

A quick glance showed he'd succeeded better than planned. The zombie lay on its back, curling, twisting, kicking its bony stumps. The shadeling clung to it like morning cobwebs, like darksome mist. The image of Sunbright had shrunken to half its size. Instead of drawing life from a living man, the soul sucker tapped a dead thing, losing its corporeal existence in the process. The stolen image of Sunbright shriveled as the magic sputtered and died and curled in on itself. The barbarian had no clue what would result, but was glad to be free.

Another quick glance showed him that the dumpy, four-armed manling was dead, poisoned through feet turned black.

That left only the yarn ball, and Wulgreth.

With his right hand, the barbarian reached under his left armpit, caught a squirming clutch near the core, and wrenched savagely. Arms, tentacles, branches, and whips popped and tore, ripping his vest and shirt and skin as they were pried loose. The shredded beast seemed stunned, for it hung in his hand a moment like a fish on a hook, gathering strength to flap anew.

Sunbright didn't give it time. Jumping up on the tree trunk, he advanced on Wulgreth, who backed away with Knucklebones dangling in front as a partial shield.

"Let's trade," Sunbright rasped, his voice as scarred and scraped as his mind and body. "My bundle for yours!"

"*Noooo!*"

But Sunbright trailed out his right hand and slung the black dripping mass of wounded arms. The squishy clump slapped on Wulgreth's shoulder and upper arms, and immediately they grabbed hold, whipping, coiling, curling and grasping, burying the lich lord's head and smothering his upper torso. Instinctively Wulgreth let go of Knucklebones to grapple with the writhing tangle that was trapping him.

As he did, the small thief bounced light as thistledown, bunched her legs, and bounded away. A good thing too, for Sunbright had regained Harvester of Blood.

Lunging, diving over the trunk, Sunbright grabbed the pommel two-handed, slung the long glowing blade far behind, and swung.

The keen steel slammed into Wulgreth's side just below the ribs. The blow knocked him sideways, staggering him. Hissing through his teeth, Sunbright ripped the blade loose and gave him another shot. Two more blows rained, as if the barbarian chopped a tree. There was no blood, but the meaty smacks chopped Wulgreth's thick skin and dried organs to hash. Then Sunbright lined up to cut a leg out from under the undead tyrant.

Wulgreth had had enough. Clawing tentacles free to peek out, he whirled, and ran for the deepest stand of mutant brush and drooping trees.

Sunbright stood, chest heaving, blood dripping, and let him go. It could take him all day to chop the lich to fist sized chunks, and he wasn't even sure those would be dead.

So he let Wulgreth go. He'd won. He and Knucklebones.

And the natural, growing, living magic that was part of this land.

Sunbright panted, even dropped Harvester's point on bare ground. He pulled up the hem of his spattered red shirt to mop blood off his face. Sweat stung in the scrapes, but he didn't mind, for he was glad to be alive. And to see Knucklebones with a rare smile.

"So the country mouse is a timber wolf on his home ground," she teased. She ripped loose a sucker-covered arm still stuck to his neck.

He grinned back, examining his arms and hands. The green glow was indistinct in the sunrise, but he knew it had faded.

"More like a firefly," he said. "I've used up the magic."

"So it's gone?"

"No," he answered, "it's still here, an ocean of it. Down there." Moving around the tree trunk, he walked to the fire pit, saw a crack in the earth yards long and wide enough to admit his hand. "I came up through there, somehow. The magic came with me. Feel it?" He waved a hand as if over a campfire.

Knucklebones shook her head. All she felt were the warm rays of the day's sun slanting through the mutant trees. But she was glad Sunbright could feel the magic, for it meant he'd remain a shaman, and she wanted it so.

"No matter," he told her. "I think—I'm sure the nature magic only needed a conduit, someone to care for it, ask its help. It's hard to explain, but from this spot, I believe the nature magic will begin to heal the land, until the corrupt magic of Karsus has leeched away and the forest is balanced again."

The thief turned at a scuffle and shuffle. Creeping from huts and bushes came the mutants, eyeless, limbless, warty, alligator-skinned, deformed. In the darkness, they'd tortured Sunbright to death and beyond, but by day they looked pathetic and harmless.

"And them?" she asked.

The barbarian hoisted his sword, wiped the blade clean, and marched to the mutants, who cowered before him. Even the testy raptors in their makeshift corrals were quiet, almost docile. Standing tall, arms on hips, Sunbright asked, "Who's the eldest here?"

A withered crone with blind eyes raised a shaking hand and said, "I, sir."

"Then you're chief now, for Wulgreth won't be back. This forest will no longer tolerate him. Nor will it abide torture any more, or raids on your neighbors. You are to become a people of peace from now on, at one with the land. Nurture it, care for it, and it will care for you. The elders can teach you, for they remember when this land was healthy and alive, liked the feel of human feet, and nourished its dwellers. Will you do this thing?"

The old crone bobbed her head and told him, "We shall, your highness. We shall."

Sunbright nodded, satisfied. Knucklebones was more skeptical, but realized the mutants probably thought Sunbright a glowing god risen from the earth itself. Certainly they'd seen it, would tell one another and their children in years to come, and so they'd believe, and obey.

Sunbright took Knucklebones's small hand with the brassy bars adorning it and led her to the far side of the camp, where a path wended into the diseased forest. Up high a bird sang, and was answered from afar. Liking the feel of his strong, gentle fist, she asked, "So they'll heal, get better?"

"No." The barbarian shook his head as he answered. "These scars, on people and plants, will remain, and die out slowly, naturally. But the children will be normal, and the seedlings. Nature moves slowly, like a glacier, but nothing can stand before it."

"That sounds like something a prophet would say," she half kidded.

He grinned in answer, saying, "It does, doesn't it? *Ooh!*"

"What?"

He touched the back of his neck where his horsetail rested.

"Besides all my other aches and pains, now I'm burned on my scalp. Candlemas must be signaling me, as I called him. We'll have to go see.

"But I think I'll wash first," he added, studying his bloody arms and hands.

"Candlemas?" Knucklebones frowned. "He's up in the city. How will we get there?"

Sunbright studied the high treeline as if reading the weather. Distantly, he asked, "Why don't we fly?"

Chapter 19

The game had gotten out of hand. War blazed between Karsus and Ioulaum, and people died by the
hundreds.

Candlemas crouched with Aquesita in her rose-
painted carriage. They'd tried to cross the city, spiraling
out from the castle mound, but the driver kept stalling
at obstacles: fallen trees, torn up roads, shattered
buildings, bodies, and marching columns of soldiers and
city guards. Time and again they had to circle. Aquesita
had promised a friend aid, to fetch her from her mansion to Karsus's castle, where no destruction had yet
struck, or would. Candlemas had tried to dissuade her,
but she refused, stubborn as her famous cousin, and
he'd come to watch over her.

But the danger and disasters were more serious than

either of them had reckoned, and growing worse all the time.

No one was even sure what the attacks were. Candlemas knew about the super heavy magic exploding runes, and he'd seen many graceful ballista shafts, like arrows from the gods, arc over the city, fall, and explode with tremendous force, tearing up stone and people and trees. The heat ray, too, he'd seen at close hand, and many city towers had been turned to molten slag that coursed down the buildings like candle wax to set innumerable fires below.

Fires raged throughout both cities, far more than city guards with water or mages with spells could ever put out. Smoke roiled along the ground, stung the eyes, dirtied everything it touched. Other magics had been visited upon Karsus's city, and even normal weapons. Something in Ioulaum could hurl rocks the size of houses that crushed whole blocks. And there were many more weapons.

"How can this happen?"

Aquesita cowered in Candlemas's arms as the carriage rattled through back streets. Frightened and angry faces passed by the small windows, some weeping, others cursing and waving their fists. Candlemas knew the throngs were no danger, for the carriage was warded against unwanted entry. But a huge boulder falling from the sky could hash them, along with their carriage and wards. The woman insisted, "It's not possible the war has gone this badly. Karsus wouldn't let it. He'll stop it. I know he's working on it right now."

Candlemas said nothing, for he knew Karsus had caused this nightmare. And since nothing rained on *his* castle, he wouldn't care much, might even be oblivious to it all.

The carriage rattled on, but stopped abruptly and began to back awkwardly. The passengers heard the driver curse. When they stalled completely, Aquesita opened the trap door at the front of the compartment and called, "What's happening, driver?"

The man's worried face filled the square hole. "Beg pardon, milady," he said, "but they're riotin' again. We can't go for'ard, but I'm hopin'—"

"Rioting?" interrupted the noblewoman. "Again? Over what?"

"I couldn't say, milady. Malcontents, is all. The guards are seein' to 'em. We'll be right on our way shortly."

He slapped the trap door shut.

Aquesita plucked a handkerchief from her embroidered sleeve and mopped her brow as she said, "What could they riot about? Surely even the poor support our efforts in the war. Don't they, Candlemas?"

The mage didn't answer, for he didn't want to lie to his ladylove. He stared out the window at a brick wall. But, no fool, Aquesita demanded an answer, so he finally said, "They riot for food, Sita. There isn't any for the poor. It's finally run out."

"What? What do you mean, finally?" She stared at her friend and lover with a blank face. "How can there be no food?"

Candlemas shrugged helplessly. "There hasn't been enough for a long time," he told her. "Since before I arrived here, they say. Something wrong with the distribution. . . ." He was hedging, as if breaking bad news to Lady Polaris, and he hated it.

"The, uh, nobility was somewhat . . . shortsighted in its goals," he continued, "and misjudged the amounts needed to feed everyone. Now with war here and on the ground, the supply of food has stopped completely, and there are no reserves. So the poor riot in hopes of . . . I don't know what. Justice, I suppose."

"Justice? This is abominable! No food? Do children go

hungry too? That's insufferable! I'll see that Karsus fixes *that* problem first thing!"

"Karsus is—" again Candlemas swallowed his words, "—too busy."

"Not to see me, his only living relation, he's not! I'll be busy too, filling his ear with what's right and what's wrong! But we can't just sit here. Come, Candy. We'll walk!"

"Walk?" the mage balked, grabbing her hands. "No, Sita, you can't do that! It's not safe!" By the gods, he knew Aquesita was misinformed about her cousin's true nature, but for any noble to show her face in the streets now would be certain death. Wards or not, the crowds would tear her apart. "No, Sita! We must remain here! We shouldn't even have come—"

"Nonsense! The empire needs us, and so does my friend, and the poor. Come!"

Before he could stop her, short of knocking her flat and trussing her, Aquesita had popped open the carriage door and hopped out, skirts flapping. Candlemas scrambled after her, shouting as did her driver and footmen over a greater roaring.

Aquesita stamped into the street, then stood frozen, pointing, disbelieving.

Down at a crossroads, past a barrier of rubble and furniture, raged the riot. Ragged poor suffered under the brutal hands of city guards and soldiers. None of the guards plied silver-tipped clubs any more. It was all blade work. As Candlemas watched, unable to turn away, some fifty guards and soldiers with long lances chopped into the crowd while a hedge wizard in a garish uniform sent lightning crackling amidst them. The terrified mob boiled and bled and fled down the street toward the city center, leaving twitching victims and leaking corpses behind. Some of the slowest had been children.

The screaming and shouting was awful, but the crying of Aquesita was the worst for Candlemas.

"Love of Mystryl, Lady of Love," she whispered. "I didn't know it had come to this. I didn't know . . . but Karsus knew, didn't he?"

Gently Candlemas put his arms around her, but she pushed him away. She wanted truth, not dumb comfort.

"Yes, Sita. He knew. All the leading nobles knew. But they did nothing about it, and it just got worse. I'm sorry."

"I'm sorry too," she sobbed. Tears coursed down her cheeks, but her plump mouth was firmly set. "Sorry I've been so blind, so coddled, and so stupid. But no more. I'll see Karsus, and this will stop—"

Her voice seemed to rise into a high, whining scream that no human made. It was a missile arcing across the sky. Candlemas grabbed Aquesita's head and pulled her down just as a rollicking explosion jarred them both off their feet. Not far off, screams filled the air. The bomb had landed smack in the city's center.

With a short cry, Aquesita grabbed her skirts and ran toward the site of the disaster. Candlemas jogged after her, puffing. City guards, blood-spattered and weary unto death, tried to stop her, but she evaded them and ran on. By the time Candlemas caught up, she'd gotten to the end of the street and stopped cold.

What he saw made his blood run just as cold.

The great fountain at the center of town, a high fluted, complicated affair of many spouts and cherubs and fans, boiled red. Rose-colored spray filled the air, staining white marble, and a frothy pink bubbled in the many pools. Candlemas's jaw dropped at the horrific sight, but Aquesita's words were even more chilling.

"The prophecy! The sign. A fountain of blood. Oh, and look!"

Weeping, Aquesita stepped over a dead man. Rubble

and corpses littered the plaza, but Aquesita picked up a ratty bundle of white feathers. Candlemas didn't even recognize it until her voice came faintly, "Our storks. The guardians of the heights, the wings of Mystryl, our feathered friends. This is a sign, too."

Reverently she laid the bird down, as if laying the entire empire to rest. For the first time she saw the limits of the devastation. The fountain had pumped itself clear, spraying clear and merrily again, but blood spots lingered everywhere like the fingerprints of mischievous imps.

"It's the end, Candlemas." Her haunting tones chilled the mage. "The end of the end, the end of everything. The Netherese Empire will fall now, and no one can prevent it."

Not even Karsus, thought Candlemas. Not even him.

* * * * *

Much later, as the sun set, they got back to the castle. Their driver had finally abandoned the carriage, cut the traces, and mounted Candlemas and Aquesita bareback on the horses. As they wolfed soup and bread in the kitchen, servants and hangers-on buzzed about the portents of disaster.

Even the feared "rain of skulls" had come true earlier when a stray explosion on the underside of Ioulaum opened a forgotten cavern. Bones and skulls had gushed in a stream like snowmelt, and only then had people recalled that Ioulaum had cut his enclave from the Rampant Peaks, either Bone Hill or Thunder Peak, where tens of thousands of orcs had been exterminated in a war lasting sixteen months.

Yet no one knew Ioulaum's thoughts, for the ancient and venerable mage had gone missing. Great Karsus himself had tried to contact Ioulaum with his strongest palantir and drawn a blank. The sages of Ioulaum proclaimed that their master was not dead, but, they hinted darkly, he might have abandoned the city because "sinners" had "resisted his will." Faint hearts and weak resolve had disappointed the master, they warned. As penance, to appease Ioulaum and show their true devotion, everyone must reapply himself to his work and carry out the archwizard's final orders: intensify the war and destroy the city of Karsus. And this too matched prophecy, for wasn't the loss of Ioulaum be "the disappearance of the first of the brightest?"

But what, they asked, did it mean for the empire, if these were portents of its demise? Prophecies had come and gone, and little changed. The city had not winked out of existence. So perhaps they meant nothing, and the church sages would invent new ones?

Fatigued, fretful, Candlemas excused himself from Aquesita. He had an idea to offer Karsus, he explained, one that might stop the hostilities. Aquesita asked what, but Candlemas didn't want to "dilute the magic" by repeating it. Kissing her smudged forehead, he left her wondering.

He wondered himself if his idea would work. He hoped Karsus was still listening. He needed just one more favor from the mad mage.

* * * * *

Candlemas found Karsus in the highest workshop overlooking what remained of the city and the distant enemy, Ioulaum. The madman still wore his ridiculous general's costume, though he'd abandoned the drooping helmet. He was surrounded, as usual, by slavering to adies who complimented his every notion and laughed at his feeble jokes.

Nor were any dissuaded by the destruction so visible

from the balcony. In fact, they planned more mischief. Two apprentices were explaining their latest fiendish invention. By thinning heavy magic with a grease spell, they could form a slush. Into the slush they could sprinkle fleas containing the blood of cows sickened with anthrax. Once flung into the city, the slush would ooze down gutters and storm drains. At the least, rats at the lowest levels of the city would be plagued with anthrax. At the best, the ooze might filter into water reservoirs and sicken hundreds at one stroke. Karsus loved the idea, whooping with delight, and ordered the pair to develop it immediately.

Candlemas stood stock still, fists clenched tightly at his sides to keep from screaming and slamming the apprentices' heads together. He was not a violent man, had never warred or fought, but he could see sometimes justice needed to be dealt swiftly with a sword or club. Pounding these capricious fools to death would be a good start. Bashing Karsus over the head, locking him in a chest, and tilting it off the city's precipice might be wise, too.

But he had to be polite, smile, even praise Great—no, General—Karsus if he hoped to save himself and Aquesita, and Sunbright, if he could locate him. So when the mages bustled away, and other sycophants clamored for Karsus's attention, Candlemas raised his voice. "Gr—General Karsus, I believe I have the ultimate weapon, one to banish Ioulaum from the sky!"

"What's that?" Karsus asked, stifling the mages at hand and raising his swirling golden eyes to Candlemas. "Ultimate weapon? What could that be? You intrigue me, Eadelmas."

Lucke's Love, thought the mage, now he's even forgotten my name. But he bulled on. "I'd need to relate it in secret, General Karsus, Greatest of Any Who Ever Led Us."

The archwizard preened at the flattery, smoothing his tangled, tattered hair with one hand. The other hand fiddled with his belt buckle. "Very well," he decided. "Begone, you lot! Shoo, shoo! Anvilmast and I shall talk privately of wizardly things."

The disgruntled mages dispersed, passing Candlemas with black looks. He ignored them, trotted to Karsus and caught his elbow, talking fast to keep the flighty archwizard's attention. "Time, milord, time! Consider this: if you could reach back in time—the same way you grabbed the fallen star, and the barbarian and myself—you could seize Ioulaum when he's just beginning his magic research! If you dragged him here, you could imprison him! He'd never become a great mage, one they whisper is almost as great as you. He'd never create the flying enclave of Ioulaum, and you'd have won the war without ever leaving this room! You'd be the most famous of this, and every other epoch in the empire! No one would speak of any archwizard without first mentioning Karsus the All Mighty!"

The mad golden eyes lit like lanterns. "Why, it's true! We never thought of that. Of course! Why couldn't it work?" (Candlemas could think of many reasons, including that if the first flying enclave were never created, this one might not be either. But he wasn't pursuing logic. . . .) "Oh, yes! Yes! We'll do it. I'll do it—"

"Sire," interjected Candlemas loudly, giving the archwizard's elbow a small shake. "It wouldn't be mete for you to pursue such a path yourself. For one thing, it might be dangerous, and nothing must endanger the life of Karsus the All High. Rather, sire, I suggest you assign someone—me, perhaps, who's already moved through time once—to perform the task. I'd see you got all the credit, for I live to serve only your greatness. So, if you tell me the secret time travel spell you so cleverly employed . . ."

Flattery, fast talk, simple, twisted logic, and a conspiratorial tone all worked. Within minutes, Karsus was gabbling about how he'd imagined the fallen star and twitched his fingers to summon it. From there, Candlemas led him to the hypothetical reversal of the spell: how to send something or someone *back,* to that same spot.

* * * * *

Candlemas's brain whirled with spells, cantras, lists of potential materials, and the overall weirdness that was Karsus. The combined spells he'd outlined seemed just too illogical to work. Candlemas had pried and prodded, desperate to grasp every nuance, but Karsus grew bored, wanted to move on to the next subject.

Candlemas mentally shrugged. He'd tried his best to retain it all, but would have to experiment, muddle through. He was about to beg his leave to get started when Karsus caught *his* elbow.

"I must tell you, dear Carpalmen, that you're a clever fellow, but a mere birdbrain compared to He Who Knows Everything and Tells Naught."

"He Who—?"

"Me!" Karsus beamed. "Because what you've outlined is fine, but *I've* conceived a *true* ultimate weapon!"

Candlemas felt faint and cold, as if all his blood had run out his feet. Pockall's Hex, what now? Calm as possible, he asked the source of this ultimate weapon.

"Myself!" Karsus cried and slapped his chest, giggling so hard he almost fell over. "Myself! Us, Great Karsus! I'll turn *myself* into a weapon! That's the secret project I've been working on. Think, Niselmutt! What's the greatest living thing in all the empire? Me, of course! And what's the most potent magical source in the empire? My super heavy magic! So it's logical—

though only I could think of it—to *combine* them!"

Candlemas couldn't even squeak, so frozen was he.

"I, we, Karsus the One and Only, intend to infuse ourselves with super heavy magic! If I were to eat some while, say, bathing in it, or just—I don't know—pour a ton of it over my head, who knows what power I might attain! With the power of the stars in me, I might become a god!"

At that notion, Karsus fell over laughing, hugging himself and crying hysterically with glee.

But Candlemas wasn't there to pick him up. The pudgy mage was already running through the corridors as fast as his tight boots would allow.

He had to fetch Sita. And Sunbright. And figure out this time travel spell.

And get the hell out of this city!

* * * * *

Back in his tiny workshop, frantic and fumbling, Candlemas burned the sun-blond lock of Sunbright's hair. His hand shook so badly he singed his fingers in the flame, but it would alert the barbarian that he needed help, desperately. Candlemas was going to need all the help he could summon.

And for now, he had to gather supplies, even steal them from other mages. There wasn't a second to lose.

Except that he must send word to Aquesita.

* * * * *

Riding the winds with the residual nature magic, Sunbright and Knucklebones soared toward the floating city.

Her knuckles were white as she clung to Sunbright's baldric and belt. Even though she was barefoot, she squinched her toes in reflex, for there was nothing under them for a mile or more. The ground was a misty yellow-brown patchwork, mountains only soft blue mounds. She'd never been more terrified.

By contrast, Sunbright's face was placid as an angel's. His horsetail stood out behind, his green eyes were bright, and his nose quivered like a hunting hound's as he watched the floating city of Karsus come closer. He even smiled at his accomplishment. Strangely, he wasn't worried. But then, he'd been dead, or near it, and life still seemed unreal to him, as if he still dreamwalked.

"W-we won't be fl-flying often, w-will we?" asked the thief.

Sunbright actually laughed, "I'm afraid not. The nature magic in me is almost spent. This will probably be the last time I ever fly, though shamans fly in their dreams. For this, I thought of how geese move and mimicked them, but I'm not sure exactly how I do it, to tell the truth."

Knucklebones wasn't encouraged, and clung tight as a tick to his iron frame. She wanted to squeeze her eye shut, but didn't dare to for fear of missing something. She bleated, "When we took off in the glider, Candlemas said the city was warded against people shifting in. Will that stop us from flying in?" Most specifically, just when we reach the edge of the city? she worried.

"I don't think so," he told her, "but I'm sure we'll find out." He squinted against the rush of wind. He didn't flap his arms like wings, simply held them stiffly outright, soaring like a hawk. "The city seems busy."

Stiffly, Knucklebones craned to see. In the distance floated another, smaller city, and red and blue gushes of smoke burst from it. Karsus returned hails of arrows, whirling balls of lightning, and misty, sparkling gasses of yellow and orange. As they rose higher, she saw that several buildings had corners and bites knocked from them. Obviously the two cities were at war, though she couldn't guess why. More nobles' foolishness. She wondered if her friends in the lower depths were safe.

Then the upside-down mountain slid past them like a cloud bank. The mountain had mostly been scoured clean by wind and rain, but in clefts and pockets nature hung on, and red pine trees and gorse bushes sprouted. The mountain filled her limited vision, then the edge showed, clean cut as if by a knife, and they looked at high stone walls surrounding ornate gardens. A prosperous neighborhood where nobles preferred to live on an edge rather than the hills. Naturally, this side was turned away from the enemy's fire. The docks were launching pads for magic infused ballistae and spells. Whatever engineers controlled the slow spin of the city must have arrested it during the war. Just was well, for Sunbright could steer to this quiet side.

Yet even here there was damage. One corner of a house had been knocked off, so two walls in an upper bedroom showed, and red tiles littered a flagstone walk. The missile had shorn limbs from a willow tree and gouged the earth. Gardeners worked like bumblebees to clear the debris.

But here their toes lifted over the wall, so Sunbright called, "Hang on! We'll land in the—"

They dropped.

Knucklebones had time for one short scream before she slammed onto grassy turf and lost her wind. Immediately she was up, crouching, feeling the grass. It was real. She was home.

At that stomach lurching drop, in a few seconds, she'd seen a lifetime of nightmares, imagining the long plummet to the earth below. But Sunbright had steered them over a wall and garden before the wards—they *were* in place—negated his flying spell.

But where was—

A thrashing sounded behind her. Sunbright had crashed into a bush with shiny leaves and red blossoms. Groggily he clambered free of branches, sucking a gash on his wrist. He leaned on a stone wall behind, then paused to look at it.

Knucklebones saw his gaze, said, "That's the last wall. On the other side is nothing but a long drop."

"Yes," Sunbright drawled. Ever so carefully, as if he'd sink through the soil, he stepped out of the flower bed onto the grass, straightened his tackle, and took a deep breath. "We're back."

The thief nodded, grinning all over with relief. She nodded toward the house and street beyond. "We better move if we're to find Candlemas."

"Hey, you! Halt!"

A stone's throw away, at the entrance to the garden, stood a trio of heavyset men in a house livery of purple and tan tunics. They waved short swords. "Come here!" one of them shouted. "You're trespassing! We'll have you flogged and quartered, you . . ."

Sunbright and Knucklebones walked toward them, the barbarian with his tall, panther's glide, the thief high stepping and quick. Knucklebones waggled her thumb at the house guards and said, "We make for the street. Get out of our way."

The guards balked, reached for their pommels, took another look at the dangerous, scarred pair, and stepped aside. Knucklebones didn't even sniff as she passed. She was home.

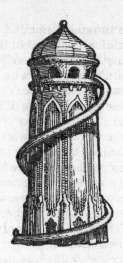

Chapter 20

Candlemas rubbed his burning eyes and aching head, and flexed cramped fingers. He'd gone without sleep night and day, without food, without rest, trying desperately to comprehend the muddled references and esoteric spells Karsus had mentioned might allow time travel.

The pudgy mage was alone in his borrowed workshop. A dozen books stolen from the library lay open, and handfuls and jarfuls and heaps of materials were scattered about: quicksilver, henbane, brimstone, lead, creeping thyme, chalk, a fish fossilized in a slate, an egg, an acorn, sand, a bottle of rare air.

The spells he listed were a jumble, some old, some new, some sprung from Karsus's addled brain. Protect from getting lost (in space). Immunity to gasses (if there were any in the ether). Spell at maximum effect (he'd need it). Valdick's spheresail (if time had currents). Shatter barrier (time barrier?). Trebbe's invulnerability (couldn't hurt, but was it necessary?). Dimensional folding (no clue). Stoca's wings (to say the least). One of Xanad's power words (if he could think of one). Yturn's feather fall (backward?).

But the words blurred together while he read the list over and over, no closer to the true path, if there was one. With a genius (mad or not) like Karsus, anything was possible. For a while, Candlemas had considered simply asking Karsus to return them to their time, but sensed the answer would be no, he was needed. Or worse, sure, and they'd be mistakenly transported to the gods knew where or when.

But he had to try something, so he had prepared a scroll. Grinding various materials as finely as he could, he dissolved them in ink and inscribed the spells, hoping he got the right elements and spells in the right order. First was Stoca's wings, thickened with egg yolk for bird wings. Then shatter barrier, with iron filings to mimic a sledgehammer. Then Valdick's spheresail, with dandelion fluff that clotted the quill and made his letters smeary.

And so on.

But there was something else, he knew. The biggest element. He must recite the spell while touching the fallen star, for it was to its landing spot they wished to return. That was the only way to guarantee the right time and place. Otherwise they might find themselves a thousand feet in the air, or deep underground, or in some foreign land without a clue or—

The possibilities for mishap were endless, so he brushed them aside. He'd try his best, and hope for the best.

Except he wouldn't be allowed to conjure at the star,

because it was guarded by mages night and day to see no one tapped its awesome power, reserved exclusively for Karsus. Aquesita might be able to dismiss the mages, but—

But she was the other problem. Candlemas still hadn't told her of his plan to get himself and Sunbright back to their own time. Would she go with him? Why should she? She was the highest noblewoman in the empire here, with a world at her fingertips: mansions, servants, gardens, treasures from countless worlds. Why would she accompany Candlemas to Castle Delia, where he had a dusty workshop and a small room with a straw pallet? He owned nothing, though he was rich by most standards, with a trunk full of coins gathered over the years and never spent. He'd never wanted to buy anything. He'd only studied magic.

And wasn't that the problem? That he was a dumpy, bald, dusty little man of no importance? Why would Aquesita go with him? Why did she even associate with him now, when she could summon the most fascinating people in the empire to her tea table?

Yet, he hoped, she loved him. As he loved her.

But was love enough to leave her homeland and treasures and status? Or were such sacrifices the codswallop of softheaded romances?

In short, would she say goodbye when he left?

* * * * *

Far below the earth, diamond-tipped tornados of stone tilted and swayed and bobbed in agitation.

This is not what we planned.

We did not plan anything. We only gave the humans enough magic to destroy themselves.

That works. But this Karsus plans to become a god. No human can do that and live.

So? Better for us. He will flare like a candle and extinguish.

The Phaerimm stumbled over one another's thoughts, interrupting, questioning, demanding, a thing unheard of in their history, for they were old as time and had decades to converse. But danger loomed like a moon eclipsing the sun.

His flare might shake the stars. He would use all the magic in one fell swoop. He could blow a crater the width of the empire. And as deep. Even down to here.

Impossible.

Nothing is impossible with magic, and this source is the greatest.

Are you saying we erred in giving it?

I say, men with fire can burn down a forest. Men with star magic can burn a world.

Then we are in danger.

No.

Yes.

Never, not us.

It could be.

It cannot be.

I am not sure.

Whatever, we must act.

To act would require us to go above ground, shift fully into the humans' dimension! That causes us to explode! That is why we gave the humans magic indirectly!

We did not foresee personal danger.

We will pay for that shortsightedness with our lives. We, the oldest of the old, may cease to be and not the humans.

It is written in the stars that all things pass.

Not us. We were before the world was.

No, impossible.

Blasphemy!

Stop! Think! If we could act, what action would we take?

Silence was the only answer.

* * * * *

Blearily, Candlemas stumbled through the maze of corridors toward the star workshop. He clutched the scroll in his hand. It was smeary, crossed out repeatedly, highly dubious, but finished. It was a masterpiece, really, though no one would know. He only hoped it worked. If they got home safely, he might never ensorcell again.

To complete the spell, he needed to be touching the star. Before that he had to find Sunbright, and talk to Aquesita, to ask her the most important question of his life. But before *that*, he needed another look. Mages tinkered with the fallen star day and night. He needed to know its current makeup, size, potency. Or perhaps he was just avoiding Sita. He wished he knew what to do or say, but he wasn't a strong-jawed hero from a chivalric romance, just a tired old mage, awkward with women. There was no magic for knowing the way to a woman's heart. Or perhaps they possessed their own magic. Certainly they were entrancing. . . .

But he was drifting, and here was the chamber, and Karsus's gleeful, manic giggling.

Rounding the corner, Candlemas stopped cold.

Karsus was surrounded by apprentices, as usual, but also a trio of tailors with needles and thread in their mouths. The mad mage wore a startling white gown embroidered with silver thread. Someone had cleaned his face, scrubbed his neck, even combed and trimmed his hair. He stood with arms out as the tailors closed seams and smoothed pleats. Karsus giggled all the while.

"It's not often you dress a god, is it? You'll have something to tell your friends. How you served Great Karsus when he was still human!"

The tailors smiled weakly, but averted their eyes. Their usually nimble fingers shook, and they dropped pins and scissors. Lesser mages and apprentices, some twenty, puttered at the tables or else halfheartedly tapped the gray lump of star-metal with silver hammers. Everyone was uneasy, not giggling and chuckling at Karsus's every remark. It was the first time Candlemas had seen quiet around Karsus.

The pudgy mage was sweating suddenly, his mouth dry, his knees trembling. He was surprised at his calm voice. "Great Karsus, might you enlighten me, who would learn from the Highest of the High? What exactly are you planning to do? And when?"

"Oh, I decided now's as good a time as any." Karsus waved vaguely toward the fallen star as he said, "My helpers think all is ready—not that they really understand what I plan. And the war goes badly, a maid said.

"And I'm tired of being human. So I'll become an avatar, which is a being created from a god's body, in case you don't know. Karsus's avatar, named after myself. I figure to sit on the star, imagine myself ascending to godhood, and draw all the remaining energy through my spine into my brain. I'll use the same spell that temporarily disrupted the magic of this room, for I'll want every iota drawn into my body. But I'll steal it so quickly you'll hardly notice. And who knows what will happen then? I might grow huge, or move to another plane—don't worry, I'll come back to visit—or find myself taking tea with Mystryl and the other gods. We'll talk about how to better tap the Weave, so that privileged individuals—new godlings!—can use it directly! It should be fun! All done there? Good!"

The tailors weren't done, but Karsus pulled away, so one undone sleeve trailed needles and thread. Pushing past his timid apprentices, he climbed on a stool, then up onto the table, circling the fallen star like a child stealing sweets from a cupboard. Spreading his trailing robes like a clown, he perched on the star, smoothed back his hair, and began to chant.

Candlemas stood paralyzed. This was insanity of the purest form. Idiot toadies standing by while their master made ready to tear down a dam holding unfathomable magic. Karsus could unleash a firestorm that could sear the world from horizon to horizon, and everyone just stood gape-mouthed and watched him.

Somehow Candlemas knew this would end in disaster. And at the very least, the magic of the fallen star would be dispelled, and he and Sunbright (and Aquesita?) would be stuck in the self-consuming kingdom of an idiot genius—or mad god. Yet what to do? He couldn't attack Karsus personally. Shields would reduce him to cinders. He couldn't block Karsus's spell. He couldn't—

Karsus raised his voice, chanting in earnest now. The air in the room began to shimmer, like heat waves over a blacksmith's forge. Jars and pots on tables began to jiggle. One shattered into redware shards.

Candlemas stopped thinking, and reacted.

Charging, he bowled mages aside and scrambled onto the table. In his panic, he never noticed that he dropped his smeary, crumpled scroll. Diving, he shoved Karsus off the star with both arms.

The little madman squawked as he crashed on his back on the tabletop. Toadies shouted Karsus's name. Three of them grabbed Candlemas's red-striped robe and jerked him back off the table. Frowning, dazed, Karsus lay and shook his head.

It was the first time Candlemas had ever seen him angry. The great archwizard pointed a bony finger and snarled.

Candlemas's world exploded in red fire.

* * * * *

As the odd pair, big barbarian and tiny thief, threaded the nobles' district, they saw increasing signs of devastation and chaos, and a complete breakdown of city authority.

Whole buildings had collapsed, some into cellars and some into the street. Streets had in turn collapsed under the weight of the fallen buildings, so craters revealed sewers. Broken water lines gushed, and Knucklebones whiffed effluvia, the deadly gas piped into homes for heating and cooking. Horse skeletons lay in their traces, stripped of flesh by the starving poor. Garbage was strewn about, and rats feasted. In alleys and behind bushes were glimpsed riddled skeletons of humans while nonhumans—half-elves, gnomes, dwarves—were lynched or nailed to walls and left to rot. Time and again they saw humans wandering in a daze, vacant, haunted looks etched in their faces.

"By the Earthmother," muttered Sunbright. "You wouldn't know where to start to help. Where are the guards? The body haulers? The dung shovelers?"

Knucklebones crouched, pointed one way, then shoved Sunbright the other. In a street of shops, most closed, he saw blue and silver guards looting a gold-smith's shop. The owner lay dead on her own threshold. The thief whispered, "It looks like the end of the end. What the sages have threatened for centuries."

"I hope we can enter Karsus's compound." Sunbright said, reaching over his shoulder to loosen Harvester in its scabbard and adjusting Dorlas's warhammer riding on his hip. "I hope your little charges there, Aba and Zykta and Rolon, keep their heads down. I once promised Rolon I'd take him to the ground—"

"He's there now."

Knucklebones hunted a certain alley. She knew them all, but many were blocked by rubble or abandoned carriages or garbage.

She answered Sunbright's surprised look by telling him, "That's why I sent them to Sleeping Gunn. He lives over the warehouses at the docks because he's a smuggler. Since I've disappeared and there's been war here, he'll have ferried the children to a stronghold on the ground." Her voice sounded wistful, missing them. Sunbright gave her thin shoulder a squeeze, and she touched his broad, scarred hand.

"Come on." She said choosing an alley. "We'll go over ground a while, then underground. I know a back way into Karsus's mansions, if it's still open."

They were blocked repeatedly, and often had to hunker for guards or refugees to pass, but backtracking and retracing eventually brought them into the garden beneath Candlemas's suite. Sunbright boosted Knucklebones, who pronounced a short word and fractured all the glass in one window. Sunbright used Harvester's hook to drag the lead frame down like a gray metal spiderweb. Then they were inside.

Knucklebones signaled to wait while she listened. Then she dashed from the room quick as a hare. A bleat was stifled, and Sunbright tramped after.

The thief sat atop a plump maid jackknifed over the bed. Candlemas's bed was bare to the striped ticking. Fresh silk sheets and blankets awaited. Piled by the door like rubbish lay the mage's plain wool smock, rope belt, and warped sandals that retained the imprint of his broad feet.

Sunbright was in a hurry, but told the terrified maid, "No harm if you answer. What happened to the mage who dwelt here? Why do you discard his things?"

"He-he's locked in the cellars, sir! He's wounded horrible! They've left him to die! He—I don't know what he did exactly, but he defied Great Karsus and they've—"

Knucklebones tweaked her ear to silence her, said, "Tell us how to get there!"

"No time!" Sunbright countermanded. He grabbed up fresh sheets, tossed them to Knucklebones, and swaddled himself like a servant buried in laundry. "Take us!"

Trained to stay out of sight, the gasping maid brought them down servants' stairwells to the cellars. With a quivering finger she pointed along a dim corridor lined with stone and lit only by a distant window. Four city guards idled, pitching coins against a stout wooden door, grousing at the boring duty.

"Wait here." Knucklebones told Sunbright. "I'll circle around to take them from behind." Towing the trembling maid, she backed away and down the corridor.

But the barbarian couldn't wait. Something impelled him to move quickly, as if he smelled doom in the wind. Drawing Harvester, he stepped full into the corridor. Knucklebones could catch up.

"You guards! Stand away from that door! We've no quarrel with you, we only want Candlemas!"

At his first words, the guards cinched helmet straps and snatched swords from scabbards. Now they assessed their enemy: a barbarian, a big one, armed with a huge scythe of a sword. They knew too that the prisoner Candlemas was important. They didn't know why, but anyone who'd come to rescue him might fetch a large bonus. One of them growled and two guards—a man and a woman—trotted off to circle behind Sunbright, where they'd run smack into Knucklebones.

The guard called, "You can't get out. You'd best lay down your sword quietly."

"I'm sorry, but no."

Sunbright advanced slowly, sword tilted across his chest but ready to sweep down and around.

"I need the man you hold. It's not worth your lives to protect him, so begone."

The guard puffed, shifted to let his partner join him, and both drew silver tipped clubs in their left hands as makeshift shields. They were brawny men, but nothing to compare with Sunbright's height and breadth. The first one, with a yellow beard, craned over his shoulder where the other two guards had gone. A scuffle sounded. The guard muttered something to his partner, then growled, "Rush!"

They charged low, clubs outthrust, swords ready. Sunbright dropped his right foot and shoulder back, cocked Harvester, and waited.

Obviously practiced, the guards swung clubs at the same time, one high, one low, to trap and block Harvester so their short swords could stab for guts. But the barbarian was faster with his trusty weapon. As the right-hand guard struck with ironwood, Sunbright flicked out the barbed tip of Harvester, snagged the man's wrist, and tugged. Razor steel split skin and severed a tendon. Instantly the man's hand went limp, and the club fell. Within a second, the great blade spanked to bat the other club down. So hard was the rap that the guard staggered at the blow. But he lunged on, jabbing with his sword.

Sunbright hadn't time to disarm them. Flicking sideways, he smacked the guard alongside the head just below the helmet. Skin split along his jaw as the strap was cut. Blood spouted from under his chin and he stumbled.

Dismissing that foe, dragging Harvester back quickly, sideways across his gut, the barbarian banged down the upthrusting blade of the other guard. At the same time, he kicked savagely, either for thigh or crotch. His moose-hide boot knocked the man's knee out from under him. Two-handed, Sunbright helped him fall by bashing Harvester's pommel on the back of his helmet. The man's face hit the floor, helmet clanging. Sunbright recovered his footing and kicked the man's head, not caring if he snapped his neck or not. The man lay still.

The bleeding guard clutched his neck with both hands. Blood spurted between his fingers, gradually slowed, and the red hands fell away.

Chest heaving, wiping his sword on a dead man's sleeve and then sheathing it, Sunbright toed over the guards until he found a key on a rawhide thong on a belt. Ripping it loose, he strode to the door, unlocked it, slammed it back.

Inside was dark, but before his eyes adjusted he heard a scrape and gurgle. Stepping into cool darkness, Sunbright latched onto a hairy, thick arm and towed the prisoner out. Knucklebones came, bosom puffing and blood on both hands and her dark elven blade. Sunbright laid his burden down for a look.

Candlemas was a mess. His face was red and blistered, his eyebrows and beard and mustache singed to stubble, his bald head scabbed and seeping fluid. The yellow-red robe was spattered with his own blood.

"Forest of Fire!" rumbled Sunbright. "What happened to you?"

"I tried to . . . stop Karsus." The mage's voice wheezed, husky, for his mouth and lungs were scorched. "I was lucky. Someone pulled me . . . over backward . . . just before th-the . . . burning hands got me. But Karsus is spelling . . . to be a god!"

"Be a god?" asked Sunbright. "Become a *god?*"

"Can he do that?" Knucklebones gasped.

"He can . . . do anything."

Wincing, Candlemas plied blistered hands to lever himself up, but fell back, coughing and gagging, strangling on fluid gumming his seared lungs. Blood burbled at the corners of his mouth.

"Oh, it hurts! He's using the . . . the star . . . stealing its power. Anything could happen."

Squatting, Sunbright touched Candlemas on both sides of his face, cooed to him as if to a child. The mage stared as if hypnotized. Then his eyes widened in surprise and he took a deep breath without coughing.

"My!" snorted Candlemas. He hawked and spat, with

no trace of blood in the phlegm. "Where have you been studying?"

Sunbright helped him rise and told him, "I'm finally a shaman. I've learned the secrets of nature magic. But I had to die, or almost, to gain the knowledge."

"Great knowledge indeed." Candlemas snorted. But his knees buckled and he fell. "Oh, I'm weak as a kitten."

Stooping, Sunbright grabbed a seared wrist and ankle. There was no time to heal all the mage's wounds, only the internal, dangerous ones. Grunting, the barbarian hoisted the heavy man across his shoulders.

"No, I'm too fat," Candlemas protested. "And your sword gouges my ribs."

Shifting, shoving, Sunbright ignored the protests and slid Candlemas behind his neck. But the barbarian suddenly weaved sideways and struck the wall. "Whoa! You *are* heavy!"

"That's not you!" Knucklebones bleated. She'd also been hurled against the wall. Fascinated, she stared as a guard's helmet spun loose of its dead owner and rolled down the corridor as if possessed by invisible mice.

The corridor tilted back, and Sunbright fell to one knee. Knucklebones was white, and her fear communicated to the barbarian and the sagging Candlemas. They both asked, "What is it?"

"It's the city!" howled the native. "It's tilting. It's never done that before. It'll fall from the sky!"

Chapter 21

"What do we do?" demanded Sunbright.

"Sita!" Candlemas called as he struggled to get off Sunbright's shoulders, kicked a tilting wall, and pitched them both to the floor. The mage banged singed flesh, but scrambled up like a squashed toad, laid a hand on a slanted wall, and found it quivering. "I must get to Sita!"

"In the name of the eternal mountains," roared Sunbright, "who's Sita?"

"She's . . ." The mage stopped. He hadn't told the barbarian. "A friend! We need to take her with us when we flee!"

"Flee where?" shrilled Knucklebones. She had to brace her feet against cracks in the cobblestones to keep upright. Another guard's helmet rolled past. Then came a

barrel, careening off the walls as it wobbled their way.
Candlemas barely jumped aside in time. "There's
nowhere on Karsus that's safe! The enclave will fall!"

"Back to our time!" Candlemas splayed both hands
against the walls to move upward against the tilt. It
was steep enough to make his booted feet slide. "I fabri-
cated a scroll, but lost it! It's with the star!"

"What star? Scroll for what?" Knucklebones screamed,
but the thief was ignored.

Sunbright caught her hand and dragged her after
them. " 'Mas knows what he's doing!" he told her.

"I wish!" the mage hissed to himself. Candlemas had
gained the stairs, where the door flapped as if from a
capricious wind. But there wasn't any wind in this dim
corridor, only the earth betraying their feet. Painfully,
with scorched fingers, Candlemas hauled himself up
the slanted stairwell, in danger of toppling at every
step. Cursing, Sunbright climbed after, with Knucklebones the nimblest of all. She almost skipped like a
mountain goat in Sunbright's ponderous wake.

The servant's stairs gave out onto a wide, sumptuous
hallway, but everything in it was skewed. As they
watched, a vase wobbled and struck a wall with a
crash. A table bunched against a rug and slid slowly. A
mirror swung off its hook and shattered in a thousand
jeweled shards on polished oak flooring. When Candlemas tried to walk, he slid uncontrollably. Braced in the
doorframe, Sunbright caught him.

"You can't go uphill!" the barbarian shouted, "We'll
have to skid down and go around! Where are we going?"

They yelled because sliding, grinding furniture destroyed itself, and throughout the mansion people
screamed, called questions, hollered for help.

"A white mansion on the grounds, downhill and . . ."

Directions failed Candlemas, so he just pointed.
Shrugging out of Sunbright's iron grip, he swung onto

the floor and slid on his bottom until he banged a corner already crowded with tumbled furniture. Skidding treacherously in his moosehide boots, Sunbright slid after. Knucklebones crowded so close to the barbarian that her feet rapped his kidneys when they struck a wall. They tried to use their hands as brakes, but broken glass and splinters cut their skin, even the ironlike soles of Knucklebones's bare feet.

In a main hall, the mess was worse. Tables, chairs, benches, statuary, and one dead body, a maid who'd struck her head. Skittering crabwise, they found the wreckage didn't lie still, but kept moving, for in addition to the tilt, the enclave was rotating again so debris inched around corners and cascaded anew.

Finally, inching and grabbing and gasping, they got to a wide pair of outside doors. Candlemas grabbed the doorframe and almost had his fingers smashed as the door swung back with a smash. Sunbright had to climb over the mage and muscle the door open. They fell more than jumped out the door.

Outside, they could at least get a grip on gravel walks and flower beds and grass, as if they negotiated a hill. Sunbright paused to check that his weapons were still strapped tight. Knucklebones ripped a splinter long as a pencil from her bleeding foot. "Where are we going?"

But Candlemas only stared. Nowhere was the landscape flat, and that betrayal was terrifying. In the city below, a tall, black tower, the Shadow Consortium, waggled like a nagging finger, then broke in the middle and plunged down like the arrow of Targus, God of War. Scores of people inhabited that building, he'd heard, and now it snapped like a twig and crashed onto scores more structures below. He'd just witnessed the death of hundreds of people. With more to come, for other buildings wobbled just as disastrously. Distant screams came from below and behind. Servants and nobles alike ran onto lawns to shout and cry.

Candlemas recalled his mission and shouted, "Come on!"

Sunbright and Knucklebones jogged as Candlemas crossed a grassy sward and bulled through a forsythia hedge. Knucklebones was hurled back by thick branches, so Sunbright had to grab her and lob her over, then crash through on his own. Catching up as Candlemas trotted along crushed clamshells, he yelled, "Karsus is causing this? Making the city tip and fall?"

"Yes!" Candlemas gulped, his lungs afire. He was no runner. "He's out to make himself a god! But I think he's siphoning all the magic in the enclave! If the mythallars can't keep up the city will plummet! Nothing can save it!"

"But you can get us back to our own time?"

"If there's enough magic! If it's gone, if the star's power is used up, we'll be stranded, and die with the city!"

Trotting right behind, Knucklebones demanded, "What's this about returning to your own time?"

"Candlemas can get us back!" Sunbright vaulted the trunk of a fallen tree as he said, "To where we belong!"

"Where *you* belong!" the thief corrected. "I'm Karsus enclave born and bred!"

Sunbright cast her a sidelong glance. Her ratty hair bobbed about her head, tickled her pointed ears. Despite running hard, she was not winded, and stared boldly with her one green eye. "You'll die with the city if you don't get out!"

"Instead, I should go with you?" she asked. The boldness in her voice turned hard.

"Yes! I-I want you . . . to go with me!" Sunbright found himself fumbling for words.

A statue of a man ahorse had toppled, smashing amidst a thick stand of cedars, blocking their way. Candlemas yelled a word, flicked his fingers, and the water in the trees exploded with a bang. Green specks floated around them as he rammed through denuded branches.

Yet Sunbright paused to catch Knucklebones's thin hand. "Will you go with me? Please?"

"Why should I?" she asked. Her stance was wide-legged, her hips cocked, her chin tipped to stare with a green eye. "What am I to you?"

Women picked the damnedest times to argue, Sunbright thought. Greenwillow had been the same way. It had been during such a crisis, besieged in a burning hell, that they had first bespoken their love. And as if Greenwillow's ghost breathed the words in his ear, Sunbright found himself saying, "I need you. I love you."

The boldness was wiped away with one stroke, and a mistiness possessed Knucklebones's eye. Softly, she told him, "Good. Because I love you too."

They had time for a quick kiss. Her lips were soft and firm, cool and wet. His, strong and hard. Then they were running after Candlemas as branches whipped in a wind that was not a wind.

But the mage stopped on a path at the brow of a hill. Arms outflung, he called, "Sita! I was so worried!"

The plump noblewoman flew into his arms, slamming his chest so hard he grunted, then hugged him tight, smearing his fine blue-green robe with his blood. "Me, too, dear Candy! I love you so! Don't leave me!"

"No, no! Never again! I love you, Sita!" For the first time in his life, the pudgy mage hugged a woman and breathed the words, and many more endearments.

Still holding hands, Sunbright and Knucklebones caught up. Their eyes were shining, but their faces were worried. The ground lurched, and from behind rolled a giant ball of marble. They had to dash aside to avoid it, and it rumbled past and smashed flat a wooden gazebo.

"Oh, our empire . . ." breathed Aquesita.

The others turned to look. This brow afforded an all-encompassing view.

The enclave of Karsus was dying. Many buildings had collapsed. Fires blossomed like yellow-red flowers, spinning off spirals of smoke. Water from splintered fountains and pipes sometimes met flame and burst into steam, but in other places flooded folks off their feet. Near the tumbled walls that surrounded Castle Karsus, hordes of people, from the poorest to the noblest, dashed into the grounds to seek high ground. Too, their anger swelled as their homes and families were destroyed, and instinctively they knew Karsus was responsible. The mutter of this mob became a growl, then a roar.

But Aquesita mewed, and pointed at the sky. "Lady of Mystery!"

From tilted horizon to slanted mountains, the sky was knitting, piling up gray clouds, coalescing into a solid mass. But amongst the clouds, stretched so wide the eye couldn't see all, there began to form a face, and hair, and wide, outspread arms spanning the horizon, encompassing the empire.

A woman, a goddess, blotted out the sun.

"It's the final prophecy!" whispered Aquesita. "The last true sign of the End of the End! The end of the empire!"

Candlemas tore his eyes away, grabbed his ladylove's hand. "It's nothing! A storm, an illusion!" He didn't believe it himself, so barked louder, "Let's go! We need to find your cousin before the mob does!"

No one argued, but they had to tear Aquesita from staring at the sky, at the death knell of her beloved empire. Stumbling, running uphill, they fought the bucking earth and crashing debris to get to Karsus and his star chamber.

* * * * *

The quartet found paths that were clear, dodged fallen cornices and fences and statues and trees, and managed to scramble up polished stone steps by clinging to handholds and helping one another. The rioters were far behind, but still coming. The city tilted ever steeper. If it continued to turn at this rate, they'd be crawling on all fours.

But the worst problem came because Karsus had outsmarted himself again.

Their first inkling of trouble was a maid and butler screaming past them, bloody from scratches and slashes on heads and arms. Taking the lead, clinging to a wall, Sunbright slung Knucklebones behind to drag Harvester from its sheath, ready to battle whatever terrified the servants.

What erupted around a paneled corner was a female apprentice no higher than Sunbright's breastbone. The woman sported blood on her chin where she'd bitten her tongue and lips, other peoples' blood on her fingernails hooked like claws. Her clothing was torn where she'd shredded it herself, and her eyes were wild, inhuman. She screamed like a cougar when she saw Sunbright, and raced to tear him apart with her bare hands.

The barbarian acted instinctively and stabbed straight to keep her back. The madwoman ran her stomach onto his blade. If Sunbright hadn't twisted the blade to hook deep in her liver, she would have slid along it and gouged out his eyes. As it was, she was champing bloodstained teeth and slashing with fingernails when the light faded from her glazed eyes. She fell heavily, and Sunbright had to stamp on her breast to rip Harvester loose. Blood gushed over his boot and ran in a river down the sloping floor.

The barbarian's voice shook as he asked, "What is this?"

"Berserker spell," echoed Candlemas. "Karsus said once that he'd always be protected by those who loved him best. I thought he was just airing his tongue, or joking. But he meant it. He must have enchanted all his mages so that if Karsus were attacked from any direction, they'd go fighting mad, assault whatever they saw until Karsus was safe again."

Sunbright wiped his forehead. He'd hated to kill the woman, innocent and deadly as a rabid rabbit.

"But who attacks Karsus?"

Candlemas glanced over his shoulder at the gray, roiling sky. The sky woman's monumental features were hardening, growing more defined, despite a hearty wind kicking up. "*Magic* attacks him, for he's taken on too much. That and, I suspect, a goddess."

They saved their breath for running. In the lead, Sunbright had to cut down half a dozen apprentices raving under the influence of the berserker spell. Killing them was no harder than cutting daisies, but it sickened the barbarian, so he found himself hesitating. Yet they were mad dog wild, and so they died, not knowing that Karsus, their beloved master, had betrayed them, used them as pawns.

On they traveled, down sloping corridors, past smashed furniture that had staved in entire walls. Litter and glass splinters and wreckage rattled everywhere, some forming waist high barriers. They helped one another, watched out, and Sunbright killed another dozen apprentices until he was spattered with blood like smallpox.

"How many damned apprentices did Karsus have?"

"Ninety! Or nine hundred!" called back Candlemas.

They knew the star chamber was near because of the heat.

Waves gushed from the room, eye and mouth-drying heat like a blast furnace, until Sunbright felt he'd stumbled into another pocket of hell. But he didn't understand the source until he saw what transpired within.

Karsus was lit like a bonfire.

Caught in some state between man and god, Karsus hung suspended above their heads. He'd grown perhaps twelve feet tall, but looked wider because his hair stuck straight out and his arms and legs were outflung. Skin, eyes, feet, robe, all shone white and silver like an illuminated mirror. He burned with an internal flame that would have melted lead.

The workshop was a madhouse. The stone floor, scorched black in spots, tilted even worse here than the rest of the building, so steeply the heroes couldn't have stood on it. Everything loose soared and whirled and spiraled around the room, including several mages killed by the sheer fury of the magic unleashed. A whistling roar drowned out sounds as jars, chairs, and tables, all ducked and wove in the air in some insane dance. Whirling books and objects and corpses caught fire if they spun too close to Karsus.

But Karsus would soon be a corpse himself, it was obvious, for he burned his life away. The massive infusion of super heavy star magic raged inside him as if he'd swallowed molten gold. His eyes bugged, his tongue protruded, his cheeks were sunken, his fingers clawed the air, his toes curled, but he still fought for control. He shouted chant after chant, a rapid, arcane babble unlike anything they'd ever heard.

Sunbright hung onto the doorjamb, took one look, and let Candlemas pass. "This task falls to you!" he shouted.

The pudgy mage stared, said, "I don't know what to do!"

"What is Karry doing?" Aquesita sobbed, clinging to Candlemas's sleeve. "What's happening to him?"

"I don't know!" the mage hollered. "He's sucked up immeasurable power, not only from the star but from the mythallars too! That's why the city tilts! The magic generators that keep it aloft are robbed of energy! But he's internalized all that magic and—I just don't know! Is he trying to dispel it without losing all of it, so we won't fall? Or return it to the star? Or is he forging ahead, trying to tame it and become a god?"

"He can't become a god!" Aquesita countered. "The gods wouldn't allow it! Lady Mystryl herself fills the sky and frowns on us!"

Candlemas scrubbed his bald head with a singed hand. He poured sweat that was instantly whisked away by searing heat. Desperately he tried to think what to do—if anything. Perhaps Karsus could dispel the power, channel it elsewhere, save enough to right the city. But if he opposed the gods, spat in Mystryl's eye and demanded the room for a newcomer, who knew how the gods might retaliate?

In the corridor, Knucklebones gave a yell and whipped out her elven knife. Another berserk apprentice raced around the corner, then tumbled in his stupefied, zombi-fied trance. He rolled, bouncing painfully but not feeling it, then fetched up against a wall. Ignoring blood running into his eyes from a scalp wound, he snarled and swiped for Knucklebones. Latching onto Sunbright's belt with one hand, the thief neatly speared the mad apprentice's throat. He fell and tumbled on down the slanted flag-stones like a discarded doll.

But the barbarian barked an alert, for more crazed mages charged, a dozen or more, hands like claws and jaws champing. Shifting Harvester, he tried to find a foothold. Fighting madmen in a tilting city was some-thing new, but maybe mountain fighting tactics would work. He shunted Knucklebones aside so he could block the doorway with his greater bulk. The more nimble thief had to move out into the corridor and cling to flag-stones with bare toes as best she could. Over his shoul-der Sunbright bellowed, "Candlemas, *do something!*"

Candlemas and Aquesita watched Karsus burn like a
flare while shouting defiance into the teeth of the wind.
They were boxed behind, yet to enter the room would
crisp them like stepping into a blast furnace. Candlemas croaked, "I don't know—Sita, I'm sorry."

A whirling parchment caught Candlemas's eye, and
he stabbed for it. He smoothed the wrinkled folds. It
was his scroll, the time travel spell, dropped as litter
when he pushed Karsus aside. That event seemed to
have happened ages ago.

A blessing, for he finally knew what to do. "Sita! This
scroll! I fashioned it! It can return us—Sunbright and
I—to our own time! I can take you too, if you want to go!"

The plump woman stared, and Candlemas's heart
plunged into his stomach. Clearly the concept was alien
to her. To leave the empire, family and friends, journey to
another time and place with a man she barely knew. But
he saw the noble lines in her face tighten as she debated,
sifted the notion in her mind. Despairing, he guessed her
answer before she asked, "What about Karsus?"

"I can't take him with us." Candlemas had to shout
above the whistling roar, but his voice sounded like a
mouse squeak. "Just you."

"Candy . . ." said the woman. "I . . . I love you. Truly.
But I have obligations. To my family . . . and the empire."

"The empire is going to die!" Candlemas shouted in
desperation. "This is the end of the end! You said so
yourself!"

"Not if Karsus succeeds!" She gazed at her cousin,
who shouted threats at the ceiling as he floated higher.
"He *will* ascend to godhood and save the city! Save the
empire! He's the greatest mage . . ."

Candlemas only stared, unsure if his lover was trying
to convince him, or herself. Then her words were lost as
the building's ceiling blew off.

Tons of stone, slate, timber beams, granite, carved cornices, and other elements exploded upward like wheat chaff. Not a speck of dust rained in the roofless room. High up, yet almost close enough to touch, frowned the cloud face of Lady Mystryl, Controller of the Weave, the stuff of all magics. And facing her, still shouting, was the presumptuous mage who would steal her power, usurp her place, walk into the firmament and take the throne of the gods themselves.

The cloud face was *not* pleased.

The corridor had become a slaughterhouse. Seconds before, Sunbright had killed three berserkers in quick succession. With one hip propped on the door jamb, he stabbed the first one straight through the belly, didn't even hurl the body aside before twisting his thick wrists and jabbing a madwoman from behind to pierce her liver. Despite the sword protruding through his guts, the mage in his face still clawed feebly. The barbarian had to risk his footing by stamping a boot against the man's thigh and wrenching Harvester free. He only slid the gory blade loose a second before yet another apprentice charged from the side, and died with a sidelong hurl of Harvester's heavy tip.

Knucklebones had it easier, for the ensorcelled apprentices mindlessly sought to protect Karsus. More kept rushing into the corridor from all over the castle, drawn by their master's will. And all of them charged Sunbright, who stood between them and their master. Passed by, the thief could slash her elven knife across hamstrings and drop berserkers like puppets. Yet once she attacked them, they retaliated, and she was forced to slice their throats as they grabbed wildly for her. One dying berserker clutched at her naked blade, and it fetched up in bone, so she resorted to battering with her brass knuckles. A wallop to the forehead would knock them back and down, or else a smash to the bridge of the nose set them gargling blood, drowning as it filled their lungs. Yet more and more arrived, until she and Sunbright were surrounded by a sea of waving arms and clashing teeth, as if they'd fallen into a snake pit.

Then the ceiling had blown off. Plaster exploded in clouds, lathes and splinters whirled like jagged knives, a beam thundered down and crushed five mages like mice. Knucklebones could barely see for blood and dust, but she heard Sunbright calling her name, clearly worried. That he cared sent an odd thrill through her bosom, even though she was so tired she could have collapsed and slept on the debris and bodies.

With gods about to clash overhead, this place was doomed. Candlemas knew they must go. With only one way out, with no time for arguing, he yelled, "Sita, you'll have to go with us! Sunbright, grab Knucklebones and hang close! I'll read!"

Hurriedly, Candlemas looked over the smeary lines to familiarize himself with the spell, for he'd only get one chance to read it aloud. The lines would disappear as pronounced, and botching it, or halting halfway, would halt the spell, with no second chance. He couldn't get any closer to the star, thirty feet away, without shriveling. He only hoped the crazy magic washing the room didn't disrupt his spell.

Glancing back at Sunbright, yelling for Knucklebones, and sucking a deep breath, he grabbed Aquesita's hand. But the noblewoman jerked away. "You can't enchant here! Not now! You'll steal the power Karry needs! You can't—Wait! There! Feel it?"

They'd braced their backs in the doorway to keep from tumbling into the hot, whirling room, but now, slowly, like a whale surfacing under a boat, the floor tilted and came upright. Within a minute, the room had stabilized, no longer shuddering.

Sunbright spat dust and blood, slung his sword one

nore time to behead a mad apprentice, called again for
Knucklebones. Bodies writhed all around, some trapped
under debris, some crawling to reach him. Blood pow-
lered white ran across the floor under his moosehide
boots, making the tilted footing even more treacherous.
Bracing his back on the doorway, he planted a boot
against the beam to shift it lest it roll back on him.
Knucklebones, dirty as an alley rat, watched both ways
to see if more berserkers came running. Then, flicking
her hair from her face, snorting dust, she clambered over
the wreckage and grabbed Sunbright's brawny hand.

"I don't know if more will come!"

The barbarian glanced into the room over a cowering
Candlemas and Aquesita.

"They won't have anyone to protect in a moment!"
Sunbright yelled, "Look!"

Chanting, Karsus floated higher, grew larger, until
he hovered above the high, sundered walls. He was almost a god. With a few more steps he'd leave humanity
behind.

Karsus, and the star behind him, began to pulse with
white-hot light. Lightning sizzled and crackled around
his frame, and he grew bigger than ever, until he was
three times the height of a man, so bloated with magic
he must have weighed thousands of pounds. His voice
was no longer a wheezy whine, but a resounding boom
like rolling thunder. He drew magic from the star until
even his toes sparkled, and he seemed to stand on a
cloud of his own making, a cloud of star energy.

Above, the cloud face of Lady Mystryl retreated.
Even she couldn't withstand the driving force of the
star power Karsus controlled. He flared like a sun of
blistering magic, and Mystryl faded back, withdrew,
like thunderclouds pushed by a hurricane. Along the
horizon, sunlight leaked and cast long shadows across
her cloudy face. Karsus controlled the sky, moved the

elements, stole the power of a weather god, like Selûne, or Shar, or the Earthmother—or Mystryl herself.

"See!" Aquesita's cheeks were wet as she cried out, "See? He's saved the city! Everything will be all right! You needn't leave us, Candlemas!"

The pudgy mage doubted that. A world ruled by a god like Karsus would be a dangerous, messy place to live. The new god's capricious whims would make puppets and playthings of people, turn the world into a toy. Secretly, Candlemas sided with Mystryl, but even the Mother of All Magic had retreated before the former human, Karsus the Mighty, the All-High. Karsus the God.

And who knew but that this god, mounting into the sky, wouldn't let his former city drop away from his feet?

Then he jerked, for Aquesita screamed.

The room suddenly swarmed with tornados.

In an eyeblink, as if a nest of giant wasps had been smashed, tornado beings spun around the room, a dozen or more. They were impossible to see clearly, for they rotated like buzzing tops, spinning cones of gray stone except for diamond-tipped tails that winked with a thousand facets in the meager daylight.

The mad scene grew crazier as the tornados bobbed and weaved and spun. Then, before the watchers' eyes had barely focused, the Phaerimm bounced into the air and converged on Karsus.

The huge glowing mage shrieked once, a word Candlemas and Sunbright and Knucklebones and Aquesita finally understood: "My *enemies!*"

Chapter 22

Shrieking, Karsus flung out his arms and fired spells at random to protect himself. Black bolts blew holes in the walls. Frost seared floating corpses and extinguished flaming books. Pulses of rainbow light threw wild colors over spinning splinters of wood. Water jets filled the air with steam and rain.

At the same time, wrenched apart by the planar stress of passing from their dimension into the dimension of humans, four of the twelve Phaerimm exploded. Tremendous, punishing blasts, and chunks of rock-like bodies gouged craters in the stone floors, ripped holes in walls, and shattered the furniture that still whirled and fluttered around the room like demented birds.

Candlemas stood dry-mouthed, unable to believe the raw power he saw displayed. Karsus was close to becoming a god, and not a minor deity, either, but a god who could rule a world for millennia. Yet this ongoing, disastrous battle between godling, goddess, and ancient evil couldn't last. Someone had to win, and live, and someone to lose, and die.

Whatever the outcome, it was no safe place for mortals.

Candlemas barely ducked before a hunk of rocky flesh slammed the corridor wall, shattering plaster into crumbles and dust. Wildly, the mage grabbed Aquesita, Sunbright, and Knucklebones and pulled them close. The fighters had staved off the berserkers, now reduced to a gory pile in the hallway. They hunkered close to the mage, the source of their only salvation. For with the Phaerimm attack, Karsus had been distracted, and the city's floor was tilting once more.

Candlemas yelled, "Hang on to me! I'll only have one chance to read this spell!"

Aquesita stared into the room at her battling cousin, the almost god. "I don't—"

"You must!" The mage screamed and clutched her hand. In a loud, clear, shaking voice, he began to read, enchanted words vanishing as he passed them by, magic crackling in the wrinkled paper. "Realms of fire! Clouds of air! Help us mount the silver stair!"

Despite the blistering defense, the animate tornados crashed into Karsus from all sides. Magical beings themselves, they easily penetrated his personal shields, and stone-like bodies brutally crushed his bones and smashed flesh. Flailing, Karsus fell heavily, half on, half off a workshop table. The Phaerimm kept after him, driving close to sting with their tails, batter with spinning bodies, and bite with granite-edged mouths.

Yet Karsus drove back the whirling bodies, striking with lightning-laced fists as pure star magic crackled and spat. The Phaerimm whirled faster, pounding the

nage in desperate fury, as rocks on the shore slam a
hip run aground. But Karsus was infused with super
leavy magic and star-metal and genius, and gradually
le beat them back, until they whirled harmlessly,
ouzzing in angry frustration like bees. The room
smelled of ozone and brimstone, molten metal, charred
wood, and rain.

Flaring like a new star of white-hot energy, Karsus
hoisted himself into the air and drew the city back level
and flat. With a shrug, Karsus brushed the spinning
Phaerimm back dozens of feet. With another shrug, he
cast the outside walls away, so they toppled out of sight
to let the day in, as if Karsus had outgrown their con-
fines, like a moth shedding a cocoon to become a butter-
fly. The walls tipped and shattered into stones and
beams and plaster.

The heroes huddled close around the chanting Candlemas, shut their eyes in anticipation of being crushed
in rubble, but found the corridor and the rest of the
building intact, the flagstones solid under their feet. A
neat trick, almost a miracle, the first by a man almost a
god.

Floating past the ruined walls and shorn roof, Karsus
boomed his challenge, *"Mystryl! I'll have your power!"*

High above, covering the sky from horizon to horizon,
the goddess manifested as thunderclouds was in full retreat. She drew back, still remote, calm-faced, with
dark, staring eyes wide as mountain lakes. As her retreat continued, Sunbright and Knucklebones and
Aquesita wondered where she'd go, where she'd hide
from the power-stealing Karsus.

Only Candlemas couldn't see, for he doggedly read his
scroll. He was almost to the bottom, and the four humans sensed the magic take effect. Sunbright felt light-
headed and ethereal, as if he dreamed awake, the same
as when he'd been drawn into the future by that long

spell of not-time. Knucklebones hugged Sunbright's arm as her bones and heart went hollow. And Aquesita, one hand trapped by Candlemas, was torn between a distant other world she'd never known, and her familiar homeland that was falling apart before her eyes.

"Look!" cried Knucklebones. "Lady Mystryl is—"

"Gone!"

Sweeping her arms wide, closing her volcanic eyes, Mystryl, Lady of Mystery, Controller of the Weave, ceased to be.

In a flash, the sky was clear.

Where clouds had been stacked thick and dark and roiling, there was suddenly nothing, only blue sky so vast and deep the heroes thought they saw stars. A brilliant sun, sharp and hot as if rainwashed, glared overhead. It was high noon on a spring day. The heroes' shadows lay almost directly under their feet.

But their feet were lifting from the ground, for the city was dropping.

Sunbright scooped Knucklebones, Aquesita, and the still-chanting Candlemas into his brawny arms and kicked out a foot to wedge himself between corridor walls. Already debris was sliding out the doorway into the ruins of the workshop.

Half clinging, half pushing, Aquesita pointed mutely at a craggy lump in the distance. The sister city Ioulaum dropped like the rock it was.

Tiny objects like shed feathers could be seen trailing upward, left behind: pennants, tents, banners, awnings, anything that might float on a breeze. The enclave built on an inverted mountain tipped, spun, capsized, then struck the side of a mountain. A corner burst off, a hundred buildings tumbling free like ants spilled from a hill. The face of the city struck, an entire culture destroyed. The enclave skipped sideways like a flung rock and exploded into fist-sized chunks of white and yellow and red. In three seconds, buildings, universities, streets, homes and tens of thousands of people were wiped out.

As would happen now to the enclave Karsus.

In a second, the heroes understood what happened, for the goddess's act had been clear, had communicated itself to them so that all people—all survivors—might comprehend. And remember.

Rather than allow herself to be usurped, rather than have her powers stolen, rather than let Karsus become a god, the Mother of All Magic sacrificed herself. With the last powers of this greatest of gods, she wished herself out of existence, and vanished.

And took all the magic in the world with her.

The Phaerimm, who were magic to their core, disappeared.

Karsus was left alone in the room, hovering, struggling to keep the magic within himself. But the might of the fallen star was gone, vanished, as if it had never existed. The mage clenched his fists and cried in rage and frustration and sorrow. For the first time in his life, Karsus was denied something he wanted, and he would destroy his world to get it.

Having seen none of this, Candlemas had hurried, barked the last of his spell just in time. His enchantment had taken root in the past, and already the four people faded. Exhausted physically and mentally, the pudgy mage dropped the empty paper and tightened his sweaty grip on his lady's hand.

But Aquesita tore away, screaming, "*No!* I won't desert the empire in its hour of need!"

A ghostly Candlemas gave a hollow croak and grabbed for her. Only Sunbright's sturdy hand—transparent as glass—kept him from breaking the spell's enchantment.

Stumbling into the ravaged workshop, a now solid, worldly Aquesita tripped over sliding wreckage and reached high to catch the hem of her cousin's tattered white robe.

"Karry, hang on! You must save—"

That was all Candlemas, Sunbright, and Knucklebones heard, for they disappeared. Their ghostly eyes misted over, like a curtain of fog shrouding them, until Aquesita and the flaring, howling Karsus were something from a dream.

Only Aquesita, Karsus's cousin and sole living relative, the one person in the empire who loved him for himself, saw his final moments.

Struggling to retain his magical might, Karsus employed every holding spell he knew. But the mixed and fading and fluky magic betrayed him, even as he'd betrayed himself in trying to steal the powers of the goddess who controlled all magic at its roots. His cousin watched in horror as Karsus, savior of the Netherese Empire, was transformed into stone, larger than life, denser than granite, redder than blood.

By then, the enclave had tipped almost vertically. Karsus, once a god, now a red stone statue, tipped far into space and plummeted, and his loving, ill-fated cousin fell after.

For an instant, Karsus understood what had happened, how Mystryl had sacrificed herself for the common good of god and man, an unselfish sacrifice he never could have conceived of. And how his loving cousin had sacrificed herself believing in him, as the empire had believed in him.

And how he'd betrayed them all.

With this last, godlike insight, Karsus's selfish heart broke.

Even as, seconds later and far below, the statue-man drove into the ground and came to rest, while the greatest city of the empire, named after its greatest mage, exploded into fragments.

In the space of half a minute, the Netherese Empire, beloved of the gods, was snuffed out like a candle flame.

* * * * *

That was bad.
That was good. Their empire is finished.
As are we, almost.
Never. The Phaerimm are eternal.
And greatly reduced in numbers.
No matter. We survive.
With the humans reduced to flint axes and fire, we shall even prosper.
Increase in number.
And destroy humankind once and for all.
Let us so pledge.
Aye, so pledge we all.

* * * * *

On a surprisingly peaceful mountainside, miles away from the falling Empire of Netheril, sat a star-eyed girl named Mystra.

A smile crept across her face, a tingle ran through her body, and a soft voice—a cloud's voice—whispered in her ear, "Soon."

* * * * * *

Still tightly clutching Knucklebones and Candlemas, Sunbright blinked and cast about. Spring sunlight filtered through the tops of red pines and pin oaks. Scarlet cardinals and yellow goldfinches flitted through rhododendron bushes. A warm balm of pine sap and churned earth and oak tannin kissed the air. Somewhere close, a snuffling badger rooted under rocks. Behind was a low hillside cleft like a loaf of bread, marred by a shadowed crater. In the churned loam and sand before the cave were footprints of moosehide boots and warped sandals. The tracks went into the cave but didn't come out. Sunbright raised on tiptoes and peeked. Neither he, nor Candlemas, nor the star, were inside.

So they'd returned only moments after leaving.

They were home.

Blowing a great sigh of relief, Sunbright released his death grip on his two comrades. He laughed aloud, saying, "Well, Candlemas! You're a genius! You not only brought us home . . ."

His merriment died as he remembered: there had been four people when their journey back had started.

Knucklebones grunted with relief and tugged her worn leathers into place. Curiously, she stared around at the northern forest, familiarizing herself with the terrain, wary of enemies, for old habits die hard. But just as quickly, she saw to the pudgy mage.

Candlemas slumped to the ground, landing with a thump on his fat rump. With sandy hands he rubbed a face still singed by Karsus's fire blast. He wept openly, blubbering and hiccuping like a baby.

Sunbright and Knucklebones said nothing, just sat on either side of him to catch their breath. Knucklebones stroked his knee, Sunbright his back.

Eventually the mage cried himself out. Then slowly, his voice cracked and broken, he talked.

"She didn't understand. She thought Karsus could save the empire. She was as blind as him, seeing only what she wanted. She had the same dream, that the empire would always grow, always expand, forever. But nothing lasts forever."

"No," Sunbright murmured. "That was the death of the Netherese Empire, which the Neth thought would outlast the sun. In three hundred and fifty-eight years, and a few minutes, it's naught but a memory."

"Like Sita." Candlemas croaked. "I loved her so. . . ."

"And she loved you," Knucklebones cooed. "But it was not to be. The fates decided otherwise."

"Oh!" The mage snuffled. "Oh, you were right, Sunbright!"

"I was?" The shaman pondered. "That's a first. About what?"

"Magic, knowledge, life."

Candlemas sniffed and caught his breath.

"Magic is too great a force to control. You can only use a small portion of it, follow it, not bend it to your will. It's like trying to divert the tide. You'll only drown."

The forest was silent except for the cheep of tree frogs and the carol of birdsong. The three companions basked in the warm sun, resting after their labors, for once not running, fighting, killing, dying. But Candlemas shriveled inside, his heart broken as surely as Karsus's, and he knew it would never wholly mend. He'd given his heart and lost it, and his chest was hollow but for the splintered fragments.

The sun was low in the sky when Candlemas finally rose, dusted off his hands, and smoothed his scorched, filthy robe of military cut. Sunbright and Knucklebones had dozed off holding hands. Gently the mage touched their scarred arms to wake them. Both were instantly alert and up, then wondering what to do.

Candlemas stared upward. Hovering in a blue spring sky, a mile high, was the enclave of Castle Delia, a stopping ground for the young Lady Polaris. Sunbright followed the mage's stare, asked gently, "Ready to go home?"

A surprising shake of the head. Candlemas said weakly, "I was in no hurry to return, for I left nothing behind. Some money, a spare robe, rooms full of trinkets and trash. I wanted to stay with Sita, and make a home there. That's gone, and I'm back, but there's less now than there was before. There's no place for me anywhere."

Sunbright laid a broad hand on his shoulder.

"Where will you go?"

Resigned, not really caring, the mage nodded south.

"There's a small keep, leagues off, in the hills near the lakes. I know it from my stewardship. It's abandoned. Probably Lady Polaris . . ." He paused at the mention of her name, then continued, "Probably Lady Polaris doesn't even know she owns it. I'll move there in lieu of pay. She owes me enough for my years of service. From what I saw in—the enclave—I have a notion how to cure the crop blight. Maybe Polaris and the nobles don't care if a cure is found, but many innocent people still suffer. It will be a worthwhile use of magic for once, saving crops instead of tinkering with hair curlers and gambling dice."

He glanced at the high castle, then finished, "I can walk there. It'll give me time to . . . think about Aquesita. I never said goodbye. . . ."

Sunbright squeezed the mage's shoulder, said softly, "I'm afraid you must say it now. To us."

Candlemas turned woodenly.

The shaman smiled, but sadly.

"I'm bound north," he said, "It's time for me to go home, back to the tundra and my tribe. I've debts to settle and stories to tell, and my birthright to reclaim. I'm ready now to face them, now that I'm a proper shaman." He looked a question past Candlemas.

Knucklebones hitched her belt, settled her black-bladed elven knife on her hip. Her one green eye stared back.

"I'll go."

That brought a smile of thanks from Sunbright.

Slump-shouldered, infinitely weary, Candlemas only nodded.

"Then there's nothing else to say."

"One thing." Sunbright said, holding out a scarred, brown hand. "Thank you, friend."

Candlemas clasped hands, was dully surprised to find how strong his own hand felt in the barbarian's big one.

"Yes," the mage said. "Thank you, friend. You'll be a great shaman, for you've taught me much already."

"And you'll cure the crop blight magically, and save simple folk from suffering, so they'll sing praises to your name. I can prophesy that."

Candlemas smiled weakly in thanks.

They turned and walked away. Two north, one south.

The epic Netheril Trilogy that began in:

Sword Play
What starts out as a bet between the powerful Netherese wizards Candlemas and Sysquemalyn leads their playthings, the barbarian Sunbright and the elf Greenwillow to hell itself.

And not all of them come back. . . .

concludes in:

Mortal Consequences
Author **Clayton Emery** draws the Netheril Trilogy to a startling conclusion when an old enemy returns in a surprising manner, and an old friend returns in an equally surprising package.

Coming in April 1997!

For more ARCANE AGE™, *adventures* look for:

Realms of the Arcane
An anthology of all-new fiction by your favorite FORGOTTEN REALMS® authors explores Faerûn's distant past!

Coming in January 1997!